Vengeance
is Mine

Books by Reavis Z. Wortham

The Red River Mysteries
The Rock Hole
Burrows
The Right Side of Wrong
Vengeance is Mine

Vengeance is Mine

A Red River Mystery

Reavis Z. Wortham

Poisoned Pen Press

Copyright © 2014 by Reavis Z. Wortham

First Edition 2014

10 9 8 7 6 5 4 3 2 1

Library of Congress Catalog Card Number: 2014931631

ISBN: 9781464202582   Hardcover
      9781464202605   Trade Paperback

Poisoned Pen Press
6962 E. First Ave., Ste. 103
Scottsdale, AZ 85251
www.poisonedpenpress.com
info@poisonedpenpress.com

Printed in the United States of America

This book is dedicated to my good friend and mentor,
New York Times best-selling author, John Gilstrap.
John, you're a helluva guy,
and I can't thank you enough.

Acknowledgments

I've learned that I cannot do this job alone. With each novel, more and more people have stepped forward to offer advice, read, and help promote my work. Thanks to:

...my wife, Shana Kay, who is my rock and foundation. None of this would be happening if not for her...

...the folks at Poisoned Pen Press who took a chance on this voice in the wilderness, especially my editor...

...Annette Rogers, who gently guides and lifts me in praise...

...Ronda Wise, for the medical advice that keeps the plot real...

...my sister-in-law Sharon Reynolds, who worries about my sanity...

...Mike Miller for struggling through the first read...

...to authors John Gilstrap, Joe Lansdale, Sandra Brannan, T. Jefferson Parker, Craig Johnson, Jeffrey Deaver, C.J. Box, Jamie Freveletti, Jan Reid, Leo J. Maloney, Michael Morris, and Zoe Sharp, to name only a few, who collectively offered blurbs, friendship, support, and advice. You guys are cool....

...and finally, thanks to my agent Ann Hawkins, for taking a gamble on this virtually unknown author. I hope your ante pays off in spades for both of us.

Chapter One

Tony Agrioli was grateful to leave the blistering sun and dive into the cold air of Malachi Best's noisy The Desert Gold casino. Mozzarella's Italian Restaurant was past the roulette tables and the Beatles' newest hit, "Sgt. Pepper's Lonely Hearts Club Band," blared through the sound system when he arrived at the oversized table in the rear.

"You need me, Boss?"

Best handed Tony a folded piece of paper and wagged his finger over the calzone on his plate. "This needs to be done tonight, Anthony." The Vegas mob boss sipped red wine from his crystal glass and spoke distinctly. "Take care of them. You know what I want."

Anthony studied the typed list, the letters gummed from old ink and hard to read in the dim light of the casino's dining room. Two handwritten additions stood out on the grease-stained list, though.

They were the names of twelve-year-old twin boys.

Anthony's face prickled with shock, feeling like he was back in Public School 103 when the teacher called for the answer to a difficult arithmetic question. He looked up for confirmation from Best's two men and a gray-mustached individual Anthony didn't recognize. Best showed no inclination to introduce him to the uncomfortable guy trying to disappear inside his off-the-rack suit.

Built like a fireplug, Big Nose Pennacchio had been with Malachi since they were kids, and was his most trusted associate. He got the name Big Nose, not because of the size of his schnoz, but because his last name sounded like Pinocchio.

Rail-thin Seymour Burke had been with them since they opened the casino.

Both were well-heeled in custom suits cut to hide the bulges of their holsters. Neither made eye contact, as if that would absolve them of what was about to happen.

"The whole family, Mr. Best, and not just Enrique Sandoval?"

The boss' heavy eyelids drooped as they did when he intended to make a point. "They are not our kind of people. They are Cubans, and they do not play by the same rules. Those people only know one thing, and I will give it to them."

With nervous fingers, Anthony refolded the paper along the creases. "Mr. Best, again with respect, these are kids."

Malachi carefully placed his fork on the edge of his plate and leaned back. His oily black hair glistened with Vitalis. "You know, Anthony, since we moved the business to Las Vegas, I have been reading a little history about the West, when I go to bed and cannot sleep. Not too long ago I finished an interesting story about a Colonel John Chivington in Colorado who was fighting the Indians nearly a hundred years ago. When he gathered his men to wipe out an Indian camp, he said to kill them all—men, women, and children, because 'nits turn into *lice*.'" He hammered that last word, as if were the most disgusting thing in the world. "Think about that Anthony. Nits to *lice*. Kids grow into adults.

"That is what we have here with these Cubans." Best waved a forefinger for emphasis. With each word, his voice rose and his carefully crafted diction deteriorated. "They are on *our* turf, in *my* town, and they are taking away *my* business. You know, they could have gone to some other rat hole town out in the desert and started their own casino! But instead they moved in here without asking anybody in the *Family* and started cuttin' in on our *business* and they siphon off the money that we're entitled to!"

He drew a deep breath to regain his composure and the precise speech pattern he worked so hard to effect. "Cubans do not think like us. That is why those Babalus muscled in on our action and opened that place…that…"

He snapped his fingers.

Big Nose didn't take his eyes off the plate in front of him. "The Little Havana Casino." he said.

"Right. They have no respect for American tradition. This is nineteen sixty-seven and they should know better than to muscle in on our territory. At the very least they didn't come to us as they should have, hat in hand to ask permission. Then they hire away acts that have worked for the legitimate casinos for years and look at us like we cannot do anything about it. Well, we can."

Best was furious when Enrique Sandoval made friends with Frank Sinatra and convinced Ol' Blue Eyes to perform in the new Havana Club at the farthest undeveloped end of what had become known as The Strip.

When Best contacted Connie Smith to appear in The Desert Gold a month later, she declined because she was already committed to the stage in the Little Havana Club. It sent Best into a rage that took two days to cool off.

"I can tell you to take out the mom and dad, but the kids will grow up and I will have to deal with them in the future." Best reached out to pat Anthony's arm. "Cubans don't quit. I do not intend to be looking over my shoulder in twenty years. Nits turn into lice. History repeats itself. Do this for me, *mio figlio*."

Malachi Best had never referred to Anthony, as *my son*. It was a watershed moment at the worst possible time.

Trying to land on a respectful argument, Anthony focused on Malachi's thick hands. It wasn't the killing that bothered him. He was an enforcer, and the very definition of his job involved violence and death. He'd killed many times with a clear conscience, because everything he did was for the Family. But Families didn't make war on women and kids. There was honor in war back where they came from in Chicago, and it never came home to women and children.

Life in the energetic desert town had changed Malachi in a disturbing way.

"Sure, Boss."

"Good boy." Best seemed surprised to find that his fists were clinched. He flexed his fingers. "You do that, and I will have something extra for you later, and soon you will get a new position." His speech pattern slipped back to his younger days. "You won't be muscle no more. I'll make you a *caporegime*. How about t'at?"

Being a lieutenant in the organization was a significant promotion, but he didn't want the rank for whacking kids. "Mr. Best, again with all due respect, since when do we do kids?"

"Since I said so."

It wasn't the air conditioning that made Anthony feel cold. It was the set of the mob boss' jaw, and the expression on his face. Barely restrained tension crackled between them like an electrical short and Anthony knew he was straddling the line. From there, it could go either way.

Malachi Best wasn't used to being questioned. He wiped his fingers on a linen napkin and then used his thumb to scrape sweat off his eyebrow. "Let me say it again, Anthony, slow, so you can understand. That family has connections, and I do not intend to be looking over my shoulder for the rest of my life. Wipe them all out, and do not leave anything to connect me to the job."

"Yes, sir."

Best put his shoulder between them. The slight movement said the argument was over and the men at the table relaxed. "Good. You're a good boy, Ant'ny. Nits to lice."

Anthony watched Malachi's jowls quiver as he took a bite, tucked it into his cheek, and spoke to the trio beside him. "We have to make an example out of them, or else every Babalu or that crummy little island is going to come down here in *my* backyard and start taking money out of *my* pocket. I will not have it."

Then he took a long sip of wine and waved Anthony away like a bothersome fly.

Anthony's respect for Best died the minute the boss flicked his fingers in dismissal. It had been withering for a long time, but he hadn't realized it until that moment. The Family was changing. Maybe it was the desert heat, or the insane amount of money flowing into Malachi's pockets, or that Anthony was simply growing up, but he felt different.

He left the restaurant for the address on the folded paper in his coat pocket. The vein in his forehead throbbed, a lifelong indicator that he was angry or frustrated. The built-in warning system often reminded him to back off and regain control.

It was nearly four in the morning when Anthony crept through the dark backyard. The checkered wooden butt of the .45 Colt 1911 was as familiar as a spoon and he felt the familiar electric tingle of adrenaline and anticipation that sharpened his senses.

He wanted the knock-down power that came with the larger caliber in case he ran into any trouble. He also carried a Ruger .22 semi-automatic in the pocket of his coveralls. He was usually a sharp dresser, but tonight his shop coveralls had a utilitarian purpose, as did the baseball bat in his other hand.

The pool lights made navigation through the expensive landscaping easy. He paused beside the diving board to listen. Anthony didn't think the family had a dog, but in his line of work, he was prepared for anything and everything. If you worked for Malachi Best, you knew surprises and mistakes were not tolerated.

Back home in Chicago they called Anthony an "arm breaker." The term still held up in the booming desert town, where Malachi Best wound up running the The Desert Gold casino after brief stints in protection rackets, prostitution, numbers, extortion, and counterfeiting.

On that scorching August night, the Cuban crime family asleep upstairs included a mom, dad, and kids, with links back into Havana long before Fidel Castro wrested control of the island and sealed it off from the rest of the free world.

After escaping Castro's grip in 1960, the Sandovals made a successful living in southern Florida by running numbers out of a small frame house in Miami. They used the wellspring of cash to bring more relatives into the fold, and then expanded the business to include gambling and prostitution. It soon became one of the biggest operations in the Sunshine State.

Four years later the law closed in, and after losing more than one cousin to arrest and imprisonment, they moved west to drink from the tremendously deep river of money flowing into the desert town of Las Vegas. The problems began when the dad, Enrique, went straight to work in direct competition with Malachi Best's casino in the wide-open gambling town, cutting in on the Family's profits.

Enrique Sandoval's house was silent. Anthony reached the back door and found it was locked. He expected that, but it never hurt to try the simple way first. He carefully placed the bat on the Mexican tile, and unzipped his coveralls enough to slip the .45 into the shoulder holster. That done, he dug out the set of picks he'd learned to use as a kid. The cheap General lock surrendered a moment later. The door opened into a dark, spacious kitchen smelling of spices that reminded him of tamales.

The pistol back in his hand, Anthony waited for several long moments. When he was sure no one was up, he crept through the kitchen and into the dining room. Beyond, the television bathed the living room in a cold, silver light. A soft hiss accompanied the Indian Head Test Pattern.

On the couch with his back to the kitchen, a slender, dark-haired bodyguard in a shoulder rig snored loudly, his head thrown back on the cushions. Once again, Anthony holstered his pistol.

Half a dozen quick steps cushioned by thick carpet brought Anthony to the sleeping man. The angle was perfect. Planting his feet, he swung the bat as if splitting a piece of firewood with an ax. The resulting crack sounded like a home run. Shocked by the massive blow to his forehead, the bodyguard's body jerked and Anthony quickly struck again, just as hard. The sound of the second whack was softer, and wet.

Anthony listened carefully as blood soaked into the sofa. After a full minute, he wiped the bat on a cushion and crept slowly up the staircase. On the second floor, he followed the dark hallway toward the parents' bedroom, which he'd identified while waiting in the shadows across the street.

The door was partially open, probably so the sleeping couple could hear the kids. Inside, he saw them in the silver rectangle of light spilling from the window. He moved quietly to Enrique Sandoval's side of the bed.

The only sound was soft breathing. Anthony once again set his feet and swung the bat. Enrique Sandoval's skull caved under the powerful blow. The body jerked from the impact. Blood sprayed.

Wearing only a man's white t-shirt, his wife propped herself on one elbow and turned to look back over her shoulder, her mind cloudy with sleep. *"Que pasa?"*

Anthony adjusted his grip on the bat to gain distance and moved one step back, so the wall wouldn't interfere with his swing. With a mighty grunt, he swung for the bleachers. The bat cracked against the woman's head, nearly knocking her out of the bed. He hit her a second time. She fell back, bare legs twitching. He stepped backward and smashed Enrique's head once again to anchor the Cuban mobster.

A muffled voice at the other end of the house called a question as blood splatters ran down the walls. *"Miss Adriana, está todo bien?"*

Anthony pitched the bat between the bodies, drew the .22 from his pocket, and moved quickly to the door. Using one finger, he pushed it almost closed and waited in the darkness, peering into the hallway.

In khakis and an undershirt, a barefoot young man came down the hallway, hair sticking upright from sleep. Startled awake by a noise he couldn't identify, he held a revolver loosely in his hand, pointing at the floor. When he reached the doorway, he paused to listen. If they had accidentally knocked something onto the floor while engaging in what he thought of as "marital relations," it would be embarrassing to disturb the *jefe* and his missus. Hearing nothing, he respectfully lowered his head and quietly knocked with a knuckle.

"*Senor? Con permiso?*" He waited for a response. He asked a second time. "*Está todo bien?*"

Anthony jerked the door open and stuck the .22's muzzle against the startled bodyguard's forehead. The shot was sharp and loud. The man's head snapped back and he collapsed onto the floor as if his legs had turned to noodles. The carpet quickly absorbed a wash of pumping blood.

The house still lay hushed. Anthony allowed himself to relax, breathing through his mouth and listening intently for any sound. Silence meant he hadn't miscounted the bodyguards, and the children were still asleep.

Gritting his teeth and dreading the next step, he reentered the hallway and approached the boys' room. Their door was closed, and when he gently pushed it open, the kids slept deeply in separate beds. Moonlight spilled through the open blinds into the air-conditioned room. A plastic General Electric radio glowed on the nightstand between them. Tuned low, a rock 'n' roll song explained why the boys hadn't stirred at the sound of the gunshot.

The still-warm .22 hanging loosely in his sweating hand, Anthony stopped between their beds.

One slept on his stomach, facing the wall; the other was on his back with his mouth wide open. Anthony glanced around, making out baseball and travel pennants thumbtacked to the walls. Sandy Koufax and Ernie Banks posters filled the wall over one bed, held by bright thumbtacks that reflected the streetlight shining through the window. Above the other, a tattered Beatles poster joined a line of pictures ripped from *Tiger Beat* magazine. Davy Jones, Micky Dolenz, Peter Tork, and Michael Nesmith smiled in the darkness at the man who'd only moments before killed the kids' parents.

He raised the pistol that suddenly weighed a hundred pounds and placed the muzzle above the ear of the baseball-loving boy asleep on his stomach.

"*We don't do kids, Mr. Best.*"

"*Nits to lice. You work for me.*"

His stomach clenched.

If I don't do this, Malachi Best will leave what's left of my body in the desert.

Anthony was Family. The Family took care of its own, but they also exacted terrible revenge for wrongs or betrayals.

After all, they're Cuban children who don't mean anything to me.

He swallowed the bile rising in his throat and for the first time in his life, Anthony's hands shook on the job.

Do this and I'll be a lieutenant.

His temples pounded and his mouth felt dry as desert sand. He took a deep breath, trying to separate himself from what he was about to do.

Two pulls on the trigger and he could walk out to join Malachi's elite leadership team.

His mind found a safe closet, and Anthony squeezed the trigger.

A sharp snap was the only result when the firing pin struck a faulty round. Sleeping deeply as only children can, neither of the twelve-year-olds moved.

Shocked, Anthony held the pistol in the moonlight and looked at it as if he suddenly found a live snake in his hand.

With a shudder, he dropped the weapon into his pocket, hurried out of the room. He fled to the kitchen and grabbed a dishtowel.

Minutes later, his hands and face wiped clean, the dishtowel and his blood-splattered coveralls were in a neighbor's trashcan and he drove away, his life and those of the twins changed forever.

Chapter Two

Center Springs, in northeast Texas, looked just like the pictures of Kentucky I'd seen in *Field & Stream*. I crept through the woods like Daniel Boone in the newest episode from the night before. The BB gun in my hands was a poor imitation of the Tennessee long rifle Fess Parker carried in the show. Even though I was nearly fourteen, I wasn't old enough to take a rifle or shotgun yet without Grandpa, Uncle Cody, or Uncle James.

The early fall grass was soft and spongy. Dampness soaked my genuine leather Indian moccasins. Uncle Cody brought them back to me when he took Norma Faye on a trip down Route 66 for a short vacation after we all got back from south Texas a few months earlier.

In no time my feet were soaking wet, but discomfort was the way of the mountain man, so I was righteous in my misery. My Brittany spaniel, Hootie, ran around like he had good sense, sticking his nose into every bunch of grass and pile of dead limbs he could find. He'd already busted two coveys and wanted to chase them when they flushed, but I hollered him back. Hootie didn't need to get into any bad habits, or Uncle Cody wouldn't take him hunting come quail season.

I stepped into a little bunch of shin oaks. The grass underfoot gave way to leaves that crackled like a forest fire. No way could I creep up on any Indians this way, so I struck off for a low spot where pine trees grew tall and shaded the ground.

Something caught my attention. A nearby flash of blue told me the search was over. There was my prey. I took careful aim at a leg sticking out from behind a wide sycamore and pulled the trigger.

The pump action air gun cracked and the copper BB slapped Pepper's jeaned leg. "Ouch! Shit! You dumb bastard, that hurt!" My thirteen-year-old girl cousin bent to rub her calf.

"But I told you I was going to try and shoot you for an Indian, if I saw you."

Her long brown hair hung forward, barely held back by a leather headband she'd taken to wearing. "Well, I didn't think you'd actually shoot me where it'd hurt. That ain't cool, man."

"Of course it's gonna sting. What did you expect?"

"I didn't expect you to really do it." She held out a hand. "Give me that gun and let me shoot *you*, then we'll see what *you* say."

"Uh, uh." I wasn't a fool. I'd been through a lot in thirteen years on the planet, and I didn't intend to give her my air gun. "C'mon and let's hunt for a while."

I could tell she wasn't as much into our game as I was. She'd started to change a little in the last several months, and when I asked my Uncle Cody about it, he threw his head back and laughed. "I got news for you Bud, she's growing up. Girls get there faster than boys, so she's gonna be ahead of you for a while."

The whole idea of Pepper not sharing the things I liked to do bothered me a lot. She was my best friend, and had been since I came to live with Grandpa Ned and Miss Becky not long after my parents were killed in a car wreck.

After I got here, I realized that I didn't have much in common with most of the other boys in Center Springs. Like them, I enjoyed hunting and fishing, but there wasn't one other person I liked enough to hang out with, so when Pepper wasn't around, I either read books or helped Grandpa with the farm, doing the things I was big enough to handle.

Pepper dug our shared transistor radio out of her hip pocket and rolled the switch with her thumb. "Can't Buy Me Love" by the Beatles filled the air. She backed the dial down until it wasn't so loud and shoved it into her Levis. She stuck her fingers in the pockets of her jeans and followed along behind like she didn't want to be there.

We struck out past the slough where Uncle Cody and I planned to hunt ducks when they finally moved down for the winter. Like the mountain men, I again moved silently through the forest, keeping a sharp eye for squirrels in the trees above. I knew my BB gun wasn't strong enough to kill one, but it was good practice.

A covey of quail exploded under my feet with a whir, scaring me so badly I almost dropped the gun. It made me mad, and I needed to blame someone. "Hootie! How come you missed this covey and busted up them others?"

It was Pepper's turn to snicker. "Titty baby. Them little old birds scared the pee waddlin' out of you."

My temper rose fast. "You better watch your mouth. You've been cussing a lot more lately, and you're gonna get a whuppin' for it soon enough."

"I'm too big to spank now." Pepper grabbed the pockets of her shirt and squeezed. "I have these, so nobody is gonna give me another whuppin'."

I was so embarrassed my face burned at what my cousin had done. For a moment, I didn't know what to say. I stood there, mouth opening and closing like a fish. "Well, Miss Becky can still wash your mouth out with soap."

"She won't do that neither."

For a second, I studied the glint in her eye and realized that we could stand there and argue until the cows came home, and she still wouldn't listen. "C'mon, I'm thirsty. Let's go down on the branch and get a drink."

We weren't far from Center Spring Branch, where the cool water flowed pure and clear over rocks and gravel. It was our old arrowhead-hunting grounds, but we'd shied away from it since The Skinner was killing folks back a couple of years before.

Pepper followed as I led the way. "I ain't drinking that nasty water."

"It's purified when it runs over gravel and sand."

"How do you know that?"

I hated it when she questioned me, and she did it all the time because pestering me tickled her to death. "I read it somewhere."

"Most of what you read in them stupid books of yours is probably wrong."

"Don't rear up at *me*. I read it in a magazine."

"Which one?"

"*Outdoor Life*, when we went to the barbershop in Chisum."

I kept an eye out for arrowheads. Uncle Cody liked to tell stories about how the Indians had camped along this same branch when they traded with the white men who settled our community of Center Springs back around 1880. "Besides, the water we drink at the house comes right out of the ground. It's the same thing."

She quit arguing, because folks with wells not half a mile away from our house have cloudy water that tastes sandy. Sometimes in the summer, they have to let it settle before it's drinkable. Our well water is the cleanest, sweetest water in the county, according to my grandmother, Miss Becky.

The rest of the walk only took a few minutes. We crossed a pasture full of dying bull nettles and milkweed, and then came to the trees lining Center Spring Branch. A sandstone ledge full of fossilized oysters jutted over the trickling water and I dropped to my stomach to drink, sticking my face in the cold water and slurping like a horse.

I rose and brushed the sand off my shirt. "Tastes better than well water."

"Far out, but I'll drink out of the dipper when we get back to the house."

Hootie's tongue was hanging out, but instead of drinking, he stopped and perked his ears. Something rustled upstream and Pepper froze like a terrified deer. We weren't far from where The Skinner had taken us, and fear prickled my neck. A high-pitched moan floated through the air and I realized it came from my tomboy cousin, who wasn't as tough as she liked to believe. I found her hand in mine, and we backed up one terrorized step, then another. Hootie didn't growl, but he didn't wag his tail, either.

Another rustle sounded closer, and neither of us moved.

Then a skinny, half-starved calf stepped into the open and ran across the branch.

I breathed out, not realizing I'd been holding my breath. The calf bawled and crashed through the brush.

Pepper panted like Hootie for a moment, and then got hold of herself, the terror gone. "I was so scared I was about to run like a striped-ass baboon! That poor little thing. I wonder where its mama is?"

"Who knows?" We followed the calf upstream, jumping from one side to the other as the narrow trickle of water snaked through the woods.

Less than fifty yards from where I'd been drinking, the breeze shifted and brought the thick, familiar odor of death.

"The Skinner's back for sure." Pepper's voice was a high whine. Her eyes were wide and white, like a terrified animal.

"You know better'n that."

"What's that stink, then?"

We rounded a bend in the stream and found the source of the smell. The rotten carcass of a cow lay across the stream, damming it so that a small pool gathered above the body and swirled inside her gaping stomach.

Relieved at what we'd found, because dead animals are a part of life in the country, we stood there for a few seconds, trying to regain our composure.

"Shit, that stinks." Pepper pinched her nose. "I was scared for a minute there."

"Me too." With the threat gone, I gave the dead cow a good looking over. She'd been there a long time.

The action of the water flowing through the rotting body carved a hole the size of a #3 wash tub in the soft sand and gravel behind the cow. Drowned maggots roiled in the swirl before being swept downstream.

I thought about that while running my tongue over my teeth.

Then I thought about laying on my belly downstream and taking a long, deep drink that was still wet on my lips.

I thought about where that water had been, and the maggots, and the stench of the rotting cow washed over us again. Then I did what any normal person would do under those same circumstances. A jet of vomit splashed into the water and disappeared while Pepper shrieked with laughter.

My stomach clenched and I puked again.

And again.

And again.

"I've never seen anyone puke so much at one time. That's groovy." Pepper held her flat belly and laughed so hard tears rolled down her cheeks. "Hey, mountain man, does your pure, clean water taste as good coming up as it did going down?"

Hootie gave me a quizzical look, then loped a few yards upstream from the carcass and lapped long and deep.

Finally gaining control of my convulsing stomach, I turned toward our farmhouse for Miss Becky's help and the sympathy that I knew was waiting there. A soft breeze moved the leaves. The smell of rotting cow wrapped itself on my face like a physical presence, making me puke some more.

We took ten steps, and I repeated the process, accompanied by Pepper's maniacal laugh track and the Beach Boys singing "Good Vibrations." She used her thumb to roll the volume dial, probably to drown out the sound of me throwing up. "You sound like Uncle Frank that night after the dance when he tried to drink all the whiskey in Lamar County."

I needed to get away from the smell, so I launched away from the branch in a wobbly run toward fresh air. It took forever to cross the steamy meadow and work our way through the thin grove of trees lining the road.

Pepper wouldn't leave it alone. "Hey, you know, I was thinkin' them maggots looked like the rice Miss Becky cooked us for breakfast this morning."

She was right, and I gagged some more.

The meadow gave way to the thick strip of woods between us and the two-lane road that ran beside the house. Brambles and thorns tore at my jeans and shirt as I bulled through the tangle. Breaking free, I staggered onto the grass shoulder at the same time Uncle Cody slowed his El Camino to turn into Grandpa's gravel drive.

Startled at our sudden appearance, he slammed on the brakes and stopped in his lane. The fear in his face left when he saw Pepper laughing behind me, so he stuck his elbow through the open window. "Goddlemighty boy, you're a sight. What's the matter with you?"

I gulped air. "What makes you think something's wrong?"

The constable's badge on his shirt winked in the light when he leaned forward and turned his radio down, cutting off Buck Owens. "You look like you've been string-haltered, you're dragging the barrel of your air gun in the dirt, and you're white as a sheet. It looks like a bull got aholt of you."

Pepper beamed at our favorite uncle and slapped me on the shoulder. "Tell him, mountain man."

Uncle Cody flicked a finger. "First you turn that noise down in your pocket."

She frowned and lowered the volume. I opened my mouth to find the words, and the thought of what had happened caused my stomach to convulse yet again. Hands on my knees, I leaned over, but by that time, it was mostly bile followed by the dry heaves.

Concerned, Uncle Cody turned his attention to Pepper. "What?"

"He got a big ol' drink from the branch, and then when we walked upstream, we saw a rotten cow in the water. He's been puking ever since."

Uncle Cody tilted the Stetson off his forehead and threw his head back to laugh loud and long while I suffered. "Did you learn anything?"

I gulped and choked down another gag. "Yeah, after you get a drink, don't walk upstream."

Chapter Three

Barely twenty minutes after his pistol misfired, Anthony Agrioli hung up the pay phone and returned to his car. The call to the police department would get officers there before the kids woke up and found their parents.

He owed them that much.

By habit, he drove to Fremont Street and found an empty parking space between the Mint and the Horseshoe casinos. The air was still when he leaned against the fender of his Pontiac and drew a deep breath under a flashing storm of bright lights. He bit a Lucky out of the pack and snapped his Zippo alight with quivering hands.

Glitter Gulch transformed the night into day. Across the street at the Golden Nugget, coins rattled into tin receivers that beckoned people on the street to come in and try their luck.

Look, our machines are paying off!

Down the street, a giant neon cowboy named Vegas Vic loomed over the Pioneer Club. Wearing a Stetson and a red scarf, he repeatedly waved at the tourists below and blew enormous puffs of smoke from a torpedo-size cigarette.

Anthony squinted upward and simultaneously blew his own lungful of smoke into the still night air. Minutes later, he lit another from the butt, ground out the cherry with his heel, and left the car to walk past the noisy casinos. Men in rolled shirtsleeves strolled arm in arm with well-dressed women. Cars cruised Fremont Street, some looking to be seen, others gazing in wonder at the sinful city sprouting like a neon flower in the dry desert sand.

A shiny 1967 Cadillac passed slowly. Anthony recognized the driver as another one of Best's men. He saw Anthony, tapped the horn with the heel of his hand, and waved. Anthony waved back with the realization that his association with the Family was over.

Surprisingly, the revelation was calming. His stomach unclenched and he stopped on the sidewalk to take another deep breath. Leaving the Family was the most dangerous thing he could imagine. No one leaves, yet Anthony felt free and light as if he'd quit a mind-numbing job on an assembly line.

He was officially unemployed.

And on the run.

Without any particular destination in mind, he dropped into the Silver Palace, and then the Las Vegas Club, staying in each for only a few minutes before returning to the bright, scorching night. Dawn finally broke over the town.

Restless, he needed to make himself scarce. By noon Best would know that Anthony had only fulfilled half his assignment, and that was as bad as not doing it at all.

In his car once again, Anthony left the lights behind and drove to the dusty outskirts of town. He checked into Desert Villa Motel under a false name, paying for two days. He hung the plastic Do Not Disturb sign on the knob and locked the door.

Thirteen hours later, he awoke feeling fully rested for the first time in his life. A great weight was off his shoulders. Anthony stepped into the shower, singing as if he didn't have a care in the world. The sun was sinking when he walked across the small parking lot and into the detached coffee shop smelling of fried foods and onions. He slipped into a red vinyl booth and picked up a newspaper abandoned by a previous customer.

The Gangland Hit headline screamed for attention. The story below covered the murder of the Cuban casino owners with suspicious ties to Fidel Castro, and listed the bodyguards as "houseguests." It also revealed the children's safety.

To Anthony, the story confirmed that he was on the run.

It was dark when he paid the check, settled his fedora, and pushed through the glass doors. Free of his obligation to Best, he stepped lightly in his polished shoes on the searing concrete. Anthony drove south to the Strip, past the Stardust, Sahara, and the Flamingo, until his subconscious brought him to his favorite watering hole at the new Sands Tower.

Just one drink, and then I'm outta here.

He passed the Texaco station, parked near the marquee advertising Jack Carter's appearance, and walked through the noisy casino until he reached the smoky club. An empty stool invited him to sit at the rounded corner of the mahogany bar. He ordered a Glenlivet.

A happy patron dropped a nickel into the jukebox and Glenn Miller spun to life. The music made Anthony feel even better, because he hated that rock 'n' roll crap they played on the radio.

He lit a Lucky and caught the cool gaze of a good-looking blonde in the back corner booth. Anthony scanned the bar for familiar faces. His gaze passed over her once again and she made no effort to act disinterested. He said hello to his drink, draining half of it in one long swallow.

Impressed with her self-confidence, he waved the bartender over. "Send that blonde over there another of whatever it is she's having."

The experienced bartender delivered it, leaned in and spoke for a moment. She waved a hand, inviting Anthony to join her.

He slid into the booth and gave her his best crooked grin. "My name is Anthony, and I'm going to marry you someday."

The blonde shrugged, sipped at the fresh martini, and examined her new acquaintance as he pitched his hat onto the table. "Sure. Right now?"

His dark, slicked-back hair and olive complexion were nothing new in their booming city. "Nah, I gotta finish this drink first, and then I need to tell the Boss that I don't work for him no more." He knew that statement was bogus, but it felt good all the same. When the drink was gone, he planned to be on the road, possibly to Los Angeles, or maybe Florida.

She ran her soft, green eyes over his dark suit, and the coat cut to hide the automatic under his left arm. She liked the snap-brim fedora he'd worn tilted to one side when he came in, even though men's hats went out of style not long after Kennedy took office. "Your boss won't *let* you quit."

"How do you know that?"

"Because the *capo* doesn't turn loose too easily."

His smile slipped. "Oh, you know the Business?"

"I lived in Boston for a long time." She took another tiny sip. "Before that, New York."

"I'll work it out with the Boss. Then we'll get a little house with a picket fence in a country town and raise a dozen kids."

Her eyes crinkled in a way that made his knees weak, like some mug had busted him in the jaw, which happened with startling regularity in his younger years. Anthony was missing a back tooth to prove it.

She winked over her glass. "How about *half a dozen* kids to start, until we see how this goes?"

"Oh, already argumentative, huh? Think you're a tough dame?"

"Tough enough to handle you."

"Okay. I'll buy that. What about you? Job? Married? Kids? Boyfriend?"

"No, no, no, and no."

"That makes it easier. We're a match made in Heaven." A second Scotch arrived. Ceiling fans barely stirred the stale air full of cigarette smoke and spilled beer. The jukebox switched to Rosemary Clooney's clear voice. A dim shout went up through the closed doors separating the bar from the casino. Someone won at the roulette table.

She raised an eyebrow. "Now, *you* need to fess up."

He swallowed half the pour. "I'll be out of a job. Not married, no kids, and no girlfriend, or boyfriend either, for that matter. You have a name?"

She displayed a bright grin and extended her slim hand over the table. "Samantha, Samantha Chesterfield. Call me Sam."

"Anthony Agrioli." He smiled, her hand cool in his. "Your name sounds familiar."

"Oh, you mean Sam, like in 'Bewitched'?"

"Never heard of it. It was a weak joke about Chesterfield cigarettes. All right, Sam, they have a pretty good restaurant here. Let me buy you a steak and we'll get to know each other a little better before the wedding."

Her laugh was musical as Anthony paid for their drinks and led her to a quiet table in the back of the restaurant.

Chapter Four

The Spit and Whittle Club members on the front porch of Neal Box's northeast Texas country store laughed at Constable Ned Parker's story of his grandson Top and the rotting cow.

Ned shook his bald head. "I swear, it's a wonder he ain't in the hospital all the time. I'm too old to be raising kids. He's wearing me to a frazzle."

Ty Cobb Wilson leaned back in his chair with the front legs resting on the toes of his scuffed shoes and funneled a handful of peanuts into his half-full bottle of Coke. His brother, Jimmy Foxx, peeled an apple with a razor sharp pocketknife, the dark red peel dangling in one long spiral above the dusty boards at his feet.

The Wilson boys, who didn't seem to do anything but run the woods year round weren't bad, but they had a sixth sense about trouble and always showed up whenever someone was hurt or killed.

"We were worse than that, Mr. Ned, and I imagine it was the same when you was a shirttail kid yourself."

"You're probably right." Imitating Ty Cobb, Ned also leaned his cane-bottom chair back against the store on two legs. Barely nailed to the wall, the tin Prince Albert sign above his head rattled softly.

"Speaking of outlaws…" Mike Parsons jerked his chin toward the highway, where Pepper and Top were pedaling hard for the store.

Pepper waved as they coasted to a stop in the bottle cap-covered parking lot. "Hi, Grandpa."

"What are y'all doing up here?"

"Miss Becky sent us after some sugar. She's making teacakes, and ran out."

Ned jerked a thumb toward the door. "Go on in and tell Neal to put it on my account." He felt bad, because she told him she needed sugar the day before. His wife didn't drive, so he'd intended to pick up a sack, but he'd forgotten.

"Top, tell your grandma I'll be by later for a couple of them teacakes," Mike said. He farmed a few acres in the river bottoms. "She makes the best teacakes I ever et."

"She should." Ned gave a gentle swipe toward Pepper's blue-jeaned rear as she trotted up the steps and through the porch. "She's been at it a long time."

Top waited outside. "Somebody's calling you on the radio, Grandpa."

Ned thumped the chair's front legs down on the wooden porch to better hear the Motorola in his new, second-hand red Plymouth Fury. He upgraded to a new radio that wouldn't fade in and out of service when things got bad. Halfway annoyed that the youngster's ears were sharper than his, Ned cocked his head. The tinny voice coming from his dash was clearer now that he was paying attention. "Mr. Ned?"

The old constable didn't have a call number. When anyone in the Chisum dispatch office needed him, they simply asked by name and if Ned was near the radio, he answered. If he didn't, someone called his house.

He sighed and grunted off the chair. Most of the radio calls came from Cody Parker, Ned's informally adopted nephew, who'd been elected to the position of Precinct 3 constable in Center Springs. He was a dark-haired young man cut from aged oak and hard enough to bend a sharp sixteen-gauge nail if someone was to try and drive one in him.

Some calls came from Deputy John Washington, the almost mythical Lamar County lawman in charge of the "colored" section of Chisum, Texas. The giant of a man moved light as a bird a-flying.

The rest of the calls came from Martha, who handled dispatch for the Lamar County Sheriff's office, or from Judge O.C. Rains, when he was in one of his moods. It was in one of those moods that O.C. reappointed Ned as constable after a short retirement, doubling the position for the first time in Lamar County history, and annoying Sheriff Donald Griffin to no end.

He reached through the open window, plucked the microphone off the bracket, and keyed the handset. "Go ahead."

"Mr. Ned, this is Deputy Colton Stern? I'm up here at the lake where they're building this overlook on the far east side of the dam? Well, I have somebody who saw me and ran off in the woods?"

"Say he did? All right. I'll be there directly."

"I called for some more help?"

Ned wondered if everything the man said was a question.

"Mr. Ned? You there? That feller took off down toward the creek bottoms like a shot? I 'spect he was up to no good."

Without responding, Ned sighed and hung the handset back on the bracket, wishing he could go back to his seat on the porch with Parsons, Floyd Cass, Isaac Reader, and the Wilson brothers. The conversation had already turned to the upcoming quail season, which Ned dearly loved. Top was sitting on the bottom porch step, soaking up the stories. Holding the one-pound bag of sugar, Pepper leaned against a support post.

"Top, you kids hurry on back to the house. Miss Becky'll be fit to be tied if she has to wait much longer." It would also get him out of the doghouse with her, he hoped.

"Yessir." They pushed off when Ned opened the door and dropped heavily onto the cloth seat, wondering how the car could have already accumulated so much dust. Starting the engine, he shifted into gear and spun out on the bottle-cap parking lot toward the "lake."

Much of the land due to be underwater when they finished the Lake Lamar Dam was good farmland, five miles north of Center Springs. Ned raised crops on much of it for thirty years, and it bothered him to know that it would soon be owned by fish and the Corps of Engineers.

Ned didn't much like the idea of a new lake anyways. He was deathly afraid of water, and knew that within a year or two, someone would drown and he'd be pulling bodies out. He'd already convinced himself that at some point, it would likely be a family member.

He broke out of the trees on the two-lane blacktop leading from Center Springs. To the right, three large oaks on the hill marked the site of the first house he and Miss Becky had shared right after they married.

It was gone now, suffering the same fate as a dozen other homes and farms disappearing under unstoppable progress. In the devastated creek bottom below, the lake was taking shape as the Corps of Engineers and contractors dredged a huge hole in the rich dirt of the Sanders Creek bottoms. Bulldozers worked seven days a week, along with dinosaur-like draglines, knocking down every tree in a one by two-mile area that looked to have been destroyed by artillery.

Dozens of brush piles burned in the once thickly forested bottomlands. Other stacks of enormous trees waited for a match. Smoke hung low in the huge pit that looked to Ned like the inside of Hell. The smell filled the car as he passed, making him wish for cold weather. Wood smoke on a north wind always recalled his childhood days that probably weren't as pleasant as he remembered.

The finished dam rose to block the flow of upstream water. It would eventually choke off the lower section of Sanders Creek that flowed a mile from Ned's house. Broken granite served as riprap to prevent erosion on the lake side. The floodgates were still open, allowing the wounded creek a limited amount of time to run as it had done for centuries.

At the high point on the far side, two dump trucks sat beside three highway patrol cars in front of the unfinished visitor pullout. Ned drove slowly across the new dam, because the twenty-degree bend was high above the creek on the north side.

Ned pulled over to the shoulder and got out. Two local pickups passed, telling him that the new two-lane road between Center Springs and Powderly was already familiar and would soon be heavily used by those who didn't want to drive the extra five miles through Arthur City. He set his hat and nodded at the three officers waiting for him. "Howdy, boys."

Deputy Colton Stern wasn't one for pleasantries when he had something on his mind. "Mr. Ned? That feller wasn't but about eighteen, but when I slowed down to talk to him, he took off like a scared rabbit."

Ned would have preferred to visit for a minute or two before working his way around to the subject of their conversation. In his many years as constable, few things required immediate attention, and folks often found it to be rude behavior to talk business right off the bat.

To Ned, Colton's habit of ending most of his sentences with a questioning lilt annoyed him worse than houseflies annoyed his childhood friend Judge O.C. Rains. "What'd he look like?"

"Like a high school kid? But I've never seen him."

"You don't live around here, do you Colton?"

"Nossir?"

"Then I ain't surprised you ain't seen him." Removing his Stetson, he rubbed a rough hand over his bald head in exasperation. When his head was covered, a fringe of brown and gray hair gave the impression of a full head of hair. "How 'bout you boys?"

Neither of the deputies offered anything new, having only arrived moments before.

"I called for more help?" Colton waved an arm toward the thick timber opposite the lake. "It'll take a dozen men to sweep these woods."

"Won't do no good. What makes you think we need to root him out?"

"Well, he ran off, didn't he? He was up to something."

"That's what you say, but we might want to hold off calling in the army for a little while."

"I didn't call the army? I called the sheriff's office and asked for help. By the army, do you mean that I should have called the Corps of Engineers? You may be right, with all these unexploded bombs around here? It could be dangerous for a search party to go in after him."

Much of the upstream bottomland was used for artillery practice for the soldiers at Camp Maxey during World War II. Signs were popping up all around the new construction and planned campgrounds, warning of unexploded artillery shells they expected to float up when the lake filled. In the two decades after the war ended, thousands of live shells had been found and detonated in the surrounding countryside.

One of Ned's own nephews had lost a leg to one of the shells when he and two others were working under contract for the army to collect the "duds" in a wagon. A mortar shell slipped through Harvey's hands and landed on the wheel's steel rim. He was lucky the detonation took the wheel, a mule, and only one of Harvey's legs.

Ned rubbed the back of his neck for a moment, unconsciously feeling the deep crevices burned there by countless hours of riding a tractor in the sun. "I wish you'd-a let me have a few minutes before you did that."

Contacting the sheriff's department guaranteed a visit from Sheriff Griffin, a man Ned despised. Griffin grated on his nerves because he always thought he was the sharpest knife in the drawer, and usually underestimated those around him.

Ned shifted his weight and winced at a sharp pain in the side of his protruding belly, a frequent reminder of the bullet that had almost taken his life only months before down in Mexico, right at the start of summer.

"Why don't y'all give me a little while and let me see what I find out."

"We're going to make a sweep here in a minute, as soon as we round up enough men to form a search party?" Colton nodded toward the deputies. "Maybe we can track him pretty quick."

Ned studied the nearby woods beyond the pullout, glad the engineers hadn't cut down the thick stand of hardwoods. He'd hunted there since he was a kid, and the land was as familiar as the back of his hand. A thin prickly ash tree grew a distance from the taller oaks, leaning outward into the sunshine. Indians used the bark of the understory tree as a toothache remedy long before Ned hit the ground back in 1900.

A fresh slash gaped yellow in the morning light. "Um, humm. Well, y'all do what you want to." He walked back to his sedan and settled slowly into the seat. Shifting into gear, he pulled back onto the highway.

"That old man looks like he needs to retire." Deputy Bill Buchanan ducked into his own car, knocking his hat cockeyed and growling at the annoyance. The others laughed and waited for more men to arrive.

Ned drove toward Powderly, and followed the first gravel road that intersected the hardtop. It was covered with fall leaves, and more drifted from the canopy meeting far overhead. A rooster tail of dust and leaves fluttered up behind the car and settled back, a mix of multicolored confetti.

The road changed from gravel to dirt. He slowed on the narrow trace and followed it through deep-cut banks that were old when wagon wheels first ground their way through the red clay. Half a mile later, he pulled into the bare yard of an unpainted shack in the woods.

A barking pack of mongrel dogs crawled from under the porch. Ned killed the engine and waited. No one from the country ever got out of a car until someone came outside to call off the dogs. The warped screen door opened and a washed out woman in a faded dress appeared on the porch. "Shut up! Git on outta hea! Git!" She waved an arm. "You can get out now, Mr. Ned."

When he was sure the dogs were quiet, Ned stepped out into the dirt yard. "Mornin', Geneva. Frederick around?"

She pushed a wisp of brown and gray hair from her forehead. "Naw, he went squirrel huntin' this mornin' before daylight and ain't back yet. Sumpin' wrong?"

"Nooo," Ned answered in a slow voice. "What I really needed to see was if Chester was here."

She shrugged. "He's here and then he ain't. He's been running these hills and hollers so much I don't see him 'til suppertime. If he saw you drive up, he might have run. You know how he is, Mr. Ned, about bein' nervous 'n-all."

"That I do."

He waited as she wiped her wet hands on a dingy dishtowel and faced the woods. "Chesterrrrr! Wooooo!" Her screeching voice echoed. She turned back to Ned. "He'll be here directly, if he's within hearin' distance. There was a racket in the smokehouse a little while back, so he might be in there, too."

Seconds later, a ragged kid in overalls stepped out of the nearby smokehouse held up only by a slim chinaberry tree. Chester's yellow hair looked as if it had been cut with a dull butcher knife and his clothes hung like a scarecrow's. He had a pocketknife in one hand and a chunk of bark in the other. He tucked the yellow side of the bark against a lower molar and closed the knife without saying a word.

Ned jiggled the change in his pocket, a habit he recently acquired and wanted to break. "Got a toothache, Chester?"

The youngster shrugged.

Ned nodded, and recalled the prickly, numbing feeling that came with tucking the moist inner bark against a sore tooth or ulcer. "I used the same remedy when I was about your age, but I shoulda gone to see a dentist. Now I have to wear these dentures all the time."

Still on the porch, Geneva folded and refolded the dish towel with nervous fingers. "Well, we don't have much money for such."

The old constable considered her statement and nodded solemnly. "I reckon that's why you been away from the house for a while today, is that it?"

"Mr. Ned, you know Chester don't talk much."

He studied the young man standing hunched and still as a statue. Ned knew that if Chester was in a mood, he could talk to the youngster all day and probably wouldn't get much more of a response than a nod, if he was lucky.

"Chester, did you see a deputy sheriff out on the dam road?"

"Mr. Ned!" Geneva's voice was shocked. "You ain't got no call to talk to him like that! He ain't right, but that ain't no reason to cuss."

"I wasn't cussin' at the boy, Geneva. I meant the new road out there that goes across the Lake Lamar Dam."

Embarrassed, she gave a nervous laugh. "We're all gonna have to get used to that thang, ain't we?"

"Sure 'nough. Now, Chester, look at me." When the boy timidly raised his eyes, Ned gave him a grin. "It was you, wundn't it, that the deputy saw?"

"I didn't do it." He shifted and looked uncomfortable. "I jist run oft."

"Then it *was* you. How come you to run?"

Chester shrugged.

Knowing that was the only answer he was going to get, Ned sighed. "Sorry, Geneva, for bothering you. Can I take Chester with me for a little bit so's I can show them boys back there that he ain't no bank robber? They got it in their heads that some booger-bear is running these woods, and if I don't, somebody other than me is liable to come up here, and you don't want that."

Thankful that Ned understood her son, Geneva pursed her mouth in the familiar way that had etched deep lines around her mouth through the years. She gave him a quick nod. "You'll bring him back, d'rectly?"

"Sure will, after we get some ice cream. That sound good to you, hoss? We'll go to the store and get you a banana bar."

Instead of answering, Chester shuffled to the car and climbed in the front seat, still working the bark against his aching gum. Ned slammed his own door and turned around to the tune of barking dogs.

Four more cars were parked on the side of the road when they returned to the unfinished overlook. One of them belonged to

Sheriff Donald Griffin. Ned coasted to a stop in his lane and killed the engine. "Y'all having a meetin'?"

The sheriff walked up to Ned's car and rested his hand on the open window. "You forget something?"

Ned glared at the mustached man in his large Stetson, fancy gun belt, Colt .45 revolver, and shiny black boots. He had no intention of exchanging pleasantries in the middle of the road with the pompous ass. He jerked a thumb toward his passenger. "Did your bad guy look like this?"

The sheriff set his jaw at the snub. Without taking his eyes off the young man in Ned's car, Griffin waved. "Deputy Stern. The constable has a prisoner. Come take a look and see if you can identify him."

Frowning, Colton joined them and bent to look into the car. "Well, I'll be damned. You done caught him? Hey, boys? Ned's done caught our fugitive. Why ain't he cuffed?"

"Don't need no cuffs. This here's Frederick and Geneva Humphrey's boy, Chester, and he didn't run off, at least not the way you think. Chester here runs off from everybody. He's been nervous a long time."

Before Deputy Colton could say another word, Sheriff Griffin interrupted. "I don't believe he'd-a run if he hadn't done something wrong. We don't even know it was him here, for sure, now do we? Since you say he's not right, he probably got in your car when you told him to, and the fugitive is still hiding in the woods somewhere, isn't that right, *Constable* Parker?"

Ned's attempt at a smile surrendered and froze on his face. "Me being constable still gets your goat, don't it Donald?" With an effort, he crooked his finger in a "come here" move. "Stick your hand out toward the boy there."

Puzzled, the sheriff bent down, stretched his arm across Ned and waited. Ned tapped his cheek and pointed at the open hand. "Put it there, right now."

With a look of terror, Chester dug out the soggy chunk of bark from his cheek. He placed it in the sheriff's hand. With a disgusted start, Griffin jerked up right and stared at the soaked wood leaking into his palm.

Ned shifted into gear and jerked his thumb toward the passenger window. "Now, if you'll get your team of crack investigators on the stick, Sheriff, you'll see that piece of toothache bark in your hand fits that little bitty trunk behind Colton there. So I reckon I'll rest my case. If you don' believe me, you can go ahead on with your manhunt by yourselves. We'll be up at the store eatin' a banana ice cream if y'all need anything else."

Chapter Five

In Los Angeles, Anthony watched the tanned young girls swimming in a small pool behind the bright white Hotel Continental, on Sunset and Benedict.

He and Samantha sat at a metal table beneath a white shade structure near the busy pool bar. "You should get a bikini like that."

Samantha glanced down at her much more modest one-piece swimsuit and wiggled her painted toes. "I'm not that kind of girl." She sipped her drink after removing the little paper umbrella.

For some reason, her comment pleased him. "You're not like any other woman I've ever known."

"Is that a compliment?"

"It is."

She spun the umbrella handle with two fingers. The colors were a blur. "I think I'm falling for you, Mr. Anthony Agrioli."

He thought about his feelings the night before in the Cheetah Club, their nighttime hangout. "You don't know much about me."

She watched a barefoot young woman walk by and grin at Anthony. She idly wondered what the woman's flip hairdo and false eyelashes would look like if she kicked her into the pool. "You don't know much about me, either." She paused. "I'm sure of one thing. You're a good man."

"I'm not sure that's true."

"It is."

In the past week their relationship grew in depth and understanding, despite holding large chunks of themselves back. After talking for hours on end, it was obvious there were certain holes in both their lives they avoided filling.

Anthony found the similarity appealing, because he always played his cards close to the vest. This time was no exception, even when he realized he was in love with the little blonde.

He lit two cigarettes and handed one to her. "We can't stay here forever."

"I won't go back home. There's nothing for me there."

He bit the question off. If a woman holds things back, a man doesn't need to know the details. He drew heavily on a cigarette and exhaled through his nose. "I don't have any marketable skills, Doll. No matter where we go, I'm afraid I'll make a lousy handyman."

"You might surprise us both. How are you at pumping gas?"

"I was good at stealing it when I was a kid."

She laughed.

"I'll have to find something else with a better future. So where do you want to go?"

Samantha threw her head back, puffed her own cigarette, and watched the smoke dissipate in the warm air. "Somewhere away from all this concrete. I want a house with a picket fence and a barbecue in the back."

"You'll get bored. The city is in your blood."

"I need a transfusion."

They sat silent, watching the tourists. Anthony pulled at his hula shirt to adjust the shoulders. "We'll need to go back to Vegas to get our things."

"And then what?"

"I have an idea."

Best flew to New York or Kansas City on a regular basis, and even more frequently when summoned. Anthony remembered hearing about a meeting scheduled for the next night. He picked up a paper menu and handed it to Sam. "Let's order lunch, and after that, we'll check out. It's time to leave."

Chapter Six

I crawled behind Pepper underneath the Ordway house. "We're gonna get in trouble in here."

Sitting about a hundred and fifty yards behind Neal Box's country store, the two-story was built back in the 1890s and had been empty for the last few years. It had a huge wraparound porch and giant burr oaks shaded the entire house. There was even a cherry tree in the front yard, and we stopped by each year to grab a handful when they were ripe.

Uncle Cody tells a story about when he spent the night there as a kid, and watched ghosts come down the dark wood stairs and leave through the front door to get into a phantom buggy pulled by spirit horses.

Pepper stopped beside a pipe jutting up through the floor above. "C'mon. It's easy." She reached up and slid a peeling piece of plywood out of the way. She stood and pulled herself inside.

When her feet disappeared, I followed, climbing up into the kitchen. "How'd you know about the floor?"

"I saw it when Daddy let me come in with him last week. He heard it was for rent, so we came over to look around. He said it needs a lot of work." She stepped over to the painted plywood cabinets and jumped up and down on the floor. The linoleum bounced like a trampoline. "See?"

We walked down the hallway from the kitchen. The temperature inside was surprisingly cool, making me think the last heat wave of the year was long gone. The place smelled of dust, mice, and dried leaves. We wandered through two bedrooms and found ourselves in the living room. Most of the paper blinds were down. The whole place was spooky, like those haunted houses in the movies, with old sheets draped over furniture.

We stopped in the entry hall. A set of plain, narrow stairs bent to the right at a landing. I shivered. "I ain't going up there."

She grinned and started up, but then stopped when a creak filled the air. "Uh, that's the house settling. Let's sit in the living room."

Dusty sheets covered the furniture. Pepper plopped down on a couch facing the fireplace. She dug a crumpled pack of Viceroys from her pants pocket and lit one. "This is a lot better than your stupid tree house. We can stay in here as long as we want to and no one will ever know."

I saw the smoke rise. She'd decided she liked smoking and it worried me sick. Instead of watching, I concentrated on the toes of my U.S. Keds. "I'm not sure it's a good idea. We'll get caught and they'll beat the whey out of us. You ought not smoke them things, either. You'll probably burn this house down around us."

She snorted and dug the transistor radio out of her back pocket. "Don't bring me down."

There she was again, talking like them California kids. "It ain't like Miss Becky won't be able to smell the smoke on you."

Instead of answering, she clicked the radio on and "White Rabbit" blared out. Pepper pitched the radio on the couch and jumped up into the middle of the room, jerking and throwing her hair and arms around.

"What are you doing?"

"Dancing. This is how the kids do it in California."

"You're not a hippie."

She kept flailing around. "They have it figured out. It's cool because they're all about love and peace. This song is far out."

"We're loved, and it's peaceful here."

Pepper stopped and glared at me. "Peaceful? Have you lost your damn mind?" She stomped over and turned the radio down.

"Have you forgot what happened to us? What about Uncle Cody and Grandpa? Things are getting worse and you don't see it."

Bad memories tried to surface, but I forced them back down into those dark rooms I kept locked away in my mind. "Grandpa and Uncle Cody will make sure nothing ever happens again."

Grandpa wasn't scared of the Devil.

"Something *always* happens, again and again. We're safe right now, but who knows what'll happen the minute we walk out that front door. Hell, for all we know there's an ax murderer creaking around upstairs."

I wished she hadn't said that, because the house popped again.

We stopped to listen. Pepper picked up the radio and dialed it up once more, but it was some dumb love song. She chewed her lip. "I asked Daddy if I could go spend Christmas with Aunt Ludie and Uncle Stant in California. Why don't you go too?"

I was only half listening to her, and half listening to the house. "No, I believe I'll stay here. I ain't interested in no dirty hippies. They all need haircuts."

Pepper flopped down on the couch again. "Long hair is anti-establishment."

"Huh?"

"Never mind." She looked around the room. "This must have been a great place back in the olden days. Bet they didn't have no Skinners, or crazy people who cut off heads and stuff." She stopped and hugged herself like I'd seen her do. It wasn't really hugging, she was trying to feel for that scar on her shoulder The Skinner burned there. "I'm so tired of this jerkwater town that I could spit. I wish we could live in Dallas, or Austin. I'd love Austin, because they don't have crazy murderers down there."

"That shows what you know. They had a guy shooting people from a tower down there last year."

"Just once." A dusty farm truck rattled down the oil road past the house. Pepper sighed. "But I guess we'll keep going to school, smelling cow shit, and watching old people grow older."

I tried to think of something good. "City people don't have horses."

She snorted. "When was the last time we rode horses? The only thing Grandpa has is that old plow horse, Jake."

"Your daddy had one 'til last year." Uncle James kept horses and cows on his place until a couple of months earlier. He sold them to make a little money, but I knew he'd buy some more soon and start all over.

Pepper started to answer, but a loud pop overhead caused us to look upward. The sound of a wooden door closing was enough to make us both stand. Her face went white. "Someone's in here with us."

We listened. A sound like light footsteps crossed the room overhead. I looked at the staircase that Uncle Cody talked about when he was a kid. "Ghosts."

"Ghosts don't walk."

That's when we heard footsteps approach the staircase and start down.

It was too much.

We charged across the living room. Pepper shot the bolt on the front door and we raced out of the house.

Once safely outside, I looked over my shoulder, but there was no one on the stairs.

Chapter Seven

It was after midnight in Las Vegas, and the temperature still hovered in the low nineties when Anthony dropped Sam off at her apartment. "I'll be back in a couple of hours, Doll."

"You're not going back to your place?"

He thought about it for a moment. "I have some business to finish, but I'll be back before daylight. Pack your grip, and we're outta here."

It was a dangerous move. They needed travel money and Anthony recalled it was one of those rare times that Best's house staff had the night off. He planned a little visit to the empty house, because Best did business by keeping large amounts of cash money on hand at all times.

He drove to a car lot owned by Best and utilized a drop system that had been in place for years. Half a dozen spaces in a fenced area behind the office held clean cars registered to fictitious people. The Ford that Anthony drove came from there over a week ago. He pulled it into an empty slot and pitched the keys in the ashtray. Selecting a Pontiac facing outward, he reached under the back bumper and located the keys. After transferring his suitcase into the new car, Anthony drove off.

When the manager arrived the next morning and found the Ford nosed into the parking slot, he wouldn't ask any questions. By that afternoon, the car would be on a carrier heading out of Vegas, replaced by another one available to any of Best's trusted employees.

Half an hour later, Anthony parked at the curb and knocked on the front door of the dark house. Despite the early morning hour, Leo Barbeau opened the door. Obviously awakened from a deep sleep, Leo lowered the pistol in his hand and scratched his mussed hair. "Ant'ny, where the hell you been? The Boss wants your ass…"

Smiling, Anthony grasped Leo's shoulder with his left hand and shoved the .22 against the older man's pajama-covered chest, pulling the trigger twice. Leo collapsed backward and Anthony stepped inside, shoving the door closed with his foot.

He kicked Leo's gun away and waited, listening. The house remained silent.

Confident the house was empty, Anthony left Leo's body where it fell and backed the car into the mob boss' empty garage. He passed through the open living room and den. The wall safe behind a heavy mahogany desk held thick stacks of bills. He'd seen it open a couple of times when Best paid him, but Anthony didn't have enough time to crack that one.

Instead, he rolled a stout two-wheeled dolly from the garage into the master bedroom's walk-in closet to load up a small free-standing Hercules safe. The guys who worked for Malachi said it was full of bills and jewelry, but by the weight, Anthony figured it contained gold, too. He had to throw his entire weight against the dolly to tilt the safe far enough to get it out of the closet and down the thickly carpeted hall.

After dragging a long crease down the sheetrock in the hall-way, he maneuvered around several corners and through the kitchen. It barely fit through the door leading into the garage. He stopped behind the Pontiac and studied the squatty little chunk of steel. There was no way he could lift it into the trunk.

Anthony found a car jack in the super-heated garage and maneuvered it underneath the Hercules. He worked the stiff handle. The black safe scraped the bumper as it rose higher, but he didn't care…the Pontiac wasn't his anyway.

Once he had it high enough, it was nothing to tilt the safe and let it fall heavily into the trunk. He figured to open it somewhere else and hoped the contents would be enough to pay him what Malachi owed, with a little left over as severance.

He picked up Samantha half an hour later. She was waiting on the sidewalk outside of her apartment and eyed the unfamiliar car.

"Nice." She pitched two bags into the backseat and they cleared out. It was almost too easy. She adjusted herself in the seat, curling up like a kitten. "When did you get the new car?"

"A couple of hours ago."

"We heading to the airport?"

"Nope. The Boss and I didn't end on good terms. You said you knew the business. I'm sure he has people out there looking for me, so we're not going where they are." It was a good bet that Best's men were watching the airport and bus station. Even the Las Vegas Holiday Special train, once called the City of Las Vegas, was off limits. The only safe way to travel was by car.

"I know how he operates. Instead of heading for California, we're driving to Texas."

She smoothed her skirt around her legs. "What's there?"

"Paradise, I've heard, and none of the Boss' people."

They didn't see the sedan driven by Pinocchio following at a safe distance.

Chapter Eight

"This world's a changin', Mr. Ned, and I don't know if I can draw a tight enough rein to hang on for the whole ride."

Pursing his lips to think, Judge O.C. Rains crossed one leg over the other and laced his fingers over his knee.

Ned studied on Deputy Sheriff John Washington's statement for a long moment. They were sitting on the concrete retaining wall north of the courthouse, beneath the crepe myrtles and a cloudy sky. "What do you mean?"

"There was a cuttin' outside of Sugar Bear's joint last night, and it weren't like no regular fight. It looked like somebody butchered a hog when this one sorry outfit got done with the other'n."

A giant of a man, John Washington was the only black deputy in Sheriff Griffin's department, and worked with virtual autonomy, something unheard of in most rural Texas cotton towns.

"Well, we've worked cuttin's before."

"Yessir, but this one was different, y'all. When the loser was down, the cutter kept at him somethin' fierce. That colored boy bled out in a lake of blood, and when I got there, the one a-doin' it stood up, folded the razor in his hand, and laid it on the dead man's forehead. When I ast him why he done it, he laughed and said the devil made him do it."

"Well, I reckon that's the truth." O.C. rocked slowly back and forth, still holding his knee. "The ol' Devil is behind most meanness, black, white, or red, as far as I'm concerned."

"Yeah, but we never had anything like that, 'til the last three or four years." John shook his great head. He dwarfed the old men sitting on either side. "Now all we got around here is one killin' after another."

Ned studied a foreign-looking man walking past them on Main. "That's true, sure 'nough. At least you got him locked up, instead of us having to run him down."

Traditionalists, they were waiting for noon to walk down the street and eat dinner at Frenchie's café. John hadn't decided if he wanted to join them in the front part of the "whites only" café, or to sit in the back with his own people. It was a difficult decision, because he'd taken coffee in the front before, though it brought stares and muttered comments from the same white citizens he would protect if they needed a lawman.

"You know what I was asked yesterday while I was working that cuttin' at Sugar Bear's?"

O.C. raised a bushy white eyebrow. "What?"

"If me and Mr. Ned went down to Mexico after The Skinner. They thought he caught Cody and tried to kill him before them Mexicans put him in jail."

Ned shook his head. "They just won't leave well enough alone, will they?"

"I reckon not. They still scared of The Skinner comin' back. The story is he's down on the Rio Grande there, skinnin' folks on *both* sides of the river. I tried to tell 'em it ain't so, but they won't believe me. If there's a murder in the next ten years, they'll lay it off on *him*."

"Folks will forget in time…who's that?" O.C. finally noticed the same stranger in a dark suit standing at the corner, taking pictures of the courthouse with a Polaroid camera. Most folks in Center Springs used Brownie Hawkeyes or those new Instamatic cameras with plastic flashcubes on top.

John squinted from under his Stetson and watched the man push three levers on the camera before peeling the picture from the open back. He waved the photo for a moment, then slipped it into his pocket and shot again. "I don't know," John said.

"I've seen him a time or two on the square these last few days, taking pictures and making notes on some papers he carries in that briefcase there."

"Could be a spy, intending to send a missile down here on us." Ned twiddled his thumbs as he thought.

O.C. blew out his lips in exasperation. "I don't reckon there's much sense in bombing *Chisum.*"

Ned immediately reddened. "The army camp's just north of us. I 'magine it could still be a target. We probably got some of them missiles of our own buried out there."

"You blamed old fool. Them Ruskies'll bomb Dallas or Wichita Falls or Houston, but I doubt they'll waste an atom bomb on Chisum, unless they know you personally and have had all they can take. I could understand it, then. I just hope I have time to get gone far enough away from you so I don't get any on me."

"Well, Top and Pepper tell me they practice what they call them duck-and-cover drills under their desks ever couple of weeks or so, like a little 'ol school desk is gonna be enough cover if somebody drops an atom bomb on us. So I reckon the government still thinks them damn fools over there are liable to shoot at us."

John grinned, and cut off further argument between the two old friends who enjoyed arguing as much as eating. "Yessir, but Maxey ain't much camp no more, not like back in the war. They mostly jus' chicken houses there now. I'll drop by and get two or three dozen eggs from 'em every now and then when I'm heading over to Rachel Lea's house."

John had met her back in the spring. After finding out that her husband left her in a shack to raise her own two children and her dead sister's kids, he began to visit two or three times a week. At first it was to bring groceries to the struggling family, but later, he finally admitted it was to see the attractive woman with the deepest, prettiest dimples in all of Lamar County, in his opinion.

"Her young'uns eat a lot?"

"Right smart, Mr. O.C. They all growing like weeds."

"Well, you a good man, John, for taking up with a woman with so many kids. Besides, her cookin' must be somethin' else."

The old men exchanged looks and laughed.

O.C. reached deep into his pants pocket, thumbed through a fold of limp bills, and handed several over to John. "Use this for 'em. I got a boy's life of stoop labor behind me, and would hate to see them kids working the fields if they don't have to."

The big deputy knew better than to argue, especially after Ned added to the collection. John nodded, stuffed the cash into his shirt pocket, and buttoned the top down.

"Thankee."

"That'll dry up once you marry that gal." O.C.'s eyes twinkled.

John bit back a grin. "There ain't no talk about marryin' up."

"I bet there ain't much talk no how," Ned said and they laughed.

"Mr. Ned, they's so many kids around, all we *can* do is talk."

"Don't let Griffin hear about you being over there too much during the day," Ned warned. The sheriff was about as popular as the Itch. "He'll make something up about you, if you do, and it might come around and cost you your badge."

O.C. sobered quickly and spoke, making sure no one was within hearing distance. "Y'all, I'm hearing more things that ain't settin' well with me about Griffin."

All three men despised Chisum's sheriff. He was crooked as a dog's hind leg, in Ned's opinion, and it proved true when they traced a direct line of illegal drugs from Mexico to the Red River, all covered by Griffin and one or more of his deputies.

Cody found out the truth while he was held in a Mexican prison. The final confirmation came from a couple of offhand photos shot by Top when he was playing spy outside the Lamar County Courthouse one snowy day. One captured Griffin taking a thick envelope from the hand of a known drug-runner.

Judge Rains leaned in to Ned. John shifted to listen. "Y'all, I hear he's keeping the highway hot between here and Dallas. You know Deputy White. Well, he's told me that Griffin spends a lot of time on the phone in his office, and White's seen him go home two or three times a day. He said he went over there one day so's he could ask him a question, and Griffin was on the phone. He hung up real quick and gave White a chewing out for coming by."

"Hell, O.C., that's a lot of…What do you call it?"

"Supposition, and you're right. That's all it is, but it's more than that. It's a feeling I have from being around that sorry bastard for so long. Y'all keep an eye out for him, and watch your back when he's around. I can protect you most of the time, but when it's you and him out on the highway somewhere, I'm out of the loop."

Their dark mood fled when Wade Reidel hurried up the sidewalk, waving his arms in agitation. Wade always needed a haircut, and the hair growing down the back of his neck and into his collar was almost as long as his cowlick in the front.

Ned sighed. "Uh, oh. This ain't gonna be good."

Wade jerked his chin upward in a hello. "Ned, we got a problem."

"What's that?"

"Well, I think my in-laws are in cahoots with my wife to keep me out of the house."

"That ain't against the law." O.C. always hated trying to pull information out of someone who, in his opinion, should offer up the story and be done with it.

"Hidy, Mr. O.C., sorry I didn't speak. How you doin'?"

"Fair to middlin'."

"Mr. Ned, I'm so riled up it's eating a hole in my stomach. I don't like to hang my dirty laundry out in public, but me and Karen Ann started having troubles about July and things have been rough since then."

He paused, as if expecting one of the men to say something sympathetic. Instead they waited.

Wade cleared his throat and dug at the wax in his ear. "Okay, I wanted to move out, but I held on 'cause, you know, folks tend to think things'll work themselves out. But that ain't gonna happen as long as she keeps stringin' off across the river two or three nights a week to drink in Cody's club."

"Careful there, Wade." O.C. held up a hand. "Just cause Cody owns the Sportsman, it don't mean he's at fault. There's half a dozen other joints over there with jukeboxes and drinkin', and I doubt his is the only beer hall she visits."

"Didn't mean no disrespect to one of your constables, Mr. O.C." He examined the exploratory results under the nail of his little finger. "Mr. Ned. Anyways, I guess I shoulda seen things were changing when she started sleeping in the living room all the time. She said it was because her back hurt and our cotton mattress was too hard, but that old couch has springs coming up through the cushions, though you can't see 'em because of that bedspread she keeps on it…"

"Can you get to the point, Wade?" Ned was half listening, half watching the well-dressed man with the camera. He'd changed positions and was shooting down north Main toward Frenchie's Café, and maybe including their little cluster on the retaining wall. From the corner of his eye, Ned saw O.C.'s attention was on the man, too.

"All right. Anyways, I'm a nervous wreck over all this and they always say the husband is the last one to know…Hey, did either of y'all know that Karen Ann is running around with Bud Templeton? I believe they're sleeping together, too."

No one made eye contact. Bud Templeton was so far down the list of Karen Ann's bed partners that they didn't have the heart to bring up the others that stretched back through their stormy marriage. She was a knockout, all right. The young men in Lamar County stopped what they were doing to watch her walk by. The truth was, not all of them just looked. Ned knew why her back ached, and it wasn't their hard cotton mattress.

"Anyways, okay, both of us have a tendency to get mad real quick, so we might both be guilty of something, but certain third parties got involved—well, it was her sister for one, who talked Karen Ann into pitching my clothes out in the yard and changing the locks. Said I was doing her wrong. So I marched myself right over to the courthouse to see if somebody can help me and to hire a lawyer, cause they keep telling her what to say and every time I call the house, her mama's listening in on the party line 'cause you know they live down the road a piece, though I think her daddy likes me well enough. I ain't against him or nothin'…"

The young man simply stopped, as if he'd run out of energy.

Ned took the opportunity and stood.

Wade gathered himself. "Are you leaving, Mr. Ned?"

"I'm trying to. I'll drop by and talk to Karen Ann and her folks, but if they haven't done anything other than change the locks, there ain't much I can do right now."

"Well now, I'd be proud if you did that." He started to leave, then dug in his pants pocket and came out with a handful of silver dollars. He handed one to each of the surprised men. "I'd like to buy y'all dinner today. I'll see you soon."

After he left, the three lawmen frowned and shook their heads. "How come him to do that?" Ned asked.

"People do funny things," O.C. stood. "Let's go eat." He handed the silver dollar to John and Ned did the same, both knowing the money would go to Rachel for food or clothing for her kids.

Before they could step off the curb, Cody pulled up in his red and white El Camino and spoke through the open passenger window. "Ned, we need to go to work. Howdy, Judge, John."

Ned leaned forward and peered into the window. "What is it?"

"Gene Stark called and said he found his brother shot to death up out toward Bill Stiles' place. Tommy Lee's still sitting in his truck, with the side of his head blowed off."

John struck out across the lot between them and the courthouse, where his car was parked next to the "colored" bathroom. "I'll meet y'all out there." Center Springs was far out of his assigned area, but John had long ago adopted the Parkers as part of his own family and was always willing to help.

"All right, then. We'll see you there." Ned screwed himself into the front seat of the El Camino's cab. "Dammit, boy, when are you gonna get you something decent to drive?"

They were still arguing when Cody pulled away from the curb to take Ned to his own car parked on the square. O.C. stood alone on the sidewalk and shivered, worried that a dark train might be coming for them once again.

Finally, he walked toward Frenchie's to eat alone.

Chapter Nine

They drove east down Route 66 through Santa Fe before Anthony whipped the Plymouth into a dismal used car lot on the outskirts of town. A salesman in a drugstore cowboy hat and a gaudy bolo tie had Anthony's door open almost before he could kill the engine. "Howdy, folks! How can I help you?"

Anthony shouldered himself out of the car, forcing the aggressive ducktailed salesman to back up. "I need to trade this car in, but I have a problem." He winked. "How about I give you the keys and pay you half again what that fifty-eight Buick there is worth?"

Bolo Tie squinted one eye, noting the suit and Anthony's flat eyes. "You must be in a hurry."

Anthony leaned close and spoke in a conspirator's whisper. "Yeah. Her husband is looking for us and…well, you know the story."

Tilting his hat back, Bolo Tie rocked on his heels with a lascivious look on his face. "I see. A young couple in love is it? No title?"

It was all Anthony could do not to punch him in the mouth. He shrugged.

Bolo Tie scratched his cheek. "Well, I could get in trouble for this, but I know how young love is. That Buick might be a tad more than half again, but I bet we can come to an agreement." He jerked his head toward the tiny office. "C'mon on and let's get this done."

Anthony leaned into the car. "Doll, pull around to the back and we'll unload the trunk after I make this deal. It'll take both of us because there's something in there that you can't lift."

"That's what's making the rear end sag so heavy?"

He smiled. "Sure is. I think there's a safe in there."

"Um hum. Yours?"

"Ours."

"Don't you think it'll be a little obvious, moving a safe between cars?"

Anthony jerked his head toward the office. "After I finish in there, our new friend won't look out the window until we leave. He'll be counting his money."

"How are we going to move a safe?"

"No worries. A place like this will have an engine hoist."

He winked and followed the salesman inside. Twenty minutes later Anthony handed the man a wad of cash and plucked the new title from his hand. "Now, give me a minute to move some stuff over."

Bolo Tie started to follow him out the door. Anthony stopped him with a look. "No. I said give me a minute while we move some stuff. The keys will be in the ignition when we leave, and then it's yours."

Bolo Tie rocked back on his heels again, and built an awkward grin. "All righty, Mr. Smith." When Anthony stepped outside and started the Buick, the dealer picked up the phone and dialed. "Kenneth. Get on over here and bring your tools. We got a hot one."

He hung up, stared out the front window, and didn't move from behind his desk, even when he heard the chains rattle on his engine hoist not ten feet away. The Buick finally appeared from around the corner and pulled onto the highway. Bolo Tie breathed a sigh of relief and once again counted the cash in his hand.

He stuffed several bills into his pocket and recalled the look Anthony gave him. He watched a car full of rough men pull slowly out of the parking lot across the street. It followed the couple down Route 66. He shuddered, glad the young man was gone.

◇◇◇

Feeling comfortable in the new car, the couple took their time and stopped at trading posts doing business behind giant papier-mâché Apache Indians and teepees, slept in a water-cooled motel with giant arrows in the courtyard, and ate in greasy spoon cafés serving overdone hamburgers, unidentifiable chicken entrees, and tasteless strawberry shortcake desserts.

Their pursuers, if they existed, had no idea which direction they chose. The obvious direction was west to California, to disappear into the crowded cities of Los Angeles or San Francisco. Most of the gamblers in Vegas would have bet against Texas.

Route 66 led through the wasteland of eastern New Mexico and the barren Texas Panhandle until they finally reached a small country town of Shamrock, less than a hundred miles from the geographic ground zero of the Dust Bowl. Dusk fell on the small town surrounded by irrigated fields that stretched as far as the eye could see. An art deco tower, thirty feet high, jutted up from twin filling bays of a futuristic Conoco station, glowing in the late evening light. Anthony pulled in to gas up, and the smell of frying food from the U-Drop Inn filled the air.

Though it was dusk, and hotter than hell, they left the station and cruised down the burg's main street. Samantha saw a movie poster in the lighted frames on either side of the ticket kiosk at the Liberty Theater.

"Look. *The Good, The Bad, and the Ugly*. I'm tired of driving, and I've been wanting to see that picture."

"Doll, we're on the lam."

"You said yourself they're looking somewhere else. Besides, they have air conditioning. I want to sit for a while and look at something besides the desert or movie fan magazines."

Anthony quickly realized he couldn't talk her out of seeing the spaghetti Western. He gave in when he realized he was tired, too. He drove on past the Liberty and at the edge of town, steered into the Clay Court Motor motel for the night.

Swimming Pool! blinked under the neon sign.

Below that, another sign announced, Kid Friendly!

A chatty little old man with gray hair totally unfamiliar with a comb lurked behind the counter. "Mr. and Mrs. Smith. Glad to have you." He licked his peeling lips, scratched deeply into the tangled mass on his head, and gave them a key attached to a large green plastic fob. "Y'all want the room for a couple of hours, or all night?"

Anthony thought about knocking his old block off. "We want it for the night."

"I bet. I wish I was that young again."

"Hey, buddy, give me the keys without the commentary." He felt his forehead throb and dialed back the rising anger.

The old man frowned and stared down at the twenty-dollar bill in his hand. "Well, hell, I didn't mean no harm. We don't get many out-of-town folks named Smith that don't want a short-term discount."

Without another word, Anthony held out his hand for the change, glad Samantha was waiting in the car. A minute later, back at the wheel, his frown prompted her to reach for his shoulder. "Something wrong?" she asked.

"That old man in there is too nosy."

She grinned and glanced back into the tiny office. "There probably isn't much excitement around here."

"He was about to get more excitement than he bargained for." They pulled around the tiny swimming pool enclosed by the U-shaped motel and backed the Buick into the slot directly in front of their room. The warped door was stubborn. Anthony put his shoulder against it and shoved. It snapped open with a pop and they found themselves inside the stifling room smelling of stale cigarette smoke and Pine-Sol.

The water cooler wheezed when Samantha punched the switch, but a trickle of cool air told them it would be a comfortable night in the spacious room, if they only used the threadbare sheet as cover. "It feels good to be out of the car for a while."

Anthony pitched their suitcases on the sagging bed and closed the cheap curtains. "You hungry?"

"For anything but a hamburger."

He thought about leaving his .45 in the room, but old habits die hard. Remembering the good smells drifting on the dry air while he pumped the gas, Anthony simply unbuttoned his suit coat and said, "Let's walk back to the Conoco. The diner looks like the place to eat around here."

Without changing out of her high heels, Samantha led the way outside. They left the motel and strolled arm in arm down the scorching sidewalk. Anthony watched her honey-colored hair glow in the setting sun.

The U-Drop Inn served a good seventy-five cent open-faced steak sandwich. Anthony wasn't sure about the idea, but Sam explained it was nothing more than a chicken-fried steak on a piece of toast and covered with cream gravy. Their plates were empty an hour later when they left the little diner, full and fighting drowsiness. They walked to the Liberty Theater in the dark.

The movie was unnaturally long, but comfortable in the air conditioning. Anthony went through half a pack of Luckies, the smoke mixing with others and spiraling in the projector's strong beam. The young actor from Rawhide was only one of three characters in the Italian Western whose lips synched with the words, and they left laughing at the strangely quirky movie.

Outside under the bright theater lights, Anthony lit two toonies, passing her the first. The high plains evening air was finally cool. Well-dressed couples passed on their way home.

Samantha took a long drag and waved the cigarette toward the empty ticket booth. "I could get a job selling tickets and we could live here."

He'd already learned how quickly she made decisions. "This the one? They don't have anything but flat here."

"I like this town. It fits me."

"All right." Anthony realized he wanted to give her everything she desired. He'd never felt that way about anyone before and it left him light and cheerful. "I had a different town in mind, but we can look around tomorrow for a house, if you want." He didn't care where they settled, as long as it was far away from Vegas.

It was nearly midnight when they strolled through the darkness back to the motor court. As usual, Anthony couldn't relax his guard, keeping an eye out for Malachi's goons. He wasn't convinced they'd be easy to find so far out there in the sticks, but he learned long ago that no one in his business could ever be too careful.

When they reached the motel, Anthony was surprised to see the manager's office was dark, a neon No Vacancy sign sputtering fitfully in the window. They continued under the awning covering the office's entrance, past the dark pool and playground.

Clearly unnerved, Anthony paused and scanned the parking lot. "We have a problem. There aren't enough other cars here for that no vacancy sign to be lit."

"It's probably a slow night. It *is* Wednesday."

"Uh uh. Something isn't right. Stay close and be ready to move if I say so."

Samantha picked up on the nervousness that radiated from the young man like a wave of electricity. Frightened for the first time since they left Vegas, she kept a hand on his back of his suit coat as they cautiously approached their room. In the dim parking lot, Anthony saw the lock on the Buick's trunk was broken. The lid was halfway open.

He slipped the Colt from the rig under his left arm and handed Samantha the key, keeping an eye on their surroundings. "Open the door and get inside while I keep an eye out. Grab our bags and let's get out of here."

Sam was a quick study and didn't ask any questions. She reached for the lock at the same instant Anthony gave it a quick glance.

The knob twisted, opening from the inside. The stubborn door once again stuck, giving Anthony a half second to respond.

He pushed Sam sideways off the high heels he'd been admiring all evening. She fell hard on the concrete walk with a surprised yelp. The door opened a crack, throwing a long rectangle of yellow light into the lot and revealing a barrel of a man standing there in his boxers.

There was no time to wonder why the familiar man was in his drawers. The .38 in his hand was answer enough. Anthony hit the door with everything he had, like he was shoulder-blocking a linebacker. The man inside didn't expect an attack.

The wooden door caught Big Nose Pennacchio smack in the head, slapping him back into the room. He dropped the cocked revolver and fell backward, howling. Big Nose had fallen onto a little kid's chair that matched two others around a scarred wooden table barely eighteen inches tall, part of the motel's "kid friendly" advertisement. Two taller-backed support posts stuck up and he landed directly onto one of them. The thick post punched through his thin shorts, and into a place designated as an exit.

Big Nose didn't yell long, because Anthony shot him twice, the .45 deafening in the enclosed room. Big Nose's presence immediately told Anthony they were there to kill him for leaving the business. The guys waiting in their room had done the same many times before, for lesser reasons, and Anthony had been a part of it on a number of occasions.

Slick and shiny with sweat, two other goons leaped up from peeling the Boss' safe and grabbed for weapons. They were also stripped down to their boxers and sleeveless undershirts in the stifling room after shutting off the swamp cooler to better hear what was going on outside.

The gangsters must have been at it five minutes after the couple entered the café. The table beside the pole lamp in the corner was full of tools, beer cans, fedoras, and guns.

Anthony swung the automatic's muzzle and hammered them both. Red bloomed on their thin undershirts as they dropped to the floor like limp rag dolls.

The last guy was stuck all the way to his elbow in the safe. The last time Anthony saw Seymour Burke and Big Nose was the night Best ordered him to kill the Sandoval family. Tufts of hair escaped his dingy undershirt. Burke tried to yank his hand back, and if he'd gotten it free, would have had a better chance at killing Anthony than the others, because the table was between them and Anthony couldn't get a good shot. If Burke'd been up and ready for a fight, Anthony would have probably taken a slug.

Instead, the man hesitated when he saw the young woman over Anthony's shoulder. "Samantha?"

Anthony quickly stepped to the side for a clear shot.

Recovering from his surprise, Burke awkwardly reached for a pistol with his left hand. Anthony shot him in the head.

Shocked by what he'd heard, Anthony spun to see Samantha in the open door, half expecting to look down the barrel of a gun in her manicured fingers. It wouldn't have surprised him, because their business was one of double and *triple* crosses.

Instead, she stood immobile, stunned at the sudden and deadly violence. He realized his pistol was pointed at her. When he didn't see a gun, he lowered the muzzle, realizing he'd have been a dead man if she'd been heeled. His automatic was empty, the slide locked back. He quickly thumbed the empty magazine free, drove a fresh one home, and released the slide.

Anthony stepped over the bodies to make sure no one else was hiding in the room. The closet was empty, but the dead motel owner sat against the bathroom wall with his legs splayed around the toilet. The Sealed For Your Protection slip from the cracked lid was stuffed in his mouth.

Anthony turned back to the carnage. "You *know* these guys?"

She spoke softly. "They work for Daddy."

Ears ringing, he thought for a moment that he'd heard her wrong. "Malachi Best is your old man?"

Her voice trembled. "Yes."

"He's the guy I worked for."

"I didn't know." Her blue eyes opened wide.

"You said your last name was Chesterfield."

"Mother was a Chesterfield. She kept it so I wouldn't be tied to dad by name."

"I've worked for Best for years. I never saw you before."

"He always kept me at arm's length, so nobody could use us as leverage. He lived in Vegas, and we lived in New York."

Anthony thought for a moment, weighing the pistol in his hand. "So they were after *you*? And the safe was extra candy?"

"I don't think so. I was only in Vegas for a few days to visit. Daddy thinks I'm going to be in Chicago all month."

"So it's like I thought. They wanted *me*." Anthony chewed his lip. And the safe was *still* candy.

He took a good look at the peeled safe. It was the classic double cross in a dishonorable business. Obviously, the men inside their room were sent to kill Anthony and bring back the safe. The kick was their ambition. They planned to empty the safe, split the contents, and then tell the Boss that Anthony had taken the money and either spent it, or hidden it before they gunned him down.

They'd tried to smoke the lock first, using a key blank and candle smoke to find the tumblers. The dead candle and blank lay discarded on the table, beside several empty Schlitz cans, because those guys were thugs, not safe crackers. They finally resorted to using a sledge hammer to peel it open, an ugly but effective way to open one up.

Peelers hammer at a corner, any corner, until it bends enough for them to work a chisel under the outer layer of steel and pry it out of the way. That reveals the next dented sheet, which they also roll back. Like peeling back the layers of an onion, they continue the slow and tedious process until finally levering a hole big enough to drain the safe's contents.

Anthony and Samantha had walked into the stifling room the moment Burke had stuck his hand inside.

"Quick, get our stuff into the car. Those shots will bring the cops even in this burg." He jerked his head toward the bathroom. "He won't be calling the cops, though."

"We take their car?"

Anthony shook his head and holstered the .45. "No. That one is recognizable to Best's men. It's a cinch they haven't called in yet to say they found us, and I can't figure out how they hell they did that, but they'd take the money first, and then rat us out."

The room reeked of blood, gunsmoke, and released bowels. Trying not to look at the dead men, Samantha grabbed the suitcases from the corner where the gangsters had pitched them. Anthony collected all the guns, especially a drum-fed Thompson lying on the bed, and stacked them on the table by the door. He hadn't seen one of those Chicago Pianos in years, and knew it might come in handy somewhere down the road.

"We were lucky. If one of them had gotten to *that* killing machine, it would have been all over but the crying." He peeked outside. Half a dozen sleepy tourists milled uncertainly in their doorways, looking for the source of the noise.

They were quickly running out of time.

Anthony struggled to raise the body of the man with his arm in the safe. Holding it upright, he grabbed the thick forearm and tugged it out of the triangular hole, peeling dead skin in the process.

With a grunt, he pitched the gangster aside, rolled up his own sleeve, and carefully reached into the safe. His thinner forearm passed easily through the opening. At first he couldn't feel anything, making him wonder if he was wrong and they'd already cleared the safe's contents, but then his fingers tickled the edge of a thick envelope lying in the corner. He knew it had to be money. He gripped it between his middle and index fingers, carefully drew it into the open, and stuffed it into his coat pocket.

"I can't believe this is all there was in that heavy sonofabitch."

Samantha had the suitcases and guns in the damaged trunk by the time Anthony rummaged through the goons' clothes and emptied their wallets. Their cash came to more than two thousand, enough for travel money. Giving the room one last look, he hurried outside. Samantha had already slammed her door by the time he slipped behind the steering wheel.

A siren shrieked in the distance.

"We need to go." Anthony gave the room's closed door one last look before pushing the clutch and shifting into first. They gunned it onto the highway and sped away from the siren.

Moments later they came to a four-way intersection in front of the Conoco. He took the highway leading south out of town and accelerated smoothly. Once they were past the city limits, he floored it and the engine roared as they shot down the highway, using the full moon's glow to drive headlights.

For the next two hours they zigzagged their way across the state line into Oklahoma on a skinny two-lane road. The dry high plains air was chilly under a starry night punctuated by streaks of meteorites. They passed through dark farm towns and continued to follow tiny rural highways running east until they reached El Reno, not far from Oklahoma City. The horizon was glowing yellow when Anthony passed a closed Stripes gas station and stopped in front of a local café not far from the Owl Courts motel. There was an Open sign on the door.

Samantha was deep asleep, curled up on the seat, her head on his leg. He gave her a little shake. "Wake up."

It took her a second to get oriented, then she sat upright. "Where are we?"

"Not far from Oklahoma City."

She looked over her shoulder. "We made it?"

"Looks like it. This time. Want some breakfast?"

She rubbed the stubble on his cheek. "We aren't very presentable after spending all night in the car."

He watched a farmer in overalls push the door open and go inside. "I think we're fine."

"Breakfast sounds good. I'm hungry."

"Me too." Anthony reached for the thick envelope from the safe. "We'll use some of your old man's cash for ham and eggs."

They were both surprised when he tore the seal to reveal the envelope's contents.

Anthony's eyes widened. It wasn't stuffed with cash, but thick with clipped pieces of paper. He shuffled through the sheaf, and realized they were all recipes. He laughed, tilting his hat back. "Look at this!"

Samantha took the envelope. "These are my mother's recipes. They're all Daddy kept after she died. He loved her cooking."

She selected a slip. "This one is for German chocolate pie. It was his favorite."

"We have a little cash, but not what I expected to get from the safe. Those guys died for *recipes*."

"It doesn't matter. I have money."

"A few thousand won't get us far with your old man's goons chasing us." Anthony shook out a fresh toonie from a pack of smokes he'd picked up off the table back in the motel room and lipped one from the deck. Camels weren't his favorite, but they'd do. He pushed in the lighter on the dash.

Samantha flashed him a grin and reached into the backseat. She pulled a blue grip into her lap, one he thought was full of makeup and stockings. She unzipped the hard case, opened it, and angled it toward him. It was packed full of money, and the bills he saw were all hundreds.

"Dad has another safe…"

"…in his den. I know about that one in the wall."

She threw back her head and laughed. "I know the combination. I took this when I knew you and I were leaving for Los Angeles. There's enough here to hide out and buy that house we've been talking about."

The lighter popped out and Anthony held the glowing end to his cig, then hers. "They would have had us if they hadn't gotten greedy."

"I bet that's not the first time it's happened."

"And it won't be the last, Doll."

Wide awake, they found a table in the middle of a café full of farmers and truck drivers. The experienced waitress was fast. After ordering, Samantha extended both hands across the table. "Where are we going now?"

Anthony reached out and took them. "A couple of years ago I met these newlyweds in the Flamingo. They were real hicks, but I liked 'em both. She was a redheaded looker and he was some kind of sheriff or something not far out of Dallas." He let go of her hands and pulled a highway map from his back pocket. He unfolded it on the empty table and after a moment, pointed a finger at a tiny dot on the Red River. "This is it. Center Springs."

Samantha peered at the upside down map. "It sure is small."

"Yep. That's what we want. From the way that guy…Cody was his name…described it, the place is perfect to settle down and get married. Besides, if it's too small, we can live in Chisum." He pointed again at a much larger dot. "He said it's an old cotton town with grand houses and white picket fences."

"That's what I want."

"I know it, Doll. We'll live somewhere around here and have kids."

Her face clouded. "Do you think they'll find us again?"

Anthony shook his head. "The only reason they showed up in Shamrock is because I told Pinocchio about Center Springs once."

"We could have gone anywhere, like back to California. But he found us in…"

"Shamrock. Think about it. Only one good highway leads this direction, and that's Route 66. It made sense that he followed it right behind us. All he had to do was check the motels until he found us. There aren't that many between here and there."

"We could have taken any little road heading east, like we did last night."

Completely wrong, he shrugged. "He knew me well enough. I'm a city boy, and I don't like those roads. I was stupid and Pinocchio put himself in my shoes. We needed some place out of the way to lay low and he put two and two together, but he's gone now, so we don't have to worry."

"He didn't know which car we were driving."

"It's not hard to stop in a motel office and ask about us. We're pretty recognizable out here in the sticks."

Someone behind the counter dropped a stack of plates, startling everyone in the café. Samantha held her chest and laughed. "Do you remember his wife's name?"

"Pinocchio's?"

"No, silly. Your friend Cody."

"Her name is Norma Faye."

"Norma Faye." She let it roll off her tongue. "That's country all right. I'd like to have a friend like that."

The waitress brought steaming coffee in thick mugs and they sipped and talked leisurely about a quiet life in a small town.

It was the perfect place to settle down and raise a family.

Chapter Ten

A thick stand of persimmon trees looked golden in the warm sun. Gene Stark and a crowd of men milled not far from his dead brother's truck when Ned pulled up on the dirt track.

Ty Cobb and Jimmy Foxx stood near the tree line with Gene beside his old beat-up Ford truck. Isaac Reader was there also, cleaning his fingernails with a penknife. Conversations with Isaac Reader always made Ned tired. He shut off the engine and caught Gene's eye.

"Yonder he is," Gene said to himself and waved him back toward the car in the hope he wouldn't have to deal with anyone else for a few moments.

Cody coasted to a stop behind. He slammed his door at the sight of so many people stomping around the crime scene, and joined Ned at his door. "I'll go over there and run them off from the truck, but I doubt there'll be any tracks we can use after they all get through traipsing around here looking in at him."

Ned stepped out and watched Gene approach. Eyes downcast, the square, good-looking man walked through the weeds as if carrying a great weight on his shoulders. "He's gone, Ned."

Cody gave him a sympathetic pat as he passed without stopping.

Ned stayed where he was, intending to avoid the crowd as long as possible. "What happened, Hoss?"

Gene wiped his eyes with a blue bandana. "Tommy Lee left early day before yestiddy mornin' to go huntin'. He always likes...liked...to get out in the woods 'fore daylight and set up on the creek down there."

"That's where I'd go for fox squirrels." Ned was a squirrel hunter from way back, and always looked forward to the first day of the season. The lawman portion of his brain worked on the problem at hand, but another part thought it would be a good idea to take Top hunting some morning soon.

Gene looked uncomfortable. "He, uh, he wasn't after no squirrels. Said he was going deer huntin'."

"Deer season ain't open. He was poaching, then."

"He never paid much attention to seasons. You know that."

"Yeah, I suspect he didn't pay much attention to anything except what he wanted to do when he wanted to do it."

Tommy Lee Stark led a troubled life that existed solely inside the swirl of a tornado. No matter what he did or touched, it always fell apart. He wasn't a true bad boy, but he'd been in and out of trouble with the law more times than most folks. Tommy Lee even served a short term in the Huntsville state pen, too, but six months in a Louisiana lockup cured him of hardcore meanness.

Frequent arguments with his ex-wives over money often resulted in a call to Ned's house in the middle of the night. He'd lost count of how many times Tommy Lee was married, but it was more than a few.

"Any idea why somebody'd want to shoot 'im?"

Gene shrugged, his face vacant. "He didn't owe money to anybody as far as I know of. He's been working pretty hard lately, mowing the Methodist cemetery and cutting fence posts to make ends meet. You know, that little house of his ain't got no electricity nor water, so his bills is low. He ain't been messin' around with nobody that I know of neither, and for sure nobody's wife, not since he got caught across the river with Bill Adkins' ol' lady. Bill damn near beat him to death with an axe handle out in the parking lot of the Western Club, and he's shied away from married women ever since."

Ned wondered if he was fooling around with Wade Reidel's wife, Karen. In his state of mind, it would make perfect sense for Wade to take revenge on Tommy Lee, or anyone else he took a notion to punish. Now he had two people to question.

"I'd steer clear, too, after that. I'll talk to Bill. I doubt he did it, but it needs lookin' in to. Was Tommy Lee meat hunting?"

"Yessir." He blew his nose in the bandana, folded it, and put in the back pocket of his khakis. "Beef costs, and deer's cheap when it only takes one bullet." He waved an arm. "He likes to hunt up thataways, just up a piece from us."

"I haven't seen him in a while, not since Miss Lina called and said he was peeking in her winder one night last year."

Gene flushed red. "I believe besides drinkin', that's the only vice he had. He couldn't help himself, and that's why we moved out of Chisum when we was kids, to get him out of the neighborhoods. Dad said the only thing he knew was to get him away from as many winders as possible."

"You think he mighta peeked in somebody's winder-light and they caught him at it? Maybe they came out here to settle up."

Gene shrugged and studied his shoes.

"Did he owe any gamblin' money? You know, he spent a lot of time across the river."

"Nossir. Like I said, things have been quiet."

Ned recalled his recent battle with a gang of outlaws who tried to establish a drug pipeline thought Lamar county. "Did he start messin' with drugs, that marijuana?"

"Not that I know of."

"Well, *somebody* killed him." Cody rejoined them beside the car. "I can't tell what he was shot with, but it was big enough to blow out the side of his hea…I'm sorry, Gene. I didn't mean to say so much."

"That's all right. I done seen him."

"He wasn't killed here. There ain't no blood on the seat, and there's leaves and trash in the wound. He was killed somewhere else and then somebody put him in the cab."

"That makes a sure 'nough murder, then." Ned watched John Washington arrive and get out of his patrol car. "Who found him?"

Gene waved a hand toward a cluster of men. "Isaac Reader. I went up to the store after dinner, because I was worried Tommy Lee hadn't come in. Him and me were going to Hugo for a load of feed this morning, and he didn't show up. Being gone two days wasn't like him. I went to the house and he wasn't there, so I came up to the store. The Wilson boys showed up, so me and them and Isaac took different roads and went looking."

"All right." Ned motioned for John and tugged on Cody's sleeve. "Y'all come here a minute."

They left Gene's body, and walked back to John's car. Ned absently studied a cluster of sandburs stuck in the side of the tires while John crossed his thick arms and leaned against the fender. "Mr. Ned, from the looks of all these folks trampin' around here, I think the only evidence might be that hole in his head, and I doubt we can tie *that* to anyone in particular."

Ned used the sole of his shoe to scrape the stickers off the tire. "John, I can't explain why, other than I dislike the man, but this looks like a murder that Griffin might have something to do with. Tommy Lee never was no angel, and he might have got tangled up in some of them drugs coming up here. He may even have been helping him move that marijuana. We need to be careful how we handle this. It might be the thing we need to connect it all with Griffin."

"It looks like a herd of horses came through here." John scanned the beaten grass. "You can't even see where he drove in from all the cars and feet, and the bullet went plumb through."

Cody saw the game warden's truck bumping down the dirt track. "Here comes Roland, and I called to get someone out here to pronounce Tommy Lee, not that we don't know."

"Good." Ned waved an arm. "You men come away from the truck and leave Tommy Lee alone. Y'all stay back here and let us do our work." He rubbed the back of his neck. "Tommy Lee wasn't no angel, that's for sure. I know for a fact he's run whiskey for Doak Looney who's back at it again. For all I know, *he* might have something to do with it."

Isaac Reader paced up and down in the grass, fit to be tied and almost busting with the need to talk. Any amount of time with Ike always sapped Ned's energy, but he didn't have any choice. He crooked a finger and called the jerky little farmer over. "Ike, come over here and tell me what happened."

As fast as a calf released from a squeeze chute, Isaac hurried over. "Listen, listen, I was up at the store with the Wilson boys there when Gene come and got us to help him find Tommy Lee. We split up in our trucks, and I run acrost him there, all shot up and dead."

"Yep, he's dead all right. Did you see anything when you pulled up?"

"Him dead in the truck. There wasn't nobody running off or nothin'. He's been dead a while, I can tell. He was already cold."

"No, I mean any other tire tracks coming in and out of here?"

"Weren't looking for that. I's driving and looking to find him. His truck was setting right there and him dead in it. Half his head's gone, you know."

"Cody, did you see Tommy Lee's rifle?"

"Yessir, muzzle down in the floorboard."

"What is it?"

"Looks to me like a lever action Winchester thirty-thirty, but I ain't picked it up." Cody pointed toward Roland and went to speak with the game warden.

Ned nodded an answer. "Ike, did you touch anything?"

"Naw, I learned my lesson when I found Onie Mae and them dead last year." It was Ike who discovered the murdered family when he went by for a dinner invitation. Josh's body was still in his chair on the porch. His mama, Onie Mae, and his wife, Beth, were carefully positioned side by side on the living room rug.

"Yes you did. You already said he was cold. You wouldn't know unless you checked."

"Well, I mashed on his neck to see if I could feel his heart beating, but he was stone dead. Listen, I think I got a curse on me. I keep finding too many dead people. This here's three times in the last three years."

"Two."

"*Three.*"

Ned sighed, removed his hat, and rubbed his bald head, a sure sign of exasperation. "One was Cody's bird dog. That don't count."

"Well." Isaac backed off. "It don't make no difference now. I done found another one and listen, I'm thinkin' of moving to Chisum where things are a lot quieter. In fact, I believe I'm gonna move in my sister's house on North Lamar."

Ned stared off toward the river bottom and thought about how peaceful it would be without Isaac always jabbering at him. "I wouldn't blame you if you did."

Chapter Eleven

They were back on the road after sleeping the entire day in an Oklahoma City motor court. Anthony rolled down the windows so the moist, night air could blow through. He drove with his elbow in the wind and his right wrist over the steering wheel, a smoking cigarette almost forgotten in his fingers.

"So I worked my way up as a wise guy in the Family. I was raised by a man who'd worked for Nicolas Marsala. He built an empire on a sense of honor, despite the nature of our business." They'd been talking nonstop, learning about each other and wanting more. "From the time I was eighteen, and a runner for Marsala, I knew to stay away from harming families, especially kids. Wives are another thing, they can be tough and dangerous, but I never harmed a child."

For several long minutes, the only sound was the wind, and the whoosh of an occasional car passing in the opposite direction. When Samantha didn't answer, Anthony felt compelled to fill the silence. "I kill people."

Finally, Samantha reached across the seat to pluck away the cigarette. She drew deep and the cherry glowed red. "I *figured* you were one of Daddy's wise guys. I knew it when they recognized you back in the motel."

"Probably when I shot them, too."

"That too." Sam surprised herself that she could discuss it so calmly. She knew what her dad's world was like, but had never seen the dark side. Instead of feeling horrified, or thrilled, she was surprised to find nothing but ambivalence.

"I liked it. That's the problem. I was good at my job."

She thought back to Anthony's quick, violent response to the gangsters. "You know what, pal? You still are." Resting against the passenger door, Samantha thought she should have been scared, but instead, the conversation cleared the last bit of fog between them. "You liked being a made man?"

Anthony ran nicotine-stained fingers through his oiled hair. "Yes. I liked killing the people Mr. Best wanted gone. There was always a reason, a good reason for it."

His comments were so nonchalant that she thought her new boyfriend might be kidding. Instead of waiting, Anthony plowed ahead. "I'm good at it, or was. The people I rubbed out were all soldiers for other gangs, or for business reasons. Some of them were murderers…"

"…like you?"

"Yeah. Like me. But I'm different."

"How?"

He struggled to explain. "I don't know for sure. I made my bones in a war with people who were trying to muscle in on the Family. I did what Mr. Best ordered, but other than that, I never bothered anyone unless they crossed a certain…line. Then, like any soldier, I did my duty."

For the first time in his life, Anthony had voiced how he felt. Right or wrong, he was a soldier in Mr. Best's army. He thought of the escalating war in Vietnam. "Soldiers kill, because that's their job. When men go to war, they don't ask if it's all right to kill the enemy, they do it because they're trained and the enemy will kill them first, if they get the chance. That's what happens in a war. That's how it is with Mr. Best. His enemies are my enemies." He paused. "Or were. Not now. Not anymore. It looks like his friends are *my* enemies, now."

Enough light glowed from the dash for Samantha to see Anthony's eyes. She expected them to be moist, but they were clear and steady, almost cold. "I know what Daddy is. He tried to keep all that away from me, but when you grow up in the life, you find out things and know what's going on. The problem is, growing up with it makes you immune." She pushed in the cigarette lighter and waited for it to pop out. "You haven't told me what made you quit."

Anthony took his eyes off the pool of light they were chasing down the highway. "Because he wanted me to kill kids."

Shocked that her father had ordered the deaths of children, Samantha shook her blond head. "He wouldn't do that."

"He would, if they were from Cuba. Another family moved into Vegas and cut in on our…his territory. They brought their kids, and settled in for a long fight. Mr. Best wanted them gone. All of them. 'Nits turn into lice' is what he said. It's a quote from some book on the old west."

Samantha's fingers trembled. "I gave him that book for Christmas last year. Good Christ, if it hadn't been for you, those children would have died because of me."

"No, they would have died because I pulled the trigger." He didn't mention the dead round. Truthfully, he had a tough time recalling those moments in the children's bedroom. Maybe it was a way of blocking that traumatic incident, or it might have been mental self-preservation. Whatever the reason, he'd pushed it far back in his mind and left it.

Sam watched his face. "But there are other men in the organization that will pull the trigger in a heartbeat."

"No. The kids are safe. Probably on their way back to Florida to live with their relatives."

Nits to lice. Anthony didn't want to think about what Best said about looking over his shoulder. Neither realized they'd been listening to static on the radio until it abruptly broke off and Johnny Rivers' "Poor Side of Town" came through the tinny dashboard speaker. Overhead, stars shimmered in the clear sky, stretching to the ragged black treetops.

"Without their parents." Sam's voice was flat.

Anthony barely turned the radio's knob, trying to dial a station in. "They're alive, that's the important part. Look, you don't have to stay with me. I wanted you to know what kind of man you're traveling with. If you want, I'll stop in the next town with a bus station and let you out."

The Righteous Brothers overrode Johnny Rivers, but abruptly quit when they lost the signal. Static again filled the air.

"No."

A car approached, the headlights nearly blinding them. Then it swept past and peaceful darkness wrapped their car once again. The air smelled…green…to Samantha. She enjoyed the earthy, moist breeze coming through the open window. She flicked the butt out into the slipstream. "I have a question for you."

"Shoot."

"You think you're ever going to kill anyone again, now that you're away from Daddy and the Family?"

His answer came back like a snap. "If I have to."

It wasn't the answer she expected. She knew right then that Anthony always spoke what was on his mind. "But you don't *need* to kill people do you? It was a job, right, not a compulsion?"

He paused, thinking. "The truth is, I like to take care of problems in a permanent way. Some people are good at solving business problems. Others work out what they're calling New Math. Others build houses, weld, or bake bread. I killed people because I was good at it, and they had it coming, according to what I believed at the time, but I'm not a complete ass."

Tires whined on the highway, the only sound other than wind blowing through the window. Sam shook two smokes from the pack as they passed a country store, lit only by a pole light. Tony pushed the lighter in again.

The dim light from the dash revealed a grin on Anthony's face. Sam watched him for a moment. "What are you smiling about?"

"I just remembered something Cody said. He's the one who lives down in Texas. He said his uncle raised him to believe…" He paused. "How did he put it? Some people just need killing." They were silent for a moment. "That's where we're going, to where Cody Parker lives. We're getting close, and I think it might be a good place to stay for a while. That is, if you still want to stay with me. If you don't, I understand."

The lighter popped out. Sam put two cigarettes in her mouth and pressed the glowing end to the tips. Puffing them alive, she passed one to Anthony. "We shouldn't have any more problems, now that we're so far away from Daddy. How about you try not to shoot anyone anymore, and I'll stay with you."

"You must really like me."

"You're all right."

"Good, then we're a couple, I guess."

You don't get to choose who you fall in love with.

She shivered as the car cut through the Oklahoma darkness.

Chapter Twelve

On Saturday, Pepper and I went looking for Hootie. He'd been missing for most of the morning, but that wasn't unusual. He liked to roam by himself. Miss Becky called him after dinner, but she got worried when he didn't come home to eat.

Miss Becky's my grandmother, but everybody always called her "Miss" instead of Grandma or some of those stupid names kids hang on them, like Gaga or whatever. Even Grandpa and Uncle Cody called her Miss Becky.

Not a soul in the world ever met that old lady that didn't love her. The soft voice, her love for people, and her dedication to the Lord and her church, all defined that little old full-blood Choctaw woman. She gently and unconsciously shaped the lives of all those near her, and could always be relied on to remain calm in a crisis.

Pearl Henson didn't have a cow, but she always had fresh milk from Miss Becky's cow. Wayne Clark was a successful business-man in Dallas, because he lived in the Parker's spare bedroom for his senior year of high school when his parents died. She was constantly sending food and clothes to those in need, and there wasn't a person in Center Springs who hadn't set a table with fruit, meat, or vegetables she canned in her kitchen.

Miss Becky tithed more than most, after she made sure the preacher at the Center Springs Assembly of God used a portion of that money for those who couldn't afford food. Each year under her close supervision, another slice of that tithe went to the kids at church for their Christmas stocking full of fruit, nuts, candy, and a small toy.

I was always fascinated by her rough, work-hardened hands that felt velvet soft when she touched us. Those hands planted and harvested food in the garden that went on our table and to others in need. They cradled babies, cooked, sewed, cleaned, and clasped together in prayer.

There was no other person like her in our community.

Me and Pepper stopped by Uncle Cody's house, but Norma Faye said she hadn't seen him. We ate a fried peach pie apiece, and then pedaled up to the store, thinking he might have followed Grandpa up there.

We passed Oak Peterson's general store, but I never liked to go in there. It was too dark, and Oak's wandering left eye always scared me. The long hairs growing from the top of his nose weren't right, neither.

We coasted to Uncle Neal's store, past the domino hall where someone rattled the rocks on the other side of the open door. The usual members of the Spit and Whittle Club were on the porch, talking about a murder. We leaned our bikes against the side of the building and listened for a minute.

"I 'magine Tommy Lee got killed because he's been into just about everything that ain't legal."

"I heard he was selling drugs."

"It was whiskey."

"He got to stealing car batteries and such…"

"He didn't do no such of a thing…"

Pepper leaned in close. "These old windbags are talking to hear their heads rattle. They don't know any more than we do. Let's go in and get a Dr Pepper."

For once we agreed, but I didn't even have a nickel in my pocket. "I ain't got no money."

"We'll put it on Grandpa's credit. I watched how he paid it up last time. Neal gave him a number, and he handed him the cash. He won't notice two more cold drinks."

"That don't sound right. It's kinda like stealin'."

"It ain't stealing, *knothead*. Stealing is if we snitch a couple of drinks out of the cooler and don't pay for them. If Grandpa was here, he'd say all right and give us the money, so what's the difference? It's like when we came up here the other day and bought that sugar."

She was right, and at the same time wrong, but I couldn't come up with a good argument for that kind of logic. None of the men at the top of the wooden steps paid us much attention, because kids were like dogs and always underfoot, at least until she held up two fingers and said, "Peace."

"Howdy, Uncle Top!" Neal Box always called me that for some reason.

I waved and went straight toward the red chest-cooler beside the door on our left. I heard one of the men behind me. "What's she mean, victory?" It was several years later that I learned the peace sign was also the victory sign during World War II.

Pepper raised the lid on the cooler. "We're getting a couple of drinks. Grandpa will pay for it later." Inside, the metal tracks full of chilled bottles were mixed together, so it took a second to find the bottle cap we wanted.

"That'll be fine." Neal flipped the pages of a notepad and noted the purchases with a stubby yellow pencil.

We pulled them on the opener mounted to the front of the cooler and left. I felt as guilty as if I'd hidden the sweating bottle under my shirt. Despite her attitude, Pepper must have felt the same way too, because we slipped off the porch and went around to the side to drink them. I'll have to admit, though—that Dr Pepper tasted sweeter than any I'd ever drank.

Ross Dyer was sitting on the porch with his back against the corner support post. I glanced up at him and nudged Pepper, knowing she'd take off on him. I was right.

Her forehead wrinkled. "That man has the hairiest ear holes of anyone I've ever seen. He don't take the trouble to trim them at all, and I'm not sure he spends much time washing 'em, neither."

She didn't bother to lower her voice, and I began to worry that he'd hear her, but she probably thought he couldn't because of his ears. They looked like hairy spider holes in the ground. Maybe that's why he didn't wash them good, because he was afraid to stick a finger in there.

"That man's disgusting! He stinks, too. He needs to throw some powder under them arms. Shit, I imagine they're worse than his damn ear."

The fun was gone, because I knew somebody on the porch would hear her. I pulled her around behind the store. "Pepper!"

I'd forgotten the colored men on the loading dock. Uncle Neal sold feed and a few men loafed around back there until he needed somebody to load a truck. They made a few cents a sack, that Uncle Neal tacked onto the price of the feed.

I wondered time and again why Grandpa didn't buy his feed there. He'd get a sack or two, maybe to help Uncle Neal, but for the most part, Grandpa traded in Hugo, across the river in Oklahoma.

Them colored fellers didn't seem to be paying us no mind, but Pepper was talking loud enough for them to hear. "Well, I bet if Miss Becky had half a chance, she'd give 'em a good scrubbing, after she barbered at 'em for a while. I don't know why Uncle Willie don't take his scissors to 'em when he finally gets around to gettin' his hair cut…"

"Pepper, now that is enough!"

I don't think she'd ever heard me use that tone of voice, and to me I sounded like Miss Becky. I saw one of the colored men hide a smile behind his hand, and knew they heard that last part, at least.

We were standing under the chinaberry tree when I noticed a lot of activity at Doc Ordway's spooky two-story house. I shivered, recalling the ghostly footsteps on the second floor. "Looks like somebody's moving in."

Pepper perked up like a bird dog pointing quail. "Let's go see who it is."

"We don't know them people."

"We didn't know Mr. Bell, neither, until we dropped by for a visit."

I didn't want to think too much about Mr. Tom, because the hurt was still there after what happened down in Mexico when him, Grandpa, and Mr. John Washington went to get Uncle Cody out of that Mexican prison. They got in a shooting war down there, but everyone except Mr. Tom made it back. Uncle Cody said it was Mr. Tom that saved them all and the last time he saw the eighty-six-year-old man he was bad-wounded but still fighting to cover their escape.

We pushed our bikes down the road, so's not to spill our cold drinks. A dark-complected man was lifting two boxes out of the trunk of his fancy car when we came up the long dirt driveway. He looked out of place in Center Springs, dressed in a suit and tie on a Saturday. Most of the men in our community either wore overalls, coveralls, khakis, or jeans. This feller looked like he was going to a funeral.

He gave us a wide grin. "Hello."

"Ain't he purdy?" Pepper straightened and stood taller. "That's the purdiest Indian I've ever seen. He must be Sioux or something exotic."

With his slicked-back hair and dimples, I realized he was almost as good looking as Uncle Cody, but I wasn't going to admit that to anyone. "That must be his wife."

One of the most beautiful blond-headed women I'd ever seen came out the front door and stopped on the porch. She was even prettier than Norma Faye, and that's going some. She smiled and waved, a pleated dress dancing around her legs.

We stopped our bikes beside the man. "I'm Pepper and this here's my cousin Top, and we ain't twins like most people think. Who're you?"

The stranger wasn't a bit surprised at such a pointed question from a kid. "Name's Anth.. uh, Tony. This is my…wife, Samantha."

"Like in 'Bewitched'?" As soon as the words were out of my mouth, I felt like a five-year-old, throwing out such a stupid question.

The blond lady came down from the porch and walked across the sandy yard. "Yes, but I'm not a witch."

"You put a spell on *my* heart." Tony gave her a wink.

The line would have sounded stupid coming from anyone else in Center Springs or Chisum, but from a stranger in a suit, it was perfect, despite his Yankee accent.

"What are y'all doing here?"

Samantha stepped closer and put her hand on Tony's arm. She was dressed like a movie star, and wore the tallest heels I'd ever seen on a woman. I imagined Miss Becky or Aunt Ida Belle in them, instead of the thick-soled shoes they always wore, and had to choke down a grin.

"We've rented this house until we find one to buy."

"This old place will fall down around your ears. You need to be careful. The floor is mush under the linoleum in the kitchen." Pepper took a long drink of her Dr Pepper as punctuation. "They say it's haunted."

I wished she'd shut up.

Samantha didn't seem to mind. "We've heard. We had someone repair the floor, so it isn't too bad. The inside is nice, and it's furnished, too, which is good for us, because we don't even own a table yet."

"Furnished with everything including dust, I imagine."

"It's pretty clean now." Samantha's eyes glittered with her smile. "We had someone come in yesterday before we got here."

Pepper wouldn't quit. "Hope you ain't afraid of mice. How can y'all be married and not have furniture?"

I wanted to throttle her. She always asks too many questions.

Miss Samantha wasn't a bit fazed, though. "We haven't been married long."

Pepper cocked her head. "What tribe are you?"

"Huh?" Mr. Tony tilted the city hat back on his head. We usually don't see hats like that in Center Springs. Most men around our parts lean toward Stetsons with what they call a sheriff's crease. His looked like those the gangsters wore on "The Untouchables."

I tried to step in for my aggravating cousin. "We're part Choctaw, about a third I guess. Miss Becky is full-blood Indian, but Grandpa's barely any Comanche at all. That's why they get along so good. If he was more Comanche, I imagine they'd be fighting all the time."

Miss Samantha laughed, her teeth white behind bright red lipstick. "He's not Indian."

"I'm half Italian." Mr. Tony grinned.

"There's lots of Indians across the river in Oklahoma."

The couple exchanged a smile and Mr. Tony shrugged his shoulders at Pepper's statement. "Do either of you know someone named Cody Parker?"

The name surprised me. "Sure do. That's our uncle."

"Isn't that something? Well, he's the reason we came to Center Springs. I met him and his wife when they were in Las Vegas, and their enthusiasm about this place made it sound like Heaven, so we decided to come see for ourselves. Would you tell him we're here when you see him again?"

"Sure will." Pepper can't answer a simple question without wandering around. "He'll come by the house pretty soon for dinner."

"Good. Tell him tonight that Tony Agrioli from Las Vegas is in town and says hello."

"I said he'd come for dinner." Pepper jerked her head back and forth from me and Mr. Tony. Her hair was held back in a ponytail with a rubber band, and it occurred to me that she was twitching that tail so he'd pay attention to her.

"Okay. If it isn't tonight, then it'll be tomorrow night maybe?"

"Where you from? We don't eat dinner at *night*. We eat it at noon."

Mr. Tony frowned. "I'm not sure I understand. Your dinner is during lunch?"

I rubbed my Boy's Regular haircut, and realized I probably look like Grandpa when he's frustrated. "We have lunch at school, but at home, we eat dinner at noon. We have supper at five or six at night."

Mr. Tony and his wife exchanged looks again, and they busted out laughing. "We're in 'Green Acres' for sure." He leaned into the trunk.

I didn't much like being compared to that silly television show, but we'd been dismissed even though it didn't seem as if he wanted to get rid of us. Mr. Tony handed his wife a little suitcase I recognized as what they call a valise and his coat was caught for a moment under her hand. It pulled to the side and I saw a Colt 1911 in a shoulder holster, like Uncle Cody's pistol. Mr. Tony tugged free without noticing, and reached back inside for another valise the same size. He slammed the trunk hard to get it to catch, but before he did, I saw something else in there.

It was the round drum attached to a Thompson machine gun. I knew what they looked like because I'd seen them in gangster movies with George Raft, who called his a Chicago Typewriter. One time Grandpa Ned took me to Judge O.C. Rains' office and showed me a Tommy Gun that once belonged to a crooked old Chisum Sheriff named Poole.

Mr. Tony and Miss Samantha flashed Hollywood smiles at us and walked toward the house. He made a gun with his fingers and dropped his thumb at us. "Tell your Uncle Cody to stop by when he gets the chance."

Chapter Thirteen

Tony dropped his valise on the house's wide porch and watched the kids ride away. He flipped his Zippo alight, lit a Lucky, drew deep, and let the smoke out slowly. "That's the kind of childhood I wish I'd had." He clicked the lighter shut with a metallic snap and slipped it into his pocket.

"It's different here." Samantha took the cigarette from his hand and leaned against the peeling square support column. It was peaceful, and they felt the same with each other.

A truck passed on the narrow oil road. The driver waved a hand in greeting at the young couple standing on the porch. Samantha waved back. "I wonder who he is. We don't know anyone here."

"That's the way it's been since we got here. Everybody waves. It's a friendly place."

She cocked her head to listen, breathing the fresh scent of warm earth. "It sure is quiet. All I hear are birds when there aren't any cars or trucks passing. I think I'm going to like it here."

"Cody said this is about the top speed for this little burg." Tony nodded toward the rear of the wood frame country store barely two hundred yards away. "I'm out of smokes. While you unpack, I'm going to walk over and see if anyone knows where he lives." He started to leave, then stopped and shrugged out of his suit coat. He removed the shoulder holster, placing the .45 on the porch rail beside Samantha. "Would you put that inside for me? I think we found a place where I won't have to carry it anymore."

"Are you sure?"

He slipped back into his coat and patted the pocket of his slacks, reminding her of the .38 he always carried.

She held the half-smoked cigarette in two fingers and crossed her free arm under her breasts, watching the little puffs of dust under his feet as Tony walked down the long driveway. His tailored suit was out of place in such a setting. She looked down at her own skirt and blouse. They'd have to buy new clothes to blend in.

Another farm truck rattled down the oil road and the driver waved at Sam. It was quickly gone. She listened to what she thought of as rural silence. Blue jays cried in the trees. A slender bird she'd eventually learn was a mockingbird sang through its repertoire from atop a nearby power pole.

In the distance, someone chopped wood.

A cow mooed in the adjoining pasture.

Sam thumped the cigarette butt to death, sighed deeply, and spoke aloud. "I'm going to like it here." She went inside to see if she had anything to wear besides a skirt.

Chapter Fourteen

Tony stopped at the loading dock in back. The door was closed and the men who'd been there earlier were gone. Voices drifted around the corner and Tony followed the sound.

"Lordy, Daddy spent his whole life walking behind a mule down there in the creek bottoms. Now it'll all be underwater by this time next year, and I don't like it one little bit."

"It didn't get better until the war started."

"It was hard times on us all till it started raining regular."

"Yeah, and if it don't rain again soon, we're all gonna burn up."

The loafers stopped talking when Tony appeared beside the porch. It was one thing to see a man in a coat and tie coming up Neal's steps. It was entirely different for him to appear from nowhere, without a car.

Floyd Cass, with his pencil-thin Hollywood mustache, sat hunched forward in a cane-bottom chair, one leg crossed over the other. Jimmy Foxx and Ty Cobb rested on the two-by-six porch rail. Isaac Reader, Emory Daniels, and T.D. Stacker were there, too. Emory was the sorriest of the bunch. Ned Parker had no use for the no'count loafer who ate Moon Pies every day but wouldn't take his children sweets when he went home.

Floyd nodded in the sudden silence. "Howdy."

Tony passed below and climbed the steps. "Gentlemen." He nodded hello back and went inside.

"Come on in!" Neal Box's voice boomed through the open door.

Tony stopped inside and tilted his fedora back. "Hello." He paused to take in the shelves stacked with canned goods, folded clothes, hardware, and farm implements. He'd never seen anything like it. Aging harness hung from the rafters, along with buckets of all shapes and sizes. One had a long, rubber nipple about six inches long sticking out at a right angle from the bottom. Tony wanted to ask about it, but other items caught his attention. Rope, hats, and bonnets shared wall space with out of date calendars and advertisements.

"What can I do you for?" Sitting atop his customary stool, Neal leaned forward and rested his elbows on the worn counter. Beside him in a one-gallon jar with a glass lid, pickled eggs floated in dingy liquid.

They reminded Tony of eyeballs. "Huh?"

Neal immediately realized the city fellow didn't understand. "How can I help you?"

"I'd like a pack of Luckies and a couple of sodas." Tony walked up to the cluttered oak and glass case of candy, cigarettes, cigars, and gum. On the shelf below, horse liniment and salve gathered dust. Tony idly wondered about Bag Balm. The green square can with a cow's udder was a mystery.

Neal produced the white pack of Lucky Strikes from a dispenser mounted on the wall behind him. "Baking soda is there on the shelf, but if you're wanting something like a chocolate soda or malt, you'll have to go to town."

"No. I, uh, would like a soda." He paused at Neal's puzzlement. "A cola."

"Ohhh." Neal scratched his curly white hair. "Shoot. Cokes are in the cooler there by the door."

"Is that all you have? Coca Colas?"

"Why no. We have strawberries, grapes, oranges, Dr Peppers….whatever you want."

"No fruit, thank you. I'm not sure what a Dr Pepper is, either."

Neal placed both palms on the counter and leaned forward with a smile. "Why don't you lift the lid there and see for yourself?"

Tony quickly realized the fruit suggestions were soft drinks, and Dr Pepper was a local favorite. He made his selection and placed two sweating bottles on the counter. Neal produced a pencil and wrote the items in a notebook.

"Let's see, toonies are thirty cents, and twenty cents for the Cokes. That'll be four bits, plus four cents for the deposit on the bottles, and you can pull them there on the front of the box."

Tony counted out the change. "Thanks. Pull them?"

"Yeah, the opener is there on the front."

Tony scratched his jaw. "Say, we moved into the two-story behind the store here this morning. I'm looking for someone I met a while back, name of Cody Parker. Do you know him?"

Neal laughed loud and long. "Well, somebody finally moved into the old Ordway place huh? I was wondering why May Murphy was in there working these past couple of days. She's the best gal at housekeeping I've ever seen. Why sure. Everybody in Center Springs knows Cody. He's been coming through that door since he was in diapers. He's the constable now. Shares the job with his Uncle Ned Parker."

"Could you tell me where he lives?"

"Sure. Go east on the highway here, past Henry Arnie's place for about half a mile. About the same time you see a white house on the hill off to your left, that'd be Ned's place, but take the dirt road past the corral on your right. It leads down to Cody's house, but I doubt he's there. We had a killin' here awhile back and Cody and Ned have been making the rounds, trying to find out who done it."

The idea stopped Tony for a moment. He felt the Colt's absence under his arm. "I wouldn't expect a murder in such a nice place."

"Didn't used to be that way, but it seems like more and more meanness is showing up these days. I'm afraid it's gonna get worse when they widen highway two-seventy-one to four lanes. It'll bring in even more traffic and people, with all their ideas and troubles." Neal looked sad for a moment. "I'm afraid things are changing. Cody dang near got killed last winter. It's probably something to do with them hippies."

"I hope it doesn't change too much. My wife and I were looking for somewhere quiet to settle down."

"Oh, it's quiet all right, for the most part. I'm Neal Box, by the way, and I appreciate your business." He stuck out his hand and they shook.

"Tony, Tony Agrioli. My wife's name is Samantha."

"Glad to have you Tony…" Neal glanced at the door. "Why, looky here. There's Cody now."

Tony turned to find the young constable stomping the dirt off the soles of his boots before coming through the door. Cody looked the same as when they met in the casino two years earlier, only he was frowning.

Tony's own face lit up. "Cody!"

Surprised at hearing his name called by the well-dressed stranger he didn't recognize, the young constable stopped and tried to place him.

Tony quickly crossed to the door and stuck out his hand. Cody instinctively took it and was taken aback when the stranger slapped his arm. "Good to see you, Cody. Do you remember me?"

"No, I can't say as I have…"

"It's Tony, Anthony Agrioli. We met in the Flamingo, when you came to Vegas."

The frown disappeared from Cody's face. "Oh, yeah. I remember you. What are you doing here?"

"I had enough bright lights and the desert. I'm married now and the wife and I rented the house back here." Tony pointed at the back wall. "I want to try and make a go of it here in Center Springs."

"Y'all rented the old Ordway place?"

"I guess, if that's the two-story right back there."

"Well, glad to have you."

Tony kept shaking his hand. "You talked about this place so much, Sam and I decided to come on out."

"Sam? I thought you said you were married."

"I am. Sam is short for Samantha."

"Oh." Trying to bring himself out of his thoughts and back into the reason he was there, Cody retrieved his hand. "Say, have you seen the kids, Neal?"

"Top and Pepper? Yep, they were in here not fifteen minutes ago looking for Hootie."

"Yeah, that's why I'm here. I'm trying to run 'em down cause I found him, and he's in bad shape."

"Oh, no." Neal's shoulders slumped. "Did somebody hit him with a car? I bet it was Donny Foster. He'll take to the ditch to run over a dog, if he gets half the chance. That whole Foster bunch is bad."

"Naw. He's been chewed up by dogs. I found him in an armadillo hole under some sheet iron out back of my barn and took him to Miss Becky."

Neal shook his head. "I bet it was them dogs that tried to eat you that time." He realized he needed to explain to the city man. "Town people get tired of their animals and bring them out here to throw 'em out, usually down by the creek bridge for some reason. They figure country folks'll take them in, I guess. But we have our own dogs and nobody wants them, so they pack together to survive. Cody damn near got et by 'em when he had a car wreck and the dogs found him."

Cody waved at Tony. "Look, it's good to see you. Let me deal with this and when I can, me and Norma Faye'll have y'all over for supper."

Tony nodded, understanding more than he would have twenty minutes earlier. "Of course. You know where we live."

"Fine." Cody left, and made a mental note to tell Tony that a suit in Center Springs was for weddings or funerals.

Chapter Fifteen

Me and Pepper were almost home from the store and pedaling down the highway at a pretty good clip when I saw Norma Faye walking up the dirt road from their house. She waited beside the corral and waved us down. When we got closer, the look on her face told me something was bad-wrong.

We stopped on the shoulder and braced our bikes with one leg. Norma Faye looked like she was carrying something heavy on her shoulders. She got right to it. "Top, your Uncle Cody found Hootie out by the barn."

In our world, when somebody said they "found" a dog, or cat, or horse, in a sentence like that, it usually meant the worst. A wave of dread washed over me and my eyes immediately burned. I wanted to reach for the asthma puffer in my back pocket, but remembered it was on Miss Becky's kitchen table.

I'd felt something was coming, but I didn't know what. Some of us Parkers have the gift of second sight, and most of the time it comes through dreams, and they usually come true, though they don't make sense to us at the time. It's only after things happen that we realize what they were about. As far as I'm concerned it ain't no gift. It's a curse.

Miss Becky calls it a Poisoned Gift.

I'd been having dreams again, and this time I was standing in the middle of a pasture with Hootie lying at my feet. From different directions all around me, dark streaks were coming, like I was the hub of a wagon wheel. A horse kept whispering in my ear, but I couldn't understand what it was saying.

I took a deep breath. "Is he dead?"

Norma Faye shook her head and her eyes were full of hurt. It made me want to cry. "No, but he's in bad shape. Dogs or coyotes backed him into an armadillo hole and he fought 'em off, but it cost him."

"Where is he?"

"Cody pulled him out and took him up to your house. I came back to get some monkey blood." We used the red liquid, really called mercurochrome, to treat cuts and scrapes. It stung like the devil, and stained everything it touched. "Your Uncle Wilbert is on the way. Hootie needs sewing up."

Pepper gasped behind me. The full effect of what had happened finally fell on her and she started crying. "I hate this place! It's all killing and dying and hurt!"

I didn't have time to listen to her. I jumped on the pedals and took off for the house, pumping hard to see about my dog that saved my life two years ago.

Chapter Sixteen

Martha Wells' calm voice on Ned's Motorola belied the urgency she felt. "All units. All units! Robbery in progress at the First National Bank. Two individuals. One man, one woman, driving a late model green Ford sedan. They are armed and dangerous."

Ned was parked on the dirt road next to his cotton field in the river bottoms, studying his straight rows and the green plants growing strong in the rich soil. Looking at his crops always eased his troubled mind and helped him think.

He'd stopped by one of the unpainted shacks not far away to visit with the farmer and his wife who lived there. Tommy Lee's murder still weighed heavily, because Ned could find no reason, and though their community was tiny, no one had a clue as to what happened. It seemed impossible, because folks in small towns always knew everyone's business.

He flicked to a different channel and keyed the microphone. "Cody."

His voice came back quickly. "I heard. Where do we need to go?"

"Head for Arthur City. We'll set up there in case they make a run for Oklahoma." Like spokes on a wheel, nine hardtop roads led out of Chisum. "Griffin'll try and sew the town up, but they'll already be gone."

"Okay. Got some bad news. Hootie's been chewed up by dogs."

Ned held the microphone away from his mouth for a moment. "Sonofabitch."

"Did you get that?"

Ned keyed the mike. "Yep. How bad?"

"Pretty rough. I took him to the house." Cody looked down at the dog's blood on his shirt cuffs, and under his fingernails. "Miss Becky called Wilbert Johns to come over and doctor him. I've been looking for the kids."

Thick and built like a stump, Wilbert had a way with sick animals. Top once called him to remove a fishhook from Hootie's leg when he tangled with a cane pole stored in the smokehouse. Though in considerable pain, Hootie settled down to the sound of Wilbert's calm voice and allowed him to push the sharp point completely through the meat, then skin, of his right foreleg, clip off the barb, and then pull the shank back out.

Cody made a U-turn on the highway, stomped on the foot-feed, and the El Camino's engine roared. He cleared his throat. "He's gonna have to do a lot of sewing on that poor pup. Even then I don't know if he's gonna live."

Despite the tiny speaker and wind noise in the background, Ned heard the young man's voice tremble.

"You Parkers need to clear this channel for official business!"

Cody bit his lip instead of answering Sheriff Griffin's curt interruption. Hanging the mike in its bracket, he passed Ned's farmhouse on the hill. From the brief glimpse as he zipped by, he saw Wilbert working on the dog, using the tailgate of his old truck as a makeshift table. Miss Becky held Hootie's head, and the kids sat on the bed rails.

Cody wanted to stop, but the robbery took precedence. Highway 271 was an obvious escape route from Chisum and the only one within miles leading to Oklahoma. He skipped over the Sanders Creek Bridge and nearly bottomed out when the road rose sharply. He barely hit the high spots in the winding, tree-lined road leading from the creek bottoms. Cody tapped the brakes when he reached the Arthur City railroad crossing, and shot across the empty lane coming out of Oklahoma.

Ned's car engine ticked as it cooled under an oak tree south of the Oklahoma bridge. Cody was surprised to find him waiting so close to the river. If the robbers saw him in time, they could turn and shoot toward Center Springs. Cody pulled up and stopped with enough room to maneuver if the green Ford appeared.

He met Ned between the cars. "Why did you park here? Shouldn't we be a little further south, so they can't dodge around us and head toward the creek?"

"I'd rather have them go that way. If they see a chance to get away instead of crossing the river, they'll head west, and them windin' roads'll slow 'em down enough so we can stay on 'em. John's visiting his lady friend out by Forest Chapel. If they come by, I can call him up on the radio and catch 'em between us."

"Radio said there was two of them."

"You think one of them might have been that stranger you saw at the courthouse taking pictures the other day?"

"Could be." Cody positioned himself to see down the highway. In the distance, a cream-colored 1955 Chevy came over the hill and down the tiered incline leading to the river. It passed at a sedate speed, driven by a man they both knew. He raised a hand in greeting, and the Parkers did the same.

Cody nodded his head toward the oncoming traffic. "We'll see them before they realize we're waiting here."

"That's the idea...look, here comes a sheriff's car now. I guess that means they went another way, or he'd be lit up like a Christmas tree."

The constables watched the black and white Chevrolet hiss down the hill and roll to a stop at Cody's bumper. Deputy White killed the engine and stepped out from behind the wheel at the same time Sheriff Griffin emerged from the other side.

Cody quickly cut his eyes toward Ned, watching the muscles swell in his jaw.

Griffin strolled up and stuck his thumbs in his hand-tooled gun belt. "Looks like they got away. Probably while y'all were talking about dogs."

"What are you doing here?" Ned squinted at the man he despised. "Don't you need to be back in town?"

Before Griffin could answer, Deputy White stepped in. "Our first reports said they originally headed this way out of town, but then they disappeared. The sheriff thought we'd make a run this direction and see if y'all saw anything."

"That's what the Motorola's for." Ned wasn't buying it. "I'd-a thought you'd be back in your office, running things from there."

Griffin pushed upward on his toes and bounced lightly, thumbs still in his belt. "I have men working every highway out of Chisum. I'll head back that way, directly. The FBI is on the way from Dallas, along with the Rangers. Pretty soon, it'll mostly be out of my hands."

For once, Ned had to agree with the paper sheriff. The feds and Rangers had the reputation of quickly taking over investigations. "Anybody get hurt?"

"Naw." White preferred to answer as many questions as possible, to keep Ned and Griffin from tangling. He'd once been in the fledgling K-9 Corps, but lost his enthusiasm for nearly everything after his dog, Shep, was killed in the Cotton Exchange. "They were in and out pretty quick. Nobody got shot, so that's a blessing. I hear that someone you know was in the bank when they hit it."

"Who was that?"

"Isaac Reader. He was the only customer when it was robbed."

Cody grinned at the thought, and Ned rubbed the back of his neck. "I reckon I'll hear about that for the rest of my life. Do you have a good description of these two?"

Griffin rocked back on his heels and cut White off. "The man wore a dark suit, white shirt, and a city hat. The woman was a little taller and in a dress so tight the window clerk said it looked like it was painted on her. Both had pistols, and the woman carried a pump gun.

"Neither one said much more than get your hands up. The rest of it went like they'd planned it for months. We haven't had a bank robbery here since the forties. It makes me look bad to have one now."

"You being sheriff don't have nothin' to do with a robbery." Ned's eyes flicked to a farm truck coming over the hill. "I don't reckon outlaws vote on who they want in the sheriff's office before they rob a bank."

In an effort to keep Ned and Griffin from tangling, White re-directed the conversation. "Hey, I heard your grandboy's dog's in bad shape. I'm sorry." The thought of an injured dog dug at the deputy. "He gonna make it?"

"We'll see."

"I know you set a lot of store behind that pup."

"Yeah, he saved Top's butt…" Ned trailed off when he realized he was talking out of school. No one knew of Hootie's involvement when The Skinner disappeared a couple of years earlier. Ned's frustration grew a little each time he let something slip about that night at the Rock Hole. "…a couple of times out running the woods. He's a good…snake dog."

"Well, I hope he makes it. Dogs are special."

"White, we need to go." Griffin had lost interest in the conversation. "I figured it'd be a good idea to check on the oldest constable in the county. Wanted to make sure the bad guys didn't get through here into the territories."

Ned bristled. "I don't believe that's why you're here at all. You know we can handle whatever comes down the highway."

Griffin bristled right back. "Maybe they're headed to Cody's joint over there to divvy up the money."

The young constable raised an eyebrow. "You saying I had something to do with it?!"

Deputy White held out a calming hand. "Now, Cody, take it easy. The sheriff said he wanted to make sure things were all right is all. One of the robbers looked Indian, so he figured they'd head this way."

"You better be careful, Griffin." Ned recalled Top's photographs in his safe deposit box in the bank. His breath caught when he realized what the bank robbers might have taken.

"They say a picture's worth a thousand words, and I reckon we got about nine hundred and ninety nine of them words put up safe. The last word we're looking for is 'guilty.'"

Griffin stopped and frowned. The old constable seldom said anything without meaning.

Ned ignored the sheriff. Instead, he addressed White. "Did the robbers open the safe deposit boxes, too?"

"They only got into a couple of the boxes before they got scared and took off."

"Find out who owned 'em." Ned breathed slow and lowered his voice. "I'd like to know. They may have stole from folks up here on the river."

"It looks like they were after certain boxes, that's a fact." White caught a glare from Griffin, but didn't understand why he couldn't tell the facts to the two lawmen. "They went straight to work on them. They're comparing the numbers right now to the records."

Ned felt his stomach sink. To make it seem like he didn't care about the boxes, he crossed his arms and leaned back on the hood. "How much cash was took?"

White shook his head. "They're counting now, but it was somewhere in the neighborhood of sixty or seventy thousand or so."

Griffin was ready to go. "White, we'll head on back, if these two have things in hand."

"We do."

A deputy sheriff's car coming from Center Springs stopped at the railroad track as the driver studied the three cars beside the road. A hundred yards away, three well-dressed men photographed each other beside the Texas state marker. Griffin had been watching them since he arrived. He redirected his anger toward the vehicle. "Is that Washington?"

Ned barely gave the car a glance. "I believe it is."

"Why's he coming from that direction?" Washington and the Parker clan had a bond that went as deep as family. It annoyed Griffin to no end that all of them were beyond his reach, protected by Judge O.C. Rains. The cranky old judge was a fixture in Chisum, and would be until the day he died. Until then, he was Griffin's second-worst enemy.

Ned was the first.

They watched the deputy's car crossed the highway and joined the cluster of cars. Big John Washington stepped out and opened the rear passenger door. A well-dressed young man emerged, hands cuffed behind his back.

John pointed at the group of lawmen, and his prisoner walked in their direction.

Cody tilted his Stetson back and raised his eyebrows. "Hello, Tony."

Chapter Seventeen

Still conscious, Hootie whimpered from the pain as Uncle Wilbert washed his deep wounds with warm, soapy water from the dishpan Miss Becky brought out of the kitchen. "Becky, bring me a needle and some thread, and Ned's shaving razor."

I sat on the tailgate with Hootie's bloody head in my lap. He was cut up bad by the wild dogs, and I couldn't see how he was still alive. Warm tears kept running down my cheeks, but I wasn't bawling like Pepper. It sounded like she was chewed up herself.

"Do you think he's gonna make it?"

Uncle Wilbert's heavy face was a blank mask. His thick hands worked through the open wounds, probing and scrubbing with the now bloody dish rag. "Can't tell you, son. I see bone here, and guts through there." He washed a long tear in Hootie's front leg. "These bluish things are tendons." He shook his shaggy head. "I don't see how he's still alive."

I glanced up to see Pepper with both hands over her mouth and a horrified look in her eyes. He could have gone all day without telling me the truth, but Uncle Wilbert never was much on hiding his thoughts. In fact, none of the men in town held back on what they were thinking. They lived in a real world of hurt and fact. There wasn't a lot of gray.

Miss Becky came down the steps with her sewing box and a half full quart fruit jar of Doak Looney's white lighting from Grandpa's evidence collection in the smokehouse. She set it on the tailgate and opened the box's lid. "Did you look at them guts? Are they cut?"

Uncle Wilbert grunted at the little Choctaw woman who'd spent hours on her knees, praying for him to quit drinking. "I don't believe so. They didn't get inside to start chewing on him. This is one smart little dog to use that hole to keep his backside safe. Other than this long tear in his stomach, the rest of the bites are on his head, shoulders, and front legs."

"Praise the Lord." Miss Becky sorted through the wooden spools of color. "I got this waxed thread here." She threaded a needle and held it out.

"No, ma'am." Uncle Wilbert raised a thick hand, like warding off something that scared him. "This is gonna hurt awful bad, and he might bite *me*. I doubt he'll do the same to you, since he knows you." He wiggled his wet, bloody fingers. "Besides, these are too fat to do that kind of work. Horses and cows are one thing, but sewing this dog up is sump'n else. Top, you keep a-holt of his head while I finish cleanin' up around these cuts, and then you get to work, Becky."

My grandmother sewed all the time, but it was on quilts stretched and rolled on the rack dangling from the living room ceiling, or material pinned to the thin Simplicity or Butterick patterns on the kitchen table. She made the blue dress she wore. "This'll make me a nervous wreck."

Uncle Wilbert carefully shaved around the deepest cuts and tears with Grandpa's Gillette safety razor, and then washed more blood and hair away. He unscrewed the lid off the jar and took a long sip. Miss Becky didn't say a word about his drinking. One day she'd testify against liquor, and the next, she'd hand someone a bottle or jar of white lightning if she figured they needed it. After a second swallow, he held the jar over the Hootie's wounds and let the clear alcohol dribble over the cuts and tears.

It must have stung like the Dickens, but Hootie only whimpered. He buried his head in the crook of my arm, as if to hide from the fear and pain. I thought Uncle Wilbert would never get through washing those dog bites, but I didn't expect what came next. He finally moved aside and Miss Becky took his place at the tailgate.

I watched her wrinkled face. Her chin quivered. She wasn't scared, just tenderhearted. She carefully smoothed a large flap of skin back into place on Hootie's shoulder and held it for a moment. "All right, baby. This is gonna hurt."

She thought for a moment, and instead of sewing his shoulder first, Miss Becky started with the rip in his stomach. I was glad. I was afraid his intestines would pooch out if he started thrashing around.

Hootie's shriek cut the air the first time she pushed the needle through the raw skin of the deepest slash. Her eyes filled.

Somehow he got my thumb in his mouth and bit down hard enough to dent the skin. He could have chewed it off, but he didn't shower down on it at all. I knew better than to try and yank it away, so instead, I held him and whispered in his split ear until he quit thrashing. Hootie settled down, but he whined like a hurt baby each time she pushed the needle into the flesh. His muscles quivered in a terrible way while my tears dripped down onto the old scar on his head.

Miss Becky blinked quickly to dry her own eyes and moved a little to the side so the bright sun could shine directly where she was working. When she finished that first tear, the tight little stitches pulling the wound together would have made Dr. Heinz, our family doctor, proud. Her chin had quit quivering by that time, and she started the shoulder slash. Watery blood and clear fluid leaked from more than a dozen other holes in his skin.

She kept up a stream of soft baby talk while she worked. Miss Becky didn't usually talk that way, but I figured she did it to keep Hootie calm. It made me feel better, all the same.

Pepper sat on the truck's bed rail in silence, staring off in the distance toward Oklahoma through puffy eyes. She looked like a mainspring that was wound so tight it would swarm if the pressure was released. Every minute or so, she wiped tears away with the palm of her hand and dried it on her jeans.

When Miss Becky finally finished and stepped back, Hootie sighed, closed his eyes, and was still. I thought my dog was dead until his good ear twitched. Uncle Wilbert opened an old leather shaving kit and took out a shot needle and a bottle of white liquid.

I thought I recognized the contents. "What's that?"

"Penicillin. It's supposed to help keep those wounds from getting infected, but I don't know how much to use, so I'll draw this much and we'll see what happens."

I knew all about that thick, white medicine. Dr. Heinz used it on me when I got really sick, and it ached like the devil when he gave me a shot. Hootie barely whimpered when Uncle Wilbert stuck the needle in his hip, so I knew my little Brittany was about out.

Uncle Wilbert packed his small bag and carefully picked Hootie up like he was carrying a baby. "Where do you want him?"

"In the living room, beside the heater. I'll need to make him a pallet." Miss Becky led the way, and Uncle Wilbert followed her into the house. Pepper didn't move to follow, and I stayed where I was on the tailgate. We didn't talk, because there wasn't anything to say. Pepper wiped her eyes again when Uncle Wilbert came back outside.

He stepped off the porch with his jaw set. He crossed the yard and reached into the open window on his truck. I like to have died when I saw a .22 rifle in his hands, because I'd seen a lot of men in Center Springs put dogs out of their misery with the little rifles. Grandpa used them to kill hogs, when the weather turned cold enough.

Uncle Wilbert came around to where I was still sitting on the tailgate and held the rifle out to me. "This is a J. C. Higgins automatic. The safety is here. Push it in with your finger and she's ready to fire." He placed the butt on the ground and twisted the grooved knob on the magazine under the barrel. "Twist this and pull the rod almost all the way out. You put the hulls in here, see, the hole is shaped like the bullet, and then push the rod back down and twist it closed. She holds fifteen rounds."

He held it out. I took the rifle from his hand and rested the butt on my thigh. I checked the safety, like I was taught. Uncle Wilbert nodded. He picked up the open, half-empty jar of white lighting and took another long swallow like he was starving to death for a drink.

Pepper walked across the truck bed and sat beside me on the tailgate. "What are you gonna do with that?"

Uncle Wilbert drew a deep breath, replaced the lid, and screwed on the ring. "Vengeance is mine, I will repay, sayeth the Lord."

Our eyes met.

"Romans twelve, nineteen."

My cousin's eyes widened. "You're gonna let him go off with that rifle?"

"I would, if a pack of dogs chewed up *my* bird dog."

I wondered what Grandpa and Uncle Cody would say. Uncle Wilbert must have read my mind. "I'll tell Ned. I saw him do the same thing once. A bunch of dogs killed his little house dog, Cricket. It took him nearly a month to get 'em all." He reached into the pocket of his baggy jeans and handed me a full paper box of shells.

I never knew they had a house dog.

I slipped off the tailgate and tucked the little box in my jeans. "I know where they hang out during the day. It won't take me that long."

Pepper slid down toward the tailgate. "What are you doing?"

I took off across the pasture and heard Uncle Wilbert behind me.

"He's fixin' to go huntin'."

Chapter Eighteen

Standing in handcuffs on the side of the highway, Tony Agrioli gave Cody a sheepish grin. "Hello, gentlemen."

John looked truly surprised. "Well, you *do* know Cody."

"I told you, officer. We met in Las Vegas, and that's why I'm here." Tony's eyes narrowed when he saw Griffin. He'd seen him somewhere before.

Griffin felt the same thing, but he couldn't place the stranger. "Why is this man under arrest, Washington?"

John was surprised at the tone of Griffin's voice. He allowed himself a deep, not very well-concealed breath before willing his temper down. He worked for Griffin, and it wouldn't do to make him mad with what he longed to say. "The bank robbery's all over the radio, and when I come past the Center Springs store, I saw this dark-complected feller standing outside. He matches the description of one of the robbers, so I'm taking him in for questioning."

"You can cut him loose." Cody dug in his shirt pocket for a toothpick. "He was with me at the store when the bank was robbed. He moved to Center Springs today."

Tony grinned. "That's what I told this officer, but he was insistent. Kind, but insistent."

"Now hold on," Griffin's tone changed. "He might know something about the bank job. They might have split up."

"The boy's done told you, Griffin." Ned's voice was firm. "This Tony feller just got here."

John unlocked the cuffs and Tony rubbed his wrists. He gave Griffin a shy grin and explained how he knew Cody and Center Springs. "It's an honest mistake, and I'm glad to see that the law around here is on their toes." He was glad he'd left his Colt back at the house with Samantha. It would have been hard to explain to the deputy back at the store. It was funny, really, to be cuffed for a robbery he didn't commit. They'd have a stroke if they knew the things he'd done in the past, and had never been in bracelets before in his life.

Worried that he couldn't place the olive-skinned newcomer, Griffin simply nodded. "All right, then. White, let's go."

With a long-suffering look of apology, White slipped back behind the wheel and as soon as Griffin slammed his door, they left in a quick U-turn.

Ned squinted at Tony. "Tony how much?"

At his look of bafflement, Cody stepped in. "His last name is Agrioli."

"You Indian?"

Tony had already been down that road. "My family is Italian, but they live in New York. I live in Vegas."

"That explains why you're dressed for a funeral." Ned held out his rough, sun-browned hand and they shook. "Ned Parker. I'm constable here in Center Springs, and Cody's uncle."

"I thought Cody was constable."

"He is. It's a long story."

John waited to shake. "No hard feelings. Just doing my job."

Tony returned a solid grip that told of immense power resting behind the gigantic deputy's quiet demeanor. "None at all, but my wife might be worried by now. Can you take me back?"

"Sure 'nough." John smiled. "Mr. Ned, what's going on at your house? I saw Mr. Wilbert there when I passed, drinking out of a fruit jar."

"Hootie's hurt. We need to get back over there and check on him."

The smile disappeared. "I'll meet y'all there after I drop Mr. Tony off."

Cody grinned up at the deputy, despite his worry about the dog. "You sure you won't go on back where you were…checking on folks?"

John knew Cody had already figured out he'd been at Rachel's house, dropping off a few bags of groceries for her children and the nieces and nephews that lived with her. "Well, since things is all right at Rachel's, I figure I can spare a few minutes at yours. Don't let on to Sheriff Griffin about it, though. C'mon my eye-talian, you can ride in the front this time."

Chapter Nineteen

As they left the river bottoms behind, Griffin looked back over his shoulder at the parked cars receding in the distance. "I didn't expect them to be waiting there like that."

White's eyes flicked to the rearview mirror. "I did. Ned's been at this a long time. It was a sure bet he'd seal up that road."

"I can expect Cody to be with him. Those two are like peas in a pod, but Washington had no business being out there."

"Sheriff, you had John working last night till late, serving warrants with Dolph and Van, remember?"

"So?" Griffin didn't think twice about sending his deputies out at all-hours. Deputies Washington, Dolph Wicker, and Van Simmons were used to leaving their families well after dark to serve at the sheriff's whim.

"Well, I imagine he probably figured he could spare an hour or two and run up here to see Rachel. He talks about her a lot. She must be some punkin'."

"That's misuse of county property." Griffin stroked his white mustache thoughtfully. "A man could get himself in trouble using tax dollars to run around with country whores."

White frowned. "Sir, I believe she's a decent woman. Her husband run off a while back, and she's taking care of her dead sister's kids along with her own."

"And how does she pay for that? I know for a fact she ain't got a job. Probably on her back."

"I don't know how she made ends meet before she met John. But Mr. Ned hired her to work in his field and I think she's taking in washing now, too." White wondered how Griffin knew about Rachel's business. "Sheriff, why'd we come out here in the first place? There's half a dozen other ways them robbers coulda gone. If it'd been me, I'd-of headed toward Dallas. Robbing banks is one thing, but crossing state lines is another."

They drove for a full minute before Griffin answered. "I had a feeling they went north. I wanted to look around up here, in case they headed for the river. Instead, we come up here and find them Parkers loafing on the side of the road."

"I don't believe they were loafing. They were parked out of the way. It wouldn't-a took a second for them to pull their cars across the highway, if the bad guys was to come along."

Martha Wells' voice crackled over the radio. "Sheriff, you close by?"

He picked up the handset. "Pretty close. Why?"

"You have visitors. The FBI boys want to see you."

"Put 'em in my office and I'll be there in five minutes."

White glanced down at the speedometer. There was no way they'd be at the courthouse so fast.

"They're in with Judge Rains." Martha's tinny voice almost sounded as if she were laughing.

Griffin hissed like he'd cut his finger. "Shit." He keyed the handset. "All right. Any updates on the fugitives?"

"No, sir. I expect you'd have heard on the radio if we'd found anything."

White bit the inside of his lip to keep from grinning. Only a handful of people could be so short with the sheriff, and Martha was the third of three, behind Ned Parker and Judge O.C. Rains.

Griffin didn't answer. Instead he slapped the handset into the metal bracket and steamed for a minute. They passed Gate 5, the main entrance to Camp Maxey, a World War II infantry training camp that had bustled with activity in the 1940s. Griffin glanced up at the curved iron sign over the stone columned entry and idly pictured how it would look if they had lights on it. In one of those light bulb moments, it reminded him of the flashing, colorful neon in Las Vegas, which took him back to the man John Washington had detained...

...who said he was from Vegas...

...and Griffin clicked on the flicker in the man's eyes when they met.

Griffin remembered seeing "Tony" in Vegas only two weeks earlier. It was at the table with Malachi Best, when they were hammering out the last details of a laundering process for his newfound drug money.

Tony was the man Best ordered to kill an entire family, while Griffin sat numb, wondering what he'd gotten himself into. Now Best's professional killer was in Center Springs, looking for him.

Nearly panicked, Griffin could barely sit still. His heart pounded. He wanted to throw White out of the car and drive off, lights and siren running, until he was in Mexico. But he'd already ripped his britches with the cruel men down there who would also kill him in a New York minute if they had the chance. As it was, he was fortunate they hadn't sent anyone to Chisum already.

With the Mexican connection gone, Griffin found a way to launder the money through the Vegas mob. He thought it worked after he "salted" them with the first suitcase full of legitimate bills, but they'd apparently already discovered his deception.

So they sent Tony, a hit man, to kill him. Griffin first ran across the definition only a year earlier from an FBI letter. Now he had to find a way to eliminate the assassin and get gone before someone else came after him. He was still alive only because Tony Agrioli hadn't gotten a good chance at him, yet.

Maybe it was because he was constantly surrounded by deputies and lawmen. No one knew it, but Griffin only slept in his house once or twice a week. Other nights he sacked out on a cot in the courthouse. Every now and then he stayed with a widow woman who allowed him into her bed only when she was overpoweringly lonely, after he worked on her for days over the phone, and promised to take her on an occasional weekend to Dallas for shopping and restaurants.

His hand unconsciously slid to the butt of his pearl-handled pistol, to make sure it was still in the holster. He'd have to come up with a plan now. Griffin needed to think of a way to deal with Tony first, then he could get his hands on those prints. He only learned of them when R.B. at the drugstore mentioned he'd developed some pictures that Top Parker shot of him and a man named Whitlatch.

He didn't think anyone was around when he met with Whitlatch that snowy morning in front of the courthouse to take his usual cut from their smuggling operation. Who'd expect a kid to see them beside the Confederate statue on the snowiest day in years?

Griffin grinned. He had an idea. A setup, so Washington or one of the Parkers could do the work for him and take out that Yankee, or the other way around. If he could get them after one another, *somebody* would get shot, and he'd come out ahead, no matter who it was.

Chapter Twenty

"Where's Top?"

Miss Becky shook her head. She could tell Ned was mad about something. She didn't know if it was because dogs had nearly killed Hootie, or maybe it was law work. "He didn't come in after Wilbert brought Hootie inside."

Pepper sat in Ned's rocker, pressing one foot barely enough to move. Hootie slept fitfully on the pallet.

"Pepper. You're up to something. Where's Top?"

Startled, she nearly jumped off the rocker. "Why'd you say that? I'm sittin' here minding my own business."

"That's the reason." Ned studied his granddaughter. "The only time I see you sitting on your hands is when y'all think you're into something. Now, where is he?"

She figured the truth was the best idea. "Uncle Wilbert gave him a twenty-two and sent him out after that pack of dogs that hurt Hootie."

"Lands!" Miss Becky threw up her hands. "Ned, them twenty-two bullets can go a mile. He'll shoot somebody, or hisself with that gun."

"No he won't. He's old enough to handle a rifle. I've been thinking about giving him one myself." He knew exactly what Top had in mind. "How long has he been gone?"

"An hour or so." Pepper rocked harder under the questioning. "Right after we came in. Uncle Wilbert told him 'vengeance is mine,' and Top took that rifle and was gone."

Miss Becky shook her head. "That ain't right, to blaspheme the scriptures like that. The good Lord will take care of what needs doing Himself."

Ned snorted. "Sounds like He's using Top to do it. Y'all hear any shootin'?"

"No, but we been inside with the fans going ninety to nothing." It was unseasonably warm for October, and everyone looked forward to a good cool front to make it feel like fall.

"All right, then." Ned spun on his heel and went out on the back porch. Hands in his pockets, he stared toward the roof of Cody's house, barely half a mile away. While he was thinking, a ragged pickup truck crept down the highway and up the drive.

Ned felt himself deflate.

Isaac Reader again. He killed the engine and leaned out the window. "Listen, listen, Ned! I guess you know about the bank robbery, and I think I done figgered out who killed Tommy Lee Stark."

Even though he hated to be hollered at, Ned walked out to meet him. "You seen Top?"

Derailed from his train of thought, Isaac paused. "Not since yesterday. Why?"

"He's off with a twenty-two."

"What's he huntin'?"

"Dogs."

"With that killer out there?"

"What do you know about it, Ike?"

"Listen, listen. I figgered it out, like I said. It's The Skinner."

Frustrated at so much being out of his control, Ned scrubbed a hand across his head. "Tell me what you think you know."

"The Skinner is back and settling up with the last of us. Looks like he started with Tommy Lee."

The Skinner had terrorized Center Springs two years earlier, first killing and then mutilating animals. As the months progressed, he moved from torture to skinning, from animals to people, and when he targeted Ned's grandchildren, all hell broke loose on the Red River. The killing spree abruptly ended one stormy night, but the community feared his return.

Ned sighed. "Have you seen him?"

"No, but listen, you know he's been a-layin' low. I think he decided to come back and start killin' again, and this time he's a-usin' guns and shootin' people in the head. You know, they kill quicker than cuttin' throats. Cleaner, too."

"Well, that's true, but I doubt he's back."

Isaac paused didn't seem to hear. "Listen, listen. Some folks is saying that you and Cody settled up with him down there in Mexico. I know y'all don't want to talk about it, but I don't believe y'all did what they're saying."

"No. Cody chased some other bad folks down to the Valley, but it wasn't The Skinner. He's gone. I'm gettin' worried that things are coming unraveled around here. Now tell me about that bank robbery you saw."

"I done told the sheriff and the FBI."

"Tell *me*."

"Listen, I's standin' there in line to get me some cash when they come sashayin' in the revolving door like nobody's business. One of 'em hollered for everybody to put their hands up..."

"Which one?" Ned interrupted.

"Why, I believe it was the man."

"You don't know the difference between a man's voice and a woman's?"

"Why, of course I know. It was the man. Anyway, listen, listen, everybody throwed their hands up and them two went to work. They split up, with her holding ever'body with that shotgun and he took off inside with the bank manager to where the safe deposit boxes are."

Isaac stopped, as if waiting for Ned to ask a question.

"Go on, Ike."

"Listen, listen, he knew what to do. He was in there a-bangin' away for a minute and then he came running out with a bag full of money."

Ned interrupted him again. "Did you see him put money in there?"

"Why no."

"Then you don't have any idea what was in that bag. It could have been full of newspapers for all you know."

"Why would somebody keep newspapers in the safe?"

"That ain't what I said, Ike. Never mind. Go on."

Ike pulled his ear. "I don't believe I ever heard of anybody saving newspapers like that. Anyway, they headed for the door at a trot, and I thought for a minute the manager was going to get that gal's gun, because she dang-near fell off them high heels of hers on that slick tile floor, but she caught her balance."

"Tell me what she looked like."

Reader thought for a moment. "Listen, she was hard lookin', but not hard to look at, if you know what I mean. Lots of makeup, poufy blond hair, bright red lipstick, and wearin' clothes so tight I thought the seams would bust. That gal's built like Sofie Watkins out by Razor."

Ned once heard Miss Becky say Sophie was "blessed." Him and every other farmer in the county knew what that meant. "Was her chest really big like Sofie's?"

Ike smiled. "Sure was."

"Could you see the tops of 'em?"

"Huh?"

"I'm asking because you sometimes say things like you really know what you're talking about. Did you see skin? They might have made her up to draw more attention to her chest than to notice what them robbers really looked like. Was her top low enough you could you see between 'em?"

Isaac's mouth worked like a fish. "Why, why, listen, I wasn't *tryin'* to look down her shirt."

"Did you see 'em, or not?"

"Well, listen, I guess I noticed. Why?"

"Because she might have been made up to look different."

"Oh, naw, They was real all right."

"All right. How old were they?"

"Her titties? I reckon they were as old as her, though I guess if you take off a few years before she grew 'em…"

Ned rubbed his head some more. "This is what makes me tired when I'm-a talking to you. How old were them *bank robbers*?"

"Oh, thirties, I reckon."

"Tell me about the other'n, the man."

"Slender, in a suit and hat."

"How'd his clothes fit?"

"Listen, it was hanging off of him like it had fit once, but he'd lost weight. It reminded me of Jeeter Rhodes, you know how skinny he is and…"

"Anything else?"

"Didn't pay no attention. I was busy looking down the barrel of that pistol he was waving around…wait, he had a white bandage on the side of his face."

"A bandage?" Ned felt his face redden. Talking to Isaac also raised his blood pressure. "Don't you think that's something you should have thought of at first?"

"Listen, listen, I been so rattled since then that I'm a nervous wreck."

"What did it look like, the bandage?"

"Big, white piece of gauze taped to his face. It had a little blood seeping through."

"Did you tell that to Griffin, or the FBI?"

"I…I don't remember. I reckon I did."

Seeing the worry in Isaac's eyes, Ned let him off the hook. He gave Reader's arm a pat. "All right. And back to what we was talkin' about at first. I don't know why Tommy Lee was murdered, but if there's somebody else running these bottoms doing them kind of things, we need to keep everybody close to the house."

"All right, Ned. Listen, *you* keep an eye out for The Skinner. It can't be nobody else." Isaac paused. "You know one thing I'm proud of, though…."

"What's that?"

"Them bank robbers weren't clowns. I saw a picture show a while back where the bank robbers dressed up like clowns. I don't know what I'd-a done if they'd been dressed thataway, and all that makeup. You never know what people are like under all that paint. You know, I'm afraid of clowns." Isaac shifted into reverse and backed up. "I'm gone."

Hands in his pockets, Ned stared at the red gravel under his feet.

Minutes later, he heard the distinctive crack of a .22 rifle.

Chapter Twenty-one

"We got a problem, Mr. Best."

The casino owner glanced up from a sheaf of papers on his desk. He propped the horn-rimmed reading glasses on top of his head. Chris Champion was one of his most trusted men. He'd moved up since the recent loss of his older, more experienced men in the Texas shootout in the Shamrock motel. "Talk to me."

"A couple of weeks ago we had a large number of counterfeit bills show up at one of our high-stakes tables. We haven't had a problem with funny money in a couple of years, and I thought the stupid bums who print this stuff finally learned it was bad business to launder their paper through our casino."

"How much is considerable?"

Champion looked uncomfortable. "Someone dumped five-thousand in one night, on one table."

Best glowered and plucked the butt from his lips. He crushed it out in the crystal ashtray beside the papers. "So that means a lot more could have come through here that night."

"Right. We checked the other tables, and the total came to more than twenty thousand."

"How the hell did we miss something like *that*?"

"It's good paper. Some of the best I've ever seen." He pulled a sheaf of bills from his pocket and gently placed it on Best's reports.

Best slipped the rubber band off and flicked his fingers so that it rolled onto his wrist like a bracelet. He squinted at the top bill and held it up to the light. He rubbed it between his fingers, then sniffed it. He shuffled through the remaining bills and selected another one for the same treatment. A tickle of recognition in the back of his mind warned him of what was coming next. "All right. I can see how it got through. Do you have any idea who brought it in? A high roller dumping that much cash should be remembered by somebody here."

Champion swallowed. "It wasn't just one night. It happened three nights in a row, and not only here at The Desert Gold. I checked some of the other guys, and even a couple of clip joints out on the edge of town. They all report the same thing, only not as much. For some reason, this mug liked us...a lot."

Best didn't say anything.

"So we went back and looked around some. You know, since we kinda...keep...cash stocked, I had one of my best men check back through the dates."

Best was the only casino operator on the strip to keep cash in rotation, instead of banking it like the others. He was the last of the old-timers who funneled money back to the Family, but he did it in a different way. Unimaginable amounts of money were stored in a monstrous vault deep below the casino. There, stacks of bills from weeks past rested on carefully numbered and labeled steel shelves.

"We ran the numbers. Then I cross-checked the tables and talked to the dealers and pit bosses to see who bought in, lost a little, and then cashed out. You know the dodge, change a counterfeit thousand into chips, lose a little, and then cash out with real money. Every time I checked, I came up with a guy they all remembered."

Best's patience was almost at an end. "All right. I believe you. So who was it?"

"I think it was that Texan, Griffin."

Best's eyes went cold. That wasn't the two-part deal he had with the north Texas sheriff. Griffin was supposed to bring the funny money in and exchange it for a percentage, a very small percentage, so he could walk away clean with fresh cash. Best was going to funnel the fake paper back east into another organization. It was a beautiful idea that would keep his enemies fighting and too preoccupied to make any significant push into Vegas.

For the second half of the deal Griffin brought legit one hundred dollar bills to use in creating a front company that dealt in precious metals, jewelry, art, and antiques. The entire operation looked good to Best, since Griffin agreed to an eighty-twenty split using what Best suspected was drug money that flowed up through Texas.

They also planned to combine the front company with a land scheme handled by an associate Best had known for years. They would purchase property in the desert well below market value and slip the cash difference to the seller. Then, a few months later, the idea was to resell at the true value, getting that cash back as a perfectly legal profit.

The best part, as Best liked to think, was that he'd orchestrated everything to point directly at Griffin. If the scam went south, he could walk away with clean hands and no loss.

But the criminal had double-crossed the criminals.

Chris shifted uneasily from one foot to the other. He never knew what bit of information would set Best off. "But the way we nailed him was simple. Remember those two suitcases full of cash he left?"

"Of course."

"What about it?"

"Half that was counterfeit, too, Boss."

Best felt his face redden. "So I have been taken by a rube."

"Sorry, Boss, but look at it this way—your cash system worked like it was supposed to. We won't get caught again."

"You are right about that." Best reached for the phone. He punched one of the buttons lining the bottom. "Ann, get me Leo Caifano in Kansas City."

Chapter Twenty-two

I was filled with a white rage that drove me to the edge of the woods.

A dozen dogs worked across the pasture a hundred yards below, sniffing the grass in hopes of startling a rabbit from cover. A skinny German shepherd with prominent ribs stopped and raised his nose to the air.

For the second time that day, Uncle Wilbert's rifle rose to my shoulder. I'd already killed two strays down by the creek. My cheek found the smooth stock. The iron sights lined up down the barrel.

Squeeze the trigger. Never yank it. Squeeze until the shot surprises you.

The sharp crack echoed off the trees. The good smell of burned gun powder filled the air.

The half-starved German shepherd lay on the ground, kicking weakly. In the back of my head, I thought I was doing him a favor, dying quickly instead of starving to death in the coming winter.

I shifted my aim at the pack of fleeing dogs. The next shot missed a running mixed-breed, and I remembered the .22 was a semi-automatic. I led the dog and squeezed the trigger as quick as I could. The little rifle spat over and over again, almost spraying like a machine gun. Bullets plowed into the sand behind the dog. I led even further, and the mutt rolled.

It was hard to see through the tears blurring my eyes. Another, slower dog settled into my sights and it rolled and lay still. I was on automatic, mind and body working together without conscious thought.

Prickly anger took over when the rifle ran dry and my chest tightened. Through the tears, I fumbled a few shells out of my pocket to reload, but I dropped most of them. I fought the deep sobs that tried to surface. I wanted to be like the men in Center Springs, and hold it inward. None of them cried over dogs.

"Dang, that's good shooting," Ty Cobb Wilson said, stepping out of the tree line twenty yards away. I was shaking when I saw Jimmy Foxx there with him. Both men were holding rifles, though Jimmy's rested over his shoulder, and Ty Cobb held his own 30.30, pointed muzzle down.

"Y'all can shoot, too, you know."

They joined me. "We could, Top. But we ain't mad at them like you, even though I suspect they've killed a calf or two around here."

"They hurt Hootie." Tears welled.

"I know. We heard. That's why we're here."

"He's a good dog. He was so smart…" My voice broke.

Jimmy Foxx gave my shoulder a pat. "He ain't dead yet, leastways he wasn't when we went by the house."

For the first time since I saw Hootie, all cut up on that tailgate, I broke down and cried. I hadn't cried so hard when The Skinner took me and Pepper. I didn't cry much when Mama and Daddy were killed in a car wreck. But with two tough outdoorsmen watching, I bawled like a baby over my dog. Maybe it was because they were hunters and understood, because they loved their bird dogs. I don't know, but it felt like everything inside me flowed out with those tears.

I wrapped my arms around Ty Cobb for no reason except he was closer, and bawled, letting all the pain and anger out. It didn't seem like I could ever stop.

He took the rifle from my hands and passed it to his brother and pulled me against the brush pants covering his legs, getting my jeans muddy, but I didn't care.

Jimmy Foxx dug a handful of .22 hulls from his pants and reloaded my rifle. I wondered later why he had them. Neither of the Wilson boys were carrying .22s that day, but he had enough to fill the rifle's magazine.

I finally cried myself out and felt curiously relaxed, like a pressure valve had released something that had been building a long time. I wiped my runny nose. "I'm sorry."

"No need to be sorry." Jimmy Foxx handed the loaded rifle back. "We're pretty close to Cody's house. Why don't we run by there for a few minutes?"

"I'm still hunting."

"I know you are, but them dogs'll keep hightailing it for a while. They'll come back. Right now we need to let folks know you're all right. They're looking for you."

The pasture was empty, except for the dead dogs. A light breeze moved the nearby leaves, and the long grass swayed. I didn't feel bad about killing them. I didn't feel anything at all, except kind of empty for crying so hard. Killing the dogs wouldn't make Hootie any better, but it was something I had to do for myself.

My chest hitched, but I finally regained control. "All right."

I followed the brothers through the woods. They moved like the animals they hunted, quiet and without wasted motion. My footsteps sounded loud as a bull stomping through broken glass.

When we arrived a while later, Norma Faye and Uncle Cody were in their front yard near the blackened ring where Mr. Tom Bell burned lumber scraps. He'd worked for months to restore the house. When he didn't come back from Mexico, they found he'd willed it to them.

The Wilson boys led the way out of the woods. Uncle Cody nodded to the brothers. "Thanks, boys."

Norma Faye knelt and opened her arms. "Come here, baby. It's gonna be all right." Her soft voice cracked and I couldn't help it. I found myself rushing toward her and for the second time that day I broke down. Maybe it was because I needed to cry some more, or maybe because I needed a woman to hold me, but I stuck my face in her mane of wild red hair and she held me close, crying herself.

The men pretended not to see.

Chapter Twenty-three

Three well-dressed men stepped off the plane from Kansas City and rented a blue Ford Galaxie at Dallas' Love Field airport. A bald bull of a man named Michael Braccaro drove. "I hate this city. How long will it take us to get out of here and to wherever we're going?"

His olive-skinned associate in the passenger seat glanced up at the red flying horse on top of the Magnolia Building, high above downtown Dallas. Jack Machino, known as Johnny Machine, was the toughest gangster Kansas City had ever seen. "They call this burg a city?"

In the backseat, Nicky didn't bother to look up from the open map in his lap. "It's what passes for a city in Texas." He traced a line leading east with a forefinger. "Michael, you went the wrong way. If we keep going in this direction, you'll come to Northwest Highway. Turn right and stay on it until Buckner Boulevard. That'll take us to Highway 66. Then we go east."

Michael Braccaro shrugged and checked his rearview mirror, knowing he could never be too careful when it came to the local constabulary. "Don't expect me to remember all that. Tell me what to do when we get there."

The distinctly northern accents were completely out of place in a state full of slow drawls. Johnny Machine patted his coat pocket. "Anyone got any butts?"

A half-empty pack sailed over the seat. "You need to buy your own smokes next time. It'll only cost you thirty-five cents."

Johnny tapped one loose. "Hell, Nicky, you bum off me all the time. I didn't bring a whole *carton* for cryin' out loud. I buy 'em by the pack just like Michael."

Michael rested his wrist across the steering wheel. "How far away is that town?"

"Chisum?" Nicky examined the map. "It doesn't look far. Half an hour maybe?"

The Machine drew a lung full of smoke. He released it and the slipstream sent it to the back where it mixed with Nicky's own cloud. "This ain't Kansas City. I know because the last time I came to this lousy state, I found out the hard way. The distance between towns is a lot farther than the way it looks on that map."

Ten minutes later, Nicky sat forward and spoke over the seat. "The next street is Buckner Boulevard. Hang a right. You were right, Johnny. It adds up to about an hour and a half, depending on traffic."

"There won't be any traffic after we get out of the city." The Machine glanced toward White Rock Lake as they passed. Sailboats tacked across the small Dallas water source. Closer to the bank, two men fished from a V-hull aluminum boat.

Michael turned at the light. "The place we're looking for is tiny, at least that's what Mr. Best says."

They drove in silence for fifteen minutes, until the Machine couldn't take it anymore. He had no idea why they were heading for a small town in northeast Texas. "Are you going to tell us our orders?"

"Relax." Michael slowed for a stoplight. "We gotta good opportunity here. We do something for Mr. Best, and he takes care of us, right?" The light changed before the car came to a complete stop, and they passed through the intersection. The four small shopping centers at each corner were roofed in red Mexican tile. A red Pegasus glowed atop a corner gas station. "Casa Linda. What's with that stupid flying horse everywhere?"

"Mobile stations are popular around here…uh, oh. Everybody sit tight. A cop's behind us."

"Relax. We ain't wanted for anything." The Machine didn't like cops either, but he knew better than to catch their attention by watching through the back glass. He shifted so he could better see the side mirror. "But I don't like cops."

Michael grinned. "How do you feel about sheriffs?"

"Don't like 'em either, why?"

"We're going to meet the town sheriff in Chisum."

The other two perked up. "What for?"

"Because Mr. Best said so, that's why."

"Left here." Nicky resisted the impulse to check behind them. "This is Highway 66. It takes us halfway there, and then when we're way out in the sticks, Tighway 24 takes us to Chisum."

The police car continued straight down Buckner. The Machine sagged back into the seat. "Mr. Best didn't fly us all the way out here just to talk with a local sheriff."

"That's right. When we leave, he won't be sheriff no more."

"Will he be breathing?"

"Nope."

"And then?"

"Then we call Mr. Best and tell him it's finished."

"These are the kinds of jobs I like," Johnny Machine said. "Quick and easy."

Chapter Twenty-four

Ned Parker opened the screen door busy with flies. Frenchie's Café smelled of frying onions and bacon. Since O.C. Rains wasn't in his office, Ned knew he'd be in the back booth he used as an office away from the courthouse. As he'd suspected, the judge was there, facing the door.

He walked the length of the café and slid into the booth across from his old friend. He put his Stetson on the counter beside O.C.'s hat to keep anyone from sitting there. "Don't you ever stay in your office anymore?"

"Too many federal agents in the courthouse, working on the robbery. They make me nervous, and you know I get edgy when I get that way, so I thought I'd come over here and maybe eat a bite in peace…and then you show up. How's Hootie?"

"He'll live. We weren't sure at first, but he's come through all right."

"Top?"

"Dog huntin' again, I imagine."

"Figured. You making any headway on your killing?"

"Working on it. Nothing smells right about it."

"You ever see a murder that did smell right?"

"Nope, and that's a fact."

Frenchie slipped a daily menu between them, set a cup of coffee in front of Ned, and gave his shoulder a squeeze. He absently took the mimeographed sheet. "I'll probably never figure this one out. It reminds me of when we found Dev Hardin laying in his chicken house. I still don't have any idea how he got a twenty-two bullet in his head, and that was five years ago."

"I remember that one. I always figured somebody might have shot at something else and missed, and it wound up in Dev."

"I've heard of that happening, but not while somebody was *inside* of anything. For that to have happened, the bullet had to have flown through the window, without hitting the chicken wire."

Always a lawyer first, Judge O.C. sipped his coffee. "Well, from what I remember, the evidence showed that open window in the chicken house is in a direct line with that road."

"Yep, and everybody in the country owns a twenty-two, and none of 'em admitted shooting that day."

"Didn't expect they did."

They sat in comfortable silence for a long minute. O.C. squinted at the little menu while Ned wiped at an invisible crumb on the table with a calloused hand. On the opposite side of the booth, softer hands belied a life of intellectual work. "What do you hear on your bank robbery?"

"It ain't mine." O.C. shrugged. "Nothing. Some folks keep pointing at your new couple there in Center Springs, because they ain't from around here, but no one has brought any evidence to support the theory. The FBI has the police and sheriff's department looking everywhere but under Miss Ida's dress, but they can't find hide nor hair of the two that done it. The money and the robbers are *gone.*"

Ned leaned in. "I imagine they were out of town ten minutes after the robbery. But here's the thing, I believe they were after my deposit box there in the bank. Now, I don't know how they found out about it, but I have a sneakin' suspicion Griffin's in on it."

O.C. rested his elbows on the table and lowered his head, eyes flicking around to see if anyone was paying attention. His voice lowered. "Did they get it?"

"Nope. There's two boxes, one in my name, and one in Cody's. But they didn't know enough to look for Miss Becky under her maiden name. My empty box and Cody's was took, but not hers."

"Somebody wants them pictures that Top shot?"

While playing spy one snowy day less than a year earlier, Top snapped a photo of a drug dealer named Whitlatch passing a mysterious packet to Sheriff Griffin. It was obvious the pictures were incriminating, but not enough to proceed with formal charges against Griffin.

Ned laced his fingers. "He wants 'em bad, 'cause he knows I got him by the short hairs, and I'm waitin' for that last piece of the puzzle to put him away."

"What is it?"

Ned shrugged. "I don't have any idea. I'll know when I see it. But even then I ain't telling you. I don't want you to have any reason to recuse yourself when a certain person comes to trial."

"That's a mighty legal term for a country constable."

"I learned from you."

They chuckled.

Ned cut his blue eyes toward the other customers and lowered his voice. "I need to do something about Griffin, for sure."

"I know."

"He's been on my mind a lot lately."

"I know."

"He's almost killed me, Cody, and John, and he's ruining this county, but I can't get enough on him other than them pictures."

"I know, but this ain't about vengeance, Ned. It's about right and wrong. You'll get what you need soon enough, and then you can turn it over to me. But remember, Ned, vengeance is mine sayeth the Lord."

"Yeah, I keep hearing that." Ned motioned for Frenchie. She saw him and raised a finger in a silent 'wait a minute.' "Pepper's started listening to that hippie music and I keep hearing her talk about California and the war, and peace signs, love, and happiness."

"What does that mean?"

"It means they don't live in the real world. I'd like peace and love too, but I doubt it's gonna come to a bunch of raggedy ass dope-head kids sitting in a circle somewhere. Wait a minute, you know, they may have something. They'll have peace and love until they have to work for it, then things'll look different."

They paused again. O.C. squinted at the typed menu for a long moment. He angled it to better see by the schoolhouse lights hanging overhead. "I believe I'll order the chopped steak."

Taken aback at the sudden change in subject, Ned frowned. "I thought we were talking about them long-hairs and their music."

O.C. didn't raise his eyes from the menus. "We were, but I'm hungry."

"You just ate a piece of pie."

"I know it, but I'm still hungry."

"You know chopped steak ain't nothin' but hamburger meat mashed into a patty."

O.C. grunted. "Why wouldn't I know that?"

"Well, if you want a steak, you oughta order one that ain't all mashed up."

"I want a hamburger steak. Look, it ain't but sixty-five cents."

"You can get a hamburger for that price, and it comes with everything on it."

O.C. poked at the menu. "This comes with a side salad, and that's more than a leaf or two and a mushy tomato slice, besides, if you're right, hamburger meat is the same thing."

"Goddamnit O.C., sometimes you're so bull-headed you make me want to dip snuff. I'm sayin' that a good steak beats chopped up meat any day."

"I know it." O.C. looked around to make sure nobody was paying attention. "But I got a tooth that's sore as the dickens. I can chew chopped steak easier, at least until I get Doc Bryson to pull it."

Ned cleared his throat. "Well, why didn't you say so, then, instead of arguing with me?"

"Because I like to get your goat, that's why."

Frenchie finally came by with a fresh pot of coffee.

O.C. slid his mug closet to the edge. "I believe I might, and bring me the chopped steak special."

She rubbed a strand of stray hair away from her eyes with the back of her hand. "All right, hon. Ned, you want anything to eat?"

He grinned. "Yeah, bring me that little lunch sirloin."

O.C. glowered at him. As their coffee cooled enough to drink, three men in a rented Ford cruised slowly past the courthouse, and then Frenchie's place. They parallel-parked on the street and took their time coming through the café's screen door.

"More foreigners. They don't know no better than to hold the screen open and let all the flies in. We don't need no more flies in here." O.C. waved his hand at one that had been particularly annoying. "We already got enough."

Ned threw a glance over his shoulder. "They sound like Yankees to me."

"Like I said, foreigners."

The trio took a booth beside the front window. Frenchie joined them and answered a dozen questions about her menu. They finally settled on hamburgers, fries, and when they couldn't get shakes, ordered Cokes.

All through lunch, the strangers talked quietly and kept watch through the window. Ned and O.C. finished their meal and stood. Ned selected four dollars from his worn billfold, and slipped it under his plate. "I'll get this. You can get the next one, after you finish paying for your tooth."

O.C. grunted in response and, putting on their hats, they waved good-bye to Frenchie and left.

When they passed the stranger, the bald man stiffened at Ned's badge. He caught Ned's cold blue eyes and nodded. His friend with snake-dead eyes didn't change expression. The third man concentrated on his plate. Instead of stopping to talk, Ned left, knowing many people responded strangely to the sight of a badge or holstered pistol.

On the sidewalk, they strolled down to the town square as the three men watched until they were out of sight.

Chapter Twenty-five

"We bought a Curtis Mathes television set." Miss Sam took the tiniest bite I've ever seen by an adult. "Color."

In the living room, Pepper leaned over close to me, careful not to knock over her TV tray. "Do you think they'll let us come over and watch 'Bonanza'? I'm so damned tired of fuzzy black and white pictures I can't stand it."

Grandpa was at the head of the table, and Miss Becky was in her usual place on his left. Hootie dozed on a pallet beside the cold space heater. He was getting better, day by day, but it still hurt to look at him, all shaved and stitched up like he sat.

Pepper was furious at being so far away. Miss Becky's new hand-me-down chrome-trimmed table was smaller than her old one, so me and Pepper ate in the living room. "I hate it when they treat us like kids."

"We *are* kids."

"That don't mean they can stick us off at the other end of the house."

It always tickled me when she got mad and said things like that. "It's a small house. We can spit from one end to the other."

"I'd like to spit all the way in there and see what happens."

"We might find out what happens if you'd shut up." I didn't much like it either, and wished we were in the kitchen with the adults. It was hard enough to hear their conversation without Pepper's grumbling. I'd gotten up once to lower the volume on the television. There wasn't much to watch on the snowy screen anyway, except for a boring Saturday baseball game.

Somebody said something funny and everybody around the table laughed.

"Cattle rustling?" Mr. Tony leaned back in his chair. "There are still rustlers out here?"

I could see him and Miss Sam from where I ate in Grandpa's rocker.

"Cattle rustling ain't only in the movies." Uncle Cody was facing us, so his voice was a lot clearer than those of Miss Becky, Uncle James, and Aunt Ida Belle. "We deal with it all the time. Someday I'll introduce you to Lee Berry, and you can meet a real stock ranger."

Miss Sam carefully laid down her fork. "I'd like that. I'd also like to see a *Texas* Ranger."

"Hang around long enough." Grandpa broke a biscuit in half and sopped the gravy on his plate. "There's a Ranger working over in the courthouse right now on that bank robbery. I'll take you over to meet him one of these days, if y'ont to."

Mr. Tony rolled the sleeves of his shirt in the warm, moist kitchen. "Rustling. It sounds like we live in a western now."

Miss Sam laughed and pulled at the collar of her shirt. "I don't think we're westerners, even though we look the part. These clothes still don't feel right."

"You look fine," Miss Becky and Aunt Ida Belle said almost at the same time. Miss Sam wore the same kind of skirt and top the women in Center Springs liked, except her's was cut lower and more western than most. Mr. Tony was in khakis and a blue shirt with a cowboy yoke on the back. They were both a little hokey, but then again, they weren't from Lamar County.

"I have some things that'll fit you," Norma Fay said. "If you don't mind hand-me-downs."

Miss Sam laughed. "I've never worn hand-me-downs, but I'd like that. Your clothes look so…soft."

"They've been washed a hundred times. I have a few things

that aren't as worn out. They don't fit me too well in the...certain places. You come on over and we'll see what suits you."

Miss Sam took a little sip of tea. "After only a few days here in the country, we realized we needed new clothes. We went to Duke and Ayers to buy these, but we couldn't take the leap and buy dungarees."

Pepper hollered. "We call them jeans!"

They all laughed and Mr. Tony shook his head. "Jeans, then, Pepper. After we changed behind a curtain, we spent the rest of the day shopping in town. The Sears store was interesting, since they mostly carry only washing machines, dryers, and refrigerators. They said we needed to order what we wanted from their catalogue. That thing is thick as a phone book."

"Not for Chisum," Uncle Cody said. "Our phone book's not much thicker than when the war ended. There hasn't been a lot of change around here. The square even looks like it did back in the 1930s. Come to think of it, nothing's changed much since the war."

When adults say, "The War," they're always talking about World War Two. For the others, they say, "the First World War," or "Korea," or "Vietnam."

Mr. Tony ticked off on his fingers. "It's different from where we come from. Let's see, in Chisum we saw two movie theaters, a five and dime, a drugstore with a soda fountain, three banks, a couple of furniture stores, a hardware store, and a few other businesses. It didn't take long for us to realize there isn't much to do in a cotton town. Maybe that's why they're rustling cattle, they're bored."

I could tell Mr. Tony liked to say "rustling," because of the way he rolled the word around in his mouth. It sounded a little different each time.

Norma Faye shook her head. "This isn't Las Vegas, is it?"

"No, and I'm glad." Miss Sam put her fork down. "It was so nice of you to invite us over, Mr. Parker. Miss Becky, this is the first good meal I've had since we left Nevada. I'm not much of a cook, and even Reeves' restaurant doesn't come close to this."

Reeves' was the best place to eat in Chisum, and I'd heard them talk about eating there several times since moving to Center Springs.

Miss Becky waved her hand with nails cut short that had never, and *would* never, see polish. "Hon, this ain't much, but we're proud to share what we have."

"We really appreciate the invitation for lunch," Tony said.

"Dinner." Uncle Cody corrected him, but with a smile so it didn't sound sharp or mean.

Miss Becky got up and came back to the table with another pan of biscuits. "It's all right if you call it lunch." During the meal, Miss Becky was constantly leaving the table for one reason or another. "We're glad to have you."

Eyes bright, Mr. Tony shook his head in wonder. "Cattle rustling, cowboy hats, horses everywhere. This really is the wild west!"

"Not what you'd think."

"So you get a lot of bank robberies and shoot-outs too?"

Uncle Cody reached behind him for the tea pitcher sitting on the chest-style deep freeze. "Well, you remember almost being arrested for the bank robbery…"

Everyone around the table laughed.

Grandpa held out his empty glass to be refilled. "So *that* happens, but it was the first one since the Depression. Even Bonnie and Clyde steered clear of devilment in Chisum back in the day and drove on through. Most of our work is small stuff, drunks and people yammering at one another over the least little thing."

"Were you involved in a shoot-out last year?"

Uncle Cody sighed. "They do like to talk up at the store, don't they? Yeah, we had some trouble here a while back. It seems like we're seeing more and more problems lately. But that's not normal. This is a quiet place, like I told you in Vegas. Ned mostly rides a tractor during the day and handles calls at night. I do the same, except I don't run a tractor."

"Things are changing." Grandpa dipped a spoon full of pinto beans from the bowl an arm's reach away. "I may still sit on a tractor, but those days are gonna be gone pretty soon. Things are changing here and in town, too. We've had three Yankees hanging around, taking pictures and asking who owns what, then the other day there were three more hard-looking fellers in Frenchie's that I figure don't have no business in our town. Now we have at my table a New Yorker through Vegas."

Mr. Tony's head snapped toward Grandpa. "Yankees? I haven't heard that word pitched around much until we got to Texas."

They all laughed. Grandpa studied his empty plate. "Didn't mean to be rude, but that's what we still call anybody who comes from north of Oklahoma. I knew right off they weren't from around here when I saw the first three in town, because they wore suits. I was sure when one of 'em opened his head and talked like you. I hear they're looking to invest. Ain't that a kick? This town is drying up and the kids are leaving as fast as they graduate high school, then right on their heels, other folks from up north come in to buy up what the kids don't want. It's a strange world."

"What'd these new guys look like? We might be related."

"Which ones?"

"Oh, the first three with the camera."

"Nah." Grandpa shook his head. "They don't favor you at all. They all favor one-another, so I imagine they're brothers."

Mr. Tony reached out and rubbed Miss Sam's shoulder like she had a knot in it and was trying to work it out. "What about the other three at the café?"

"One's a bald-headed bull, but the other two *are* dark com- plected, black hair."

"You notice everybody who comes through?"

"We try."

I ate till I was full, and that included everything on my plate, so I carried it into the kitchen. Uncle Cody stood and opened a door on Miss Becky's homemade china cabinet. He pulled out a bundle of folded papers. I knew what was on them, because every now and then I'd take out the wanted posters and study the bad guys in case I might run across one in town.

Uncle Cody handed them to Mr. Tony. "We keep an eye out. These FBI flyers come in the mail every week. I always look them over and then watch out to see if any of these people are coming through."

Mr. Tony shuffled through the folded flyers. Each was headed Wanted by the FBI in bold letters. Underneath, two rows of fingerprints capped another row of mug shots, front, back, and side. Below, a description of the fugitive filled the remainder of the page.

From the photos, they all looked hard, sullen, and dangerous to me.

"I swear, every time we sit down at this table, it's either law work or cattle." Aunt Ida Belle picked at the remains of a bony piece of chicken. "Tony, tell us about Las Vegas and what you did for a living there. We don't get out of this town very much, and I dearly love to hear about exotic places. Did you work in one of them gambling houses, or have you met Dean Martin?"

Mr. Tony passed the wanted flyers to Miss Sam. I saw them make eye contact for a second, and it was a whole conversation. "They call them casinos. I've seen him and the rest of the Rat Pack, but I've never met any of them. I worked for a guy who owns the casino where I met Cody and Norma Faye."

Aunt Ida Belle was shocked to find her suspicions were right. "So you *did* meet Cody and Norma Faye in a gambling house?"

Me and Pepper slid through the kitchen and put our dirty plates on the counter. Mr. Tony gave me and Pepper a smile as she followed me out on the porch. The screen door didn't block what we could hear, so we stopped outside to listen. It was better than sitting in the living room.

Mr. Tony's voice was as clear as if I was sitting at the table with them. "That's right. Mr. Best is a casino manager. If you work in the business, you're always near where the players are, but I'm not a gambler."

"Well, Cody and Norma Faye should have stayed out of those sinful places." To Aunt Ida Belle, everything was sinful. "I hear they drink in there, too. I bet you can have a good time in Las Vegas somewhere other than a casino. Sam, what did you do?"

"Mostly secretarial work...keypunch...things like that."

The conversation drifted for a while until they all grew quiet for a minute. I stepped to the screen door. "Uncle Cody?"

"What do you need, hoss, another biscuit?"

"Nossir. Do you think we can go frog giggin' sometime soon?"

"What's frog gigging?" Miss Sam asked.

Beside me, Pepper put her nose against the screen. "You don't know?"

"No honey, I don't."

"Have you ever been on a snipe hunt?"

Uncle Cody shook his head at the glint in her eye. "Oh no you don't, missy. Sam, don't let these two outlaws get you out on a snipe hunt, we'd never see you again. There's no such thing. They'll take you out in the dark woods and leave you."

We came back inside while everybody around the table laughed at the look on Miss Sam's face.

"It isn't to be mean," Norma Faye explained. "Snipe-hunting is more of a rite of passage around here that young folks play on those who don't know."

Grandpa joined in. "But frog giggin's different. You either walk a creek or pool bank with a flashlight and sticker, or float the creek in a boat and stick the frogs from there."

Miss Sam's forehead wrinkled. "Stick them?"

"Yeah!" Pepper couldn't wait to join in. "We have these long poles with sharp tines on one end, and you jab them into the frog that sits there while you do it." She wrapped her hands around an invisible pole and jabbed hard, her eyes bright and almost mean.

"Then what do you do with them?" Miss Sam's own eyes were wide.

It tickled me. "Why, you skin 'em and eat 'em, of course."

"The whole frog?"

"Nope, the legs, but a big old bullfrog has a lot of meat in them legs, and when you fry them up, they make a good meal." Pepper couldn't resist aggravating Mr. Tony and Miss Sam. "The thing you gotta remember is that fresh frog legs will jump out of the frying pan if you ain't careful."

Unsure of the truth, Miss Sam looked for help. "Is she kidding?"

Miss Becky laughed. "Hon, a lot of wild game does strange things in a frying pan. Frog legs will twitch, and fresh rabbit is bad about quiverin' while you're cutting it up. We don't pay too much attention to it, though."

Miss Sam blanched at the thought of eating frogs, but Mr. Tony perked up. "I hear the French like frog legs. That sounds like fun. I'd like to go with you some time."

"How about tonight?" Uncle Cody asked. "The weather is good, and the skeeters haven't been too bad this fall."

"Deal." Mr. Tony leaned back and stuck out his chest. "I'm going frog gigging."

"Oh, Lordy," Norma Faye said.

Chapter Twenty-six

In the car on the way back to their rented house, Tony lit a cigarette and blew smoke through his nose. "I suppose you caught that talk about new people here in town."

Samantha watched the crooked fence posts pass by. She loved the tiny community and felt like she could spend the rest of her life in a place that seemed to be frozen in time and reluctant to emerge. "You think they're from Daddy?"

Tony wondered if the trio in the café was sent by Malachi Best. He couldn't imagine how they'd found him in such a backwater place, if they were really after him at all. But then again, they found them in Shamrock.

He shrugged. Those guys could simply be traveling through, the way he and Samantha passed through a dozen towns of similar size on their way to Chisum. "There is that possibility. I'd like to get a look at those guys. If Malachi sent them from Vegas, I'll know them. If they're contractors from somewhere else, I'll probably recognize their look."

"How did he know where we are?"

"That's the thing that's bothering me. None of it makes sense."

Instead of heading directly back toward the Ordway place, he took the first dirt road they passed and soon found himself driving between fields of cotton and harvested corn stalks.

Cicadas shrieked from the trees. Tony slowed on the dirt road when a narrow plank bridge spanned a dry ditch. They crept over the dusty boards. He and Sam leaned their heads out the open windows to see dried Johnson grass dying in the cracked mud of the wash. When he looked back up, half a dozen dogs broke from the nearby trees where they'd been lying in the shade. They darted down the rows of green cotton.

"Did you see that?"

"What a different world." Sam started to flick her cigarette butt out the window, and then thought about the dried grass. Instead, she stubbed it out in the ashtray. "Those guys showing up here has to be a coincidence."

"I'd like to think that, but more folks like us in Chisum? Look, I don't think your dad could have put us together at any time. I think they've figured out where I am, and are here for me, not you. Pinocchio must have told someone about this place."

The sickening odor of rotting meat filled the car. Something nearby had died. Samantha waved her hand in front of her face. "Ugh."

Tony accelerated, raising a rooster tail of dust, but getting into fresh air. Samantha punched the lighter into the dash. It popped out and she lit two more cigarettes, more to kill the stench in the car and their sinuses than anything else. "So you think my old man sent people to Chisum looking for you? That's crazy."

Tony sighed. "You're right. I'm being paranoid, but something's up. There are too many *somethings* going on here. I still can't shake the idea that I've seen this Sheriff Griffin somewhere. He looked so familiar…"

A puzzle piece fell into place.

"Sonofabitch!" Tony slammed the brakes and the dust cloud that had been following them caught up, wrapping the car in a mini-sandstorm.

Sam waved at the dust rolling through the open windows. "What?"

"I remember seeing him now. This sheriff was sitting at a table with Malachi when he ordered me to take out that family, the one I couldn't do."

"The family and kids?"

"That's the one."

Tony let off the brakes and steered off the sunny dirt road to park in the shade of a wide oak tree where other vehicles had obviously parked before. Only a few feet away, a pipe crowned with a hand pump jutted from the sandy ground. He had no idea he was parked exactly on top of Cody's bird dog killed by The Skinner three years earlier.

"Sheriff Griffin was at the table in Vegas when I was there to talk with Best. The man didn't say a word, he just kept staring at me. I bet he remembered and called Malachi when he saw me in cuffs on the side of the road." He snapped his fingers. "Then Malachi sent the squad in the café they were talking about."

"What do you think he was doing in Vegas with Daddy? It doesn't make sense."

"Stranger things have happened. Who knows why he was there, but I can promise you these guys are here for me."

"You don't know that for sure."

"I'll find out."

"How?"

"I'll figure it out." He chuckled as they made their way from the bottoms.

"Something funny?"

"Yeah, I was thinking about the city and the Family, and now here I am getting ready to go frog gigging with a bunch of country hicks."

"They're nice people."

He nodded and chuckled again at the incongruity of it all. He'd graduated from clocking people to bumping off frogs.

Chapter Twenty-seven

It was full dark by the time Uncle Cody and Mr. Tony backed the El Camino under one of the hay barn's wings to load the flat bottom johnboat. It was going to be the four of us, because Miss Sam said she'd rather watch color television and catch up on her magazine reading.

Uncle Cody tied the boat into the back so it wouldn't slide out. "Hold this flashlight, Top, so I can see. Ned'll meet us in a couple of hours down close to the river."

I held it and Mr. Tony watched him snug down a half hitch. "How will he know where to pick us up?"

"We've done this for years. You kids, climb in there and let's go."

We went over the tailgate and sat in the boat. The El Camino's engine caught. Grandpa was waiting by the gate when we drove down from the barn. Once past, he closed and locked it behind us.

"Y'all do what they tell you," Grandpa warned us as we drove past.

"What does he think we're gonna do?" Pepper asked me. "Run around these dark woods like chickens with our heads cut off?"

"Adults always say that. They think they have to."

"I wish Miss Sam had asked me to watch TV with her." Pepper's long hair was parted in the middle and tied with a leather headband. It blew in the wind as we rode down the highway, and she kept pulling it out of her face.

"This was your idea for the most part. You were the one talking it up to Mr. Tony."

"Well, that's before I knew Miss Sam wasn't going with us. I'm thinking I'm getting too old to be a tomboy anymore. A different scene is calling me."

"What?"

"A cool new scene, man. Think about what it's like out there. Wouldn't it be far out to split this town and hitchhike to somewhere else, like Vegas or California and...?"

"I don't know who you are," I interrupted. "You're talking like a Dutchman. I don't understand a thing you're saying."

She shot me that look that was worse than her cussing. Uncle Cody pulled off the road and under the creek bridge. He backed the truck to the creek and killed the engine.

Pepper thumbed the switch on her flashlight and we saw the muddy water swirling past. A water moccasin slid off a nearby log and plopped into the current. "Did Mr. Tony see that?"

He was looking the other way. "No, but this is going to be fun."

Pepper handed me the flashlight and tugged the transistor radio from the pocket of her jeans. She rolled the on switch with her thumb. The Byrds were singing "Tambourine Man."

"Get rid of that crap or get us some good country music." Uncle Cody came around to the tailgate. "Y'all get out of there so we can unload the boat. Tony, you're gonna get them shoes all muddy."

He looked down and shined his flashlight on the bank. "I didn't think about that."

"It'll wash off," Pepper rolled the dial wheel, looking for a different channel. Johnny Wright's "Hello Vietnam" came on.

Uncle Cody shook his head and pulled the light boat out of the back. "Not that neither."

"Girl on the Billboard" filled the night. Everyone but Mr. Tony sang along while we loaded the boat with the frog gigs and 'toe sacks.

"Tony, you get in the bow and we'll put the kids between us."

"That's the front, right?"

"That's it." We were barely settled when Uncle Cody pushed us into the sluggish current. He dipped a paddle into the dark water and pointed us downstream. The late October waning moon was still bright overhead, and if we didn't need the flashlights to light up the frogs, we could have read a book in the bright glow.

Pepper shined her light forward and I passed Mr. Tony the frog gig. He held it sideways. "What am I going to do with this?"

"Job the frogs with it when we see 'em." Pepper made a jabbing motion.

"*Jab* them? Kid, why don't you move up here and do it."

"Because you're company."

"Huh?"

Uncle Cody angled us toward the right bank. "She means that you're our guest, so you get to have the fun. Pepper, on your right." Her beam steadied on a large frog. "Tony, see that bullfrog's eyes shining right there beside that pin oak?"

"What's a pin oak?"

We tried not to laugh, but frog gigging with a city boy was fun. I added my flashlight to Pepper's beam. "That tree closest to the water."

He finally found the frog's bright, reflective eyes. "That's the biggest frog I've ever seen."

"He's a good 'un. Now, when we get close enough, stick 'im with that gig."

We drifted into position and I couldn't stand it anymore. "Now!"

Mr. Tony lunged with the gig, and missed by a mile. With a yip, the frog jumped into the water and vanished.

Pepper had to duck to miss the long pole waving over her head when Mr. Tony yanked it free of the mud. "Shit! Careful. We're back here."

Uncle Cody cracked her in the back of her head with his knuckle. "Watch it, missy."

"Ow!"

Mr. Tony ducked his head, embarrassed. "Sorry."

"No problem." Uncle Cody steered us back into the middle of the creek. "You'll get the next one."

We heard a deep croak. I found the next bullfrog with my light. "Right here."

Uncle Cody dipped his paddle again and we drifted toward the frog.

"Like this?" Mr. Tony held the gig like a spear.

"Whatever works for you."

"Letting one of these kids do it works for me." With a grunt, he lunged with the gig again. "Got him!" He held the limp frog up high. "Now what?"

I opened the wet 'toe sack. "Pass him back here."

Mr. Tony spun the gig so I could reach the frog. "This thing is nasty."

I grabbed the pole to steady it, and pulled the dead frog off the long tines. Pepper shifted on her seat to see around me. "You think *frogs* look nasty, wait'll you see an old mud-cat."

Mr. Tony didn't know what to say, but I knew he was trying to figure out what a mud-cat was. He beamed. "This is all right."

Uncle Cody pushed his Stetson back and laughed. "I knew you'd like it." His face changed when he saw a second water moccasin unwrap itself from an overhanging limb. It took a looong time to slide into the water and swam ahead of us.

Mr. Tony saw it and the next thing I knew, he was holding a .38 revolver.

"Can you hit him with that?" Uncle Cody asked.

It looked like Mr. Tony was surprised to find the gun in his hand. He hesitated. "Yeah."

"Well, shoot him them."

Me and Pepper kept the snake lit up. Without waiting, Mr. Tony straightened his arm and fired. A flame shot from the cylinder and the barrel. The bullet struck the snake about two inches from behind its head in an explosion of water.

Uncle Cody whistled. "Damn, that was good shooting."

Mr. Tony nodded. "I used to practice a lot out in the desert."

"Well, it paid off."

"I don't like snakes."

"Neither do we."

I saw Pepper shudder. She hates snakes with a passion. "You can kill all of them you want."

He slipped the revolver back into his pocket and transferred the gig into his right hand. "That was fun. Who's next?"

I held out my hand. "Me."

Instead of changing places, I moved up beside Mr. Tony and got ready. In the next half hour, we drifted downstream, adding one frog after another to the sack. Pepper wasn't interested in gigging, which was fine by me.

Uncle Cody steered us into the middle of the channel. "Kids, I'm afraid we won't recognize this creek in a few years. That new dam'll choke the water off and we'll only get to float when they open the gates after it rains."

Pepper's flashlight beam skipped across the bank and through the dark trees. "Grandpa hates the idea of that lake."

I hated the idea of it killing this creek, myself.

A few minutes later, we drifted through the Rock Hole. I shined my flashlight up on the tall sandstone cliff jutting high overhead on our right. Then I moved it to the other side and the shallow bank where The Skinner kept me and Pepper tied up when he took us. It was the first time we'd been back since that stormy night.

I shivered.

Pepper clammed up and when the silence got to her, switched her radio back on. I didn't recognize the song, but it didn't matter, because I wasn't listening anyway. Uncle Cody paddled hard to get us out of there and the old swimming hole disappeared into the gloom.

Mr. Tony noticed something was different, but he didn't say anything.

Uncle Cody rapped on the side of the aluminum boat. "Knock knock."

I knew what he was trying to do. "Who's there?"

"Madam."

"Madam who?"

"Open up. Ma-dam foot got caught in the door!"

It wasn't real cussing, but it was enough to break our sad spell. We kept floating and telling knock knock jokes until we came up on a tree laying across the creek. The low banks held the trunk only inches above the water.

"Well, hell." Uncle Cody let us drift up parallel to the trunk. "We're gonna have to climb out and drag the boat over to the other side."

Mr. Tony rested his hand on the rough bark. "It doesn't look too stable."

"It'll hold us. Pepper, shine your light over there." Uncle Cody put his hand over hers and directed the beam onto a mass of roots still anchored in the ground. He followed the trunk to the other side. "This thing is as solid as a bridge." He grabbed a stout limb. "Okay kids. Y'all climb up and get a good hold out of the way. Shut off them lights and you'll be able to see and still keep your hands free."

He was right. In no time our eyes adjusted enough to climb out of the boat and work our way onto the log. I didn't stand up. Instead, I straddled it like a saddle and took the sack of frogs from Uncle Cody. Pepper scrambled up beside me like a monkey and squatted on the log to show she wasn't scared of falling off.

Mr. Tony was next. I shifted out of the way. One tall limb stuck straight up in the air, so he climbed out of the boat and stood beside it, holding onto it like a fencepost.

Uncle Cody was last. He handed me the paddle and carefully pulled himself out of the boat to sit astraddle of the log like me. I looked up to see limbs and dying leaves towering overhead in the bright moonlight. "Now, we'll pull the boat over onto the other side and climb back in."

The boat was halfway out of the water when everything went to pieces.

Standing above me, Mr. Tony jumped and reached for his collar. "Snake! Snake! Snake fell down my back!"

He was twisting and twitching in horror. It looked like Pepper's new dancing style. The worst thing I could imagine had happened, a water moccasin falling down someone's shirt to bite him over and over. I did the only thing I could do. I swung the paddle one-handed against Mr. Tony's back, hoping to kill the snake so it couldn't bite him any more than it already had.

With one hand, the blow wasn't hard, but he turned and it caught him in the stomach making him double over with a whoosh of air.

"Goddlemighty!" Uncle Cody let go of the boat and barely managed to catch Mr. Tony's collar to keep him from falling in. The boat landed with a splash, upside down.

It was all too much for Pepper. Terrified of snakes, she jumped into the water to get away from what she probably imagined was a tree full of cottonmouth moccasins.

"Well. Shit!" The radio in her pocket immediately went silent, emphasizing the nighttime sounds around the creek. I looked over to see my cousin standing in the chest-deep water and holding onto a limb.

Uncle Cody grabbed Mr. Tony's shirt and gave it a yank, pulling it out of his britches. When he did, it was bright enough to see a lizard plop down onto the tree trunk beside me before it skittered away.

We were all silent for a long moment, and then Uncle Cody started laughing. It looked like Mr. Tony thought about it, and then he joined in. Before long, we were all laughing at Mr. Tony's lizard.

Chapter Twenty-eight

Ned had a couple of hours to kill while Cody and the kids gigged frogs with Tony. The take-out point wasn't that far away, but the bends and twists in the creek stretched their float to a country mile. Instead of going back home, he steered toward Gene Stark's house not far off Razor Road. His brother's murder had been worrying Ned, because none of it made any sense.

Though Tommy Lee was pretty much a no'count in the community, to Ned's knowledge he hadn't done anything bad enough to get shot in the head for. He figured to spend a little time visiting with Gene. Maybe he'd say something to give Ned a clue as to where to look next. The old constable was running out of ideas, and didn't have lead one to follow.

Ned took his time driving between the moonlit fields and pastures of the river bottoms, enjoying the night and familiar scents of earth, vegetation, and leftover cotton poison. With the windows open, Ned followed his headlights through the darkness, driving with his left elbow hanging out the window.

His mind was in neutral, sifting through dusty files of information, when his headlights lit up the reflectors on a car parked off the dirt road. He slowed, flicked on the red spotlight mounted on the door post beside the windshield, and painted the car with the strong light.

The 1954 Dodge Coronet was empty, but a flicker of motion beside the stock tank on the other side of the vehicle caught his attention. He twisted the handle and moved the light in time to catch a flash of white slipping down below the water's surface. A second flash of well-developed white ducked down to join the first as he passed.

Ned braked, shifted into reverse, and backed up past a two-track dirt cut-off leading to the stock pond. Stopping beside an unfamiliar car, he maneuvered the strong beam beyond the open barbed-wire gate and onto two heads that seemed to be floating in the pond.

Ned checked the area. Insects fluttered in the light. The Dodge was empty. Clothes were scattered across the hood.

With the red spotlight fixed on the surface of the water, he left the car and flicked on his heavy silver flashlight. He was startled to see the heads belonged to females. "How's the water?"

Both women used a hand to shade their eyes from the white light. The squinting brunette beamed him with a smile. "Feels good, but it's a little thick."

"That don't surprise me none. You're swimmin' in a mud hole, you know. I ain't in the habit of talking to two heads floating on the water, not without knowing who they are."

"Can you lower that light a little? We've been out here for a while and you're blinding us."

Ned tilted the beam to illuminate a stack of empty Jax cans.

"Now, would you move to your left a little bit," the brunette asked, "to block that spotlight?"

When Ned shifted, the brunette raised up until her shoulders were above the water. "Thanks. My name's Pearl."

More creamy white reflecting the moonlight told Ned they'd been hunkering in the water because they weren't wearing bathing suits.

The blonde stood a little higher, too. "I'm Liz."

"Good to meet you, Liz and Pearl. Do you know whose pool you're in?"

They exchanged looks. "Not really. We're not from around here."

"That's about the only thing I know right now." Ned tilted his hat back and shined the flashlight onto the badge pinned to his shirt. "I'm the constable here in Center Springs, and y'all probably need to know that Frank Suttle won't be expecting two nekked women to be out here in his pool, scaring his cattle who probably need a drink right about now."

Liz tilted her head. "How do you know we're nekked?"

He jerked the beam toward the pile of clothes on the hood and half a dozen more empty Jax cans. "It's a good guess, I 'spect, from what there is to see."

"What's *your* name?" Pearl asked. They alternated in the conversation, giving Ned a good idea that the two had been running together for a long time, if they weren't sisters.

"Ned Parker. Constable Ned Parker."

It was Liz's turn again. "Good lord. Somebody's done called the law on us. I've heard of you, but I thought you'd be a lot younger."

"That'd be Cody. He's constable, too. Now, what are y'all doing out here in this water?"

Both women were standing higher as they talked. Even poorly lit, their shoulders glowed red, indicating they'd been in the sun for a long time. The muddy water barely covered their breasts, and Ned had a hard time keeping his eyes and the flashlight beam where they belonged.

Pearl's hand shaded her eyes. "We're from Dallas."

Liz took over. "We're staying at Gene Stark's house right over there. We heard that Tommy Lee got killed, and came to see if we could help Gene in any way."

"Um hum. And did Gene have anything for you to do?"

"Sure did!" Liz laughed. "We've been doing it all afternoon."

"Gurrrlll," Pearl cautioned. "What she means is that we cleaned his house for him, and then we all came down here for a swim after dinner and wound up staying. We both blistered, and Gene left a little while ago to go across the river and get us some more beer. Somebody drank all we had." They laughed. "I wish he could drive into town and get some Unguentine, but it's too damn late. We been staying here in the water while he's gone, 'cause it's cool and that helps take out the sting."

"Spirits of camphor'll take the heat out, but Resinol salve works, too."

"I've never heard that. Mr. Ned, you better shine that flashlight beam a little higher."

With a start, he realized the girls were standing completely upright in the waist deep water. He quickly moved the beam once again. "All right, y'all need to get on out of there and go someplace else, to Gene's, or home, I don't care, but you can't stay out there."

They waded toward him.

"Whoa! Y'all wait till I'm gone, and then git."

Ned went back to his car and heard them splash onto the bank. "Y'all don't forget to close this gate back and wire it shut," he called over his shoulder. "I don't want to get a call later tonight from Frank telling me his cows are out and to come here after 'em."

"We will."

When he slammed the door, switched off the spotlight, and started the engine, Ned caught a glimpse of the women in the bright moonlight.

Making sure they were unarmed, he shifted into gear and left with a wave.

◇◇◇

Ned's headlights led him down the dirt road past Love Thicket. Straight rows of harvested corn ran right up against a line of thick trees that trimmed the edge of a small trickle of water. The road bent, following a patchwork quilt of different-sized fields.

When the beams swept across a patch of winter wheat, half a dozen pairs of eyes glowed. The deer raised their heads to watch the car pass, and then resumed grazing. Ned slowed for a plank bridge, and the road paralleled another stand of trees. Once again, an unnatural glint in the darkness caught his attention.

He backed up, and aimed his spotlight toward the base of a tree, lighting two men that he recognized immediately. One waved, and they made their way through a tangle of blackberry vines to the side of the car.

"Howdy, Mr. Ned." Jimmy Foxx stepped across the strong beam. His waders were muddy up to his knees. "What are you doing down here this time a'night?"

A quick jolt of dread made Ned feel sick, making him wonder if the brothers, though good friends of his, were the ones who might have accidentally, or otherwise, killed Tommy Lee Stark.

Rifle over his shoulder, Ty Cobb joined them. "Howdy, Ned."

"What are you boys doing?"

Ty Cobb jerked a thumb at the silver moon. "Perfect night for coon huntin', but I'll be damned if I know where the dogs are. They been trailing an old boar coon, but then they got away from us and I ain't heard 'em bark in half an hour."

"The hell of it is, we got one treed in this pin oak back here, but neither one of us can get a shot." Jimmy Foxx spread his hands.

The absence of dogs worried Ned. "How'd you tree a coon by yourselves?" The boys laughed so casually he felt a little better.

Ty Cobb pointed his flashlight toward the tree. "The last time we heard the dogs barking was in this direction, so we hoofed it over from Love Thicket and saw a tree limb shake. When I shined my light up there, a coon blinked at me. Ain't that hell? We're better coon dogs than our coon dogs."

"That's the way it is sometimes." Ned waved an annoying mosquito away. "I never did ask you boys, were y'all out huntin' the day Tommy Lee Stark got killed?"

They shook their heads in synchronization. Ty Cobb spoke up. "Ned, that was one of the few days when we *weren't* out. Dumbass here cut hisself on a bobwire fence so bad I had to take him in to see old Doc Heinz. He sewed his arm up and made him take a tetanus shot."

"That damn thing hurt worse than the cut or the stitches." Jimmy Foxx pulled up his shirtsleeve to show Ned the long, barely healed gash near his left armpit.

"What'd you do, rassle with the fence?"

He gave Ned a wry grin. "Naw, I's climbing one running along the top of a gully over in the army camp. My feet slipped, I fell straight down, and it raked my arm open."

Ty Cobb cocked an ear away from the car to listen for his dogs. "We hadn't no more than got back when Isaac Reader came and saw us up at the store and told us Gene was looking for his brother, so we joined in."

Before Ned could answer, Jimmy Foxx held up one hand. "Lissen." The sound of barking dogs echoed through the woods. "There's your dumbass coon dogs."

"I done heard 'em before you," Ty Cobb nudged his brother, "and half of 'em's yours, to boot."

"You didn't do no such of a thing. I heard 'em first."

It was hard to tell how far off the dogs were, but their baying quickly increased in volume, growing stronger and clearer as they approached. Feeling better, Ned shifted into gear. "They're probably after that coon y'all already treed."

The brothers laughed and stepped back. "Don't run over 'em if they cross the road."

Ned waved, and drove off.

A pair of headlights met him a mile down the dirt road. "I-god, these bottoms are busy tonight." Ned shook his head at the amount of traffic in the river bottoms when, in his opinion, everyone should be home in bed. He steered to the side and waited. When the other car slowed, Ned's red light lit the face of Gene Stark, who grinned and waved. He pulled up door-to-door so they could speak between the cars.

"Howdy, Mr. Ned. What are you doing down here at night?"

"I was going to see you, when I ran across a couple of your friends back there in their all-togethers."

Gene rolled his eyes. "Those girls are a couple of ring-tailed tooters, that's for sure. Did you need something from me?"

"I don't know. I thought maybe something new about Tommy Lee might have come to mind, and I figured we could visit for a while. I've about run out of ideas."

A cloud immediately fell over Gene's face. "Mr. Ned, you know I'd-a called you if I thought of anything else."

"Well, did you see anybody around his house that you didn't know before he was killed?"

"Nawsir. Oh, Tommy Lee always had folks over. For some reason I never figgered out, gals seem to like him, but it wasn't anybody we didn't know."

June bugs flew through the headlights of their parked cars, striking the windshields with hard-shelled thumps. Other insects joined the mosquitoes and buzzed in and out of their open windows.

Ned waved a bug from his face. "Have you thought of anything Tommy Lee might have said or done to make somebody mad enough to kill him?"

Gene shook his head. "I done tol' you. He's stayed out of trouble."

"Could he have got to sneaking around other folks' windows again, and lookin' in? Maybe some husband or daddy caught him and settled up."

"Not that I know of, Mr. Ned, 'course I don't…didn't…see him all the time. He coulda' been doing anything for all I know."

"You think he coulda got into them drugs? Maybe he started selling *that* stuff."

"I wouldn't-a knowed it if he did."

"Maybe he went hunting with somebody that had a bone to pick with him. You ever think of that?"

"If he did, he didn't say nothin' to me about anybody being sore at him."

Ned took off his hat and put it on the seat beside him so he could rub his head to help him think. The engines idled quietly in the wide darkness between cotton and corn fields. "Well, keep studying on it. I can't help but feel like we're missing something right here under our noses."

"Sure will. Mr. Ned, were them gals still in the water when you left?"

"Most of 'em."

"You didn't give 'em no ticket or nothin', didja?"

"Naw, but I told 'em to get out and git after I was gone."

Gene looked disappointed for a moment. "They been in there so long, I reckon they're probably pruney anyways."

"I didn't get that close." Ned shifted into gear. "But the next time they come...visit, you need to take them swimming down at the Rock Hole, where decent folks go."

Gene waved a hand and depressed the foot feed. "Who said they was decent?"

Chapter Twenty-nine

Griffin had been on Tony's mind a lot since that afternoon when he stood in handcuffs on the side of the road. The frog gigging trip took his mind off of it only as long as they were floating down the creek. The puzzle of Griffin's appearance in Vegas resumed the moment they pulled the flat bottomed johnboat onto the muddy bank.

He remembered the sheriff sitting in the restaurant that night in Vegas. Of course the man looked different, dressed in a business suit and tie, instead of his Stetson and khakis. The puzzle was the relationship between Griffin and Best. Tony couldn't believe his bad luck, running into probably the only man in Texas who knew the same mob boss that put out a hit on him.

Tony's biggest worry was a simple phone call. If Griffin remembered Tony from that night, he could drop a dime on him and Best would be overjoyed to send a few professionals to his front door.

He had to find out what was going on.

It wasn't too late when the float was over and Ned picked them up not far from the confluence of Sanders Creek and the Red River. He plucked at Pepper's wet shirt in the fading light of dimming flashlight batteries. "I can't wait to hear why you're all wet."

She laughed. "It was funny! Mr. Tony thought he got a snake down his back, but it was only a stupid little ol' lizard."

She and Top took turns telling the story while they loaded the boat into the back of the truck using Ned's fresh flashlight.

He shook his head. "I wouldn't expect anything else from this crew." Once it was secured, the adults squeezed into the cab and the kids once again rode in the back. They dropped Cody off to get his El Camino, and drove on up to the house.

Despite the hour, Miss Becky was waiting when they pulled up the drive. Yellow light from the windows spilled onto the porch when she opened the door and stepped outside. The kids boiled out of the back, shouting stories.

Cody stopped beside Ned's truck. He reached in and lifted out the 'toe sack full of frogs. "Now the messy part, Mr. Tony."

"What's that?"

"We have to clean them before we can be through."

Tony shrugged. "It shouldn't take long to wash them off."

The adults exchanged looks, then burst out laughing. Miss Becky gave him a pat on the shoulder. "Oh, Hon, what Cody means is that we have to cut their legs off and get 'em ready for the skillet."

He grimaced. "You know, I don't think I have the stomach for that."

"It's part of it," Top explained. "You have to finish the job."

Miss Becky gave her grandson a light shove toward the house. "You two go in and wash up. You don't get to tell adults what to do. Pepper, you need to get out of them wet clothes before you catch double pneumonia."

They went inside without argument. "Uh, if you don't mind, I'd rather not stay for this part." Tony gave them an embarrassed look. "I have a weak stomach."

For those who lived by the land, the idea of being affected by blood was alien, but no one wanted to embarrass him. Miss Becky hugged Tony. "You go on home and be with that pretty little wife of yours. We'll take care of this."

Tony left, but instead of going home, he drove into Chisum.

Chapter Thirty

Griffin lived alone in an older Craftsman-style house on the east side of town. It was after midnight when Tony drove past. Lights glowed through the paper shades. At the intersection, he made a right, drove half a block farther, and parked against the curb.

Inconspicuous in the clothing he still wore after the float trip, and with the .38 deep in his front pocket, Tony strolled down the street. The neighborhood didn't have alleys. The only access was from the front. When he reached the house, the street out front was empty, as was the garage. Glancing around to make sure he wasn't observed, Tony hurried up one concrete strip of the drive and into the shadows under the living room window.

He pushed behind the shrubs growing against the frame pier-and-beam house and peeked through the two-inch gap below the pull down shade. A man sat in a chair with his back to the window. He was obviously not Sheriff Griffin. A woman on her knees in the adjoining dining room rummaged through the lower drawer of a cheap buffet. Their heated voices came through the screen of a partially opened window.

The woman turned and pointed a finger. "You had only one thing to do, and you blew it."

"Blew it, hell!" The agitated man moved his head in anger. "Our job was to hit the bank, get as much money as possible, and to take box one-thirty-eight and two-sixty-four. It's not my fault Griffin shorted us on our part of the take."

"You got the wrong boxes is why!"

He threw his hands in the air and leaned back. "We don't *know* that. We got away with what you said you wanted."

She stood and put her hands on her hips. "There were supposed to be pictures. That's what he told us to get, a packet of pictures."

"Well, we didn't have much time to stand there and talk to the guy with the keys. He was so nervous I thought he'd fall out, and I punched them boxes as fast as I could."

He referred to a homemade device that he learned to use only days before. While she kept everyone in the bank down on the floor, his job was to knock out the locks and find the packet of photos. It was surprisingly simple to clamp the rig onto the box with a steel pin positioned directly over the lock, hit the plunger with a hammer from the bag at his feet, and pop the mechanism.

"Well, there were supposed to be pictures."

"All right. I believe you, but they weren't in there. Let's find the rest of our share of the bank money and go before we get caught. It's a wonder we ain't in jail already." She disappeared into the kitchen. The man shook his head and shifted forward to sit on the edge of the couch. "I've already looked in there."

She came back into the living room after several minutes, her face bright, carrying several packages wrapped in white butcher paper. "I told you."

"What are you gonna do with steaks?"

"This is the money, you idiot. It might say 'steak' on the outside, but he wrapped the bills in this and stored them in his deep freeze."

The man launched himself from the chair, grabbed one of the packages, and unwrapped it.

She wiped her damp forehead with one hand and carefully patted her hair. "You don't trust me?"

"You've got to be kidding."

She shook her head as he thumbed through the sheaf.

He opened another stack of bills. "You think this is all?"

"It's enough to make up what he owes us for our share."

Their mood swiftly changed from argumentative to positively happy. He hugged her and she beamed up at him. In the shadows outside, Tony realized their stormy relationship was as full of ups and downs as a roller coaster ride.

The man laughed. "This is a sweet deal. We're getting paid at least twice for the same job."

"That bank robbery was a great cover for a couple of lock boxes."

"You planned it, baby!" He rushed into the bedroom and returned with a pillow case.

She dropped the white packages inside and wiped her hands on her jeans. "All right."

"Let's get that last job done and get out of here."

The woman's face fell. The man held his hand toward her. "Yeah, I know you think it's a bad idea, but it won't take but a few minutes and then we're gone."

"I don't think it's a good idea for us to hang around anymore."

"It'll be all right. Griffin wants me to take someone out."

"Is this for Griffin, or you?"

He nodded. "Griffin. I agreed to do two jobs and I'm going to finish the second, come hell or high water."

She gave a harsh laugh. "We robbed a bank, broke in a sheriff's house to steal the money back that he wouldn't give us because he said we didn't get the right box, and now you want to do him a favor and shoot someone? Ridiculous."

He glowered at the woman. "I do have a little honor left."

This time she threw her head back and laughed. "My God! That word. There's no honor among *thieves*. Haven't you ever heard that before?"

"There is as far as I'm concerned. You might have learned something different, showing your tits in the Carousel Club there in Dallas, but I'm going to do what I said and take the guy out. If you want to stay with me, you'll do what I say."

She shook her head and rolled her large, almost almond-shaped eyes. "I thought Jack Ruby was a nutcase when he was my boss before he went and got himself a nice prison cell, but I think I've hooked up with someone worse than him." The words were there, but the look in her eyes told Tony that her interest in the man was deeper than she acted.

"Don't worry. No one will figure out who we are. I think those stupid disguises worked. Let's go check in at the Holiday Inn and get some sleep. We'll do the job and be in Hot Springs before you know it. How does that sound?"

Tony recalled the description of the bank robbers that he'd heard on television. When the couple went through the First National door, they were dressed as conspicuously as possible. The man wore a bright blue suit with a tie painted with a hula girl. His hair was long, greasy, and combed back in a ducktail. A bloodstained bandage covered half of his face. The woman stood out like a sore thumb in a skin tight shirt and black pedal pushers, and hair teased into a blond bouffant.

Now, his face was completely smooth and his hair was much shorter. Hers was also short, brunette, and flipped. They could have been any young couple living in town or traveling through Chisum.

Had they been staying with Griffin? It could explain why they hadn't yet been found, hiding out with the man looking for them. Tony shook his head at the strategy that didn't make sense, but worked. *That also cleared up the reason why Griffin came north toward Oklahoma. While he sent deputies and police in all directions, those two probably drove right to the house to hide out until things cooled off in Chisum.*

Brilliant.

She turned off a lamp. "I don't like it."

"I don't care. Shut up."

They flicked off the last lamp and left. Tony watched the couple hurry down the street to a sedan parked on the next block. Their headlights came on and the car pulled away. Still in the shadows, Tony thought about waiting for Griffin to get home. It would be a simple matter to kill him and leave. He'd done it many times in other cities.

But there was no way to know how long Griffin would be gone, or if he'd even show up before dawn. Standing around only risked discovery.

He left the shadows and walked down the street. A car approached and the headlights split the darkness. He waved and squinted straight ahead, trying not to lose his night vision. Everyone waved in Chisum. There was no way to know if anyone waved back behind the headlights, but he didn't care. They passed without slowing.

Tony got into his own vehicle and drove home to Center Springs.

Chapter Thirty-one

"Sonofabitch!"

In the dark car, Johnny Machine frowned at Michael. "What?"

"When the headlights hit that guy, the one that waved at us like we're family, he looked like Anthony Agrioli."

The Machine looked over his shoulder. "Who's 'at?"

"Agrioli is one of Best's lieutenants."

In the backseat, Nicky looked over his shoulder. "You think Best sent someone else out here for Griffin, too?"

Michael shrugged. "Maybe."

Nicky couldn't figure it out. "So he waved at us like he knew we were gonna be here?"

"I guess." Michael slowed to pass between two parked cars. "I wouldn't have noticed him until he did that."

"Where do you know him from?"

"He worked for Nunzio Perfetto in Chicago for a while, before Best called him out to Vegas. I knew him there, and then I saw him a couple of times when I was in the casino. He's a good man."

"It can't be him. Maybe the guy only looks like Agrioli." The Machine settled back into the bench seat and worried the radio. "I can't find anything except for this hillbilly shit."

"No, that was him. I'm sure of it."

"So what?" Nicky took off his hat and leaned his head back

to look through the sloped rear window at the moon. "Best sent someone else."

"That don't make no sense." Michael shook his head. "The Boss wouldn't fly us out here, then send one of his own men without telling me."

The Machine was tough and frightening, but his thought processes were sometimes a little slow. "Maybe he's here to keep an eye on us."

"I don't think so. Mr. Best never did that before." Michael steered around the corner and cruised the block, passing Griffin's now-dark house.

Nicky unconsciously adjusted his hat on the seat beside him. "So what are we gonna do now?"

Michael looped back toward Main Street. "Nothin'. I don't wanna screw nothin' up. If Mr. Best sent Agrioli, then he has his reasons."

"Hey," the Machine scratched his chin. "Do you think Agrioli already did the hit? Maybe he tapped Griffin and left."

"Could be." Michael came to a decision. "We hold off tonight, go back to the motel, and give Mr. Best a call in the morning."

Nicky sighed. "He ain't gonna be happy."

Michael flicked a glowing butt into the darkness. "I ain't gonna be happy to stay in that stinking Holiday Inn another night, either."

Chapter Thirty-two

The next morning at breakfast, Tony and Samantha heard a knock on their screen door. Tony left the table and stepped into the entry hall to see past the staircase. The screen diffused a backlit shape and it took a moment for his eyes to adjust.

Sheriff Griffin raised his hand in greeting. "Good morning."

Tony waited, the ten feet between them an unsecure cushion. "Good morning. How can I help you, Sheriff?"

Griffin stuck his thumbs behind the hand-tooled leather gun belt and rocked back on his heels. "Can I speak to you, Mr. Agrioli?"

Tony didn't want to talk to the sheriff, but even more, he didn't want the man in his house. He crossed the short distance, pushed through the door, and stepped uncomfortably close, intending to push Griffin back.

Instead, Griffin used Agrioli's momentum and jerked his head toward the car. "Come on."

Tony found himself following the sheriff away from the two-story house. It made him nervous, because his .45 was on the living room mantle. He didn't even have the .38 revolver in his pocket that morning.

His nervousness faded when Griffin stopped by his car and stuck both hands in his pockets. "Mr. Agrioli, I remember you."

"I don't think we ever met before, Sheriff." Tony noticed the stubble on Griffin's cheeks, and his puffy eyes that told a story of little sleep.

"Yes we have. I know you, and you know me. It took a minute to place your face the other day on the side of the highway when Washington had you in cuffs, but I did."

It was obvious Griffin didn't want to say where they'd seen each other, wanting Tony to fill in the blanks.

Tony hated playing games, wishing Griffin would come out and say what he meant, because there was always the chance the crooked sheriff was simply fishing for information. "Sheriff, my wife and I have only recently moved in."

"I know that. And I know you ain't got a job, and that's unusual for a man in this community. I'm surprised Parker hasn't been around here asking questions."

"The constable and I have talked about a lot of things. There are many job possibilities to explore. What can I do for you? Have I broken the law in any way? Am I under arrest?"

Griffin looked genuinely surprised. "Why, no, I don't have anything to arrest you for, right now. I came out to see if you wanted a job, before you moved."

Tony squinted. "I don't need a job right now, and I didn't say I was going anywhere."

"Sure you are. I believe you're going to do something for me, and then you're leaving north Texas for good. When you do, I won't come after you or your woman."

"What do you want?"

"I know what you do for a living, and I know you've been sent here for me. But I'll make you a better deal. I'll give you twenty thousand dollars to leave me alone and do a job for *me*. You kill Ned Parker and that nigger deputy who arrested you. Then you can tell Best that I run off." Griffin spread his hands. "Ain't that simple? Killing me will bring all kinds of hell down on your head, but you can put those two down and nobody around here will come looking because I'll cover for you. You'll get paid twice, once from Best and once from me, and go on back to Vegas with money in your pocket when I disappear. What your boss don't know won't hurt him."

Tony raised an eyebrow at the idea. "People read newspapers. If someone hired a guy to kill you, he'll be checking the papers, or he'll have someone watch the news. You can't get away like that."

"They'll read that I *disappeared*. That happens around here. I had a deputy vanish into thin air a couple or three years ago, and he ain't been found *yet*."

A farm truck passed on the oil road beside the house. The driver raised a finger from the steering wheel in a wave. Griffin threw up a hand, knowing it was expected.

"He saw us together." Tony nodded toward the retreating truck. "If I've learned anything about this place, it's that people talk about the littlest things with each other."

"Who cares? We'll both be gone from this one-horse town when it's all over, because this has to happen quick."

"I'm not here for you and I don't want to be gone. We like where we are. Sam and I may want to spend the rest of our lives in this house."

"You can quit with that story. I know better."

"It isn't a story and you aren't as good as you think you are. I'm out of the business."

Griffin threw his hands up in exasperation. He always felt that he was the smartest guy in the room. "Look boy, you can't con a con man. Y'all don't belong in Texas, and you stick out like a sore thumb. Besides, that isn't why you're in Center Springs." He lowered his voice in a conspiratorial whisper. "Like I said, we both know, and I don't think either of us wants that. I'm making you a good deal. I'm giving you the chance to pocket two salaries, and go back to Best a hero." Griffin snapped his fingers. "Better yet, here's what I'll do. I'll give you another twenty thousand to go back and kill Best. Whaddaya think of that?"

That unbelievable suggestion finally confirmed what Tony already knew. Griffin was either completely insane or out of touch with reality. A feeling boiled up in Tony, feeding the urge to kill someone. It was an almost overwhelming injection of adrenaline.

Silence stretched so long that sweat beaded on Griffin's forehead, the only sign of nervousness. The sheriff wiped a trickle from his cheek. "Look, I'll make this even easier for you. I'll have someone help you with Washington. He'll be the toughest to take down. He's seeing a woman named Rachel. Her house is about five miles down a dirt road south of Reid's store in Forest Chapel. Washington shows up there every day about five in the evening and he won't be expecting you. Go there, shoot the big bastard, and leave. I'll have the money ready for you when you're finished. You've done this before. Twenty thousand, Saturday afternoon, at five."

The vein throbbed in Tony's forehead. His hand clenched, and he wished for a baseball bat. Three good whacks. Three. It would eliminate the problem standing before him, and give him the release he desperately needed. It had been too long. He knew then that he would soon kill Griffin. With that thought, the pressure immediately lessened. Relieved, Tony winked at Griffin. It was his promise to put the man in a shallow grave very, very soon.

Griffin mistook the wink for agreement and relaxed just as the Parker kids coasted past the store on their bicycles. They pedaled hard for the two men standing under the ancient oak trees in Tony's front yard.

"Mister Tony!" Top called. "Did you hear what happened?"

The kids' enthusiasm dimmed when they recognized the sheriff. Neither liked the man, but they couldn't explain why, even if asked.

Pepper stopped her bike beside them. "Hidy, Sheriff. Mr. Tony, the Wilson boys rounded up a bunch of men and they all went dog hunting."

For a moment, Tony didn't know what to say. Did these people organize dog hunts, like a deer hunt? "Tell me about it."

Before Pepper could answer, Top spoke up. "Before daylight this morning Ty Cobb and Jimmy Foxx caught some more dogs killing a calf out in Mister Bronson's pasture and shot two of them. Then they came up to the store and gathered up a bunch of men to help. They trailed them down to the creek bottoms."

Pepper broke in with the exciting conclusion. "Them Wilson boys was waiting, and when the rest of the men ran the dogs in their direction, they opened up on 'em. Mr. Ike said it was like a deer drive they have back east, whatever that means. They killed them all."

Tony chewed the inside of his lip in thought. "So I guess that gets you off the hook, doesn't it, Top?"

"I did my share."

"It looks like it's over for you now."

"Yessir."

"And when it's over, you hang up your guns, isn't that right, Sheriff?"

Griffin tried to read Tony's face. "A smart man knows when things are over, but he also knows some things aren't over until they're done."

Pepper frowned. "What?"

Tony looked down at Pepper. "*He* knows. Let's go to the store and get a soda…a Coke. How's that?" Without a glance at Griffin, he paced the kids as they walked their bikes down his long, dusty drive.

Griffin's voice was clear in the still air. "Remember the time, Mr. Agrioli! And don't pay too much attention to those two little nits, they'll pester you to death if you let 'em."

Tony felt a catch his throat.

Oh my god, Griffin and Best have been talking.

Nits.

Moments later, Griffin caught them and slowed the car. "Best, to you and that pretty wife of yours." He raised one finger in a wave.

The kids waved back. Feeling his temple throb again with renewed savagery, Tony swallowed down the growing rage burning deep inside. He watched him drive away.

Best to your wife.

Best.

Tony watched the car disappear and vowed to go back to Vegas and beat the sonofabitch into jelly if Best included the kids, the Parkers, or especially Sam in his vendetta.

He didn't care if he *was* Sam's father.

Chapter Thirty-three

Something kept nagging Ned about Tommy Lee's murder, but he couldn't put his finger on it. His mind kept going back to his conversation with Wade Reidel on the day Tommy Lee's body was found. He decided to visit Wade or Karen Ann. Either would work for the moment. Ned picked up the microphone. "Cody Parker."

A moment later, Cody's voice came through the little speaker. "Go ahead, Ned."

"Where are you?"

"Leaving the courthouse. I dropped off a prisoner."

"You want to run by Bill Adkins' house and talk to him about Tommy Lee?"

Cody knew exactly what he meant. Bill spent a lot of time rubbing bellies with Karen Ann in the honky-tonks across the river. "You bet. I been planning to go over there anyway."

"Good. I have a stop to make. I'll meet you there in an hour."

"Ten-four."

The nearly twenty-year-old ten-code always annoyed Ned to no end. He preferred to talk in plain English. "All right, then."

Passing the Plaza Theater, Ned traveled west to a neighborhood of tired frame houses not far from the red brick train station. The splintered boards on the railroad crossing rattled as his tires rolled over the tracks.

Though many of the houses were tired and needed mowing, the neighborhood itself was tidy. Most porches had chairs or swings. A few were occupied by folks who either watched him with suspicious eyes, or old folks who waved whether they knew him or not.

Checking the address scribbled on the Harold Hodges Insurance notepad, Ned steered to the curb in front of a cheaply constructed Texas bungalow that probably looked worn out ten years after it was built. The eaves drooped and the yard hadn't felt a lawnmower blade at any time during the summer.

Ned slammed the car door and studied the house for a moment. A rusty, unsupported water cooler sagged from a window on one side, actually pulling the wall out of plumb. An even rustier screen leaned against the peeling shiplap. The porch contained two chairs and a dead washing machine.

The wooden steps creaked underfoot as Ned stepped into the shade. He opened the warped screen and knocked loudly on the front door. He squinted through the dirty windows. The interior was surprisingly neat. The living room contained an overstuffed sofa, a chair, an upright piano, coffee, and end tables. Each of the tables wore a white doily.

He hammered the door again with his fist, but by that time, Ned was sure nobody was home. He didn't expect Bill Adkins to be there at that time of the day, but he figured he'd give him a try anyway. A minute later he stopped at the top of the steps to think.

"Bill ain't home. He has a job, you know."

The statement came from a tiny gray-haired woman on the porch next door. Her home was the exact opposite of Bill's rented house. The green yard, blooming plants hugging the foundation, and a variety of hanging and potted plants gave it a cool, jungle feel. "You know Bill pretty well?"

"Who're you? The Law?"

"Yes ma'am."

"Well, walk over here. I don't aim to holler across at you."

Trying not to grin, Ned took a moment to cross the yard. He paused halfway up the steps, still not invited all the way onto her porch. "I'm Constable Ned Parker."

"I can see that, now. My eyes is getting cloudy and I can't make out things from a distance like I used to. I've seen you before. I've lived here all my life."

"Yessum." Ned removed his hat and wiped his head with a soft handkerchief from his back pocket. "I'm looking for Bill Adkins. They say he rents that house."

"Sure 'nuff. Been living there for nigh onto twenty years, and he ain't struck a lick at that yard the whole time."

"I can see that. Yours looks nice, though."

She sat as straight as her age would allow. "Thank you. It don't take much more than some water and a handful of fertilizer ever now and then. I scatter my morning coffee grounds on the yard and in my flower bed, too. You ain't asked me my name."

"No, I haven't."

"Don't you want to know it for your report?"

"Well, I don't reckon I'll make a report on this visit, but I'd like to know who I'm talking to."

"You should. I'm Olivia Rose Owens. My husband was the late Walter Cooley Owens. He was the ticket master for the railroad. That's why we lived right 'chere, 'cause he could walk over to the depot each morning after breakfast. He only had one cup of coffee a day, too. You shouldn't have anything to excess."

"No ma'am. Did he know Bill?"

"Oh, no. Mr. Owens was called to glory near thirty years ago."

"You been living here by yourself all that time since? I'll vow you're a strong woman."

Her eyes twinkled. "Strong enough. Now, question me so I can get back to my sewing. I see better this time of the day, and I don't want to lose the light."

"I'm trying to find Bill Adkins."

"Answer me this. Is it about that bank robbery I read about in the paper?"

"I can't say, but it ain't about the robbery."

"Are you married?"

Startled by the sudden conversational shift, Ned was for a moment at a loss for words. "Yes, ma'am."

"Oh well. I like them blue eyes of yours. Bill works down the street at Mack's Garage. You can generally find him there during the day, but you'll play the devil catching him here. He comes home to scrub off some of the grease, and then heads north across the river nearly every night to them honky-tonks. I hear he likes the Sportsman and the Texoma Club the best." She leaned forward and lowered her voice. "Sometimes he brings one of them low-class Oklahoma hussies back with him." She wrinkled her nose in disgust. "Sometimes they're even Indian. I can tell by them cheekbones and that black hair jist a-shinin'.'"

Ned felt his face redden and wondered what she'd say if she met Miss Becky. "You don't say?"

"I do, and they don't make no bones about it in the mornings when they come-a struttin' out of the house, pretty as you please, to go back across the river."

He wondered how she knew the names of the joints across the Red River. "Mack's tarage."

"Yep. Constable, you're as good as that 'Dragnet' feller Sergeant Friday that I used to watch back before it went off the air."

"Thank you. I hear it's coming back on again next year."

She brightened as if that was the best news she'd heard in years. "Is that a fact?"

"It's what I heard, and took it for the truth."

"Well, I hope you're right. There ain't nothing on the television set anymore, except a lamp and a bunch of silliness." She expelled what she felt was a girlish giggle.

Ned replaced his hat. "Thanks for the information."

"Don't you let that man drag you down to his level. He's as sorry as the day is long."

Bill was under an International pickup in the garage bay when Ned lightly kicked the sole of his shoe. "You Bill?"

"Uh huh." Bill continued to work. "I'm kinda busy here. I got a bolt all boogered up and I need to get this sonofabitch fixed before dark."

"I need to talk to you now, and I ain't got time to wait. C'mon out so we can both get back to what needs doin'."

Bill rolled out from under the truck on a creepy crawler and squinted upward. "You the law?"

"I am."

"I ain't done nothin'."

"Didn't say you did. I have a couple of questions."

Bill sat up and rested his greasy hands on the knees of his blue work pants. "Go ahead."

Ned wasn't sure if there was more grease on his hands, or in his unwashed hair. "Do you know Tommy Lee Stark?"

"I did. Somebody killed him, I believe. If you're here about that, it wasn't me. I's with somebody then."

"You don't know when he was killed, and neither do I."

Bill's eyes drifted down to Ned's badge, and the .38 on his hip. "Well, I mean if I ain't here, I'm gen'lly with somebody."

"I've heard. Sometimes it's with somebody's wife."

"Ain't against the law."

"No, it's not. But didn't you get in a fight a while back over some other man's woman?"

Bill stood quickly, expecting Ned to back away, but the old constable stood his ground. His lack of response took some of the wind out of Bill's aggression. "That was across the river. Do you have some kind of warrant from Oklahoma?"

"I already told you, I want to ask a couple of questions. Have you been running around with Karen Ann Reidel?"

Bill's eyes were answer enough. "Why?"

"Well, she's married to Wade Reidel, ain't she?"

"What of it?"

"She was also running around with Tommy Lee, too." Ned hadn't heard any such of a thing, but he wasn't above a little white lie every now and then to jolt somebody into spilling a little information. "Y'all didn't have words over her, did you?"

Once again, Bill's eyes gave him away, and this time they got him off the hook. "I didn't know she was having anything to do with Tommy Lee. But I can promise you this, I wouldn't kill another man over a woman like that. What she has ain't that special."

Ned watched another lead fizzle out and he completely lost his spirit. "All right." He started to go, and then faced Bill again. "By the way, do you have a rifle?"

"A twenty-two."

"Not a deer rifle?"

"Nope."

Ned studied him for another moment. "If I's to get a warrant right now and go to your place, I wouldn't find a two-seventy, or a thirty-thirty, or a thirty-aught-six?"

"You'd find a twenty-two, like I said."

"All right. Now, if I's you, I'd stay away from Karen Ann. Her husband came by to see me here a while back about her and them honky-tonks, and I don't want any trouble over it."

"There won't be none." Bill absently scratched his cheek, leaving a black smear of grease. "She's done moved on to somebody else."

"Who?"

"I ain't tellin'. She may come back sniffing around again, and I don't want to make her mad."

"Even though what she has ain't special?"

"It ain't bad, neither."

Chapter Thirty-four

Cody was already parked in front of Wade's house and leaning against the El Camino when Ned pulled in behind. "What are we doing here?"

Ned jerked his head toward the house. "I didn't tell you, because it didn't make much difference until now, but Wade came by to talk to me and John…and O.C. the day they found Tommy Lee's body. Wade said Karen Ann was running around on him, and Tommy Lee was one of them at one time or another'n."

"I knew that. I see her at the Sportsman every now and then, or hear tell of her over at Pop's club."

"Joints. They're joints, and why didn't you tell me?"

"What difference does it make? There's always folks he'n and she'n across the river. That's the point of a honky-tonk to begin with, to sell beer and dancing."

Ned reddened. "That's why you need to get shut of that place."

"I don't want to talk about it right now out here in the sun. What I meant is Karen Ann's been over there with more folks than you can shake a stick at. So we're here because you figure Wade decided to kill Tommy Lee out of that whole crowd?"

"I won't say he did, and I won't say he didn't, but he wouldn't be the first man to kill a feller for fooling around with his wife."

"I can see your point, but why Tommy Lee in particular?"

Ned started for the door. "I don't know, but I intend to find out."

"Why am I here? Wade ain't no dangerous man."

"You need the practice."

Wade must have been watching through the window, because the door opened as soon as they stepped up on the porch. He spoke softly. "Y'all come on in. Good to see you Cody, Mr. Ned." He moved back to let them in. "What can I do for y'all?"

Both constables removed their hats when they stepped through the door. Ned glanced around the empty living room. The house was silent except for a clock ticking in the kitchen. "Karen Ann here?" He matched Wade's soft voice.

Wade smiled. "Yessir, she's in the bedroom."

"Can you get her out here?" Cody asked.

"Why, she's asleep, but I reckon I can wake her up."

"Hang on a minute." Ned held up his hand. "Let's talk for a little bit, then we might let you go get her."

Wade settled easily in a blue chair. "All righty. Y'all set."

Ned placed his hat upside down on the coffee table and sat on the bedspread-covered couch. "Wade, you came by the courthouse to see me not too long ago."

Wade continued to smile, but the corners slipped. "Yessir."

The room was silent for a long moment. The ticking clock filled the emptiness.

Cody rested an elbow on his knee. "You had something to tell Ned that day?"

"Well, yeah, me and Karen Ann were having some troubles, but that's all cleared up now."

"How so?"

"Well, Mr. Ned, she stays home more than she did, and when she leaves, she usually goes over to her mama's house, or spends the night with first one girlfriend and then another, you know, to talk girl talk, I suppose."

It was all Ned could do not to shake his head. "She still spends a lot of time away from home like that?"

"Oh, it ain't what you think. She's not gone on the weekends anymore. We made up. She only goes when I have to work the third shift, 'cause she don't like being home alone. See, we don't have a television set, yet, so she gets kinda lonesome with nothin' but the radio to keep her company."

Ned and Cody exchanged looks.

"How often do you work third shift?"

"Oh, couple nights a week, I reckon, more if they want me to. See that's why I do it, I work second, and when they offer third, why, I take it 'cause we're saving for a color Zenith."

Cody glanced around the living room and saw only a waist-high wooden Philco radio. He jerked a thumb toward the street. "You only have the one car?"

Wade smiled. "Right now. We're saving up for that, too."

"How does Karen Ann get around when you're at work?"

"She usually drops me off. That way she can have the car. And the good thing about that gal is that she's always waitin' in the parking lot when I get off, or if she ain't there, she has someone take her home and leaves the car with the keys. I'm working second *and* third again tonight, so she'll take me then."

"When did she settle down?" Ned asked, softly. He felt so sorry for Wade that his eyes were stinging.

"It wasn't but a day or so after I came and talked to you, Mr. Ned. I kinda figured you had something to do with it, that maybe you talked to her and made her understand."

It was so pitiful that Cody couldn't decide whether to laugh or cry. "Wade, you ever hear of Tommy Lee Stark?"

"No, why?"

The constables traded glances once again, knowing Wade was telling the truth.

"Do you get the paper?"

"No. It costs."

Ned wondered how anyone could be so innocent, so simple when it came to women and the facts of life.

"How about Bill Adkins?"

"Sure, Cody. If it weren't for Mack's Garage, I wouldn't be able to keep that car rolling. I've knowed Mack for years, and he cuts me a lot of deals. Shoot, he even gave me the set of tires out there, because he took 'em in trade, but said they didn't have enough tread to sell, so one day I went by there and he put 'em on for me and all I had to do was clean up the shop for him."

Ned stood and picked up his hat. "Why are you still up? You need to get some sleep or you won't be able to work."

Wade shrugged. "I don't want to go in and wake her up. I was just ginnin' around for a little bit, and I'll lay down on the couch there in a while. She says it sleeps pretty good. Y'all still want to talk to Karen Ann?"

Cody waited for Ned to answer. "Naw, we wanted to drop by and make sure everything was all right for you, after you came by that day and talked...." He drifted off to allow Wade to answer.

"We're good now, Mr. Ned. Thanks for listening, and for what you've done for me."

They shook hands, and left.

Outside by the cars, Cody looked back at the house. "You didn't have much to ask."

"Didn't need to. That poor feller didn't kill Tommy Lee."

"I'm not so sure. He said things quieted down, and that was right after Tommy Lee died. He might-a done it."

"Nope. You have to learn to look in a man's eyes to see the truth. I'god, I wouldn't be surprised if someday they come up with a way to tell when somebody's lying by looking at their eyes, or the way they act. I know for a fact that man wouldn't hurt a fly."

"Why didn't you drag Karen Ann's ass out of the bed and question *her*?"

"Because I got no reason to suspect she killed Tommy Lee, either, and things are good for Wade right now. It won't last for long. He oughta be happy for as long as he can, and besides, you're gonna question her the next time she rolls into your... club."

Chapter Thirty-five

Like I mentioned a ways back, Miss Becky always said some of us Parkers had what she called a Poisoned Gift, the ability to dream what was going to happen in the future. I always thought it was me, then one day Uncle Cody said that he dreamed about things that came true, too.

The problem is that the dreams aren't so clear that we know what's going to happen. Sometimes I have to see something and then it reminds me of the dream. I had nightmares about the Rock Hole for months before that night came true. The only thing that saved me and Pepper when it did was that I'd talked to Grandpa and Miss Becky about 'em.

Uncle Cody had nightmares about the Cotton Exchange until it happened, and after that night, they shut off like somebody had throwed a switch. Then he started dreaming about snowstorms and Mexico.

I couldn't get it out of my head that Miss Becky said Grandpa had The Poisoned Gift, too. He was always pretty close-mouthed about everything, especially law work. But she said when they were first married he dreamed of horses, Model A cars, and a little girl named Pickles, until it all came true. She quit talking about it after that one time. I knew better than to ask Grandpa, so all I could do was keep rolling it around in my head.

That's what Miss Becky called "borrowing trouble." There were a lot of folks in Center Springs who worried all the time about things that didn't need worrying on, but they went right

ahead, spinning these gray ideas over and over in their minds
until it about drove 'em crazy.

I tried not to do the same, but then my own dreams started
again, and it was the same one, might-near once a week. I was
sitting on the hub of a giant wagon wheel laying on the ground.
The spokes stretched out in all directions, almost disappearing
into the distance. One led up into Oklahoma and the thick
grasslands there. Another one went west, through the yucca and
prickly pear, until it disappeared in the desert full of cactus that
looked like "The High Chaparral," that new television show.

Then each one of them spokes became a road, and people I
knew and people I didn't know were walking toward me. Some
were laughing. Some were crying. Some were mad, and others
looked like they had the weight of the world on their shoulders.

I told Miss Becky one Saturday morning after breakfast. She
was sitting in her rocker beside the open window, sewing a rip
in one knee of my jeans. She stopped, her sewing forgotten in
her lap. "Do you recognize them people?"

I was laying on the cool linoleum floor with the funny papers
open in front of me. Snoopy was on his doghouse again, chasing
the Red Baron.

"No ma'am."

"What else, besides the wagon wheel and roads?"

"Stars. Stars up in the sky that I see from Mama and Daddy's
old house in Dallas. I'm standing in the yard, looking up and
see 'em bright and clear. Then they start to swirl and get into
formations, and then spaceships come across the sky and trum-
pets and angels and Mama's standing there with tears running
down her face and she's normal."

Miss Becky looked so sad then. "Your mama *is* normal now,
because she's in Heaven with your daddy. Is what you see the
Lord coming down and Gabriel blowing his horn?"

I flipped the page to see what was showing at the movies. "I
don't know. I think it might be, but then the air is full of thunder
and flashes and screams, and falling stars shoot down toward the
house, like those tracer bullets in war movies."

"That's in Revelations."

Brother Ross at the Holiness church across the pasture liked to preach about once a month out of Revelations, and it always scared me to death. Sometimes, especially after church on Wednesday nights, I'd go to bed listening to the whippoorwills outside the house and wonder if the world was going to end before I got up the next morning.

"I don't think I'm dreaming of the Bible. I'm only dreaming. I remembered, sometimes there are three black birds that show up and land on top of the house, and there are three more circling in the distance, all high up in the sky and not much more than pinpricks."

"You need to get right with the Lord about all that."

"Yessum." I figured I was as right as I was gonna get with Him, but I knew that short answers would get me out of the conversation I'd gotten myself into.

She went back to her sewing. "Well, you need to pray every night when you go to bed that you don't have any more of them dreams. I'll have them pray for you at church, too."

We let it go, though I imagine she studied on it long and hard. Later that day, Uncle James brought Pepper by and she spent the night with us.

I was lazy that next morning and stayed in bed with a good book. Grandpa was up at the store and Miss Becky was humming a sacred song to herself in the kitchen because she didn't go to church on account of she didn't like the visiting preacher. Pepper was in there with her, talking about making cookies. I hoped they'd make chocolate chip.

Miss Becky and Grandpa always hit the floor at daylight, 'cause that's what farmers do. It was second nature to wake up at daylight, even on Sunday mornings.

Covered with nothing more than a sheet, I was propped with my head against the footboard, reading a good book called *Henry Reed's Journey*. We slept with our heads at the foot of the bed, to catch whatever breezes came through the screens.

It's funny, the book covered Henry's travel from California to New Jersey, and the parts where they followed Route 66 reminded me of a trip I took with Mama and Daddy a year before she started losing her mind. While we were on that trip, Daddy stopped a couple of times to visit museums. I was fascinated by the dusty old Indian stuff in the glass cases.

The book got me to thinking I might find some artifacts like those in Center Springs. I especially remembered one dusty case full of baskets, moccasins, arrowheads, and a little baby Indian mummy. I guess that started me wanting to be an archaeologist, especially after Pepper and I found some arrowheads and spear points down on Center Springs Branch. I found a stone knife the night we ran into The Skinner.

Uncle Cody stopped us once when we were headed toward what we thought was a burial mound with shovels in hand. When we told him where we were going, he explained how we'd be digging up our kinfolk, so we gave up on that idea, but I never gave up on finding Indian stuff.

Up at the store, I overheard a couple of men talking about a new house that was going up on the far west side of Center Springs. They were hauling fill dirt for the foundation from a deep draw south of Forest Chapel, down near where the new lake would be. Back in the olden days, the draw was fed by a spring, and one of the workers said they'd found Indian burial mounds full of tools, skeletons, and artifacts.

They were finished with the foundation and didn't need any more sand. I had an idea me and Pepper could talk Mr. John Washington into taking us with him the next time he visited Miss Rachel. The draw was across the pasture behind her house and I hoped there might be a few relics left.

Artifacts and relics. I liked those words and decided right there in bed to be an archaeologist when I grew up. Someday, after I dug up all the artifacts and relics in Lamar County, I'd head out on Route 66 and dig for dinosaurs in the desert.

The screen door slammed and through the bedroom window I saw Miss Becky and Pepper walk across the yard toward the barn. Hootie followed, walking slow and sticking his nose into every clump of grass.

I'd tell Pepper my idea when they got back. I knew she'd figure out a way to get us to Miss Rachel's. The phone rang and I answered. Minutes later I dressed, grabbed the .22, and rode my bike to finish the wild dog problem for good.

Chapter Thirty-six

Miss Becky slowly eased herself down until she rested on a small stool beside Mary. Every milk cow she'd ever owned was named Mary. She set a galvanized bucket of warm water under the cow's teats and washed them one by one.

Pepper draped herself like a lazy cat across the hay barn's pipe gate. Hootie sniffed around a mound of dusty 'toe sacks. Satisfied by whatever he smelled, he turned around three times and laid down with a sigh, keeping an eye on Miss Becky.

"Girl, I expected you to be off somewhere with Top by now."

Pepper studied her grandmother's Fundamentalist bun tightly wrapped on the back of her head. She knew that when it was free from all the bobby pins and net, Miss Becky's hair reached to the old woman's waist. "He's being lazy. I 'spect that when he gets up, he'll go off killing dogs again."

The Jersey shifted restlessly while eating sweet creep feed from a metal trough. Miss Becky grunted. "I hope not. It's bad enough we didn't go to church this morning. I wish he'd be done with killin'."

Pepper frowned. "He's a drag. Hootie's all right, so I don't know why he thinks he has to kill every stray in the county."

Finished washing, Miss Becky poured the water through the litter of hay on the floor and traded for a large bucket.

The barn immediately filled with the metallic, almost musical sound of milk shooting into the bottom of the empty bucket.

"He ain't after 'em all. Just the ones that hurt Hootie. The truth is, he's probably doing most of 'em a favor. They'll starve come winter, or someone else will shoot them later on after they kill a calf. I'd have your grandpa shoot one if it came around the chicken house. I can't stand an egg-sucking dog."

"But is it right for him to go off killing like that? Y'all always said that we only kill what we eat."

The tinny sound of milk softened as the bucket filled. Soon each squirt was deeper and thick as the warm stream shot through foam. "Sometimes right and wrong can be confusing. I believe in this case, though, it ain't right, or wrong, it just is."

"That don't make no sense."

"It will one of these days."

"When Uncle Wilbert gave him that rifle, he said 'vengeance is mine.' That's from the Bible."

"It sure is. But the good Lord means that He'll settle up in his own way when the time comes."

Pepper snickered. "Uncle Cody told me the same thing, but then he said the Lord let us invent rifles, so we could settle up ourselves and He wouldn't have to bother with all the little bitty things."

"My lands. That boy. He shouldn't be making fun of the Lord's Word like that. You hear me, the Lord will take care of what we need. Sometimes he settles up for us and we don't even need to be there for it. All we need to do is pray about it."

Pepper climbed off the fence and stood behind her grandmother's shoulder, watching the pail fill as her gnarled hands stripped the milk from the cow's teat.

"Can I do that?"

"Sure. Trade places with me."

A moment later, Pepper was on the seat, her forehead against the cow's stomach. She gripped a teat in each hand and squeezed. Nothing came out. "What am I doing wrong?"

"You have to start by squeezing and stripping with your index finger, then the middle and on down to your little finger at the same time you pull." She reached out. "Like this."

Again, a thick stream shot into the foaming bucket. "Now you try."

Pepper squeezed again. "That ain't much."

"You'll get better with practice."

"How long have you been milking?"

"Oh, sixty some-odd years, I reckon."

Pepper concentrated on her job. The barn was silent for a long moment. "So, do you think what Top's doing is bad?"

"Top's doing what he has to do. He'll get done with it pretty soon. You can't stay mad forever, or it'll burn you up from the inside out. Parkers ain't like that, and neither were my folks. Good blood will win out. Besides, Parkers are tough."

Pepper stopped. "I don't think I am."

"What do you mean, Hon?"

The teenager kept her head against the cow's side. "I'm more and more afraid. I used to feel safe here, but it seems like there's always killings or people being hurt. I don't like living here anymore."

Miss Becky reached out in reassurance. The youngster stiffened, and Miss Becky realized her hand was resting on the burn scar on Pepper's shoulder.

She let go and smoothed her apron, as if to wipe off something unclean. "Hon, we all get scared from time to time, and these are hard times for us all. It'll get better."

"No it won't. People still cause problems over and over again, and then holler for help when it gets to be too much. Now it takes both Grandpa and Uncle Cody to keep the law."

The distant crack of a light rifle caused them to look up. Hootie raised his head, listened for a moment, and then rested it on his paws, uninterested.

"I wish I lived somewhere else."

"It'd be the same in town, hon."

Pepper shook her head. "I don't mean in Chisum. There's a whole world out there and all we know is cow shit and dirt roads."

Miss Becky ignored her anger. "This is where we live."

Frustrated that her grandmother wasn't interested in the world outside of northeast Texas, Pepper went back to her milking. "Someday I'm going to live in California. They have beaches there, and the weather is nice all the time." She thought of the Beach Boys and the music coming out of Los Angeles. "I was watching the news the other night and kids are running out there like ants. The guy on the radio said this year was the Summer of Love." She stopped talking, startled at how it sounded in front of Miss Becky.

"We have love in this family, and it ain't just during the summertime."

"They mean to love everyone, and to make love and not war."

"I know what they mean, child. They're talking about lust, and that ain't the same. Decent folks have families, and love them and their neighbors, but they don't go crawling under the covers with whoever's closest."

Miss Becky pondered the pasture beyond the barn, and the slope down to the gate. Fifty yards away, a wide red oak held Top's tree house. An unpainted chicken house sat an equal distance in the other direction, and straight ahead was their little farmhouse, surrounded by white sycamores and fragrant mimosa trees. In the distance, the top of the Lamar Lake dam was barely visible over the treetops to the south of their hill. She sighed, knowing that little patch of land would never be enough to hold her headstrong granddaughter.

"Hon, you need to know that these county roads nor no others will lead to golden cities. Roads only lead to the next place to live and work. That's what life is and it ain't nothin' else." She paused to study the cow's flank. "When you graduate from high school and go to college or get married, maybe you can move out to California. You could stay with Bill and Ethyl, that's grandpa's brother's daughter and her husband. They have a farm in Pixley. That tee vee show you like, 'Petticoat Junction' is about Pixley. Then you'd have the best of both worlds."

"I don't *want* to farm. That's the point of going to California, to get away from all this." Tears filled her eyes and dripped onto the hay. "I wish I could go to sleep tonight and wake up in San Francisco or Los Angeles, or maybe Hollywood. That's where the action is." Frustrated with both the conversation and milking, Pepper stood. "My wrists are tired."

"Okay, hon. You got a right smart in there. I'll finish up."

Once again solid streams shot into the bucket, raising thick foam. Pepper sat cross-legged on a bale of alfalfa beside Hootie and rubbed his ears. "I love you, Grandma."

Startled, Miss Becky stopped. "Why, I love you too, hon."

Pepper wiped away the dried tears on her cheeks and frowned at a quick series of distant shots. "But I'd love living in California, too."

Chapter Thirty-seven

I'd seen where the last of the wild dogs were using the little branch out back of the Ordway place to get to the trash barrels behind the school house. The dogs hung around there, knocking the barrels over and eating the scraps us kids threw away. They'd killed a small house dog across the road from the gym only the day before when Miss Dovey let her little Chihuahua mix out to pee.

I knew Grandpa would get my butt if he heard I was shooting up around the school or gym, so I decided to wait for them not far behind the Ordway barn. I left my bike parked beside one of the bur oak trees in the front yard, and climbed through the gate. I didn't figure Mr. Tony or Miss Samantha would care, since they'd been over to the house and were friends.

Tall summer grass dried upright in the pasture, and polk salad grew higher than my head against the prairie style barn. I'd always liked that barn with its drive-through center hall, horse stalls, and tack rooms under wide gambrel roofs. The tall, cathedral-like interior was held up with rough-cut timbers that supported the open beams. A hay loft covered the front quarter of the building.

The doors were partially open, so I avoided the tall weeds, intending to walk the length of the open hallway to the other end. Light shining through the cracks in the walls lit Mr. Tony's car he'd backed into the wide hall. There was plenty of room on each side between the car and the stalls. Dust motes filled the bright slabs of vertical beams, and the long unused barn smelled of dirt, instead of hay and manure.

I thought about going on through before I realized I could crack open one of the back doors and use the whole building as a blind. The shallow draw down the slope wasn't a hundred yards away, and I knew I could hit anything at that range.

Only a couple of minutes later, two wild dogs loped into the open. I'd seen them before and figured they were the last of the pack that hurt Hootie. A lump formed in my throat as I shouldered the rifle, clicked the safety off, and lined up on the largest of the two shaggy mutts. My finger tightened on the trigger and two shots rang out, surprising me. A second later I lowered the rifle and saw the Wilson brothers walk out of the woods.

They stood beside the bodies for a moment, then reloaded their rifles and disappeared. I clicked the safety back on, wiped my leaking eyes, and dang near had a heart attack when I turned into Mr. Tony standing only a couple of feet away.

"Oh!" I was so startled that the barrel of the .22 swung toward him.

He casually reached out and caught it with one hand. "Hello, Top."

I quickly lowered the rifle. "I'm sorry, Mr. Tony. I didn't intend to shoot you."

He nodded. "Who was that outside?"

"The Wilson boys."

"What were they shooting at?"

"Dogs, wild dogs."

"You people sure do shoot a lot."

"They finished off that pack that almost killed Hootie. Those were the last two, I believe."

He leaned past me to look through the rear doors. When he did, I noticed a bulge in the pocket of his khakis. It sure looked like a gun to me. He noticed where I was looking. "Yep, I saw someone coming in the barn and came down to check it out. I didn't know it was you."

"I left my bike beside a tree in front of the house."

"I didn't see it. I came out the back. Do people here usually wander on other people's property without permission?"

His eyes hardened, and I couldn't figure out if he was mad or not. "Nossir, but since Grandpa knows nearly everybody, I didn't think anyone would care..." I drifted off, because I knew it wasn't right the minute I decided to shoot from the barn. Most folks in Center Springs don't mind if you hunt in the fields and woods, but going into another man's barn was wrong.

Mr. Tony scratched his neck. "Well, I won't say anything to your grandpa, but it might not be smart to come around here without permission. I thought you were a burglar and you might have gotten hurt."

I couldn't meet his eyes, so I looked down at the soft, sandy floor. "I won't do it again, Mr. Tony."

"All right." He slowly scanned the wide hall between the stalls, and the open trusses overhead. "This is only the second time I've been in here."

"Uncle Cody says this was one of the fanciest barns in the county at one time. Not too many of them have built-in corn cribs and tack rooms."

"What's that?"

"This." I led him back to the front double doors and the small room to the left. The wooden floor in there was about a foot higher than the rest of the barn. It reminded me of a cage with wooden bars going sideways instead of up and down. Through the dusty horizontal slats you could see wooden boxes and barrels stacked around the edges. I opened the door.

Mr. Tony leaned in and poked at some dried up horse harnesses and bridles hanging from nails. He pointed at the outside wall. "What's that door? It looks too small for adults."

I almost laughed at the city guy. "It's there so you can reach inside without going around."

He grinned. "I guess I don't know much about your world, Top."

"You want to see something cool?"

194 Reavis Z. Wortham

"Sure."

I went inside and jumped on a small trap door set in the floor. "You know what that is?"

"No, what?"

"A tunnel that comes all the way out here from the house."

"How do you know that?"

"Me and Pepper were crawling around under there a while back and we found it."

Mr. Tony shook his head. "And why were you kids under a house?"

I decided to confide in him, because after all, we'd already told Uncle Cody. "We were looking for a way into the house through that hole in your kitchen floor. When we told Uncle Cody, he thought it was pretty funny, because he'd done the same thing with old houses when he was a kid. He told us about a trap door under the staircase that led to the tunnel that comes out right here."

"Why would anyone want a tunnel from a house to the barn?" He thought for a minute. "Oh, the weather. The farmer could get to his livestock when it was snowing or freezing."

"Nossir, moonshiners made it."

His frown told me he wasn't following. "Back during Prohibition, the Ordways started running short of money, so they built a still in here. They drove cars through, loaded them with whiskey, and drove out pretty as you please."

"An old tunnel sounds dangerous to me, after all this time."

"We peeked in with a flashlight. Whoever built it did a great job. It ain't a dirt tunnel ner-nothin'. The whole thing is lined with solid cedar planks and the supports look like bodark."

There was that frown again.

"Bodark is a tough tree that grows around here and the wood don't hardly rot. Most of the fenceposts are made out of it"

"So it's solid?"

"As a dollar."

"That's good to know. I might take a peek at it one of these days."

"Can me and Pepper go with you? I'd-a gone the first time, but she's deathly afraid of spiders, so we had to back out."

"Sure." He ruffled my hair.

Adults were always doing that, and messing up my Boy's Regular haircut. I rubbed it back into place. "I guess I need to go now. I'm sorry I bothered you. I only wanted to finish my job."

"Is your vendetta over?"

"My what?"

"Vendetta. Your blood feud with the dogs."

"Yessir. I reckon I'm done."

He studied me for a long moment. "I think you did what you needed to do. Now, why don't you go back to being a kid again?"

"I don't know if I can."

"Try. That time will be gone pretty soon, and you'll wish for childhood some day."

"I'd rather be grown up."

He sighed. "C'mon, kiddo. I'm out of cigarettes. Walk with me to the store and I'll buy you a Coke."

"I'd rather have a Dr Pepper."

He sighed again. "I'll never understand your lingo."

Chapter Thirty-eight

I finally convinced Pepper to join me on an archaeological dig late in the day on the last Saturday of the month. The weather still didn't seem like October. A couple of cool fronts pushed the heat away for a while, but it came back again. A stronger cold front was supposed to be on the way, but it wouldn't be soon enough for me.

"That sounds about like something you'd want to do," Pepper complained when I told her my idea while we were sitting in the lawn chairs under the mimosa tree. The humidity wrapped us in a great, sweaty weight.

"You're starting to remind me of Lucy."

"Huh?"

I reached over and rubbed Hootie's ears. "Lucy, from the Peanuts comic strip. You're getting more and more crabby every day."

"That's because I'm getting older. They say hormones change you."

"What's hormones?"

"When you change, you know, like growing these boobies."

My face flushed. I never liked her to talk like that, even when we were alone and the adults weren't around. "Well, you need to quit complaining so much, and I imagine Miss Becky is getting close to finding a new soap to wash your mouth out."

"I'm getting too old for that, besides, she's too busy making preserves and butter to give away."

"You ain't too big for a whuppin' across them new tight Levis of yours. And where did you get that shirt?"

She tugged at the tail. "This is called a peasant shirt. All the cool kids in the city are wearing clothes like this now."

"Well, just because you dress like one of them hippies, it don't mean you *are* one."

"They have good ideas that'll change this world for the better."

"They're nothin' but a bunch of long-hairs havin' sit-ins all day and listening to music and smoking that pot."

Pepper saw Mr. John pass on the highway at the bottom of the hill. She jumped up from her chair and ran across the yard, waving her hand. "Mr. John!"

He saw her, tapped his brakes, and pulled into our gravel drive below the house. He stopped in the yard and Pepper leaned in his open passenger window. "Mr. John, will you take us with you to Miss Rachel's?"

He raised an eyebrow and gave us a wide smile. "What for?"

"We want to meet her, and her kids."

He tilted his hat back. "Mr. Ned or Miss Becky say it was okay?"

"Sure."

I shot Pepper a look. Instead of outright lying, I tried a different tact. "We'd like to go with you. Grandpa said there may be Indian artifacts in that draw a ways behind her house. I'd like to see if I can find any."

"Artifacts?"

I wasn't sure Mr. John knew what the word meant. I'd only gotten a good grip on it in the last few days myself. "Yessir. Artifacts are stuff left over…"

He finished the thought for me. "…from a long time ago. I know what they are. They's artifacts all around this country, if you look hard enough. There's one right over there, across the road."

I was startled. "How can you see anything from here? All I can see is trees."

"Yep, and that one old tree right there that grows up about four feet and then bends to the southwest before it straightens up? That's an Indian sign."

"Bullsh…" Pepper barely caught herself, remembering who she was talking to. "What do you mean?"

"Miss Pepper, my great-granddaddy told me they'd bend small trees toward good water, like Center Springs down there, so's others could find it easy. When the trees grew, they kept that shape, and will always point toward water. They's trees like that all over this county."

I couldn't believe we lived next to an Indian signpost all that time and didn't know it. "You sure?"

"Sure as shootin'! Now, what makes you think they's artifacts behind Rachel's house?"

"We heard some men found a few while they were digging up fill dirt back there."

Mr. John grinned wide. "I kinda believe you, Mr. Top, but Miss Pepper, you want to go and be nosy. Ain't that it?"

I felt embarrassed, but Pepper whooped. "We can't put anything over on you, can we?"

Mr. John gave us a grin and raised an eyebrow. "Ummm hummm. All right, y'all get in, since Miss Becky said it was all right. I got some milk in there that don't need to get no warmer."

Even though I felt bad about Pepper lying to Mr. John, I didn't see any reason why we couldn't go, now that she'd gotten us a ride. I sent Hootie back up to the house, because he still wasn't feeling up to snuff, and he went like it was his idea. Since he got chewed up, he tended to stay close and didn't seem interested in going anywhere.

We piled in the backseat and made room between the paper sacks of groceries. Mr. John put the car in gear and drove straight up to the house. Pepper's eyes grew wide, because she knew what he intended to do.

Miss Becky heard the car and came outside to lean in Mr. John's open window. "John, did you arrest my grandkids?"

He cut a look across the car at Pepper. "I 'magine one might need it 'fore long. Pepper, go ahead on."

Knowing she was had, Pepper didn't have any choice. "Can we ride over to Miss Rachel's house with Mr. John? We ain't met her yet, and I want to go somewhere's else besides this house and ours."

The adults passed one of those looks I hate, and then they took to nodding like one of them stupid bobbing dogs that people put on their dashboards.

"All right." Miss Becky patted Mr. John's arm. "Don't let 'em wear out their welcome."

"Yessum."

A minute later, we were on the highway. "Now ain't that better, Miss Pepper, asking permission instead of sneakin' off?"

Pepper sulled up. "I guess."

Mr. John didn't take his eyes off the road. "That's right. Do things the right way and you won't get into no trouble, and you won't get others in trouble with you. Now, you don't have to answer, but think about something on the way there. Nobody knew you was gonna get in the car here with me, but both you kids need to remember that we look different, and people might think I was up to somethin' takin' y'all off. Do you see what I'm sayin'?"

Pepper didn't look at him, but she nodded.

"Times is changin', but they ain't changin' *that* fast. Colored, white, it don't matter to me, 'cause I love the both of y'all, but you don't know what folks is gonna think or say, seein' y'all with me. Now, if somebody asks, Miss Becky can set 'em straight. See?"

"I didn't think of that." Pepper's voice was small.

"Y'all ain't lived long enough to know. You'll learn."

Less than fifteen minutes later, we pulled into Miss Rachel's dirt yard. She was sitting on her porch in a cane-bottom chair, shelling peas into the apron in her lap. Two little girls about six or seven years old were playing with a toddler in the bare yard. They had a beat up old stewer and a couple of tablespoons for toys. The little girls dipped sand in the stewer, and the toddler used the handle to dump it out, laughing a deep, congested laugh each time. I'd never heard a baby with a voice so deep.

Miss Rachel dropped an empty hull into the tall pile beside her chair. She waved. "Who you got with you, John?"

"Couple of outlaws I found on the trail." We started to slide out. "Uh uh. Y'all hand me them sacks befo' you get out t'car."

I caught myself frowning at Mr. John's voice. He never sounded like that around us, but with Miss Rachel, he changed the way he talked.

"Bring them young'uns on up and lemme have a look at them little things. Boy, you po as a snake."

They sounded like Mr. John's old aunt, Miss Sweet, who was a healer. If it wasn't for her, I believe I'd have died one night from a bad asthma attack, but she mixed up a drink from leaves and roots that got me easy and opened my lungs up.

Miss Rachel's windows and doors were open to catch the breeze through the rusty, holy screens. Houses in our part of northeast Texas were built up off the ground with a crawlspace underneath, but Miss Rachel's was taller than any house I'd ever seen and I could have walked underneath by barely bending over. I bet it had never seen a paintbrush. The steps leading up to the house were raw boards on a tall stringer.

"Top, Pepper." Mr. John pointed at the kids coming around the side of the house. "Y'all meet Belle and Bubba. They're the oldest of this herd. Those two gals 'bout closest to y'all's age are Jere and Daisy. Now, let me see, the rest are Betsy, Frederick, Christian, Daisy, Josephine, Bessie, Myrlie, and Florynce." He pointed to them one by one with a thick finger. "The baby there is Bass Reeves. He's named after the first colored U.S. deputy marshal."

I knew they didn't all belong to Miss Rachel. Grandpa told Miss Becky she was also raising her sister's kids.

Miss Rachel split another hull, ran her thumb up the inside to pop the peas free, and reached for another one. "*You'll* be marshal one of these days."

Mr. John shook his head. "I don't know 'bout t'at, Rachel Lea. Don't know I'd want it if they'd give it to me. I got to likin' hangin' round this part of Lamar County."

She stood, gathering the shelled peas in her apron. "Let me get these on the stove, and I'll see what else I can find in them sacks for y'all to eat."

A voice came from inside the car. "John?"

Mr. John trotted over and picked up the microphone. "Go ahead, Cody."

"Go to channel ten."

It wasn't unusual for them to switch channels so they could talk without so many ears listening in. Grandpa and Uncle Cody did it all the time. "Hold on." Mr. John dialed the two-way. "I'm here, Cody."

"Where you at?"

Mr. John's eyes flicked toward all of us on the porch. "Rachel's."

"Good. I need you quick. There's been a wreck out here at Gate Five, and I need all the help I can get."

"Sure 'nough."

"It's some of your people, John. They're hurt bad, and more are dead than alive."

"Good thing the road is open over the dam. I can be there in fifteen minutes."

"Better make it ten. I need the help."

"I'm rollin'." Mr. John hesitated.

Miss Rachel had heard enough. "You go on. Get word to Mr. Ned that he can come pick the kids up when he's ready. They wanted to stay and play anyway. Two mo' won't make no difference in this gaggle. Besides, we need to get to know one another." She winked. "Don't we, Miss Pepper?"

Mr. John waved bye and left in a spray of gravel.

Chapter Thirty-nine

Not long after Mr. John left, me and Pepper were down in the draw a couple of hundred yards behind the house with Jere and Daisy. Bubba still had chores to finish, so that left me with the girls to poke around the crumbling banks, looking for stone war clubs or spearheads.

Some of the younger kids wanted to tag along, but Miss Rachel put a stop to that, saying there might be snakes down in the draw and one of 'em might get bit. I wasn't dumb enough to think those kids hadn't spent their lives running the hills and hollers, but she did it to give the four of us some peace.

Miss Rachel was one of those women who always knew the right thing to say or do. I could tell real quick why Mr. John had taken a liking to her, especially when she smiled. She had two deep dimples in the corners of her mouth that set off her sparkling eyes.

It was one of those days when all the excitement about looking for artifacts dissolved the minute we got down in that miserable gully. Grandpa said this spell of weather reminded him of the drought that started back in 1947 and lasted for about six years. It usually cooled by October, but not this year. All the old men up at the store kept looking at the sky and wishing for the first norther to arrive.

In my mind, it'd be easy to walk down there a little ways and pick up arrowheads like ripe persimmons. But the sun beat down on us like it was August. Dying vines and brambles covered everything else around us. The humidity and the whole vastness of the area took the wind out of my sails and I knew we wouldn't find a thing.

My attitude put Pepper into a mood, too. "Well, Mr. Archiol…archol, dammit, how do you say it?"

"Archaeologist."

"All right, Mr. Butthole Archie-ologist. You got us here. Now what?"

I sighed and looked up at the high banks around us. A small tree had fallen, taking a good chunk of land with it. I kicked at a crumbling clod. A startled lizard shot away.

Daisy looked down at her bare feet in the sand. She was a little on the heavy side, while Jere was all elbows and knees. "This air's so thick I cain't breathe. Let's go back to the house so I can worsh my hair."

Jere looked shocked. "You cain't worsh your hair this week."

"I don't know why not."

"'Cause you got your friend. You know Rachel says we don't worsh our hair then."

It didn't make any sense to me that they couldn't wash their hair because we were visiting "It don't matter none to me."

The girls shot me a look from under their frowns. "We ain't talking about you, little boy."

For a second, I saw sympathy on Pepper's face, but then she giggled. "They aren't talking about us, dummy. It's Daisy's time. Women don't wash their hair then. I'll be in the same fix pretty soon."

I scratched my sweating scalp. "Y'all are talking in circles around me."

They giggled and Jere chewed a thumbnail. "She's bleedin'."

I still didn't get it.

Pepper finally came to the rescue, probably to show that she knew for sure what they were talking about. "Her 'friend' is that time of the month."

Blank look.

204 Reavis Z. Wortham

"Period."

Another blank look.

Pepper sighed. "You know that box in the bathroom cabinet that says Kotex? Miss Becky keeps it there for women who visit."

Then I got it, and my face felt as red as if I had a bad sunburn. I wandered over to the shade spilling over the steep bank and squatted down to poke at the dirt so they couldn't see me. I was so embarrassed and listless that I wanted to curl up and go to sleep.

They giggled for a few minutes and argued over washing their hair. Finally tiring of the conversation, they joined me.

"What are we gonna do now?" Pepper waved her hands at the steep banks around us.

"Keep looking." I dug at the bank with my hand. Sand trickled onto my shoes. "Real archaeologists keep digging in the dirt until they find something."

Pepper picked up a stick and whacked the downed tree trunk. "Well, shit fire and save the matches. I knew you were gonna say that. Screw this. Let's go back to the house. At least it's cooler on the porch."

Daisy and Jere snickered. Jere twisted back and forth. "Shoot, gal. You cuss like Uncle Carter."

Pepper brightened. "Y'all ain't heard nothin' yet."

"She's right." I examined some exposed tree roots, hoping for an arrowhead. "She gets her mouth washed out about once a month these days."

The girls hid behind their hands. "You don't say!" They squealed and went off into gales of laughter.

"Daisy cusses sometimes."

"Don't do it."

"Do too." Jere looked around, as if an adult might show up. She spoke from behind her hand. "This mornin' she said...ball."

They shrieked, but it didn't make sense to me. "What does that mean?"

Daisy wrinkled her brow. "You don't know?"

"No."

Pepper was silent.

"Don't y'all ever listen to the radio?"

I realized pretty quick that Jere and Daisy liked to talk back and forth. It made me dizzy trying to keep up with who I was supposed to answer. "Of course I do."

"Y'all hear Little Richard?"

I remembered seeing him on television one night, in his loose-fitting suit. "That the guy who plays piano and wears makeup and screams?"

Jere jumped, clapped her hands. "That Miss Molly, sho' do like to ball, whooo!"

They shrieked again and Daisy finally took pity on me. "You don't really know, do you?"

I shook my head.

"It mean Miss Molly like to do it."

The blank expression on my face explained everything going on in my head, which was nothing.

Jere hugged herself. "You poor thang, you don't know nothin', do you? Ballin' means makin' babies."

"Does not."

"Sho' do! Miss Molly likes to have sex!"

All I remembered about the song was the "good golly Miss Molly" part, and the "woooo" part. My face flushed, and I knew I had to get out of that draw right then, because those girls were way beyond me. I started back toward the house.

"Ball," Pepper said, sparking shrieks from all three of them. "Balls!"

I climbed out of the gully while they dissolved into gales of laughter.

Chapter Forty

The phone rang beside Best's massive bed. It was noon and he hated phone calls the first thing in his morning. He swallowed a bite of scrambled eggs and slapped the fork onto the mahogany breakfast tray straddling his waist. Coffee sloshed onto the linen napkin.

He snatched the receiver from the cradle. "What!?"

For a long beat, there was silence on the other end. "Mr. Best, this is Michael, from Kansas City."

The frown evaporated and Best exposed his fangs when he realized the call was from Chisum, Texas. "Did you do it?"

He hesitated. "No, sir."

It was Best's turn to be silent. His face flushed and the smile vanished as quickly as it appeared. "You better have a damn good reason."

"I believe we do, sir." Michael continued before Best could start questioning him. "We had it all set up last night, but then we saw Anthony Agrioli. We figured you sent him for some reason, and we din't want to get in the way, so we waited until I could call you."

Best jerked upright, this time sloshing fresh-squeezed orange juice out of the glass. "Are you talking about my lieutenant, Anthony Agrioli?"

"Yes, sir. See, we know Anthony's reputation and we didn't…"

"Say it again and make it clear. You are in that hick town in Texas, right? What did you see?"

Michael hesitated. "Yes sir. We're at the Holiday Inn, and let me tell you, this ain't no place I wanna stay in again." The curtains on the plate glass window were open and he watched a couple walk back from the detached restaurant in front of the motel. The guy looked slimy enough that Michael immediately disliked him. The woman, though, was built the way he liked them, big-chested and nasty-looking in a way that defied description. It was mostly those smoky eyes and the willowy way she moved next to the guy.

With an effort, he turned his attention back to Best. "We were on the sheriff's street last night when our headlights hit Agrioli. He was walkin' down the street like he lived here, so we backed off until I could call you. We didn't want to screw up whatever he had planned. Did you send Anthony, too?"

Best studied the mess on his tray without seeing it. "Agrioli no longer works for me. He took something of mine and left. Are you sure it was him?"

"Yes, sir, I'm sure. I've worked with Anthony before."

"I cannot believe our good fortune. All right. Here is what you do. You have two jobs now. I want you to rub that sheriff out like I said, and Agrioli too. I will pay you double for the job, but do it today."

Michael glanced across the motel room at Nicky playing solitaire at the table under the brown plastic swag lamp dangling from the ceiling. Johnny Machine was cleaning his pistol. His constant compulsion kept him busy and focused. "Mr. Best. I need to make sure I'm hearing you right. You want us to take *Agrioli* out for you, too?"

"Right. He double-crossed me and the organization. He is now a wild card that needs to be eliminated. Who do you have with you?"

"I got Nicky Crespino and Johnny Machine."

"Those are both good men. You guys finish this job, and I will arrange for you to stay out here a week." He was so excited, his diction slipped. "How 'bout t'at?"

"We'll be happy to do it, Mr. Best. Any special instructions on how you want it done?"

"Wet. Make it wet."

"Yes, sir. I'll call you when we're finished."

"Wait a minute before you hang up. This is no reflection on your abilities, but I know Agrioli. I am sending you some help. Ray Marco is in Dallas. I will have him call you and get directions to where you are staying. He will bring some other guys, and you will coordinate with them. Got it?"

"Yes, sir, Mr. Best."

"Good. Give me the direct number to your room and then call me when it is finished." He jotted down the number and thumbed the disconnect button without saying good-bye, keeping the receiver to his ear. "Get me Dallas."

He didn't need to say anything else. The line went directly to his personal operator, and she knew who he wanted in Big D. The guys in Dallas were strictly small time, and that's why he'd opted for the boys in Kansas City at first. But now things were changing, and he needed backup *and* more firepower.

The phone rang in an office high in the Southland Life building. "Lone Star Moving. We'll take you from anywhere in Texas with a rate you won't believe."

"Who is this?"

"Ray Marco. Who's this?"

"Malachi Best."

A sharp intake of breath. "Oh, sorry, Mr. Best. I didn't recognize your voice."

"That is fine, Ray. I need you for a quick job."

"Sure, Mr. Best. I can be there tonight."

"No, not here. You ever hear of a hick town there called Chisum?"

"Sure. It ain't but a couple of hours northeast."

"Good. I have some men at the Holiday Inn there. Do you know Michael Braccaro?"

"By reputation. He's a good man."

"Yes he is, but he has an assignment that might require some help. Call him at the Holiday Inn in Chisum and get the details." He read the number written on the damp linen napkin. "Take your best men with you, but remember, Michael is my lieutenant. You do what he says. Once you are finished, I will fly you and the guys out here for a week, on my tab, and you will be paid your usual rate."

"That's fine, Mr. Best. Thank you. We'll get right on it."

"Good, and take plenty of artillery. I want this to make an impact. I want you to take an army to do this job. Do you understand?"

"Yes, sir."

"You are a good man, Ray."

Again, Best ended the call by pushing the disconnect button. His operator came on. "Yes, Mr. Best."

His eggs were cold. "Another breakfast. Right now."

Then he hung up and beamed. It was going to be a good day.

Chapter Forty-one

Mr. John's car still wasn't in the yard when I came back to the house. I already felt at home, so I wove through the clutter on the back porch and peeked through the rusty screen door to see Miss Rachel standing over her worn out table, peeling potatoes.

A colored man was singing on a plastic Titan radio about when a man loves a woman, and I found my head moving with the music. I thought she was talking to someone, and then I realized she was talking to the radio.

When he sang "a man can't keep nothin' else on his mind when he loves a woman," Miss Rachel bobbed her head. "Tha's right."

Every time he finished a line, she said something else. "Tell me honey!"

Another line.

She talked to the radio. "Yes, he can."

She saw me and clicked the radio off. "Top, you get in here and set down at this table. What'd you do with them gals?"

"They're still out there...being girls."

"Them two're 'bout as *sorry* as they come, all right." She gave me another one of them dimpled smiles that made me feel so good. "I swear I wouldn't hang around 'em no more than a minute if I didn't have to. You're smart to leave them to their devilishness. You hungry, baby?"

"Yessum." I glanced into the living room and saw three of the kids asleep on a rag pallet on the floor. "Kinda."

Behind them a bright half-finished quilt was rolled on a portable floor stand. I recognized the wedding ring pattern from the one on Miss Becky's bed and remembered her saying that only married folks slept under them. Since Miss Rachel wasn't married, I wondered who the quilt was for.

"Growin' boys is always hungry. I'm gettin' ready to start supper, but I bet you could eat a bite to hold you. How 'bout I fry you up an egg sandwich?"

I'd never thought of eating eggs after breakfast. "That'd be good."

"All right, then." She handed me a bucket that was old when Miss Becky was a baby. "I'm 'fraid you gotta work for your supper. The chicken house is out back yonder. I didn't gather the eggs this mornin', so you'll need to get 'em all fuh me."

It was my job to gather the eggs for Miss Becky, so I knew what to do. I took and carried the bucket out to a little gray shack that looked like it was about to fall down. From the smell, I knew it was the chicken house long before I got there.

It had one of them Dutch doors, and only the bottom half was open. I ducked under and peeked inside. Imagine a ladder six feet wide with only three rungs leaning against the back wall, and that was the roost. At the opposite end, directly across from the door, were twenty nesting boxes nailed to the wall. Most of the raw wooden boxes were empty, because the chickens were out scratching round the yard and pasture, but a few still had some old hens setting in there, watching me with their black eyes.

I'd have left them alone, if they were trying to hatch some chicks, but Miss Rachel said to get all the eggs. I held my breath from the stink, and went inside. The chicken shit was at least six inches deep underfoot. I thought the whole thing was going to give way under me, but it held as I crossed to the far wall. I pretty near filled up the bucket with eggs, but then had to get those from under the hens still on their nests. That slowed me down some.

My hand was under the second hen when a car door slammed. I figured it was Mr. John come back, but then it was followed by

212 Reavis Z. Wortham

another. When I glanced through the loose chicken wire on the window, I saw a woman standing beside a baby-blue Chevrolet parked in the yard at the corner of the house. I probably wouldn't have paid much attention to the car, except it had a long groove in the paint that went from the front fender on the driver side, across both doors, and dug deep into the back fender where it was bent out from the body.

A pair of legs crossed the front of the house and disappeared up the steps.

I put the warm egg in my bucket, and reached back under the hen for another when a loud shriek stopped me. The screen door banged open and Miss Rachel busted out onto the back porch. I thought she was going to run off through the yard, but she had other ideas. She grabbed a double-bit ax leaning against one of the porch posts.

The spring squealed and started to pull the screen closed again when a slimy-looking man boiled out behind her. She swung the sharp ax, but he was too close. He stepped inside the swing, grabbed the handle with his left hand, and caught her a lick with his right fist. Her head snapped back and she yelped, but she wouldn't let go of the ax handle. He jerked it twice, and then punched her in the cheek. Her knees sagged, but she grunted and threw her weight behind the ax head to drive it into him.

Instead of hitting her again, he grabbed a handful of hair and yanked her off her feet. "Don't fight me, gal!"

Miss Rachel landed hard on her back, but that feller never let go of either the handle or her hair. He dropped to one knee and slammed her hand against the porch. She finally turned loose and he threw the ax out into the yard.

He gave her head a shake. "Where's your man? We have some business."

She shrieked and used both hands to hold the fist buried in her hair. "Ain't no man lives here!"

He gave her another hard shake and spoke through gritted teeth. "Don't you *lie* to me, you black bitch! I know Washington's always sniffing around. When's he coming back?"

The little ones in the house started tuning up from the commotion. Movement caught my attention, and I saw two of the other kids standing inside the woods, stock still, like wild animals that know better than to run or else they'll be seen.

Tears ran from her eyes. "I had a husband, but he run off a while back. I ain't seen Rudolph in months."

From inside, the woman hollered. "Y'all shut up!" The kids cried louder.

The man's eyes were glassy. I've seen that when people get mad, their eyes get hot and don't look natural. He glanced around the yard, but didn't see me. I was standing too far back in the chicken house and the shade kept me hidden.

The man stood up and yanked Miss Rachel to her knees. She kept both hands on his wrist to take the pressure off her head. He put his face close to hers and spit flew. "You're *lying*! I was told he'd be here."

Miss Rachel quit fighting. "Rudolph left after he got outta jail. Said he was goin' back home to Jefferson. Said he intended to pick up where he left off with some woman he quit me for. That's all I know."

"I don't give a shit about *Rudolph*. When's *Washington* coming back?" He jerked her back and forth, and Miss Rachel's head looked like it would come off in his hand.

Her mouth opened in pain. "I don't know! He comes by to see me and bring groceries for the kids every now and then. That's all!"

A snaky-looking, big-chested woman stomped onto the back porch. She looked like what Miss Becky would call a hussy, with bleached hair and bright red lipstick. Her voice traveled as if they were standing right next to the chicken house and I could tell she was mad. "He said Washington would be here by now. I wanted to be finished with him before Agrioli showed up."

My head spun. They were looking for both Mr. John and Mr. Tony at the same time. I couldn't figure out why Mr. Tony would be at Miss Rachel's house at all. I couldn't imagine how she knew him.

The man was mad, too. "What, you don't think we can handle both of them?"

"Look, stupid, it don't matter...they aren't *here!*"

Miss Rachel cut her eyes up at the man. "I don't know no Agrilo, either."

"I's told he'd be here! Now where is he?" He gave Miss Rachel another pull. A sudden look on the hussy's face caused him to stop for a minute. "What?"

"Ralph, are you sure he said Agrioli'd be here?"

He hesitated. "Well, I *believe* he did."

The hussy threw up her hands. "Goddamn it! You either know or you don't."

"I don't remember, *Myrna*! I *think* he said he'd make sure Agrioi would be here with Washington."

Myrna used both hands to hold her head. I've seen folks do that if they're surprised or worried. "You *idiot*!" She was furious and stomped her foot. "This is just like you, to go off half-cocked without being sure of what you're doing. You don't *think*, Ralph, you're like a pinball in a machine, bouncing around and knocking into things. You hear what you want to hear, or dream it up in that empty skull of yours. What made you think Agrioli would be here?"

The man stopped yanking at Miss Rachel's head and stared off at the tree line, like he was working on a hard math problem. "I thought he might be...I don't know."

"You do this all the damn time!" She got mad and told him how the cow ate the cabbage. Ralph took it without a word, still holding Miss Rachel down and listening with his head bowed.

She slowed down and he spoke to the floor. "I remember now, he said he'd be here at five."

Like someone had thrown a switch, Myrna calmed down and studied on Miss Rachel for a minute. "Well, we're early, but what are we going to do with *her* now?"

"I ain't being paid to kill no woman, black or white. Let's tie her up and wait."

Myrna waved her hand. "Look around us. There's kids every-where. We can't sit here and twiddle our thumbs while they all run around like a bunch of chickens. Think of something else."

I wanted to cry like a little baby, watching that man handle Miss Rachel the way he did, but fear and the realization that I was no match for a grownup kept me huddled right there in that stinkin' chicken house.

Ralph was thinking, his eyes jerking first one place, then another. He yanked at Miss Rachel again. "I know for sure he's supposed to be here. Where's *Washington*?"

I swallowed down the acid rising in my throat.

Miss Rachel found some place down deep inside. She set her jaw and stared into his eyes. "I don't know what you're talking about."

He slapped her, and the sound was sharp, but instead of crying, she glared a hole through him and I knew then she'd die before she told that man anything.

"What the *hell's* going on?" Myrna worried at her hair like it was getting messed up and somebody cared. I'd seen confused old folks do the same thing. "Are we at the wrong place?"

Crying hard, little two-year-old Bass Reeves came through the door and ran to Miss Rachel. Ralph backslapped that little feller and he rolled across the back porch and lay still. Miss Rachel shrieked and punched the bad guy in the nose. Blood squirted and she twisted away and jumped to her feet, leaving him with a handful of hair.

She almost made it, but Ralph caught her by the shirt collar and yanked her hard enough that her feet left the ground. She hit on her shoulders and neck, and I thought it mighta killed her, but still laying on the floor, she swung again. That's when he commenced to beat her like a natural man.

No, he beat her like a dog.

The thing that hit me the most was how quiet they all were, him grunting each time he swung, and Miss Rachel taking it all rolled up in a ball, and that hussy woman Myrna standing there watching like it was the most common thing in the world.

I guess it finally hurt his fists too much, because he stood up and went to kicking her.

He might have kicked her to death, but he stopped when a scream cut across the yard. "Quit it! Quit it you sonofabitch!"

I knew that voice and it jolted me out of my trance. It was Pepper at the edge of the woods with Daisy and Jere.

Ralph had a wild look in his eye when he saw them. He let go of Miss Rachel and stood up. When he reached into his pocket, I knew I had to finally do something.

I realized I'd been holding my breath and let it out to draw another. "Run!" I dropped that bucket full of eggs. It bounced and fell over. I jumped to the empty window covered with chicken wire and started slapping my hands against it. "Hey! Leave them alone! Help! Mr. John, they're right here! Help!"

The wire rattled each time I hit it, and that caused the sheet iron roof to rattle too. The whole building sounded like it was about to fall down around my ears, but I couldn't stop screaming and yelling.

Bubba, the oldest boy came around the house and saw what was happening. He took off running toward the porch and saw the ax laying in the yard. He picked it up and charged at them, holding it over his shoulder like a batter getting ready to swing.

Ralph pulled a pistol out of his pocket with a shaking hand and pointed it at Bubba.

All of us suddenly appearing must have startled those two pretty bad. "Come on!" The woman yanked at his arm and jumped off the porch. "You can't kill 'em all! Let's get out of here!" A rock zinged through the air and thumped off his leg.

Those two headed for their car like the ol' Devil hisself was after them. A rock slapped the side of the house with a bang, and then another hit the man's back. Belle had joined Pepper, Daisy, and Jere, who were pelting them pretty good as they ran around the corner. Bubba stayed after them with the ax held ready for a swing.

I raced out of the chicken house and pointed, waving toward the woods like there was somebody behind me. "Here! Mr. John, they're over here and getting away! Shoot 'em!"

The car started up and shot out of the yard, tires spinning in the dirt. A cloud of dust filled the air as they sped off down the road.

It didn't take but a minute for Pepper and the girls to run up on the porch, holding onto Miss Rachel who laid there with little Bass in her arms. The slap had knocked the wind out him, but he had it back and was tellin' it with long, loud shrieks. Everyone else was squalling and sniffling, and I wanted to join them, but I couldn't. I had to stay tough with Bubba until Mr. John showed up, or Mr. Tony.

But I still couldn't figure out why Mr. Tony would be here in the first place.

Chapter Forty-two

Despite the heat and humidity, Ned and Miss Becky were enjoying the late evening under the fragrant blooms covering the umbrella-shaped mimosa tree. He watched her hands as she shelled peas into a stewer balanced in her lap. He'd never say it aloud, but Ned always loved her hands. When he'd slipped a simple gold ring on her finger, they were smooth and well-shaped. Now, decades of farm and housework had taken their toll, but he still felt a deep sense of comfort when she touched him.

Hootie lay in the grass between their shellback lawn chairs. He raised his head at thunder rumbling from ugly thunderheads rising in the distance.

Ned watched them over his shoulder. "There it is, finally. At first I thought it was heat lightning, but now I think it might storm and break this humidity."

Miss Becky watched the clouds for a moment, then went back to shelling. "From the looks of it, it's liable to go around us."

"I wish it wouldn't."

"I can smell it." She drew a deep breath. "If you can smell it coming, it won't rain."

"That's what they say, but we need the rain. I'd be satisfied if it dries the air out. Mama, what's the word for rain?"

She took a moment to flip through her mental Choctaw dictionary. "Omba. That means, 'to rain,' I believe."

"Well, I want it *omba*. That don't sound right."

"It's hard to mix both languages, but you're doing real good."

"I don't know what it matters."

"Y'all used it down in Mexico."

"We did."

An unfamiliar truck crossed the creek bridge. Moments later it passed below their hill. The driver tooted his horn and waved. Ned waved back. "Did Dan Bills get a new truck?"

Miss Becky looked up and stopped shelling for a moment in good-natured exasperation. "My stars. Now how would I know that?"

"Well, that looked like Dan driving, but it wasn't his truck."

"I heard tell up at the church that he came into some money."

Ned's eyes twinkled and he rocked backwards in the springy chair. "That sounds like gossip."

"Well, it was after preaching the other night." Miss Becky went back to her purple hulls. "Ike Reader was talking to Jeff Wright about it."

"Don't Jeff go to the Baptist church?"

"He does, but he was in the Assembly churchyard with Ike when I saw him loafing with the men waitin' on their wives."

"Ike shoulda been inside, too."

"Well, he's backslid, but the good Lord'll bring him back."

A flock of dove winged by overhead, the wind sizzling through their feathers. Ned watched them disappear toward the south and finally realized that the house behind them was quiet. "Where's Top?"

"John took him and Pepper to Rachel's. They oughta be back in a little bit." She paused for a moment, wondering whether to tell Ned about Pepper's fib to John. She heard the conversation through the open window on the porch, where she was sewing.

She thought of saying something then, but didn't want to get John involved in family business. She figured to make them pay by taking the kids to next week's revival. Seven nights of preaching would get her point across and wouldn't hurt them none.

Ned watched a hawk land on a limb holding up Top's tree

house. "Those kids running around with John could cause some troubles down the road."

"I studied on that, but I don't see much difference in them over at Rachel's, or across the creek like they wanted to do last week to eat with that Comanche family that moved into the Simmons' place."

Ned rubbed his bald head and slapped at a mosquito. "Indians is different than colored."

"We're all the same past the skin. I believe my flesh looks like John's, when it's cut, and yours too. It didn't bother us when we got married."

He studied Miss Becky and realized the little Choctaw woman was right. A lot of people raised their eyebrows when they traded vows back in 1920. The Indian wars were only forty years past. In fact, the last Indian attack came four years *after* they married, and a lot Texans had long memories.

Ned enjoyed the lightning bugs flickering over the yard in the gathering dusk. "What are you doing with all them pears in there on the table?"

"The Wilson boys brought 'em by this morning. They picked 'em somewhere down in the bottoms, and gave me five bushels for a couple of quarts of preserves when they're made."

"They probably stole from somebody's yard tree is what happened."

"It ain't my place to say. The Lord will take his vengeance if they're stole, but it looks to me like we're getting a reward for His goodness. I called Norma Faye and Samantha, they're fixin' to come over in a little bit and I'm gonna show 'em how to can."

"Then I'll probably need to be somewhere else." In the distance, a car hissed on the highway. It was moving fast, and the still air transmitted the sound as if it were only yards away.

Miss Becky stopped shelling and waited. Ned quit rocking on the springy metal chair and leaned forward. Despite their elevation, the sycamore in the corner of the yard and thick underbrush lining the barbed wire fence prevented him from seeing the oncoming car.

Ned's sixth sense kicked in. Something was up, because the car didn't slow as it neared the bend around their hill. The old lawman planted his feet, almost as if he expected to launch himself upright.

A battered two-door Ford Crestline hove into view, bouncing on worn out springs. Running wide open, the car passed the corral near Cody's house, and the driver almost immediately hit the brakes. For once, Ned stood without a grunt. It was obvious the driver was going to turn into their drive, and he hoped he'd slow enough to make it.

Almost out of control, the faded, once-blue car slid across the oncoming lane toward Ned's gravel drive.

Miss Becky stood upright, the pan full of shelled peas in her lap spilling unnoticed into the grass. "Dear God, they're not going to make it!"

Tires squalled until they left the concrete, and then scattered red gravel in a wide spray before skating across the slick grass. It almost struck the sycamore, but bounced to a stop only thirty feet from the startled constable. The smell of burned rubber filled the air as dust rolled across the lawn.

Recognizing the driver, Ned started for the car, his face flushed. "Tommy, what the *hell* are you doing!?"

Tommy Davis launched himself from behind the wheel and raced around the front, frantic after the hell on wheels drive from their farm in Razor, ten miles west. His shirt was wet and bloody. "We need to get to a doctor now!"

Ned trotted toward him when he realized the man was neither drunk nor crazy. "What fer? How bad you hurt?"

"It ain't neither of us!" Tommy's round wife, Dot, struggled out of the car with their youngest child in her arms. The little one was limp and white as a sheet. The colorful patchwork cotton blanket wrapped around the little girl was saturated with blood.

"She drank lye!"

"How long ago!?" Miss Becky shouted.

"A while. She'd thowed up and was laying in the barn when I found her and then and I couldn't find Tommy and I made her thow up some…" Dot flipped the little girl face down in her arms and started to stick her finger down the child's throat.

"Don't!" Miss Becky hurried toward them, holding out her hands "It'll burn the little thing even more."

The look on Dot's face would stay with Miss Becky until the day she went to Glory. "Becky, she's bleedin' through her *stomach*!"

Ned ran on painful knees toward his sedan parked by the house. "I'm comin' around! We ain't got time to wait for no ambulance!"

Miss Becky stopped beside Dot, struggling hard not to take the little girl. She put her hand on the child's cold forehead. "Hurry Ned! Her eyes is rolled back!"

Seeing Ned's running speed, Tommy couldn't stand it. He snatched the limp six-year-old from Dot and raced up the drive.

Ned was already behind the wheel. The car roared to life and he slammed it into reverse, then shoved it into first gear and met Tommy and Dot on the drive. He pulled up hard on the gravel. Tommy yanked the back door open. Dot fell inside, and he piled in after her.

Ned pointed his finger at Miss Becky. "We're gone to Chisum!" He twisted the wheel and grabbed up the handset from the dash. "Martha! This Ned! Holler at St. Joseph's hospital and have them ready for me to bring in a baby that's drank lye."

Harriet Stover answered the call. Martha was already home for the night. "I'll do it, Ned." He didn't pay any attention to the different voice. The engine roared when he stomped the pedal to the floor and shot away toward Chisum.

Chapter Forty-three

Cody and John Washington had their own hands full in the twilight not far from the Texas/Oklahoma border. A 1960 Dodge pickup lay on its side across the northbound lane. More than a dozen field hands thrown from the open bed lay scattered across the two lane highway and grassy ditch. Some moved weakly, but most lay still, claimed by death.

Over a dozen cars idled in the lane behind Cody's El Camino, their headlights illuminating the scene in a harsh glare. The first to arrive rendered what little assistance they could in the failing light and moved among the moaning victims, draping quilts, tarps, and even 'toe sacks over the dead. More vehicles clotted behind the accident.

A highway patrol car stopped the remaining traffic with its flashing lights, joining the wreck to completely jam the highway. Slowed by the backup out of Oklahoma, John's Ford took to the shallow ditch when he couldn't find a way around the jam, lights and siren wailing his advance.

When he reached the scene, John pulled back onto the pavement. He joined Cody as he knelt beside a still body. "What happened?"

Cody patted a young man on the shoulder. "They'll be here in a minute, Wade. Hang on." Blood reached to the rolled-up cuffs at his elbows. He stood and wiped his hands with a piece of torn shirt. "Wade was driving. He told me they were coming home from the field when a blue four-door sedan came shooting off that dirt road there." He pointed back at a strip of dirt angling between pastures to intersect with the southbound lane. "They had it wide open and didn't even slow down. Wade swerved to miss him, but they clipped him anyway. With all the weight in the back, he lost control and flipped over. It threw Wade out and rolled on top of some of 'em."

John wanted to help, but there were plenty of people tending the injured. "What kind of sedan?"

"Said it was a blue Chev-a-lay. They were heading toward Chisum when they saw this patrol car here coming at 'em, so they took *that* dirt road over yonder. That officer there only found out what happened when someone told him."

"What model was it?"

"Fifty two or three."

"He radio it in?"

"Yep, but he couldn't chase 'em by then, and neither could anybody else with all this in the way." Cody looked past John at two Chisum ambulances bypassing the back-up and rushing toward them in the empty southbound lanes. "I'm afraid they got clean away, for the time being."

The ambulances squalled to a halt as close to the victims as possible. Four men bolted from the vehicles and paused at the carnage. Two of the attendants rushed to the rear of the vehicle to get stretchers and supplies. One of the drivers threw up his hands. "They're *niggers*."

John's intention was clear when he squared his thick shoulders.

Cody stepped between them. "John." He held out his hand to stop the furious deputy and turned to the driver. "I don't know who you are, buddy, but these folks are hurt and dying. We don't have time to wait for help from Travers and Williams funeral home. If you don't start getting the worst of these people on stretchers, I'm gonna commandeer those ambulances and take them ourselves, and by *God*, John here'll start the ball rolling."

Cody recognized the driver of the second ambulance. The man took one look at the steaming deputy's hooded eyes and made the right decision. "Partridge, he means it, and we need to help these folks. Cody, who's hurt the worst?"

"Thanks, Gerald." He pointed. "That man right there." The former World War II medic immediately knelt to find a gaping wound in the victim's head beneath a crude bandage. "You ain't a-kiddin'."

The others reluctantly moved past the big deputy who stood like a tree amidst the chaos. None met his flashing eyes.

A young highway patrol officer also bypassed the stack-up and coasted to a stop beside cars parked every which way. He joined them and averted his eyes from the sight of bulging brains. "What'n hell happened here?"

John's quiet voice brought the skinny deputy up to speed. Their soft conversation was almost surreal amidst the carnage. Cody saw worse in Vietnam, but not by much. The humid air reminded him of that green country and felt wet enough to wring out gallons of water. He wiped sweat from his eyebrows as John gave him a description of the car.

The deputy's Adam's apple bobbed when he swallowed. "I'll put out an APB and add that the driver's side of the Chevrolet'll have some damage."

"It's worth a try." Cody's gaze wandered over the scene as cars and pickup trucks continued to mass around the accident scene.

The traffic situation deteriorated as the backup stretched in both directions. The northbound shoulder jammed as cars attempted to weave around the wreckage and into the grassy ditch bordered by a barbed wire fence. They soon found themselves blocked by the deep incline and were unable to back up in the soft sand.

In frustration, Cody waved his arms for them to stop. The skinny young officer waded into the grass and chiggers to straighten the traffic snarl.

A speeding sedan bouncing along the shoulder beside the blocked southbound lane caught Cody's attention. He squinted and recognized Ned's new Plymouth. "Goddlemighty. He ought not be driving so fast this late in the game. We already have this in hand."

John stepped on the painted yellow line, peering over the cars and trucks. "What's he doing?"

"Looks like trouble." Cody moved around Wade and his patient. "He needs to slow down."

At that moment, the red spotlight mounted on the Ned's doorpost came to life. The red light quickly nodded up and down as Ned worked the handle on the inside of the door. His headlights switched from low to high, as he stomped the dimmer switch in the floor.

"Goddlemighty! He ain't coming here to help." Cody raced to the shoulder. "John, help me!"

The big deputy chased Cody, frantically waving his flashlight. The only way around the stalled traffic on that side was through the shallow ditch. "Oh, Lordy, I hope there ain't nothing hid in that grass!"

Weeds slapped the undercarriage as Ned's tires threw up a rooster-tail of debris. He swung wide around the cars, coming dangerously close to the thick line of trees bordering the highway.

"Goddlemighty!" Cody stopped in shock as Ned's car roared past. In the blink of an eye, Cody registered Ned's grim expression and the white-faced couple in the backseat with a bundle lying across their laps. "Somebody's laying across them folks in the backseat!" He turned toward his car and the radio.

Ned cut back onto the highway, fishtailed on the concrete as he regained control, and once again punched the accelerator.

"Cody, was it any of us?" John was out of position to see into the car.

The young constable paused, instantly understanding the meaning. "I couldn't tell." He jogged to the El Camino and reached through the open window as a stretcher passed on the way to the ambulance. "Hang on, Wade. You'll be at the hospital before you know it." He keyed the mike. "Harriet."

"Go ahead, Cody."

"Ned just flew past us on the way to town and I didn't want to radio him as fast as he's driving. You have any idea who's in the car with him?"

"Yep. Some kid there in Center Springs drank lye and he's taking her to the hospital."

Cody relaxed a little. He knew Top and Pepper were too old to mistake lye for something good to drink.

"Cody, I was fixin to call you anyway. Judge O.C. wants to talk with you right now. Hold on." They waited for the Judge.

"Cody."

"Yessir."

"Y'all need to get home as quick as you can."

Fear gripped both men at the same time. "Can you say why?"

"I can, but I won't. Just that I got a phone call and Becky wants you there pretty quick. Everyone's all right, but go as soon as you can."

Cody surveyed the carnage behind them. "It might be a while."

"Don't take too long."

"We need to git." Cody wiped sweat from his forehead and keyed the microphone. "All right, Judge. Harriet, we need a lot more cars and ambulances out here in front of the army camp. This is a mess."

Ominous thunderheads towered over Oklahoma, reaching fifty thousand feet in the air.

Chapter Forty-four

In the gathering dusk, three frustrated hit men sweltered while cicadas sang from the nearby trees.

Michael stuck his elbow out the car window and angled his head to find the source of the backup. He slapped the steering wheel and inched through the congestion. "I hate this hick state. This is October. It's supposed to be cool and I'm sweating like a pig."

In the backseat, Nicky met his eyes in the rearview mirror. "Whatsamatta? We got traffic like this in Kansas City."

"But it ain't out in the sticks. We get stuck in *city* traffic, sometimes we can go around it on the side streets. Here, you gotta follow this one stinkin' road through the boonies, and look where it led us." Michael glanced out the window at a pasture. "Cows. Cows and trees."

"So turn around."

A steady stream of cars finally rolled in their direction. The southbound backup disappeared into the distance toward Oklahoma. There were no gaps as far as Michael could see. "And go where? The map shows we're only ten miles away."

Johnny Machine checked over his shoulder. "Back up and let's try anyway."

Headlights fill the interior. Michael tilted the rearview mirror to get the light out of his eyes. "There's a car right on our bumper."

"I'll get out and tell them to move." The Machine yanked

the handle on the front passenger door. "Guy oughta have more sense than to bright ya like that."

"Careful, in this hick state. All these people are armed." Nicky chuckled. "For all you know, it could be Agrioli back there and he'll shoot you in the face when you open the door."

"Don't matter." Michael twirled a finger in the air. "By the time we go halfway around the world to find that house, we'll be lost. This is the best way, and it'll clear up soon. Relax."

"So howdoya' know where we're goin'?"

Michael shrugged. "Simple. I used the phone book and called every number in the county that belonged to a constable. There's a list of 'em in the Government Section. They all know who's coming in and out of their towns. When I called the one for Center Springs, some kid answered, and when I asked if he knew Tony Agrioli, the kid said sure, that he'd moved into a house behind the country store."

"Where were *we?*"

"You were all asleep. Your snoring was so loud, I had to use the pay phone hanging outside the motel office. I went through an ass-load of dimes before I got the right place."

Nicky chuckled. "Wouldn't-a been able to do that in Kansas City. Nobody woulda talked to ya."

Michael shook a cigarette from the pack in his shirt pocket. "That's for sure. Looks like everybody trusts everybody out here."

"It makes our job easier." Seeing Michael's cigarettes, Nicky unconsciously shook out one of this own.

The Machine pushed in the dashboard lighter until it clicked. "So, these other guys outta Dallas. What's the deal with them?"

"I talked to them a long time on the phone, and they're all right. We do the job, they're insurance. We go in, badda boom, badda bing, and we're outta here and on the way for a week in Vegas."

The lighter popped out and the Machine lit his, passed it to Michael, and offered it over the backseat. Nicky shook his head. "Uh uh. Three on a match. That's bad luck."

The Machine looked disgusted. "This is a lighter, dummy. Don't be superstitious. Light the damn thing."

Nicky flicked his Zippo open. "It don't hurt to be careful. There ain't no need to take chances."

The Machine snickered. "So these other guys. You think they're stuck in this traffic jam with us?"

Michael killed the engine. "How do I know? I don't know 'em from Adam. They'll be there when we need 'em. Relax."

Smoke drifted to the rag ceiling overhead, crawled to the open windows, and escaped.

They waited.

Chapter Forty-five

Tony finally figured out what to do with Griffin.

He was going to shoot him.

It should have been simple. He dialed the phone. An energetic female voice answered. "Sheriff's office."

"I need to speak to Sheriff Griffin."

"He's busy. Can I take a message?"

"No. I need to speak to him. Tell him it's important."

"Just a minute." She came back on the line a minute later. "Who's calling?"

"A business associate from Vegas."

"Hold please." A click told him she was transferring the call. It took so long for Griffin to answer, that Tony almost hung up and called back.

"Sheriff Griffin here. Who is this?"

"Agrioli."

He could hear the caution in the man's voice. "What do you want?"

"I've thought about your offer. I'll take you up on it. I'll take care of the Parkers and Washington, but you have to pay me in cash. I need it tonight."

"I thought we'd already agreed on that."

Tony frowned at the comment. "Huh?"

"Never mind. Fine."

Tony sensed relief in the answer. "I'll meet you west of Center Springs. I saw a dirt road beside a barn that's about to fall down.

There are pine trees around it, the only ones I've seen around here. Drive on past, and I'll be waiting under a copse of trees around the bend."

"What's a copse?"

Frustrated, Agrioli rubbed his throbbing forehead. "A grove."

"You mean a bunch of trees. Okay, I know that barn. It's past Reid's Store."

"Yeah. I'll be waiting. Half an hour, and don't forget the money. I get paid up front, and then I disappear. I suggest you do the same."

"See you there."

Tony hung up and settled back in the overstuffed chair in Griffin's living room. Sweltering in the stifling room, Tony placed his .22 on the round end table beside him. When Griffin came home to get the money, one shot would solve all his problems.

The plan fell apart when Tony was still waiting as sundown approached. He wondered if Griffin had money stashed somewhere else and went directly to the meeting place. Frustrated that he hadn't considered such a possibility, he picked up the .22, slipped out the back door, and walked the two blocks to his car parked on the street. Minutes later, he steered toward Center Springs and home. He could always shoot Griffin first thing in the morning while the neighbors were at church, or having a quiet Sunday breakfast.

Halfway to Center Springs, he was caught in a massive traffic jam. What should have been peaceful twilight on northbound Highway 271was destroyed by a catastrophic wreck. Grinding his teeth in frustration, and not paying much attention, Tony crept almost too close to the car ahead.

There was almost no room between their bumpers when he jerked to a stop. His headlights illuminated three men in the sedan who appeared agitated at the brightness. Tony slapped the knob with his palm and they winked out. The brake lights in front blinked, and then went dark as the driver killed the engine a few moments later.

The smell of cigarette smoke wafted back from the car's open windows. A toonie sounded like a good idea. Tony snapped his Zippo alight and lit his own, enjoying both smells of lighter fluid and smoke. He killed his engine and leaned back to enjoy the smoke.

He hoped Sam had something good for…supper. He smiled. He was getting the hang of this country lingo. Despite his frustration at being stuck on the highway, he was pleasantly surprised to find that his forehead wasn't throbbing.

"That's what life in the country does for you," he said aloud, barely paying attention to the thunderheads crowding the dark horizon.

Chapter Forty-six

In the fading light, people up and down the traffic jam finally gave up and killed their engines. Little clusters of men left their cars and gathered to exchange information or speculation. All four doors of a late model Plymouth opened to discharge seven men in suits who stretched their legs.

"We shoulda took two cars."

"It's a short trip."

"It *was* a short trip."

They stood off to the side, away from the activity surrounding the accident.

"That backseat is crowded. Somebody change with me."

"Shut up."

"Turn off the headlights."

One of the men waved behind them. "Half of the cars stretching over this damn hill have their lights on."

"I wish that guy would kill his lights. We're lit up out here."

The headlights of the sedan behind them winked out. Seconds later, the car behind that one also went dark. But before it did, the man complaining of being cramped waved an arm. "Those guys have plenty of room. I oughta go take that car away from 'em, or make 'em follow you. Then I can ride with *them*."

"You idiot. What do you think, they'll just let you in? These country people are tough."

"There's only three of them in there."

"Well, take it one more step. Go on back to the next car and get *it*. I saw only see one guy in there when he lit his cigarette. That'll be easy for you, tough guy."

Ray Marco finally had enough. "You guys shut up. We have a job to do, and then we're back to Dallas. It ain't much farther."

"If I live through this aggravation."

Marco thought of what Best and Michael had told him when they discussed the hit. "Just focus. This guy we're after is tough."

"How tough can he be against seven of us?"

Marco wondered about that himself. After all, he was only one guy.

Chapter Forty-seven

Miss Rachel had control of herself faster than I would have if someone had beaten *me*. She was sitting on the porch step, holding her side. Her lips were puffy, one eye was almost swelled shut, and a cut over the other eyebrow still seeped blood.

Pepper had the baby in her lap. He'd finally quit crying and didn't seem to be hurt none. The other kids were huddled up like a bunch of puppies. We were all shaking like them little Mexican Chihuahua dogs.

Miss Rachel wiped her eyes with a wet rag and put it on the back of her neck. "The rest of y'all all right?" She rubbed on the kids nearest her and settled back when she was satisfied no one else was hurt. "Y'all did good, scaring them off, but you mighta got hurt."

"Not if I'da got here in time with this." Bubba was keeping watch with the double-bit ax over his shoulder away at the corner of the house. "Who were them people, Mama?"

Miss Rachel shook her head. "I don't know, but we need to get gone for now. I sure wish there was a telephone closer than five miles away. Bubba, you run down the road to Mr. Thurman's house and ask if he'll come pick us up."

Daisy looked startled. "Where we going?"

"To Mr. Thurman's, I reckon. We'll be safe there."

Bubba shook his head. "Mama, he's old as dirt, and I doubt we'll all fit in that little ol' shack of his."

"We ain't stayin' there. He's the only one around here with a truck."

Pepper unconsciously bounced the little Bass in her lap. He was over his scare and drooled down his bare chest while he chewed on a spoon. "We can go to my house."

I spoke up. "Uncle James went fishing up on Muddy Boggy with Mr. Scott, remember. He won't be back until tomorrow. I didn't think Aunt Ida Belle would be much help if more bad folks came around."

"Oh, yeah."

"I don't know what this is all about, but we need to go to Grandpa's house." To me, that little farmhouse was the safest place in the world. "He'll know what to do."

Bubba stood still as a statue, watching the road. Jere dug in the sand with her toes. "Won't Mr. John be back in a minute?"

Miss Rachel shook her head. "We don't never know when to expect him. Top's right, we can get word to him from Mr. Ned's house."

"Mama, Mr. Ned's white."

Her eyes looked sad. "He is, Jere, but John speaks well of him and Miss Becky both. At least we can wait outside in the yard until John shows up."

Pepper looked horrified. "Y'all don't have to wait outside. Coloreds been in Miss Becky's house before." Her jaw snapped shut with a pop when she realized how that sounded.

Miss Rachel reached out a hand and patted Pepper's knee. "I know what you mean, hon. Bubba, hand me that ax and run on down to Mr. Thurman's like I said."

"I might need to stay here with it."

"Give it here and do what I done tol' you."

He leaned the handle against Miss Rachel's thigh and took off at a jog down the road.

I couldn't stand it any longer. "Miss Rachel, I'm sorry."

She frowned and squinted at me with one eye. "What for, hon?"

"I believe I broke all them eggs in my bucket when I saw that man grab you."

She started laughing, but I couldn't figure out why.

Chapter Forty-eight

The norther rolled overhead like a wave when Mr. Thurman turned his old truck into our drive. It was full dark and I was glad, because I'd already noticed that both of Mr. Thurman's headlights were broke.

Miss Becky knew something was bad wrong the minute she saw me and Pepper riding in the back with the other kids. She came boiling out of the house with Norma Faye and Miss Sam right behind, carrying on like we all had bloody noses.

Hootie forgot he was feeling bad and set up a racket. Miss Becky hollered at him to shut up and he quieted down when we climbed over the sides and dropped to the ground.

Miss Rachel opened her door, but she couldn't get right out. She'd stiffened up from the beating and I could tell she was hurting. The others stayed put like they were waiting for an invitation, and I reckon they were.

"Lands, honey!" Miss Becky didn't ask what was wrong, probably because Miss Rachel's swole face told a pretty good story. She reached for Miss Rachel's arm.

"My babies."

"I have them." Miss Sam squeezed in to lift baby Bass out of her lap. He was almost asleep and laid his head on her shoulder. She held her hand out to Floryence, the least girl. "Come on, honey."

Miss Becky held onto Miss Rachel as she slid out of the seat. Norma Faye slipped an arm around her from the other side and they slowly walked into the house, leaving the rest of us outside.

Mr. Thurman stayed behind the wheel and we milled around the truck until Miss Sam came rushing back out the door. "Children! Everyone inside. Now."

The terror in her voice was enough to run the rest of the kids inside like a herd of calves.

Mr. Thurman sighed and spoke through his open window. "I believe I might oughta stay outside."

"Miss Becky asked that you come in." Miss Sam watched him with her soft eyes.

Nothing more than wrinkled skin and bones, the old black man wore overalls that were mostly patches, and his faded blue work shirt wasn't much more than threads. He didn't have much to do with bathing, neither.

"I'll set on the porch, if that's all right."

"All right." Miss Sam waited until he climbed the porch and settled gratefully onto a wooden straight chair. We were all still in shock, but I had to grin when she latched the screen. That little hook and eye wouldn't stop a mad five-year-old.

But the guns that appeared on the other side of the screen were enough to start a small army.

And all four of those women looked like they could use them.

Chapter Forty-nine

Taking a back route to Center Springs, Sheriff Griffin stopped his personal car at the intersection of two country roads when radio traffic told him about the massive backup from the wreck on Highway 271. With a sigh, he picked up the microphone. "Martha, this is Griffin. What happened out on two seventy-one?"

"This is Harriet, Donald."

"It don't make any difference. What do you know?"

"That Cody and John Washington are working a bad wreck at Gate Five with a couple of other deputies. I hear it's a mess. They asked for a more units." She gave him a brief report. "You going out there?"

"Washington's there?"

"Yep. Cody called him in for help since he was out that way."

Griffin felt his face redden. Wouldn't anything go right?

Washington was supposed to be at Rachel's house when Griffin's bank-robbing couple out of Dallas, Myrna Wren and Ralph Hatchlett, came by. He rubbed the stubble on his cheek. With so much on his mind, he'd forgotten to shave for two days in a row. "No. Send White and have him check back with me after a while."

Instead of answering, she clicked the talk button a couple of times in acknowledgement and called White. "Deputy White, please proceed…"

An idea occurred to Griffin as he sat at the intersection and drummed his fingers on the steering wheel. Why hadn't he thought of it before? He'd drive to Agrioli's house while the gangster was waiting out in the woods like an idiot, kill the woman, and when the gangster arrived at home, he'd simply shoot him when he came through the door.

Washington and the Parkers would be another matter, though, and so would another loose end he had to tie up. He had to do something about his bank robbers flailing around without finishing their job. Despite their performance on the day of the bank robbery, Myrna and Ralph needed to be eliminated.

His plan had worked perfectly up to that point. Avoiding the local constabulary's best efforts, the couple simply drove to Griffin's house and parked in his garage. They stayed inside until he took them to Dallas late one night when things cooled down. Then they were supposed to come back and shoot Washington and Agrioli.

He wiped nervous sweat from his forehead and thumped the steering wheel, counting off other issues.

The Mexicans screwed it all up from the beginning. He should have known better than to trust those greasers down there. The whole thing started when they paid him a butt-load of hush money to look the other way while they funneled dope into his county, except half the cash was counterfeit.

Changing the funny money in Vegas should have worked, in theory. Best's plan was sound, but Griffin couldn't resist the temptation to work the casinos at night. After giving the real cash to Best in a good-faith exchange, Griffin spent two days visiting casinos and converting his leftover paper.

He got the idea by watching the dealers at the tables. When someone handed them cash, they simply stuck it down a slot in the table and exchanged it for chips. How could that idea go wrong? He knew he was smarter than the dealers, and it was impossible to recognize the counterfeit bills with such a quick glance. But they somehow figured it out and sent Agrioli.

I could turn around right now, catch a plane at Love Field in two hours and be in Tahiti day after tomorrow.

He had enough money to live like a king in the South Pacific, despite the double cross from the Mexicans. He would have a million dollars squirreled away if it weren't for them and the Parkers, who had torn his playhouse down bit by bit.

He took a deep, satisfying breath. He'd leave for his trip to Tahiti first thing in the morning, after he was finished with the Parkers.

"By God, I'll kill them myself."

The coming thunderstorm was almost overhead. A Chevrolet sedan approached at a high rate of speed and slowed as it neared the four-way stop. It waited, idling.

In the failing light, Griffin squinted through his bug-splattered windshield at the occupants in a car so dusty it almost blended with the overgrown fencerows. They were extremely animated, and he realized the arguing couple was Myrna and Ralph.

"What the hell?" Knowing they wouldn't recognize his personal car, Griffin shifted into park and opened the door. Sensing they were ready to bolt, he stepped out and waved. "Hey, you idiots."

Recognizing him, Myrna pointed. Ralph pulled forward and stopped, headlights raking the pasture and trees. "Sheriff. How'd you know we'd be here? You following us somehow?"

"Not hardly." He noticed a long scuff mark down the side of their car. "It was you two who caused that wreck on highway two-seventy-one?" Griffin stepped away from his car and moved to the driver's window. He glanced around at the empty asphalt road. "What are y'all doing out here? Did you do it? Agrioli and Washington are dead?"

Myrna jerked her thumb toward the driver. "Ralph the tough guy here got scared."

"I'm confused."

Ralph shrugged. "We're lost."

She hit him on the shoulder with her fist. "We've been lost since we left that nigger's house. Yeah, *Stupid* here ran smack-dab into a truck full of field hands on our way out to kill Washington and Agrioli."

"So it *was* y'all that caused that wreck?" Griffin wanted to laugh. "What are y'all doing *here*?"

Griffin noticed Ralph kept plucking at a dirty towel on the seat between them with nervous fingers. He asked again, more forcefully. "You didn't kill Washington and Agrioli like I told you to?"

"No, Myrna and I tried. We really did." Ralph wouldn't meet his eyes. "We were pretty rattled after we hit that truck, and things fell apart when we got to that nigger gal's house. I was getting ready to tie her up when people started coming at us from all directions with guns. The only thing we could do was leave."

Griffin sighed and checked the highway again. "Who came with guns?"

"We don't know who they were. I think Washington set up an ambush, but we got the hell out of there."

"Did they recognize you?"

The couple exchanged glances. "They saw our faces, but they won't know who we are."

Thunder rumbled. Griffin straightened to squint toward the towering thunderheads. There was barely enough to light to inside the car. "I still don't get why y'all are here?"

"We don't have a map, and then when we *did* find the highway again, it was the same place where we caused the wreck. Every law in the county was there in the middle of the biggest traffic jam I've ever seen."

Ralph waved a hand. "It's a wonder they didn't see us, but they were all busy. We backed up, turned around like everybody else, and went looking for a way around Chisum, but that hasn't worked, 'cause these chicken-scratch trails wind around so much we keep getting lost." He squinted upward at the sheriff, sweating as if he'd run a mile. "I'm thinking we might need to let this one alone. They've already seen us."

Myrna leaned toward Ralph to better see the sheriff standing beside them. "Look, how about we give you back some of the money you gave us. That way we'll be even and you can get someone else to do the job, probably better than we could."

Resting one hand on the roof, Griffin hooked his free thumb in his gun belt. It was a familiar pose that kept his hand close to his pistol. "What are you so nervous about, Ralph?"

"I just…I'm ready to get this all over with and go home."

"Here." Myrna opened the glove box and handed Griffin a packet of money. "Just take this and let's call it even."

He took it and recognized a mark on the band holding the bills together. "We'll call the whole thing off? You give me this and drive away and that's all, huh? We call it even?"

His face a blank mask, Griffin shifted away from the car and glanced around at the dark, empty pastures and roads. When he looked back into the car, Ralph's expression in the glow of the dash told him that despite being a bumbling fool, the man had sensed what was about to happen.

Ralph reached under the towel on the seat between them.

Myrna's face was one of shock. She grabbed his hand. "Wait!"

Her interference was enough to give Griffin time to draw his .45 and shoot Ralph twice in the chest. The interior of the car flashed, freezing Myrna's terrified expression. He shifted his aim and pulled the trigger again, then again. Red bloomed on her shirt. She fell against Ralph's corpse, her head on his shoulder.

Griffin pitched the counterfeit money into Ralph's lap. "This is the funny money I paid *you* with, stupid." He checked his surroundings and smiled. Gunshots in rural Lamar County were as common as mockingbirds.

He reached in across Ralph's bloody body and picked up the towel revealing a worn revolver. Griffin used it to wipe his fingerprints from the car door and the roof, then he pitched it back through the open window.

"Now I gotta do it myself."

He drove away toward the coming storm. Their blood leaked through the seats and drenched the packets of real cash wrapped in butcher paper marked "Steak."

Chapter Fifty

A lightning bolt slashed through the thick clouds overhead. I felt the thunder rumble deep in my chest each time a rolling boom followed the lightning bolts. Pepper and me were sitting out there with Mr. Thurman and Ralston, Miss Sweet's nephew.

Miss Sweet didn't drive, and Ralston took her anywhere she wanted to go. The old healer served the poor folks in Lamar County with the folk medicine she'd learned from her grandmother. She was one of the colored folks Pepper told Miss Rachel about, who'd been in Grandpa's house.

Every light was on when Mr. John and Uncle Cody finally pulled their cars into the gravel driveway. Uncle Cody stopped behind Mr. Thurman's beat-up old Willys pickup.

Someone inside either saw their headlights or heard the car doors slam, and switched on the porch light. It spilled into the yard, making us squint.

Mr. John waited for a second before he shut off his headlights. I imagine he was studying on why Mr. Thurman's truck and Ralston's sprung car were there. Any time the old woman showed up always meant that someone was sick or hurt. Mr. John came around to the porch. "What happened? Are y'all all right?"

The kitchen door slammed open and Miss Rachel's kids rushed to meet him as soon as they saw who he was. The oldest ones led the way and they swarmed Mr. John like ants, all chattering at the same time.

Looking scared, Uncle Cody came around the front of his El Camino and we met him there. Pepper opened her mouth, but for once, nothing came out. Tears welled in her eyes. He put his hand on my shoulder. "What happened?"

"The meanest folks I've ever seen came to Miss Rachel's house and beat her, asking about Mr. John. The man hit the baby, too, when she wouldn't tell them…"

Mr. John raised his hand to the crowd around him. "Hush kids, so's I can hear. Belle, is the baby hurt?"

"I don't reckon." Belle waved a slender hand toward the house. "He's inside with the women. We wanted to stay on the porch with Mr. Thurman and Ralston, but we's told to go inside…"

Uncle Cody glanced up to see the ancient farmer sitting with his back against the asbestos shingles. He gripped my shoulder and hugged Pepper to his side. "Mr. Thurman."

"Hidy, boy." The old man's watery eyes flicked over Uncle Cody's shoulder. "Mr. Cody. Mr. John. They beat that little gal bad. Sweet say she'll be all right, and the baby too."

Mr. John took the news deep down inside. He reached out and grabbed a porch post, and I was afraid it'd snap off in his hand. "Did you see what happened?"

"Nawsir, Mr. John. I didn't know a thing about it until Bubba come a-runnin' to get me. They's all in the house bein' real quiet. I'm just settin' out here a-waitin'."

"Why didn't somebody call this in?" Uncle Cody wondered aloud.

Mr. John shook his head. "Probably 'cause Rachel told them not to. They're waitin' on *us*. This is colored business, for the most part."

Uncle Cody studied the porch and Mr. Thurman with a paper-thin towel covering an old pistol in his lap. The .22 Uncle Wilbert loaned me was leaning against the door frame beside Ralston.

Uncle Cody glanced down at me, and then back to Mr. John. "Is everybody inside? No one's off anywhere?"

"Yessir, uh, nossir. They're all in there."

Mr. John's voice rumbled deep. "All you kids get in the house, right now."

Mr. Thurman waved his left hand, but kept his right under the rag in his lap. "I'll set out here and keep an eye out, Mr. John. But would you shut off this porch light? I don't like bein' all lit up like this."

Without another word, they followed us inside. The porch light flicked off, leaving Mr. Thurman in the dark. Ralston sat down at the table, facing the door as we all trooped past into the living room.

Miss Becky's quiet command of the room held everyone in a calm. I saw her face crack for a second like she wanted to cry when she saw Uncle Cody, and then she straightened her shoulders and told what had happened to Miss Rachel. Mr. John lifted the ice bag she held to her eye. His face hardened. "We'd-a been here sooner if you'd called us."

Miss Becky shook her head. "Heavens to Betsy, it don't matter none. We weren't going anywhere anyway. Sweet doctored Rachel while we waited."

Miss Sweet rummaged through the bag of medicines at her feet. "This child ain't hurt bad, but she been beat good enough." John took Rachel's hand. "Can you see out t'at eye?"

"Not now, but Miss Sweet said it'll be all right, jus' swole shut."

"It looks bad." John swallowed, torn between rage and the need to choke down the tears threatening to crawl down his cheeks. He ran his fingers gently along her cheek.

"She got a beefsteak on it right off when she got here." Miss Sweet shook some leaves out in her hand and dropped them into a cracked mug. "Then Becky found us an ice bag. That'll help with the swelling. Miss Becky, is that water a-boilin' yet?"

"I 'magine." Miss Becky went into the kitchen and came back with a kettle. She carefully poured some into the mug. "Here, baby. I swear, them kids is still eatin' in there."

"I'm sorry," Rachel began and struggled to rise.

"Hush and lay back down, honey child. I didn't mean it that way. I meant I like to see kids eat. John, I didn't think it'd be a good idea to use the phone." She nodded toward the telephone table. "Miss Whitney would have been listening in and everybody in the county would have known. I figured we needed to keep this quiet, at least for the time being, so I just called O.C. and told him to send y'all when you could make it, then we got aholt of Sweet. Anybody listenin' in would have thought she'd come back out for Top and his asthma again."

"She's right." Miss Rachel's voice was quiet. She tentatively sipped the steaming liquid. "John, this trouble's ours."

He shook his head. "Naw, it ain't. Now I'm thinkin' this belongs to us all, but I know how to end it."

Pepper turned away, talking to herself. "God, I hate this shittin' town."

Chapter Fifty-one

When he had the full story, Cody went outside and reached through the open window of the El Camino to pluck the Motorola's microphone from the dash. Wind nearly snatched the Stetson off his head as he keyed the mike. "Ned. You there?"

The reply came only a second later. "Go ahead Cody."

"Where are you?"

"Still in the parking lot here at St. Joseph hospital. That little one I brought in is in bad shape, and I'm just getting' around to leaving."

Cody took a deep breath and spoke in Choctaw. "Listen, Ned. *Abenili anukwa n ya.*"

Hurry home.

He wasn't sure the sentence structure was right, but it should be enough for Ned to understand.

The shocked silence on the other end spoke more than words. Cody knew Ned was translating, and the use of Choctaw only meant one thing. There was news he didn't want others to hear, especially Sheriff Griffin.

Their grasp of the language was thin. Both were far from fluent, and only knew what Miss Becky taught them through the years. Much of what *she* knew came from her childhood and the ragged Choctaw Bible she inherited from her mother. The last time they used the dialect was when Cody, half Indian himself, was held prisoner in Mexico and they wanted to communicate in front of the crooked *comandante* of *Las Células,* the jail.

Ned's voice finally came back through the radio. "All right. I'm-a listenin'. What's the matter?"

"*Abeka apistikeli, bo-a.*"

Tending the sick, beaten.

"Good God. Can you say who?"

Cody had the next one down. "*Hatak lusa ohoyo.*"

A colored woman.

Another long pause while Ned studied on the phrase. The only colored woman Cody would be talking about was Rachel. "Anyone else?"

"No."

Ned stumbled, and then remembered the word. "Kat... katra...*Katimma?*"

Where?

"*Aiilli.*" Home. "Ned, *ho-miniti!*" Come on!

The wind freshened, and the sporadic light-show overhead kicked into high gear.

The old constable's next transmission was garbled, but Cody heard one thing clearly. The roar of Ned's engine.

Chapter Fifty-two

Sheriff Griffin slammed the heel of his hand against the steering wheel as he listened to the Parkers speak Choctaw.

"Shit!"

He steered through the darkness toward Center Springs.

It needed to be finished.

Chapter Fifty-three

I followed Uncle Cody into the wind and listened while he talked to Grandpa in Choctaw. I couldn't understand it, but I knew Grandpa would be at the house pretty quick.

It was time for me to help, because I knew stuff they didn't.

The porch light was still off over Mr. Thurman's head and I caught Pepper's attention. We stepped into the darkness around the corner of the house while lightning spread like bright tree roots in the roiling clouds above.

"What?"

I ducked my head back around to see where everyone was.

She grabbed my shirt, yanking me around. "Hey, *stupid*. They'll know something's up if you keep peeking around the corner like that. Just stand still and tell me what you want."

I hated that I'd never be as good a sneak as her. "Did you hear what that man was asking Miss Rachel back at her house?"

"No. I didn't hear anything. All I saw was him beating her."

"Well, he was asking where Mr. John and Mr. Tony was."

Her hair whipped in the wind. "What did he want to know that for?"

"How'm I supposed to know? All I can say is that he *really* wanted to know where they were."

"Well, we need to tell Uncle Cody."

Frustration swelled in my chest. "No, I don't think so. Something's up, and they're gonna stay here and talk about it for a long time, and then they might wait until Grandpa gets back from town before they figure out what to do."

"So?"

"So it'll be too late by then. We need to go tell Mr. Tony right now!"

She shook her head. "I don't get why we can't tell Uncle Cody."

I was thinking about that machine gun I'd seen in the trunk of Mr. Tony's car the first day they showed up in Center Springs. "Those people are after him 'cause I think he's into something that might be a little against the law."

Pepper stood there in the window light, thinking. A strong gust rattled the windowpane. Finally she sighed. "I don't think I can do that."

"You don't want to go help Mr. Tony?" I couldn't believe it was me saying something like that. Since we were little, it was always Pepper who got us in trouble, but here I was, suggesting dumb ideas I'd have expected *her* to come up with.

"I want to." Her eyes welled, reflecting the light from the windows. She wrapped her arms around herself and I knew she was touching her burn scar. "But I'm getting a really bad vibe about all of this."

I couldn't figure her out. Here was a perfect adventure. "Look, we'll get our bikes and ride on over, tell him what we know, and come home. We'll be back in twenty minutes, long before anyone misses us."

Angry, Pepper wiped her face dry. "You promise that's all?"

"Sure. What could be hard about that?"

She squinted through the slit between the windowsill and the shade. Mr. John was on the couch, sitting with his back to us and his arm around Miss Rachel. She leaned in to him and said something in his ear. Before he could answer, Miss Becky appeared and lowered the shade all the way down, and then worked her way through the house, closing them all.

"See? They're gonna sit there and talk a while." There was still enough light coming through the shade for me to see Pepper's face. "They don't know we're out here. We can get to Mr. Tony's and back before they catch us, and then we'll be all right, so all they can do is get mad and holler."

"They might not catch us." I couldn't see Pepper's face then, but her teeth were white when she finally smiled. "But this storm might."

"We've been caught in the rain before."

She wiped her tears away. "All right. I ain't no titty baby."

Chapter Fifty-four

Ned's car slid to a stop in front of the porch. He tracked around the hood. "Thurman, what are you doing here?"

"Keeping an eye out, Mr. Ned. I brought these folks."

Ned climbed the steps. "What folks? Why don't you come on in?"

"I believe I'll sit out here and watch the weather. I always did enjoy a good storm." He paused. "Sides, I didn't get a chance to clean up to be company, so I believe I'll stay right 'chere."

"All right, then." A stroke of lightning lit him up and Ned noticed the familiar outline underneath the rag over Thurman's lap. He went inside and paused.

Ralston was at the table loaded with dish pans full of peeled and sliced pears. Dirty dishes added to the cluttered the table and counter as the kids who looked like John cleaned up all the leftovers from the refrigerator. Norma Faye and Sam worked the table like waitresses, filling plates and bowls.

Ralston swallowed a bite of cold cornbread soaked in sweet milk and ducked his head. "Mr. Ned."

"Howdy Ralston. What's going…?"

"In there," Norma Faye pointed toward the living room. A revolver was tucked into the small of her back.

"Are y'all…"

Ned glanced at a shotgun lying on the chest type deep freezer. Sam smiled. "We're fine."

◇◇◇

He pitched his hat beside the shotgun and stepped into the living room. Rachel lay on the sofa, a folded rag across her forehead and over her eye. Miss Sweet rocked a sleeping baby. Two other little ones slept on a pallet in the floor.

John stood beside the couch, radiating fury. Ned had never seen the man so angry. He was reminded of a watch spring wound far too tight. With Ned there, John sat on the couch and scooped Rachel against him. Cody leaned against the door to keep an eye on the doors and most of the windows.

Miss Becky was sitting at the telephone table with her Bible open in her lap. Her shoulders slumped when Ned appeared, as if his very presence had removed a great weight. He stopped beside the television. "What happened?"

Cody pointed at Rachel, and Ned listened as she talked quietly.

When she was finished, Ned remained silent for a long moment. "John, you don't know what any of this has to do with you and Tony?"

"I have no idy, Mr. Ned."

"Has Tony ever been to your house?"

Rachel shook her head. "I never laid eyes on the man, honest. John?"

"What, baby?"

Her dimples appeared. "Do you realize you growlin'?"

The phone rang with a brash rattle, startling everyone. Miss Becky met Ned's eyes across the room. He nodded and she picked up the receiver. "Hello? Oh, hidy, Tony. Yep, she's right here. I'll hand her over."

Sam came in from the kitchen and they traded places. Her eyes softened when she took the phone. "Hey, tough guy." She listened for a long minute, her face falling. The adults watched as she remained silent, without interrupting, shrinking with every passing minute. Conversation was low in the living room, louder in the kitchen. "All right, I understand, but remember I love you." She hung up and took a deep breath, ready to give them only part of the conversation. "Tony got home a few minutes ago. He heard what happened and called to make sure I was all right."

Ned frowned. "Why wouldn't *you* be all right? Never mind, how'd he hear? No one oughta know but us."

She hesitated. "He said the kids told him."

Ned felt the blood rush from his face. "What kids?"

"Top and Pepper."

Ned blew up. "Sonofabitch!"

Lightning fractured the thunderheads, irradiating the paper shades from the outside. Thunder rattled dishes in the china cabinet. The house lights fell dark. Kids squealed, waking the smaller children who began to cry.

Miss Becky covered her mouth in shock. "*I* don't even know what's going on, and they're stringing off in this storm…!" Shaking her head, Miss Becky stood to light the oil lamps. "I can't believe we didn't know they was gone. What kind of people are we?"

Ned gave Miss Becky's arm a pat. "I know how it is. They'll get away from you before you can turn around." He caught their attention. "Cody, John, y'all come outside with me where these kids cain't hear everything we say."

Once off the porch, Ned stopped and scrubbed the back of his neck, staring into the darkness covering his pasture. John opened his trunk and lifted out his shotgun. "Mr. Ned, why don't you stay here and let Cody go find them kids? They know something we don't, and I bet a dollar it's about Tony. Maybe them that hurt Rachel has found out where he lives and gone there for some reason."

"What'll you do when you find them, John? You're too mad to think straight right now."

The deputy glared down at the older man beside him. "I'll do what I have to." He shucked a shell into the magazine and rolled half of the shells from a pasteboard box into his big hand. He dropped them into one front pocket of his khakis, then filled the other and slammed the lid. The expression on his face was one of barely restrained violence.

Anxious to get moving, Cody opened the door on his El Camino and put one foot inside.

Ned breathed heavily, considering their options. "Y'all settle down for a second. We don't know what we're getting into."

"We need to do *something!*" Cody dipped his head into the wind to keep his hat secure. When it threatened to blow off again, he yanked it off and pitched it into the seat.

Realizing he was about to lose his own Stetson, Ned took it off. The cool wind felt strange on his bald head. He studied on what to do for a long moment. "I don't expect anybody to come to the house, but one of us needs to stay here. This has something to do with Griffin and he's got something up his sleeve. Cody, you go find the kids. Right now we don't need to be running around like chickens with our heads cut off."

A truck slowed on the highway and crunched up the gravel drive, headlight beams sweeping over the house and yard. The kitchen door opened and Miss Becky stuck her head out. "Ned, that'll be Ty Cobb and Jimmy Foxx."

"What are they doing here?"

"I knew they'd be home in this storm, so I called 'em to come over and set so's y'all can go."

Ned almost grinned at the woman who'd been his rock for decades. "That was a good idea, Mama. All right." He waved at the truck. "Y'all get out and come in."

The heavily armed brothers got out. Ty Cobb took a seat on the edge of porch in front of Thurman. "Ned, y'all go do what you need to. We'll take care of things here."

Without a word, Jimmy Foxx nodded at the three lawmen, went inside, and locked the door. The kitchen went dark as he blew out the coal oil lamp on the table, leaving only a dim glow in the living room.

Cody dropped into the seat and left to go find his niece and nephew. John shifted from one foot to the next, bleeding off energy.

Ned heard John whine like a dog wanting off the leash. He realized it was the sound of frustration harnessed by the respect that John had for Ned's age and position in life.

"Mr. Ned, I believe I need to go and see what I can do to find them that hurt Rachel. I want to get my hands on 'em and anyone else who might have been a part of it. Right. Now."

Ned didn't look right, standing outside without his hat. "John, we been through a lot these last couple of years. Sometimes you have to take your time breaking up a fistfight between two men, so they'll get tired and won't be as hard to cuff."

"Yessir, you been shot, and I dang near got mushed to death in that old Cotton Exchange, but Tony and that little gal of his inside there need us. You take care of people all the time and lots of them don't even know you do it. I know you don't want to call for help, 'cause we don't know who's with us or against us, but we *got to do something*. It don't feel right to do *nothin'*."

Ned rubbed his head, muttering to himself. "I got a bad feeling about this."

"Me too. I'm afraid this is gonna be a bad night." He wasn't talking about the weather.

Norma Faye cracked the door. "Mr. Ned. There's somebody on the phone for you."

"Who is it?"

"Isaac Reader."

"What does he want?"

She tried not to roll her eyes. "To talk to you."

With that, she went back inside, but left the wooden door open. Aggravated, Ned gripped John's thick arm. "Wait here and blow a minute until I get back and we'll go together."

Instead of answering, because he wasn't sure he could trust his voice, John nodded. Ned left him to steam and followed Norma Faye inside, slamming the screen door. He threaded his way through the crowded kitchen and living room to the telephone table. "What?"

"Ned, listen, listen, this is Ike."

"I know it. What's wrong, Ike?"

"I was driving past the Ordway place, and somebody's shooting."

Ned went cold.

"Listen, listen, when I looked, I saw flashes in the house."

"You sure it wasn't lightning?"

"I'm sure."

Ned sighed, feeling his spirits fall. "All right. I'll go check it out."

"You want me to meet you there?"

"Lord, no."

Ned returned to the porch to see John's car speed down the drive. His brake lights flashed, and then he took off for Center Springs.

Chapter Fifty-five

It was one of those early fall storms, all noise and electricity. Clouds boiled in the night sky and lighting flickered almost continuously as we rode our bikes to the Ordway place. Cool wind carried the thunder around us, and it felt like we rode through the middle of an artillery battle. We knew there wouldn't be any rain, because the whole world smelled wet and Grandpa always said if you smell rain, it won't fall.

It was hard to ride fast through the flying leaves and keep up with Pepper because one hand held my .22 rifle. I wished I'd left it back there on the porch beside Mr. Thurman, but I thought I might need it if the bad folks were coming for Mr. Tony. I'd already killed out a pack of dogs, and been in the middle of a gunfight a while back. I didn't intend to go over there without something to shoot with.

That's what I figured Uncle Cody would do.

Uncle Henry's house was dark when we passed, so I knew the electricity went out like it does every time a storm comes through. With the pole lights out, the stores and domino hall looked different when we passed in the cold, harsh lightning. We pedaled hard up the drive and jumped off our bikes at the Ordway place. I knocked as loud as I could. Not even the dim light from a coal oil lamp lit the house.

It took forever for Mr. Tony to answer, and I about decided he wasn't there, until he looked out the tall, skinny little window beside the door. He opened it, reached out, and took the rifle from my hand all in the same motion, like he'd practiced it.

"Hey!"

He leaned it against the inside of the frame. "I'll give it back later. What are you two doing here in this weather?"

"We came to warn you," Pepper said.

Mr. Tony stepped back into the entry hall and motioned us to follow. He closed the door and locked it. He was back in his suit, except this time without a tie. His coat hung open, and the white shirt underneath glowed each time the lightning flashed. "Warn me about what?"

"About a man and woman who came to Miss Rachel's house looking for you." I didn't like standing in that entry hall, because it was right beside the wooden staircase leading to the second floor. That's where the ghosts lived. Lightning struck somewhere nearby and seemed to shoot right through my head. "Uh…." I struggled to focus.

Pepper shoved me. "He heard them people who beat Miss Rachel say something, didn't you?"

"The woman wanted to know where you were and when you were coming to Miss Rachel's house, like you was expected there. I didn't know you knew her."

"I don't know what you're talking about." Mr. Tony stepped closer to the little skinny window and pushed the white lace curtain back with his finger. "Tell me what happened, exactly."

"Lemme see. She said 'I wanted to be finished with this before Agrioli showed up so it wouldn't be two at the same time.'"

"Think, Top. There must have been something before that. What did she mean two at the same time?" His face was as calm as could be.

I struggled to remember the conversation. "He said 'He told us Washington would be here by now. I wanted to be finished with this before Agrioli showed up so it wouldn't be two at the same time.' That's what he said."

"Do you know who the *he* is that man was talking about?"

"Nossir. They didn't say any names but y'all's. Wait, the man was Ralph and the woman's name was Myrna."

Mr. Tony thought for a long time, then gave us a half-smile. "All right. That's fine. Now, do you two think you'll be all right to ride back to Mr. Parker's house?"

Pepper cocked her head, but not enough to make her ponytail flop like she did that first day when she was flirting with Mr. Tony. "Why don't you go with us? You can drive us there and we can get our bikes in the morning."

He patted her shoulder. "Because I think I need to stay here."

"Miss Sam probably needs you."

His smile slipped a little, and he looked sad. "She's safer with your grandfather. Now," he opened the door. Cool wind blew in, scattering leaves into the hall. "You two ride back as quickly as you can and tell your grandfather not to come over here until tomorrow, no matter what."

I didn't know why, but I felt a painful lump in my chest. Pepper looked like she wanted to cry, also. There was something terribly wrong, but we didn't know what it was. "Please go with us, Mr. Tony."

"No. You two go now, and hurry home."

He all but pushed us into the yard and the wind. Nobody in the country would turn someone out in such a storm, but we picked up our bikes and left anyway. Mr. Neal's store was dark, but there was a car parked between it and the domino hall. When the lighting flashed, I saw it was empty.

We were past Mr. Oak Peterson's store when I realized I'd forgotten my rifle. A minute later, I forgot about it when I heard gunfire behind us, almost buried in the near continuous thunder.

Chapter Fifty-six

"That's the house," Michael said as they drove slowly down the oil road past the Ordway place. He stopped. "Johnny, go in the back. We'll park and come in the front. Gimme five minutes. That should be enough time."

The door opened and closed. In a series of staccato flashes, they watched Johnny Machine cross a sagging barbed wire fence, holding his shotgun with one hand. He stepped behind a cedar and was lost from view.

Michael made a rough three-point turn at a gate and went back to the country store they saw on the way in. He parked next to a smaller building. "Let's go." He grabbed a cut-down Browning semi-automatic shotgun from the backseat and handed the humpback to Nicky, then took another one for himself.

Nicky followed past the store with its metal signs rattling in the wind, unconsciously ducking low as lightning split the clouds overhead. "I don't like this weather."

"We don't have any choice."

Leaves showered like paper snow as the towering burr oaks thrashed in the wind and egg-size acorns rattled down. One caught Nicky a glancing blow to the head. "Shit! What kind of country is this that trees throw giant walnuts at you?"

Michael glanced up. "Shhh. Come on!"

"Dammit Michael, he ain't gonna hear anything over all this thunder. Agrioli'll probably *see* us first."

Michael stopped. A flicker of motion well away from the house caught his attention. Incredulous, he thought he saw someone waving from behind an overgrown barbed wire fence. He froze and brought up his shotgun, waiting for the next flash of lightning.

It didn't take long. A man waved again and then ducked down behind the brush. "Did you see that?"

Nicky pointed his shotgun in the man's direction. "There's somebody back there."

The next flash revealed an individual standing completely upright, frantically waving them over. Michael glanced back toward the dark house. "Come on. This ain't right."

They hurried across the yard, guns ready.

"You're Michael!" The man glanced nervously at the house. "C'mere. We're the ones Mr. Best sent to help you."

The two gangsters ran to the fencerow and knelt. There was no need to whisper. The wind and crackling thunder covered their voices and no one could hear from more than a few feet away.

Michael knelt on one knee and spoke through the tangled vines. "Who're you?"

"Ray Marco, the one you talked to on the phone. We went by the motel, but you were gone. So we came on out here to meet you."

Michael thought for a moment. "How did you know where Agrioli lived? We barely found out ourselves."

"You don't remember mentioning Center Springs when we talked? I called the store over there and asked where he lived. Some guy with a loud voice damn near gave me the man's shoe size before he quit talking. So we drove out, but got caught in traffic. Can you believe it? A traffic jam out here in the boonies. We haven't been here but a few minutes, and waited for you."

Michael scratched his cheek and watched the house. "Yeah, I remember. How many of you are here?"

"Seven."

"You must have been crowded."

"It was only an hour and a half. We got a break when we got caught in a traffic jam back there. We managed."

Michael stared hard at the house and after a moment, shook his head. "Where are your guys?"

Marco scratched a chigger on his leg. "Scattered around. We've been expecting you."

Nicky kept the shotgun ready. "You seen anybody else?"

"Yeah, a couple of kids on bikes. Agrioli let them in and then they took off. The kid had a BB gun or something with him, but he left it."

"Where's your car?"

"Parked down that road beside some cows."

Michael watched the house. "All right…hey, you said you had guys scattered around? Anyone around back?"

"Yeah."

"Oh, shit…."

The flat bangs of two gunshots echoed. The sound was cut off with the crack and sizzle of lightning overhead, followed immediately by a thunderclap they felt in their chests, then another shot.

"You probably have one less now." Nicky grinned at the mistake. He didn't know them, so he couldn't care less. "The Machine's back there."

Marco's eyes widened. Johnny Machino was legendary in the Business. "You brought the Machine?"

Michael cut his eyes toward the brush beside him. They couldn't see Marco through the tangle, but both could hear the awe in his voice. "That's him."

"You sent him around back?"

"Of course I did, the same as you." Michael pointed past Nicky. "Run around to the rear and tell the Machine not to kill the rest of these idiots. They're with us."

The slender gangster crouched to run, and then stopped. "Wait, how are Marco's men gonna know I'm with them? We don't know each other."

Michael rubbed his face in disgust. "Good question. Marco, whaddya think?"

"I don't know."

Michael flicked his arm. "Run and wave your arms. They'll know you ain't Agrioli."

"But that'll give us away."

Another bang came from behind the house.

"It don't matter now."

Chapter Fifty-seven

The sharp report of a gunshot was dramatically different than the blasts of lightning. Tony drew the .45 from his shoulder holster and hurried to the largest bedroom in back of the house, wondering what Griffin was up to. The downstairs floor plan was almost exactly divided in half from front to back. From the foyer, the living room was on the right and dining room on the left. Past the staircase and dividing wall, the master bedroom was in the center of the house with another bedroom on the right. The bathroom and kitchen anchored the back left corner.

Standing against the wall beside one of three huge windows in the master bedroom, Tony peeked into the backyard. The electrical storm worked to his advantage. Lightning bathed the landscape in bleak, blue-white light. A man dragged himself behind an abandoned hog pen beyond a barbed wire fence.

What the hell???

Glass broke in the living room. Instead of charging in that direction, Tony dodged the bed and hurried to the doorway underneath the second flight of stairs. He had no idea who was outside, but from that position in the near exact center of the house, he could quickly respond to Griffin's attack.

He glanced over at the two suitcases packed and ready on the bed. It was too late to get away. He'd missed the window by only a few minutes.

Sorry, Doll.

Chapter Fifty-eight

We left our bikes beside Oak Peterson's store and snuck back toward the domino hall. One line of clouds had moved on, but another was coming quick. Grandpa called it a train of storms, one passing right after another. Storms like that are common in Texas, but they usually drop a lot of rain. This time they were full of electricity instead of water, and we didn't need flashlights to make our way to the Ordway house.

Pepper stopped beside the car. "I don't recognize this one."

"I didn't expect you to." I liked that answer. It sounded like something Grandpa might say.

"Don't be a smartass. I was just saying that it don't belong to anybody we know."

Two gunshots came from the Ordway place, immediately followed by the slap-crack of a thunderbolt.

Pepper's expression was one of pure terror. She slammed back against the plank wall of the domino hall, knocking off a metal Wrigley's chewing gum sign that banged down behind her. She screamed and jumped. The falling sign hit her legs, and still not sure what was happening, she screamed again and spun and charged into Uncle Cody, who wrapped her in his arms. He pulled her around to the front of the domino hall. "Whoa!"

"Uncle Cody, you scared me to death."

"Good." I stayed right behind them. He reached out and pulled me closer. "You two are going to be the death of me."

"We just came to warn Mr. Tony," Pepper said.

"About what?"

"What we heard at Miss Rachel's house."

"Well, why didn't you tell us when we got there?"

I didn't want Pepper to take all the trouble. "Y'all were busy with Miss Rachel. I figured we'd help and warn Mr. Tony that two bad people went to Miss Rachel's house looking for Tony and Mr. John. We were coming right back to tell you next."

Lightning split the rolling clouds and I saw Uncle Cody's grim face. "Top." He paused. "Your cousin's finally rubbed off on you."

"We're only trying to help."

"You two about got yourselves in trouble."

Pepper looked around. "Where's the El Camino?" She was a master at changing the direction of a conversation.

"I parked it right down there at Mr. Landers' house." He pointed at the farmhouse not a hundred yards away on the other side of Oak Peterson's store. "Y'all come on." Glancing back toward the Ordway place, he led the way, trotting down the highway with us following like a couple of baby ducks.

His car was parked between Mr. Landers' house and the barn. Both were painted white, and they glowed in the darkness. He was waiting on his screened side porch. "Looks like you found them, Cody."

"Yep. You two stay right up there with Mr. Landers." He slid behind the wheel and keyed the mike.

Chapter Fifty-nine

Cody powered up the Motorola and keyed the mike. "Ned."

A pause. "I'm here. Find the kids?"

"Got 'em."

"Good. Beat their little asses and then bring 'em home. I'm still here."

Cody needed to tell him about the gunshots, but he didn't want anyone, especially Griffin, to hear. "*Bamppulli.*"

Gun.

"At you?"

"No."

"Then come home."

Cody hesitated. "But you heard what I said."

"It's too dangerous."

Cody waited for a long moment. "I can't." More shots rang out, the reports distinct. "I'm leaving the kids here with Arch Landers and going somewhere to see better. Meet me at the…" He paused, struggling to find the word for store. Using Landers' name wouldn't give anything away to Griffin, but he needed to remember the right word. "Atato, no…wait. Dammit, I can't remember! Something like attoba..attit…"

"*Aiitatoba?*"

Store.

"That's it!"

"All right." Cody heard the tension in Ned's voice. "Something's going on that ain't right. We got too many irons in this fire and I don't know which of 'em are ours. And You Know Who is in this up to his neck, and I don't have any idea who he has working with him. You have the kids, and we're all here. Let's wait it out till the smoke clears and we get some help."

"No. Tony's in trouble, and I intend to help him out. Ned, you did the same for me and stepped across a line here-while-back. I don't have a line, but I have a job." Frustrated, Cody slapped the mike back on the hanger. He didn't understand why Ned insisted on waiting, but more gunshots told him to move quickly.

Chapter Sixty

Griffin lowered down the volume on his radio and pondered the dark front of Reid's store, less than three miles from Center Springs.

He was almost as frustrated as Cody, wondering what was going on. Those two Parkers were arguing about something in Choctaw, or at least he figured that's what they were talking. Ned wanted to hunker down and wait until the morning, completely out of character for the old man who usually bulled his way into everything.

But now he knew where they were. Tony Agrioli's rented house.

Unfortunately, there was also the total absence of Washington. He wasn't on the radio, and hadn't called in for some time.

He worried Griffin most of all.

For good reason.

Chapter Sixty-one

Defending a house alone was insane, and he knew it.

Tony didn't fall for the breaking glass, figuring it was a ruse. With the .45 in his hand, he peeked around the corner from the foyer to see the small utility porch off the kitchen, the only one of the three doors out of his sight.

The particularly loud bang of a strong lightning bolt was the trigger he'd been expecting. The chest-compressing thump filled the space between the storm and the ground with a monstrous concussion.

The screen door was open, swinging in the wind. A shadow moved toward him. Tony knelt on one knee and raised the Colt. He fired twice, the whip crack reports hammering his ears. A cry and the thump of something heavy striking the floor in the utility room told him the shots were accurate.

Those rounds triggered a barrage from outside. The lowered paper shades in the living room jumped and danced as slugs and shotgun pellets punched through the glass to smack into the plaster and lath walls.

These guys don't act like police or lawmen. This damned sheriff brought his own army.

Staying low, Tony duck-walked to the living room doorway. The east side of the wrap-around porch led to the other doorway, opening into the furthermost bedroom. He waited, expecting someone to rush past the windows and kick the door in.

The glass and wood front door flew back from a strong kick. It struck the wall and a figure stepped through, firing rapidly with a semi-automatic shotgun.

Tony returned fire, driving the man back. A bullet snapped past his ear. He cursed himself for assuming the guy in the utility room was out of action. He whipped around and poured it on him, forcing the wounded man deeper onto the screened porch and halting any further attack.

The battle paused. Ears ringing, Tony dodged back into the middle hallway. He ejected the spent magazine and pulled a fresh one from the shoulder holster's strap under his right arm. He slapped it in, loaded a round, and waited, expecting them to rush the house soon. He had a little surprise waiting in the corner beside the staircase.

C'mon, Griffin. I need one clear shot at you.

Chapter Sixty-two

From where we stood in the wind beside Mr. Landers' house, it sounded like a war movie. Heavier strikes and deep claps of thunder punctuated the rattle of gunfire from the Ordway place.

Pepper wanted to step around to the side so she could hear better over the wind and thrashing trees, but Mr. Landers wouldn't let her. "We got a good, solid house between us, Missy. There ain't no bullets gonna go plumb through and hit us here. If you step out there, though, no telling what might happen. Some of them bullets are liable to lob over them trees back there and hit you."

Uncle Cody was gone, and the number of shots had me worried. "Don't you think you oughta call for help?"

"Done did." Mr. Landers sounded as calm as if he were in church. "Mama called your granddaddy and told him what we heard over here, and about Cody. I imagine somebody was listening in on the line, so the switchboard's probably lit up like a Christmas tree right about now."

What we didn't know was how many people jammed the lines right away, trying to call Grandpa. Most of 'em didn't know squat about the details, but they figured they could ring him up and find out, like he'd have time to answer all their questions.

When they couldn't get through to him, folks called the sheriff's department. I imagine the phone at Uncle Cody's was ringing off the table, too.

The dominos began to fall, then. Of course Dispatch tried to call Grandpa, and when he didn't answer, they tried Uncle Cody, who was far away from his own radio. Them that knew then tried Mr. John's radio and when he didn't answer, they began to fear the worst.

Chapter Sixty-three

Tony quickly realized more men were moving into position while his attention was diverted from the rear, but it couldn't be helped. He slipped into the living room for a quick peek out the front window.

The electric storm was right on top of them, increasing in intensity. Brief, scattered raindrops slapped against the damaged windows while wind whistled thorough the bullet holes in the glass. Paper shades rapped sharply against frames.

Pressed against the wall, he crept forward. It was only a matter of time before the pull-down shades blew into the room, far enough to see out. Flickering lightning offered the only illumination inside the house. Thunder was a physical presence.

The shades hung still.

Another flicker, immediately followed by a deep crack, rattled the loose and broken windows. A chunk of glass hit the wooden floor.

Then another.

He waited, feeling alive for the first time in weeks. The throbbing in his forehead was gone.

A gust of wind reached the shades. They filled like sails on a ship, revealing two men armed with shotguns only inches away. Startled that they were so close, Tony fired a moment too soon and missed with his first shot.

Then he locked onto a target. One of the assailants folded like an empty sheet. The second happened to be left-handed, with the muzzle of the shotgun pointed toward the house. He instinctively pulled the trigger, punching a huge hole in one of the remaining windows, then immediately fired again as he lunged away. The second load of buckshot tore through the wall above Tony's head, blowing plaster and pieces of lath through the room and filling his eyes with dust.

Tony instinctively ducked and opened up with the .45, punching huge holes in the wall where he thought the shooter might be. Footsteps disappeared as the assailant rushed past the door. Enraged, Tony smacked the shade back with his left hand to reveal the first man lying on the porch and moving weakly, still holding his shotgun. Tony shot him twice more for insurance.

What the hell???

He took another quick peek at the body. The man's suit told him they weren't local.

Who did Griffin bring in?"

Glass crunching underfoot, he dodged back into the foyer and ejected the empty magazine. It hit the floor at his feet and he locked another into place, wondering who was out there.

More gunfire from the rear shattered glassware in the kitchen cabinets. Tony quick-stepped into the master bedroom again and flattened himself against the wall. The flicker of lighting was almost constant, like flashbulbs at a Hollywood movie premier. He resisted the urge to fire at the silhouette of a running man outside. Not much more than his head could be seen above the level of the window.

Thunder boomed, and gunfire erupted from outside. *Jesus, how many did they bring!* Tony knew he was significantly outnumbered. Huddled against the wall, he scooted back into the foyer and then once again, to the middle doorway.

A shadow kicked in the back bedroom door.

The front door simultaneously slammed inward.

Men charged into the kitchen from the utility porch, completing a three-pronged attack.

And the house lights blinked as the electricity came back on.

His targets clear in the bright light, Tony threw two rounds toward the front door. A doughy, pineapple-shaped man fell back, gasping. Another twisted away, grasping at his shoulder.

With those two out of commission, Tony whipped the pistol toward the bedroom and fired until the .45 ran dry. A fusillade from the kitchen drove Tony around to his original position under the stairs.

He grabbed the Thompson just as Nicky ducked into the kitchen and took cover behind the Frigidaire and motioned for one of Ray Marco's men to follow. Reluctant to step into the open, the man hesitated, but stumbled forward when The Machine roughly shoved him forward. "Go on!"

The brief glimpse told Tony everything he needed to know. *Johnny Machine! Here! This isn't Griffin. These are Best's men!*

Marco's man caught his balance, fired, and charged toward Tony's position.

His timing couldn't have been worse.

Tony leveled the drum-fed Thompson, tucked the stock snugly against his shoulder, and hosed the kitchen. Designed not for accuracy, but for volume, the heavy slugs blew out chunks of wood, plaster, and human flesh.

Huge chunks of lead blasted through the refrigerator, throwing Nicky backward. He fell in an awkward sprawl on top of Marco's almost disassembled thug. Crouched in a ball on the service porch, The Machine waited for the barrage to cease.

Senses jangling, Tony glanced over his shoulder. One of the wounded men in the far bedroom raised an arm. Tony turned and opened up with the machine gun a second time. Sensing movement behind, he spun and sprayed the front door.

The Machine had a clear view. He fired twice, and one of the shots slammed Tony into the wall. Crossfire raged from the front door and added to the din.

Tony's back went numb and his left leg buckled. Bracing against the doorframe, he directed his fire once again into the kitchen. With his left hand tight on the front grip to keep the barrel from rising, he swept the far wall, knowing they would be hiding on the other side.

The monstrous bullets chewed up their cover like balsa wood. Furious that Best had sent men after him, Tony reversed direction and again sprayed the front doorway with the same results. Ricochets whined away. His ears felt jammed full of cotton from the massive detonations. Bodies fell and pieces of men flew under the onslaught.

The roll of thunder that erupted from the killing machine in his hands drowned the storm outside.

It was a slaughter.

The Thompson finally ran dry. A scream filled the air, and Tony realized it came from his own hoarse throat. Gunsmoke and dust swirled in the room. He dropped the now useless chunk of iron and yanked the .38 from behind his belt.

The muzzle of a pistol appeared in an opening blasted apart by the .45s. Johnny Machine pulled the trigger on the automatic as fast as possible. An unheard shot caught Tony in his already numb thigh and he went down on his good knee.

Another round snapped past his ear from behind, punching through the wall and nearly hitting The Machine. Bending forward, Tony ducked his head to the right, extended his arm back, and fired until there was no one standing.

No one that is, except Johnny Machine, who stumbled back outside to wait for another chance.

Chapter Sixty-four

Gunfire rattled the night.

The bright pole light over the store sputtered to life. Startled, Ned and Cody ducked behind a pile of wooden crates full of empty soda bottles.

"Damn, Ned. I'm glad you're here, but what a helluva time for the electricity to come back on!"

Seconds later, a roll of man-made thunder filled in behind the storm.

"That's a sonofabitchin' *machine gun!*"

"Keep down." Cody aimed his own .45 toward the Ordway house and flinched as lead slapped into Neal Box's store and the domino hall. "I see people falling on the porch. There's probably more keeping an eye out back this-a-way."

"What are them fellers after Tony for?"

"That's a damn good question, but he ain't going easy."

The machine gun spoke again, and this time the storm couldn't cover the shrill screams of dying men.

They peeked over the crates. The hundred yard expanse broken only by large trees was a killing field that neither could cross. Icy raindrops pounded down for a second, and then quit.

Ned rubbed his wet head. "We need to help, but I don't know who the bad guys are, or how many."

Cody shook his head, frustrated at their position. "I don't see a way to get up there and help Tony without getting shot up ourselves. We're way outgunned."

He looked around, hoping for inspiration. The asphalt road in front of them headed off past the house and overgrown fencerow bordering the pasture. A quarter mile away, another farmhouse was once owned by Ben and Sylvia Winters, and their son Little Ben, an entire family murdered by the Whitlatch gang only months before. The house was still empty.

"Ned, I think I'm gonna swing around to the right here and come up from the back, past the barn over there."

"That'll take a few minutes."

"It's better than sitting here and doing nothing."

Wishing he was already there instead of by the store, Cody glanced down the dark road. They were stuck, unless something happened.

Lightning ripped overhead, tearing the clouds apart and flashing in the red reflectors and spotlight on a dark sedan rolling slowly their direction. Wind gusted. The electricity went off again, plunging Center Springs back into black. Cody stood higher behind the crates of bottles, squinting at the car. Gunfire inside the house backlit the paper shades. A stray round slammed into the store and they instinctively dropped.

Cody rose and Ned joined him. "Who's car is that? Is it John, or Griffin?"

Unable to figure out why it was creeping along without headlights, Cody couldn't take his eyes off the oncoming vehicle. The next flicker confirmed his suspicions. "It's a lawman's car, but from this angle I can't tell whose it is."

They watched the sedan as it crawled toward them. Two distinct flashes of gunfire lanced from the trees toward the car. The response was immediate from inside, and then again, and again.

Ned grinned. "That'd be Deputy John Washington's twelve-gauge."

Maddeningly, the electricity came back on as power lines somewhere far away made contact again. Cody pushed Ned's shoulder. "Get down!"

Instead of ducking with him, Cody charged out under the bright light, waving his arms. John's headlights came on when he recognized Cody, who sprinted for the nearest bur oak, hoping the wide trunk would give him some protection.

Realizing Cody's intent, John's engine roared as he punched the accelerator and turned past the free-standing garage. Gunfire from two different directions outside the house missed the moving target as John slid to a stop beside the oaks closest to the house. Shotgun in hand, he rolled out of the passenger side and using the car for cover, threw two shots from the pump gun toward the muzzle flashes beside the house.

Cody rammed into the side of the car beside the crouching deputy

"What's this all about, Cody?" Eyes wide, John thumbed thick red shells into the receiver. He shucked one into the chamber and finished filling the magazine. "Dispatch knows there's shootin' out here behind the store, but I didn't think I'd drive into a war!"

He glanced over his shoulder and gaped in amazement at Ned Parker walking calmly up the drive like it was a warm spring day.

Chapter Sixty-five

"Where'd Pepper go?"

I felt sorry for Mr. Landers. His one job was to keep us at the house, but Pepper disappeared like a puff of smoke the second he turned around. "She's gone to help Mr. Tony."

"Who?"

"The guy who's renting the Ordway place."

"But that's where all the shootin's coming from."

"Don't I know it."

The lights in the house came back to life. Mr. Landers' eyes widened when the wind brought a long string of shots. "Good God, that sounded like machine gun fire. I haven't heard anything like that since I was in the Pacific." He opened the screen door. "The electricity is back on. Now, you stay right there and I'll go call Ned."

I waited until he was back in the house, then I took off into the pasture Mr. Landers shared with the Ordway property. Only a few seconds later, everything behind me went dark again, but the lightning storm let me see enough to run toward the Ordway barn. I figured that's where Pepper was headed, and it was as good a place as any to see what was happening from the hay loft.

She'd be there all right, because we thought alike.

Chapter Sixty-six

Sheriff Griffin saw Cody's El Camino parked near a dark, unfamiliar house and rolled to a stop beside the car. Bolts of electricity in the low clouds overhead punctuated the gunfire a short distance away. A soft glow through one window told him somebody was home. He flicked his headlights on for a moment to let them know he was there.

Landers stepped outside and painted his flashlight over the new arrival. "Stay right there, feller." The next flash revealed a shotgun in the man's arms, and a pistol stuck in his waistband.

Griffin paused. "It's me. Sheriff Griffin."

"I don't know that. You ain't in no sheriff's car."

A quick sprinkle of rain fell, driven sideways by a gust of wind.

"Look, I'm the sheriff. I'm in my personal car. Shine your light here and you'll see my badge."

The beam moved downward and settled there. "All right. Get out sheriff, and tell me what's going on."

Relieved, Griffin stepped out and flinched as nearby gunshots echoed. "That's what I'd like to know."

"We tried to call Ned Parker again, but all the lines is busy. There's automatic fire over behind us at the Ordway place. I had Ned's grandkids here for a little bit, but them little shits snuck off and I don't know where they went."

Griffin's gut tightened with excitement. This might be it. Agrioli might have gotten his hands on a machine gun to take out the Parkers and Washington. He rubbed his palms together to bleed off nervous energy. "Any idea who's doing all the shooting?"

"Not sure." Landers stayed on the porch, keeping the house between them and the small war not far away. "Cody was here for a second, so I know he's around. Ned might be too for all I know. Past that, I can't tell you. One of them kids said a feller named Tony lives there."

Griffin thought hard, feeling even better now that he knew the Parkers were under fire. Driving away would be the smart thing to do until the battle was over, but he couldn't leave well enough alone. "Is there a way to get around back of that house?"

"Sure 'nough. Go through that gate over yonder and follow the fence a ways. It'll carry you around to the barn back behind the Ordway house."

"Much obliged. I'll be back in a little bit." Griffin lifted a pump shotgun from the backseat and jogged through the gate.

Sighing and hoping not to catch a stray bullet, Landers left the porch and crossed the yard in a crouch he'd perfected on Guadalcanal over two decades earlier. "Damn city people, don't even know enough to close the gate behind 'em."

A bullet whistled by overhead.

"Time to get to the storm cellar."

Chapter Sixty-seven

Both the .45 and .38 were empty, the Thompson lay on the floor, still smoking but useless. That left the Ruger .22 pistol in his pocket. Not enough to do the job, and surely not enough to maintain a standoff.

For a moment, the only sounds Tony heard over the ringing in his ears were thunder and the shrieks of a dying man in the kitchen. The Thompson had broken the back of their initial assault before it ran dry, but it severely damaged his hearing.

Blood ran down his back, soaking his left leg that refused to respond properly. He staggered back to the safe area beside the staircase and considered the second floor as a refuge, but it would leave no escape if they fired the house.

The front door banged against the wall and Tony expected another frontal assault. It was only the wind, but in the next flash of light, he saw Top's forgotten .22 leaning against the corner. Tony grabbed the slender rifle, and dragged himself back to the door under the stairs, leaving a trail of blood. Yanking it open, he stared into absolute darkness. A shout outside was followed by the rattle of gunfire as he pulled the door closed behind him.

Taking the Zippo from his pants pocket, he flicked the wheel with his thumb. The flame immediately drove the darkness into the corners and he saw the trap door cut into the bottom of the makeshift closet.

If nothing else, it would let him drop underneath the house. He opened it to find a ladder leading into darkness. The moonshiner's tunnel.

An escape plan formed in his mind, and a bloody grin arrived through the pain. He scrambled underground.

Tony was still in the fight.

Chapter Sixty-eight

The Machine stood outside the house with his back against the kitchen wall. On the other side, the last of Ray Marco's men, the one Johnny Machine shot beside the hog pen, tied off a tourniquet on his useless arm and leaned his head against the wall. "Shit that hurts! I can't believe you shot me."

"You're lucky you're still alive, so shut up about it."

"Whadda we do?"

"Wait a minute." The Machine peered around the corner, expecting another barrage from the Thompson. A body lay half in and half out of the utility porch. Half his head gone, Nicky's riddled corpse was draped over the man's legs. The room smelled of blood and gunpowder. "Lemme think."

He regretted shooting the man beside him. He needed someone to send in ahead to soak up some of that machinegun fire. He decided to use what he had. "Can you move?"

"Yeah, but my arm's broke and I'm dizzy." He coughed. "The bullet's in my lung. I can taste blood."

The Machine's eyes glittered. He was deep into his element, and loving every second. This was why they called him Johnny Machine. "You'll be fine. Here's what we do. I start shooting for cover, and you go in and make an immediate right through the door. That'll get us inside, and then we can flank this son-of-a-bitch."

"You'll cover me good?"

"Sure." The Machine surely expected to, but then again, what was the loss of one shot-up stranger? At the very least he'd locate Agrioli, once he opened up on the guy.

Gunfire came from the front of the house. The Machine hoped it was another frontal assault by Michael and some of the other guys. "Hey, what's your name?"

"Stanley."

"All right, Stanley, how many of you were there?"

"Seven in all."

"You all came in one *car*?"

"It was crowded."

Johnny Machine chuckled. The sound was madness amid the carnage. "That was you guys standing on the side of the road a little while ago. I hope some of them are still alive."

Stanley coughed, feeling warm blood in his mouth. "Marco might be."

"I'll bet Michael is too. Nobody can kill him. All right, you ready?"

Stanley stood on shaky legs.

"Now, go!" The Machine leaned into the doorway and gave Stanley's shoulder a rough shove. He opened up with his pistol, shooting as fast he could pull the trigger.

Moving awkwardly, Stanley blundered into the darkness and fell to his knees, expecting to hear the machine gun roar once again, and to feel the impact of a dozen bullets. Instead, there was no return fire. Using his one good hand, he crawled into the dining room and collapsed on the floor, momentarily losing his weapon. He fumbled for it, found the butt, and rolled against a wall.

Lightning exposed the room. It was clear.

Footsteps crunching on glass told Stanley that The Machine was creeping into the kitchen. "That you?"

The Machine crouched beside the bullet-riddled Frigidaire. "If you mean me, yeah."

"I think Agrioli's dead."

"We ain't that lucky. You stay right there and keep thinking. This guy's a cat, and he still has a lot of lives left."

Chapter Sixty-nine

Leaning against the car and using the engine block for cover, John and Cody couldn't believe their eyes at the sight of Ned walking up the sandy drive. His attention was fixed somewhere beyond the house. Strobes of lightning illuminated the Colt hanging loosely at his side.

Cody tried to wave him back. "Ned! Are you crazy! Get down!"

Gunshots flickered from behind the chest-high stack of firewood near the house as Michael and Marco sent bullets buzzing through the air like angry insects. The gangster's momentum failed when the lawmen arrived, forcing them toward the barn and away from escape.

John brought his shotgun to bear and fired three times, the booming reports rolling over the yard. The pellets splintered the dry wood, driving the shooters down. He shucked the empties and the hulls rattled onto the fenders with a hollow sound. Cody ducked and glanced over his shoulder, hoping to see Ned under cover behind a tree.

Instead, he stopped to aim his pistol in that peculiar manner of his that always reminded Cody of William S. Hart from the silent movie era. The men behind the firewood rose to shoot again. Ned fired over and over again, and John's shotgun boomed at the same time. The men fell back.

On one knee, the big deputy thumbed shells into the shotgun's magazine. "I ain't never seen nothin' like that!"

"He's lost his mind."

Almost casually, Ned joined them beside the car. He pushed the extractor rod on his pistol with a finger and the empties fell at his feet. "Y'all get up. We got trouble." His eyes focused on the stacked firewood as he shoved fresh rounds into the cylinder.

Stunned, Cody looked up at the old constable backlit by flickers of light in the dying storm. "What are you talking about?"

John peeked over the hood. A man dragging himself across the porch threw a wild shot toward the car. John aimed and fired. The buckshot hit with devastating effect, plucking at the man's shirt and hair.

Ned snapped the cylinder closed. "Them two guys who was shootin' at us are runnin' for the barn."

"So?"

"So I seen Top and Pepper run in there a minute ago."

"That's why you were walking out in the open?"

"I was?" Ned blinked in surprise, startled that he was so near the house. "Why, I had to do something so they wouldn't see them kids."

"Y'all gonna get us all killed." John stood and shouldered the shotgun, aiming toward the house. "Tell me when you're ready."

Chapter Seventy

"Up here!"

I hadn't no more than ducked in the pitch-black barn when Pepper called to me from the hay loft. I looked up, but it was too dark to find her. "I figured you'd be up there."

"The ladder's on the feed crib."

"I know where it is."

I felt around for a moment and found one of the worn rungs. It wasn't nothing but a piece of two by four nailed crossways between the wall studs. I was up quick as a squirrel. The Johnson grass hay on the loft floor was old and full of dust stirred up by the wind whistling through the eaves.

There was more shooting. I hadn't much more than registered the flashes when a bright bolt slashed overhead and I saw two men with their backs to us behind a stack of old firewood.

They were shooting at what I thought was a sheriff's car. Somebody shot back. A ricochet wailed off overhead, and then another. They don't sound like they do on television. Ricochets kind of have a nasty vibrating tone to them.

I shuddered. "Who-all's down there?"

Pepper squatted to see under the limbs of a nearby oak tree. "Shit, I don't know. I hope Mr. Tony's all right."

I thought about how many gunshots we'd already heard. "Well, they're still shootin', so I guess he ain't dead. But why are them people after him, I wonder?"

Pepper was quiet for a long minute because she didn't have an answer to that question, but then she backed into me and whispered. "Shit. Two of 'em ran in under us."

The lightning wasn't as strong as it had been, and we couldn't make out any details. But right behind them came two more men. I didn't think they were anyone we knew.

Pepper froze as solid as a rabbit under a bush.

I did the same, but for another reason. I felt that dizzying sense I had earlier in Mr. Tony's house, only this time it was stronger. I saw arrows of light shooting toward me from all different directions like the spokes on a wheel, only this time they met in the middle of the barn.

With a shock I knew that my dream about hubs and spokes was all about those men with guns, coming straight toward the Ordway place. My damned Poisoned Gift was finally revealed, but too late once again.

Pepper yanked my arm, pulling me back into this world. "Quiet!" she hissed.

"What?"

"You were making noises like you do when you have nightmares. It sounded like you were saying 'come in, come in.'"

"It was no such of a thing. I was seeing lights."

"Shhh."

We got quiet.

Chapter Seventy-one

The electricity came back on yet again in the Ordway house, the lights startling. The yellow glow illuminated bodies lying on the porch.

"What do you think's happening?" John asked.

Ned shook his head. "I couldn't guess, but I'm gonna go after them kids. I don't care who's inside right now. Them two men in the barn are my concern."

Cody agreed. "John, you stay out here and keep an eye on the house best you can, until help shows up. I bet there's cars on the way right now. Me'n Ned will go thataway through the gate, and see what we can do. Then you can bring some men when they get here and help us out."

"You're liable to get shot."

"So are you."

Ned patted his pockets. There was enough ammunition for one more reload. "Y'all keep an eye on the house until I get through the gate. They won't be able to see me then, and you can come on up, Cody."

"Run."

"Son, my running days are over." Ned patted his round belly where a bullet only months before had almost killed him. Throwing a glance toward the house, Ned moved in what he considered a jog toward the gate behind the tall wood pile.

When he disappeared into the darkness, Cody slapped John's shoulder, remembering that he did the same thing when Tom

Bell stayed behind to cover for him down in Mexico. He wished the old man were there now with his BAR. "Be careful."

John didn't take his eyes off the house. "You too."

Cody was barely through the gate when gunfire crackled once again in the house.

Chapter Seventy-two

We didn't make a peep when them two men came running in under us. They stopped inside the doors and we could hear them talking. One voice was thick and he had an accent I'd never heard before and he coughed like a smoker. "Dammit, Marco, what kind of lunatics do you have around here that jump into gunfights?"

"The kind that can….shoot." Marco sounded like he was out of breath. "That old man was crazy to just walk out into the open like that."

"What's wrong, you hit?"

"Yeah."

The smoker was quiet for a couple of seconds. "Bad?"

"It ain't good. Look Michael, that must be Agrioli's car. You keep an eye out while I see if I can get it started, then we'll get outta here." Marco coughed, wet and phlegmy. "Can you see what's going on out there?"

"There's a loft." It was Michael's voice, whoever he was. "I'll climb up and look.

The boards up the side of the feed crib creaked for a minute, taking his weight.

Pepper's eyes were impossibly wide. She grabbed me, trembling. A sound rose from somewhere deep inside my usually tough cousin, sounding exactly like the wind moaning through the eaves outside.

Down below, a wooden door slammed. Two beats later the sharp cracks of a .22 firing as fast someone could pull the trigger were drowned by a deep clap of thunder I could feel it in my chest.

Chapter Seventy-three

Bleeding badly, Tony struggled through the surprisingly well-constructed tunnel, ducking his head to avoid the rough timbers only inches overhead. Dusty cobwebs added to the eerie feeling pressing against the Zippo's flickering flame.

The car. All I need is the car and then I'm outta here.

He was dizzy from the loss of blood and almost completely exhausted when he reached the rungs of a short metal ladder. Wheezing, he gathered himself after a moment and started upward, hampered by his wounded leg. His head bumped against the trap door overhead. Bracing against it with his shoulder, Tony shoved upward.

His successful escape went to pieces when the trap door opened, knocking over a dusty chicken crate that collapsed with a loud bang. A flash of lightning revealed the dim shape of Michael Braccaro climbing the ladder on the other side of the feed crib's widely spaced slats.

The brief image was enough for Tony to recognize still another gangster sent by Best. Bracing himself on his good leg, he fired half a dozen shots from his Ruger .22 pistol with stunning results. The tiny rounds ripped through the dusty wood, driving splinters out the other side.

Michael fell backward, riddled with holes.

Tony saw a second man turn in his direction. He threw Top's rifle out, placed both hands on the sides of the trap door, and pulled himself clear of the entrance. Grabbing the rifle and roll-ing at the same time, Tony kicked the small access door open with his good leg, leaving a slick trail of blood behind him.

He wriggled through the opening and into a tangle of tall weeds. Pulling himself along with his elbows and one knee, he put some distance between himself and the barn. Only then did he stop, struggling to draw breath in lungs that were filling with blood. Ears full and ringing, Tony missed the telltale crackle as someone slipped through the waist-high thistles.

A second later, an incredibly hard object hit his head once, and then again.

Tony spun into a deep, dark well.

"I got you now, you sonofabitch." Sheriff Griffin hit him again with the butt of his shotgun and slipped away through the weeds.

Chapter Seventy-four

When the lights came back on, the Machine and Stanley waited for Tony to step out with the Thompson. It took a few moments to realize nothing was going to happen.

Leaving Stanley, the Machine moved away from the wall and worked his way through the house, carefully stepping on the floor slick with blood.

The closets were empty, as was the bathroom. He studied the trail of blood leading to the enclosed stairway. With no other choice, he emptied his weapon into the door, reloaded, and jerked it open. The enclosure was empty, but the blood smear leading to the trap door set in the floor told him all he needed to know.

Agrioli had escaped like a rat through a hole.

Stanley rested with his head against the wall and his pistol in an almost limp hand. "Whadda ya think? Did you get him?"

"No. He got away." The Machine looked at Stanley's bloody shirt. "I think you ain't gonna make it much longer."

The statement released whatever strings were holding Stanley's head up. His chin dropped. "He's killed me."

The Machine shrugged. "Probably. You got enough life left to keep an eye out so I can check the upstairs, just to be sure?"

"I don't know." Stanley drew a ragged breath. "Why don't you wait until Marco comes in? Don't you have anyone else with you?"

"I didn't see Michael's body, but that damned Thompson might have gotten him outside and I ain't gonna open the door to look." He thought for a minute and changed his mind. "To hell with it. I'm outta here."

"Help me. I'll go with you."

The Machine snorted. "You're nothing but meat."

"Stop. Help me or I'll…"

"Shut up!" He caught a slight movement from the corner of his eye. Stanley's gun rose, but Johnny Machine brought his pistol up first and shot him three times in the chest before Stanley could pull his own trigger. "You were already dead anyway."

Chapter Seventy-five

From outside the house, John watched the silhouettes of two men through the tattered shade. He quietly made his way to the porch, but dared not step on the creaky boards. A body sprawled under the windows, a shotgun nearby. The smell of blood and voided bowels was thick and nauseating.

One of the two men inside moved from room to room, fired several times, and finally stopped searching. He rejoined the first man. They were talking, but John could barely make out the words. He waited, watching the indistinct shapes. The room erupted into gunfire. The survivor moved toward the kitchen.

John ran around the outside and stopped, using the corner of the house as cover.

Moments later, the door opened. A muscular man stopped, scanning the darkness. "Michael?" The whispered name was almost unintelligible. "Marco? You guys out there?"

John waited.

The screen opened.

The big man came out slowly, a pistol ready.

One step down.

Two steps. Taking a deep breath, John twisted around the corner, the shotgun to his shoulder. "Sheriff's department! Hold it!"

The Machine's foot was on the way down to the next step. Off balance, he raised the pistol and fired. The slug ripped past John's head as he returned fire. There was no way he could miss with the scattergun, but he did. The Machine stumbled and fell off the last step to his knees. He brought the weapon up and shot wildly.

The strongest bolt of the night hit a tree on the other side of the fence, traveling down the trunk and lighting it from within in a shower of sparks. John flinched and time slowed. He sensed rounds slapping into the garage wall beside him and felt the pressure wave as one flicked passed his cheek.

Growling deep in his throat like a mad dog, John shucked the slide. He fired again.

It was one of those things that in hindsight, one wonders how it could have happened. The buckshot load didn't have time to spread properly and the charge missed again, tearing off one of the screen door's hinges. It fell against the Machine and he slapped it away, at the same time reaching for another pistol in the small of his back.

John saw a compact revolver rise.

Fuming that he'd missed twice, that these men were trying to kill him, that Rachel had been beaten, and he had no idea who did it, John raised the shotgun to his shoulder. "Damn you!" He aimed like he was shooting at a bottle and squeezed the trigger. This time the full load of buckshot caught the man square in the chest. The Machine's knees buckled and he fell straight down.

John shucked the empty.

The Machine's pistol rose.

"God*damn* you!" John fired again.

The pistol fell.

Still another blast shredded the body. The direct hit caused no reaction.

He shucked the hull, but the next pull of the trigger told him the shotgun was empty, and the battle temporarily over.

Digging the last of the fresh shells from his pocket and breathing hard, John jogged past the house toward the barn where he'd last seen Ned and Cody.

Chapter Seventy-six

It was silent in the dusty barn, but the storm overhead surged again with terrible power.

Pepper and I held each other, shaking. A gurgling noise down below grew softer and softer, and then quit.

Something rustled.

Someone was still down there.

Loud whispers drifted through the open loft door.

I choked down the rising terror and put my mouth to Pepper's ear. "We need to move. Slow and quiet."

She nodded.

We separated, and took a step toward the side. The floor creaked under our sneakers, and two shots roared from down below, punching through the boards and leaving holes in the tin roof.

Pepper screamed as we dove toward a stack of rotting hay bales.

Chapter Seventy-seven

Outside, Ned and Cody heard a .22 crank off several crisp shots inside the barn. Thinking at first they were aimed at them, they crouched near the outside corner and waited.

"There's folks shooting at one another in there," Ned whispered, trembling with fear for his grandkids and anxious to get inside. He knew better than to charge in, though. Getting killed wouldn't help the kids.

"I think…" Cody's response was cut off by a shot from the house, followed immediately by the heavier crump of a shotgun. They concentrated on the sounds. More deep reports told a story. He leaned close and whispered. "Looks like John's into something."

Two more shotgun blasts were followed by silence.

Ned nodded. "Sounds like he finished it, too."

A board in the loft creaked. Two shots lit the interior.

Chapter Seventy-eight

Cody had been in the Ordway barn so often when he was a kid that he knew the layout as well as he knew his own house. "Ned, count to five and hit the door with something, like you're coming in. I'm going in, around to this side through the first stall door when I hear the racket."

"Go on ahead!"

Cody spun and disappeared around the corner. With the roar of the wind and scattered explosions of thunder, he wasn't concerned with stealth. Ned felt around on the ground with his foot until he kicked up a short piece of broken board. He picked it up and swung hard, throwing it against the wall. The impact cracked loudly, drawing fire from inside.

John called from the darkness. "Right here, Mr. Ned!" He charged past the constable like an angry bull and slammed the wide door open with his shoulder. Ned followed as they darted inside. The flares of gunfire revealed the locations of both men.

John split left, and went down on one knee against the tack room wall. His twelve gauge boomed loudly in the enormous barn. Ned stutter-stepped right and used John's muzzle flash to locate the closest gangster, Michael, who was severely wounded and barely upright behind a steel barrel.

Michael threw a wild shot at Ned, who returned the favor. Cody leaped inside the pitch-black structure. Four guns opened up and the muzzle flashes briefly lit the players in a staccato string of frozen images. Cody saw Marco beside the car. The .45 bucked in his hand as he danced sideways to get a better angle.

Ned and John continued to fire. Already mortally wounded from Tony's shots, Michael fell back, his pistol discharging into the tin roof. In the sudden silence, the lawmen heard the distinctive sound of Marco's revolver clicking over and over on spent casings.

Ned also had been in that same barn dozens of times in the past. He straightened and reached up to punch the push-button switch beside the feed crib. The interior immediately flooded with light from bulbs dangling twenty feet overhead.

Two once well-dressed men lay on the dirt floor, one obviously dead. The other moved his foot, gasped, and shuddered.

Cody ran from the empty stall and kicked Marco's gun away. The gangster twitched one more time and died. "Top! Pepper! Y'all up there? Y'all all right?"

"We're okay," Top's voice quivered.

"Speak for yourself," Pepper snapped. "I think I broke my damned finger when you fell on me."

Hearing the kids argue told Ned they weren't badly hurt. "Careful boys. Cody, check that side and be careful, somebody might be behind the car. John! You all right?"

"Fine Mr. Ned!" He fed the shotgun again. "It's all over at the house. They's dead people everywhere." He leaned the gun against the feed crib.

Cody pushed through the open stall. "You kids come on down."

A voice from the opposite end of the long hallway caused everyone to jump. "Y'all stay right where you are."

Chapter Seventy-nine

Ned's rage overcame his common sense when he saw Griffin rise from behind Tony's car with a twelve gauge leveled at them. "Griffin! What-n hell are you doing pointing that thing at us?"

"I said *no* one move!" Griffin walked briskly down the hall, his footsteps silent on the hay and dirt floor. They were so close together that all the man had to do was hold the trigger down and pump one load after the other into them. Griffin was so angry he was talking to himself, mimicking Ned's longtime habit.

"If those fools had done what I told them at that nigger gal's house, I'd be long gone by now." Griffin motioned with the muzzle of the gun. "Y'all know what to do."

Cody cursed and dropped his weapon. Griffin moved the black muzzle toward John and Ned. It gaped like a culvert pipe. "Y'all think, now. Pitch down them guns."

Ned dropped his into the dirt. John reached for his sidearm.

Griffin's voice snapped. "John! Slow down and use your left hand."

The deputy didn't move. Sheriff Griffin had told him what he wanted to know. It was all he could do not to charge across the hall and beat the man to death with his bare hands. In that instant, John knew how much he loved Rachel and her kids.

Thinking about Rachel, and not knowing how she would survive if he were killed, John reached across with his left hand and plucked the revolver from his holster. Without releasing Griffin's gaze, he let it fall onto the soft floor.

"Now, Cody, walk slow over there beside them."

With no idea what was going on below, Pepper crept over to the ladder and peered down. "Grandpa?"

"Uh uh!" Griffin kept the muzzle steady on the three lawmen. "Y'all don't do nothing. You little nits get down from there. Right now!"

Ned took a step toward Griffin and Cody. "You stay away from my grand…"

A thin, disembodied voice caught Griffin's attention. "Not nits."

The sheriff's eyes flicked toward the wall on his right and caught the movement of a slender rifle barrel pointed directly at him.

Outside and barely alive, Tony shoved the barrel of Top's rifle between the wall planks. His forehead throbbed in a final burst of rage as he pulled the trigger. A crack made them all jump as a .22 round punctured the sheriff's upper right chest, destroying both lungs. In shock from the sudden sharp pain, he gasped and hunched his shoulders. Cody quickly closed the distance between them and slapped the shotgun's barrel with his left hand. Accelerating the muzzle swing, he grabbed it behind the grip and stripped the weapon from the sheriff, breaking the man's index finger in the trigger guard.

Before he could spin the weapon and fire, Griffin stumbled sideways from a string of shots that came so fast they rode on top of each other. Some missed, others found flesh.

Cody dove sideways and rolled against a stall door for cover, thinking he was going to be next.

His fury focused on Griffin, John scooped up his pistol and joined the barrage. Already bleeding from a dozen holes, Griffin fell against a rough support timber and slipped to the ground. The stubborn impulses of his dying brain tried to bring his gun to bear.

With a low growl, John shot Griffin again. The growl turned to a howl as he trembled with rage and shot Griffin's still body again.

When he thumbed back the hammer once again, Ned stepped forward and gently pushed the barrel toward the ground. "It's over, John. He's done for."

Cody plucked John's shotgun from where it leaned against the wall and rushed outside.

The smoking barrel of Top's rifle slid downward between two vertical boards. Huddled in the weeds outside the barn, Tony's last realization was that the vein in his numb temple no longer throbbed. Something popped deep inside his damaged skull. He leaned his cheek against the weathered wood, closed his eyes, and slipped away.

Ned stood over Griffin, dumped the empties from his revolver, and reloaded.

John drew a deep breath. "You're wrong, Mr. Ned."

"About what?"

"It ain't over. Someday I'll have to pay this debt."

Ned looked at the rough-cut rafters overhead, as if to collect his words from the air, but he couldn't think of a thing to say for a long moment. "John, you didn't do nothing but save our lives."

"I was mad."

He saw the anguish in John's eyes "You had every right."

"I just don't know."

A particularly loud clap of thunder rattled the barn when a bolt of lightning struck nearby. The kids peered downward at the dead sheriff from the dark loft. Top's voice was clear, but shaky. "Uncle Wilbert was right."

"Miss Becky said the Lord takes care of things in his own way." Pepper sighed as scattered raindrops on the roof sounded like falling dimes. "I wish He'd leave us the hell out of it, though."

They weren't able to talk after that, because the clouds finally opened up with rain hammering so hard on the sheet iron roof that it drowned out everything else.

Chapter Eighty

Ned pitched his hat on O.C.'s cluttered desk. "I brought us a couple of cold drinks."

The old judge eyed the sweating bottles. "I don't much care for Orange Crush."

"I'god, I don't care if you drink it or not, then."

"Settle down, son. You oughta learn to halter that temper of yours." O.C. chuckled and tilted the bottle. He really had no problem with orange, but he sure enjoyed aggravating Ned. "Thankyee anyway."

"What are you working on?"

"I was reading the paper about that killing in Las Vegas day before yesterday."

"I saw that."

"There's another story in here about the bank robbery, too. They got all the money back, after they figured out which was real and which was counterfeit."

"That's what I hear." Ned settled onto the only wooden chair not stacked with papers. "They'll be sortin' this out for months. Add in what they found at Griffin's house, the Rangers and FBI think he's been into a lot more than we'll ever know. They'll never figure out where it all came from."

"I always knew that sonofabitch was crooked."

"As a dog's hind leg." They sat in comfortable silence for a long moment. Ned picked at the painted label of his bottle with a thumbnail. "They had Tony Agrioli's funeral a couple of days ago. That little Samantha gal of his had him buried in the Methodist Cemetery, but she wasn't there. There was a good crowd anyways. I 'magine half of 'em came 'cause of nosiness, but lots of folks liked old Tony."

"Saw that in the paper, too."

"Then you saw Sam's name in the story about that Las Vegas killing. They say she was the one who shot that mobster graveyard dead in his own restaurant."

"Looks to me like another mob boss got himself killed is all."

"Most don't get shot by their own daughters."

"I reckon not. She'll probably get off."

"I hope so." Ned drained half the bottle. "I wouldn't blame her for it, after what happened to that young feller."

"They say now that Tony was a killer too. He had a whole string of dead people behind him."

Ned rubbed his head. "Probably was, but he acted right while he was here. At least till those other people showed up."

"Don't sugar coat it. There was people killed, and a bank robbery to boot." O.C. thought for a minute.

Ned was on another track entirely. "I asked her what it was all about. She said Tony worked for the Mob and was trying to get away. That's what brought the whole thing down on us."

The statement cut through O.C.'s own train of thought, surprising him. "You talked to that little gal after she left?"

"Yep. Samantha's her name. They must like her in that jail, because somebody let her get on the phone. She called us collect to talk to Becky and the kids, and then she asked for me. She told me a lot more."

"Did you get anything that'll help her out there?"

"Nope. She wanted me to know they tried to make a go of it in Center Springs is all." Something under Ned's upper denture was driving him crazy. He sucked it loose and then bit it back into place. Despite the annoyance, Ned still remembered the bad teeth he had as a younger man, and the tradeoff was worth it.

O.C. took another long drink. "I wish this world would stay out of our county. All the feds left yesterday. I reckon they're done, and I'm glad they're all out of my courthouse. Maybe things now will get back to normal." With a head full of his own teeth, O.C. leaned back in his wooden desk chair and twirled the fly-swatter between his fingers. "I sure hope it's over for a while. This kind of stuff makes me nervous."

Teeth. Ned almost heard the connections click in his head. *Nervous.* He frowned at O.C. "What did you say?"

"I said, all this makes me nervous. These past couple of years have been enough to last me for the rest of my life. Why?"

Ned ignored the question, struggling to hang onto the thread that kept pulling his attention. He knew that if he quit concentrating, he'd lose his train of thought and it was so frustratingly *close.*

Nervous.

Teeth.

A recollection tickled his memory. It was the day Chester Humphrey ran away from the highway patrol out by the lake.

When he's nervous, he runs.

He's been nervous a long time.

"You know Mr. Ned, when he's nervous, he runs."

A toothache.

O.C. quit twirling the fly-swatter and waited. It was obvious Ned had something on his mind, and they'd been running together long enough that he'd seen him worry on an idea before.

There was something...

A fly lit on a stack of papers. O.C. leaned forward and struck with the swatter.

Pop!

The slap was like a distant gunshot.

Gunshot wound.

"Now, Chester, look at me." When the boy raised his eyes, Ned gave him a grin. *"It was you, weren't it, that the deputy saw. What'd you do?"*

"I didn't do it. I 'ust run oft."

Ned came back to himself. "He said he didn't do it, he just ran off."

"Who run off?"

"Chester. I told you about getting a call from one of your deputies who saw a young boy run off the day before they found Tommy Lee Stark dead in the bottoms."

"I remember."

"I thought he ran because they saw him cutting the bark off a toothache tree that day, but I believe he ran for another reason."

"Do tell."

Ned stood and put on his hat. "I will, when I know for sure."

O.C. stood and pitched the flyswatter on his desk. "I'm going with you. I've killed enough flies for one day."

"Well, come on then."

O.C. drained his Orange Crush and followed.

Chapter Eighty-one

Pepper and I were sitting Indian style under a bare red oak on top of the hill where Great-great granddad Parker built his first house. Now there was nothing left but the shade trees overlooking the giant, smoking hole of Lake Lamar.

It was a cloudy, chilly autumn day. A skein of Canada geese flew high overhead, honking and complaining about the coming weather.

Smoke from the fires below reminded me of a dream I'd had the night before. I thought about telling Pepper about the giant pit, atomic bombs, and smoky fires, and three blackbirds that fell in at the same time three devils climbed out over the edge.

But the day was too nice, because I love cloudy days, so instead I sat back to enjoy the cries of blue jays in the bare trees. I shivered and said a quiet little prayer to keep the dream from coming true.

Pepper either didn't see it, or thought I was cold if she did. She lit a Kool she'd snitched somewhere, and clicked on her new transistor radio. The Rolling Stones were singing about a nervous breakdown number nineteen or something.

"You wanna turn that noise off?"

She shot me a look that I'd seen a thousand times before. "Why does everybody hate my music?"

I took a deep breath of the cool, clean air. "I didn't say I hated it, but it's awful loud and I don't understand that song at all."

She rolled the volume wheel with her thumb and laid the radio on the leaves. She absently played with the Surfer's Cross dangling from her neck.

She was looking more and more like those hippie kids in jeans, loose shirts, and a leather vest someone had given her. "You don't get it, bonehead. The summer of love is over and I missed it. We're missing *everything* in this hick town. This place is too damn country, and so is everybody I know. I wish we lived in California. Those kids have it together."

"Far out."

"Oh!" She slugged me in the arm. "Don't make fun of me. Do you want to spend your whole life around here with people who dip snuff? Shit!"

I thought of the sharp, pungent smell of the Garrett's Snuff that our old aunts spit into empty coffee cans on the floor. "Things are good now." I watched a car come around the bend across the dam and realized it was Grandpa's. "We have a wedding to look forward to."

For once she agreed with me. "That's cool. I ain't never been to no colored wedding before. Me and Daddy went to a colored funeral once. Shit, I hope it don't take as long for them to get married as it does to get buried."

"There's Grandpa. I wonder who's in there with him."

Pepper straightened up and stuffed the cigarette out beside her leg. She waved the smoke away and used the motion to pull a long strand of hair out of her eyes that had worked its way loose from her headband. She unconsciously checked her part down the middle to make sure it was still straight. "That looks like Judge O.C."

They were headed toward us at a pretty good clip. Grandpa saw us, threw up his hand, and then went back to driving.

I felt kinda funny, him running across us so far from the house. "He'll probably be mad at us for riding our bikes out here to the lake. You know, he already hates this thing like sin."

"Wonder where they're going?"

I shot her my own look. "It don't make no difference. I ain't gonna go stringing off behind them now or ever again."

"See? That's what I'm talking about. You never want any excitement."

"I had all I could stand. We nearly got killed again."

"Aw, those bullets missed us by a mile."

"Is that why you peed your pants a little?"

"Don't you never tell nobody about that." She punched me in the arm again, this time so hard it hurt.

"Well, I'm done adventuring. I just want to be an archaeologist and dig up bones, or maybe find gold or treasure. That's not dangerous or nothing."

A group called the Buffalo Springfield started singing about men with guns and stuff going down. Pepper rolled the volume back up, but I didn't say anything, because I kinda liked that song, even though it drowned out the blue jays.

Chapter Eighty-two

Ned piloted his car down the dirt road to Frederick and Geneva Humphrey's unpainted frame house. Parts of the gravel and dirt road were washboard rough, vibrating the car and knocking a stack of mail off the seat between them and into the floor.

O.C. grunted forward and collected the scattered envelopes. "You oughta read your mail instead of cartin' it all around the county."

"Picked it up this morning and ain't had the time or inclination to go through it."

This time only one dog crawled from under the warped porch when they arrived at the Humphrey place. It set up a howl that wasn't nearly as loud as the pack that lived there before.

Frederick was walking to the house from the barn. "Shut up, dog!" He waved. "Y'all get out."

The mutt quit barking and sat in the dirt yard to scratch. Ned and O.C. stepped out and shook hands.

Frederick shifted a chew to his other cheek and didn't seem the least bit phased about the two lawmen standing in his yard. "Mr. Ned, Judge Rains, what can I do for y'all?"

"Where's all your dogs?"

Frederick shrugged. "I couldn't tell you. About half of 'em disappeared at one time, and then the rest of them went one by one. Coyotes probably."

Another piece clicked into place, but Ned knew he'd never

tell Frederick what happened to his dogs. Top was finished, and that chapter was closed.

Frederick slipped his hands into the pockets of his overalls. "Say, Chester ain't got in any more trouble, has he?"

"No, he's been fine as far as I know." Ned waved toward the house. "I'd like to talk with him a minute, though, if he's here."

"He's been in the barn with me all day. Chester!" he called over his shoulder. "Get out here."

The youngster appeared and stood in the barn door, watching.

Ned smiled and closed the distance, but not enough to frighten the boy. "Chester, how's that bad tooth?"

He shrugged.

"We scraped up a little money." Frederick shifted from one foot to the other, uncertain what to do.

"Pulled it, huh?"

"Yessir."

Ned studied him. "Good. Now take care of them others and you'll have 'em your whole life, and not a set of dentures like these in my head. Say, listen to me for a minute, Chester. I'm-a gonna ask you a question that you can't get in trouble for, understand?"

The boy blinked once and looked down at his worn Buster Brown tennis shoes.

Ned put both hands in his own pockets to show that he wasn't going to do anything. "I believe you were in the bottoms a while back and saw something that scared you. Something that made you run, 'cause you're nervous and all."

Chester wouldn't meet his eyes.

"It's all right to say. You can nod or shake your head. I need the answer to a question, and it don't matter what you say, cause there ain't no right or wrong answer. Either way, I'll run you up to the store after 'while and get you another banana ice cream. All right?"

This time Chester nodded.

"Good. Now, you ain't gonna get in trouble at all over this, so here's the question. Did you see a feller get shot down in the bottoms here-while-back?"

O.C. and Frederick waited, still and quiet while Chester studied his feet.

Ned lowered his voice. "Did you, son?"

This time Chester nodded.

Ned sighed at the weight that suddenly rose from his shoulders. "That's all right, because you had nothin' to do with it. I believe you was just runnin' the woods and happened to be there, that about right?"

Shrug.

"That's good enough. Now, here comes another'n. You ready?"

Chester softly spoke to the ground. "You said one."

Ned held back a grin. "You're pretty smart. That's right, I did say one question, but this one is kinda part of that other'n. I guess I wasn't finished. Did you recognize the feller that shot the first one?"

From the corner of his eye, Ned saw Frederick take a breath to say something, whether it was to the boy, or Ned, he didn't know, but O.C. casually reached out and grasped his arm.

Ned scuffed the ground with his toe. "You know 'em, don't you?"

Another nod.

"Tommy Lee was one."

Nod.

"Who shot Tommy Lee?"

The silence in the yard was thick. A blue jay called nearby.

"Gene."

All at once, Ned realized he'd been holding his breath. O.C. and Frederick exhaled as one and it felt as if some crisis had passed.

"All right, then. Chester, I'm gonna have to leave for a little bit, but when I come back, I'm gonna bring you a whole box of them banana bars, is that all right?"

For the first time since he'd known the boy, Ned saw a glimmer of light in his eyes. "And a orngikle."

"A what?"

Frederick stepped forward. "That's how he saws Creamsicle, those ice cream bars that are orange on the outside and vanilla on the inside. He's taken a likin' to them, when we have a nickel to spend."

O.C. grinned wide. "I'll bring you a box of them, too, son."

Chapter Eighty-three

Ned and O.C. crossed the dam. O.C. pointed. "Is that your grandkids sitting there?"

"That's them all right. I wonder what they're up to now." Ned waved as they passed, giving them the eye.

"Looks like they're just being kids."

"Well, I know 'em. If they ain't been into anything, they'll come up with an idea before long."

"Aw hell, Ned, we was kids and ran these bottoms like wild Indians. It didn't hurt us none." O.C. rolled down the window on his side and the crosswind threatened to yank Ned's new Stetson off his head. He tugged it back down. Minutes later, they crunched up Gene Stark's gravel drive. Ned killed the engine and they waited, engine ticking.

"O.C., open the glove box there and get that .32. I doubt Gene will give me any trouble, but I don't know."

The judge opened the door, found the pistol, and checked the loads. The cylinder was full. He slapped it closed just as the back door opened and Gene dropped heavily into the rear seat of the car. Startled, O.C. nearly pulled the trigger, and Ned struggled to pull his own pistol from the holster on his hip.

"I'm ready, and you can keep that pistol in the scabbard," Gene said in a relaxed, conversational tone. They turned to look at the man sitting calmly, fingers laced in his lap. "I'm giving myself up, because it's been eatin' on me something terrible.

When the two of you got here together, I knew y'all found out. How'd you do it?"

Ned cleared his throat. "We just did."

"Well, I'm glad it's over." Gene's voice broke and he had difficulty talking. "I didn't mean to shoot Tommy Lee, but I done it. I killed my brother on accident. We's out to shoot us some table meat a little early."

Ned looked over his shoulder. "You want to tell us what happened?"

Gene took a shuddering breath. "He went across the draw, and I walked up on a little rise. When I sat down, I could see him where he was sittin' beside a tree, but kinda out in the open, you know? I always said he couldn't hide worth spit, and that's how come him to get caught peeking in winders in the first place."

Tears rolled down his cheeks. "When the sun come completely up, I lined up on his head with my rifle, to practice my aim, and thinking what a good joke it'd be when I told him I was watching him pick his nose when he didn't think no one was looking."

He broke down, crying into his hands. His sobs were deep and heartfelt. They barely made out his words. "I didn't know the safety was off. It was a pure accident, but I killed my own brother."

Ned shifted into reverse and backed the car around in the yard.

A mile from the house, Gene gained control of himself and roughly wiped the tears from his cheeks. "Man ought not to cry like that."

"You cry when you hurt." O.C. put the revolver back in the glove box. "You been hurtin' a while."

"Yessir, Judge. I wouldn't-a done it intentional for nothin'."

Ned kept his eyes on the dirt road leading out of the bottoms. "Where's your rifle?"

"Standing in the corner behind my bedroom door."

Ned picked up the microphone, aggravated that he hadn't waited to get the rifle himself. "Sheriff Parker."

Cody's voice came back. "Yessir."

"You busy?"

"Kinda. Deputy White called in with a report of three miss-ing businessmen who haven't been heard from in a week or so. They were looking for some land and haven't checked in with their wives. What's up?"

Ned recalled the town square and a man with a camera, and wondered if he'd been one of them. "I know you don't work for me, but you might want to send one of your deputies over to Gene Stark's house and get the rifle from behind his bedroom door. Handle it careful. I'm bringing him in for the accidental shooting of his brother."

The answer came a long moment later. "Yessir. Gene in there with you?"

"He is."

"Gene, I'm sorry how it turned out."

Ned concentrated on his driving while a steady stream of tears rolled down the farmer's cheeks at Cody's distant, tinny words. They struck the highway and Ned accelerated on the hardtop.

"It was an accident, Cody. It just went off. Oh God, he was dead when he hit the ground."

Ned didn't tell Gene the newly appointed sheriff couldn't hear him. The appointment wasn't easy, and O.C. had to do a lot of talking to convince the county commissioners that it was the right thing to do, but they agreed to let Cody fill Griffin's term until the next election. Both Ned and O.C. figured he'd win. "Go on, Gene."

"There weren't nothing I could do for him, so I just set with him for an hour or so."

They passed Neal's store a moment later. Half a dozen loafers on the porch threw a wave at Ned's passing car, and went back to talking.

Ned surprised himself by taking the new road to the dam. He was getting used to it whether he wanted to or not. "Then?"

"Then I threw him over my shoulder and carried him to the truck and set him up behind the wheel and walked home."

"Why'd you do that, put him behind the wheel?"

Gene's eyes went to the rearview mirror and met Ned's. "I 'on't know. I couldn't leave him in the woods for the coyotes, and it didn't feel right to put him the truck bed."

The kids were gone when they passed the old house place. At the sharp curve midway across the dam, Ned braked and his unread mail again slid into the floorboard. "Dammit." O.C. leaned over once again. He raised up with a thick packet in his hand. "Ned."

"What? Put it back on the seat and I'll take care of it later."

"Look." O.C. held out a thick envelope, reinforced with tape.

As he unconsciously took his foot from the accelerator, Ned's eyes flicked to the flowing name handwritten on the return address.

Tom Bell Parker, Hembrillo, Mexico.

"What the hell?" He slowed even more, studying on the implications of the envelope. "What's the postmark date?"

Frustratingly slow, O.C. dug a pair of reading glasses from the inside pocket of his coat. "Last week."

They stopped in the middle of the dam.

O.C. peered over the top of his glasses. "You said he was dead."

"I thought he was."

"Didn't you talk to the Rangers?"

"I did. And they won't tell me squat."

Ned's gaze slipped away and out of O.C.'s window toward the raw, gaping hole that would soon become Lake Lamar.

Unaware, Gene leaned forward. "You know what, Ned?"

"Hum?"

"You wouldn't think anybody would be so dumb, would you? To do such a thing as I did?"

Ned grunted and accelerated toward the main highway and the Lamar County courthouse. "Well, Gene, a lot of strange things happen up here on this ol' river."

To receive a free catalog of Poisoned Pen Press titles, please contact us in one of the following ways:

Phone: 1-800-421-3976
Facsimile: 1-480-949-1707
Email: info@poisonedpenpress.com
Website: www.poisonedpenpress.com

Poisoned Pen Press
6962 E. First Ave. Ste 103
Scottsdale, AZ 85251